FRONTIER EARTH:

SEARCHER

Ace Books by Bruce Boxleitner

FRONTIER EARTH

FRONTIER EARTH:

SEARCHER

BRUCE BOXLEITNER

ACE BOOKS, NEW YORK

FRONTIER EARTH: SEARCHER

An Ace Book
Published by The Berkley Publishing Group,
a division of Penguin Putnam Inc.,
375 Hudson Street, New York, New York 10014.

The Penguin Putnam Inc. World Wide Web site address is
http://www.penguinputnam.com

First edition: January 2001

Library of Congress Cataloging-in-Publication Data

Boxleitner, Bruce
    Frontier Earth : searcher / Bruce Boxleitner.
        p.   cm.
    ISBN 0-441-00799-6
    1. Tombstone (Ariz.)—Fiction. 2. Human-alien encounters—
Fiction.
    I. Title.
    PS3552.O87715 F78 2000
    813'.54—dc21   00-040174

PRINTED IN THE UNITED STATES OF AMERICA

10   9   8   7   6   5   4   3   2   1

FRONTIER EARTH:

SEARCHER

PROLOGUE

THE DESERT NIGHT SLIPPED GENTLY OUT OF THE EAST, PUR-suing the last glowing tendrils of scarlet and green lingering above the sunset. *Tzontzose*, the crescent moon, rode low in the west, waxing now in the aeons-ancient cycle.

Na-a-cha, *diyi* of the People, stood atop a worn, sandstone ledge. Taking a pinch of *hoddentin* from a buckskin pouch, he flicked the powder in the direction of the moon, a puff of yellow smoke, and addressed the sky. "*Gun-ju-li, chil-jilt, si-chi-zi, gun-ju-li, inzayu, injanale. . . .*"

"Be good, O Night; Twilight be good; do not let me die. . . ."

The chant soothed, even as he felt his Power drawing close, a familiar chill down his spine, a sense that the spirit world was near. More than once, Na-a-cha had entered trance and gone to visit *chidin-bi-kungua*, the House of Spirits, to converse with them, and learn what it was he had to do. He wondered if the spirits could help him now.

He wondered if anything could help.

Na-a-cha was a powerful man, a *diyi* who worked powerful medicine. Once, in the time of Cochise and Vittorio, he'd been a great warrior as well as a war shaman. Too old now to go on raids, he'd become a lightning shaman of the N'de, the People. To him, and to none other of the Chokonen Chiricahua that he knew of, had been granted a vision of a living *gan*, a *ga he*, one of the Mountain Spirits who were the most powerful supernatural beings in his world besides Child of the Water and White Painted Woman themselves.

He moved to the altar—the sacred place—which had rested atop that boulder for as long as Na-a-cha could remember. It was a simple affair: a low stack of stones and shingle rock, with cattail pollen sprinkled thickly across the top. In time-honed ritual, he offered pinches of *hoddentin* to the six cardinal directions of N'de belief, to the gods of the east . . . of the south . . . of the west . . . of the north . . . of the zenith . . . of the nadir, intoning low-voiced, chanted supplications to each. "*Gun-ju-li, injan-ale* . . ."

"Be good to me, do not let me die. . . ."

And as he prayed, he focused on his problem. In-che-di-jin must think himself powerful indeed, if he could question Na-a-cha's authority within the band openly. For the past three moons, the other shaman—his name meant Black Wind in the tongue of the People—had been working quietly, in the shadows, to block Na-a-cha's elevation as a lightning shaman among the Chokonen. Black Wind had never accepted Na-a-cha's vision, never trusted his counsel as shaman or *diyi*, never agreed with Na-a-cha's proclamation that the band must remain here, in the mountains of the sacred ancient homeplace.

He prayed, asking for direction, asking for clarity of thought and purpose, asking for a sign that would tell him which way to go.

Something . . . a flash of light, a flicker of movement, made him look up, and his eyes widened. There, at the zenith, three stars moved slowly, side by side, passing at a stately pace toward the west. They were too slow to be falling stars, and far, far too fast and bright to be comets; the People were quite familiar with such ordinary phenomena of the night sky and, unlike some of their superstitious neighbors, attached no particular significance to them. Their light seemed to pulse in unison in a most un-starlike way.

There'd been many signs in the sky of late. He was reminded of the sky-wagon of the *ga he* he'd seen three moons ago in his vision. Might the Mountain Spirits be returning? Whatever they were, those lights in the sky represented astonishing power and might well be portents of something incredible about to happen.

Na-a-cha wished he knew how to read them.

O N E

✧ 1 ✧

*I*T CIRCLED IN THE NIGHT SKY.

Below, the town spread out for its inspection, broad, dusty streets illuminated by pools of light cast from lanterns in the saloon windows. A steady wind blew from the southwest, carrying the chill of the encircling desert, moaning as it skirted the eroded hills beyond the town.

The Watcher—for that was how it thought of itself— was alert to each movement in the streets far beneath its wing-stretched wheelings . . . to horses nodding at their hitching posts, to drunken cowboys stumbling along the boardwalks, to a sudden fistfight in a darkened alley, to the flare of a match held to a hand-rolled cigarette.

The town was Tombstone, Arizona Territory, in the spring of 1882. Somewhere below, in one of those structures of adobe, brick, or wood slats, the Watcher's prey had taken shelter. No matter. The Watcher was patient and would continue mounting its lonely vigil. The Masters were patient, too, although lately their patience had been wearing thin.

The Watcher was not human, was not even remotely related to any creature on this world.

And neither were the Masters. . . .

✧ 2 ✧

THEY CALLED HIM MACKLIN. HE WAS ALSO KNOWN AS Johnny Waco.

"Four ball, corner pocket."

The *click-clack-click* of the billiards game in progress blended with the tinkling of the player piano in the corner, with the laughs and lightly bandied conversation filling Bob Hatch's Billiard Hall. Macklin slouched back in one of the spectators' chairs and watched Morgan Earp play the establishment's owner. For weeks, now, the two had been engaged in a friendly, ongoing series of games the two referred to as the "Billiards Championship of the World." To his left was George Berry, a Tombstone citizen, and beyond him sat the town's most famous—or, some would say, most infamous—citizen, Wyatt Earp. Several other spectators lounged about in other chairs, watching the match in the smoky haze of cigar smoke aglow in the light of oil lanterns hanging from the ceiling.

The four ball rolled into the indicated pocket with a dull thump.

"Good shot, Morg," Bob Hatch said. "But it's not gonna save you!"

"We'll see," the tall, neatly mustachioed man replied. He moved to the left side of the table, eyed his next shot, and announced, "Five in the corner."

Macklin felt the hard, sharp pressure of the carved wooden chair back against his spine and thighs, smelled the acrid muskiness of cigar smoke hanging blue-white and thick on the air, listened to the raucous laughter and piano music and clacking billiard balls, tasted the lingering bite of his last swallow of White Horse whiskey. *Sensation.* Sometimes, he felt as though he needed to submerge himself in sensation. It was the only way he knew to keep himself grounded, to maintain his sometimes scrabbling grip on an illusive reality.

I still don't know who I am. . . .

Neither Macklin nor Waco was his real name. He'd been told that his name was Ma'khleen, and that he wasn't even native to this world its inhabitants called Earth, and that he was here as a Monitor to watch and protect a planet so primitive they didn't even possess aircraft as yet, much less dream of travel among the stars.

The memory drove him to raise his glass to his lips and take another hard, burning swallow. Damn it, that stuff wasn't *real*. It couldn't be.

He'd been told a little about who he was, about why he was here . . . but being told was a long way from re-membering, from *knowing*. Except for the shadows of dis-turbingly vivid dreams, Macklin couldn't remember a thing before the night he'd awakened in the desert a few miles outside of Tombstone, been picked up by one of the animal-drawn carriages the locals called a *stagecoach*, and brought into town.

How much of all of that stuff do I believe? he asked himself. He still wasn't sure. There was plenty of evidence that everything Doris had told him was true . . . the dreams, the strange round plate set low in his chest, the . . . the *things* that had attacked them, creatures, beings indescribably horrible—walking, murderous nightmares that Doris had called Kra'agh. . . .

But then again, he'd heard that people on the brink of raving insanity saw lots of things that couldn't possibly exist. So long as Macklin couldn't connect emotionally with these fragments from a vanished past, that past would remain unreal and illusory, something heard about in frag-ments, not experienced, not felt.

No. *This* was reality, *this* was the real world . . . cloy-ing smoke and clacking billiard balls and the rough, loud good humor of the citizens of Tombstone, Arizona, this evening in March of 1882.

Click-clack-click-click. He watched the colored balls

roll across green felt, some careening off the rubber bumpers, some colliding with other balls, transferring energy and motion.

Was that all that life was, a collision of moving bodies, an inevitability of force and vector? Sometimes, he felt as though he were drifting, with no more control over his thoughts and decisions and motions than those balls had over their movements.

Something went cold and hard in Morgan's face as he straightened up from the table and reached for a block of chalk. He was staring at something, or someone, in the front of Bob Hatch's place.

Macklin knew that look and knew it well. Casually, he glanced back over his shoulder into the other half of the long, narrow room, where the Campbell & Hatch Saloon was located. Someone had just come through the swinging doors that opened onto Allen Street at the front and was making his way now past the noisy tables of cowboys and Tombstone residents to belly up to the big mahogany bar.

The man was tall, a bit gaunt, wearing a mud-splattered black overcoat against the chill March air and one of the tall, pinched-top hats known as a Montana Peak. He was ordering a drink and didn't seem at all aware of the scrutiny from the back room. Maybe he was being just a bit *too* casual.

Macklin knew him. His name was Pete Spence, and he was one of the Cowboys, that loose band of perhaps fifty cattle rustlers and hooligans who'd pretty much run things in Cochise County until the Earps and Doc Holliday had gunned down three of their number at the O.K. Corral five months ago. Spence's own wife, Marietta, had identified him as one of the holdup men in the Bisbee stage robbery the previous September, and he was known to ride with the Curly Bill Brocius–Ike Clanton gang during their cattle raids across the border down in Mexico.

Macklin turned away again. "Wyatt?" he said softly,

talking past Berry's shoulders. "Pete Spence's up front."

"I see him." Wyatt, tipping his chair back and seeming to be almost asleep, was calmly studying the reflection in the glass door at the back of the room, a door leading out into the back alley. The bottom two panes were painted white, but the top two were clear, if a bit greasy from cigar smoke, and with the night outside and the bright lamps within, they served as a fair mirror looking back into the saloon.

"We gonna take him, Wyatt?" Morgan said quietly, lightly dusting the tip of his cue with chalk. "I'll bet he knows some of the ones that took down Virg."

"I'd like to, Morg. Believe me. But we don't have a warrant, and the place is too crowded. Let's wait and see what develops, okay?"

Slowly, Morgan bent again above the pool table, but his eyes kept shifting to follow Spence's movements. "You're the boss, Wyatt. But I don't like it. Not one bit."

Click-clack-click-click.

"You scratched," Hatch said. He sounded nervous.

"Shoot. Not my lucky day, I reckon."

Wyatt said nothing but continued to watch Spence's reflection in the glass door, his eyes cold with the emotionless gaze of a rattlesnake ready to strike. Macklin drew a long breath and released it slowly. There was trouble here . . . and the possibility of sudden gunfire and death. Spence had almost certainly had a hand in the ambush of the Earps' brother Virgil, less than three months before.

On December 28, Virgil Earp, then federal marshal for the territory and still recovering from the leg wound he'd received at the O.K. Corral back in October, had been bushwhacked while going about his rounds less than a block from Bob Hatch's front door. At least five gunmen with shotguns had opened up on him from the unfinished framework of a building under construction at the southeast corner of Fifth and Allen. Virgil had survived the attack—a miracle in itself—but his left arm was shattered and a chunk had been gouged from his left leg. The doctors said he would be crippled for life.

Everyone in town knew that Virgil's bushwackers had been members of the Cowboy gang out to even the score after the shootout at the O.K. Corral, which had pitted the three Earp brothers and the colorful Doc Holliday against Ike and Billy Clanton, Frank and Tom McLaury, and Billy Claiborne, all members of the Cowboy gang. After twenty-three seconds of gunfire, both McLaury brothers and Billy Clanton lay dead. Morgan, Virgil, and Doc Holliday had all been wounded. And the power of the Curly Bill Brocius–Ike Clanton Cowboy gang had been broken in the Arizona Territory forever . . . at least, so the Earp-friendly Tombstone *Epitaph* had proclaimed. John Clum, the paper's editor, was a personal friend of the Earps, and his editorials at times were less than impartial.

When Virgil had been gunned down in the street, though, the Earps, and the men who supported them, like Macklin, had known that while the battle had been won, the outcome of the war was yet to be decided.

And it *was* a war, too, a war between two factions, each irreconcilably opposed to the other. The Earps represented law and order, the Cowboys the free and easy lawlessness of the open range, despite the fact that they had Tombstone sheriff Johnny Behan squarely in their hip pocket. The Earps were Yankees, while most of the Cowboys were Southerners with a strong, anti-Yankee bias. The Earps were Republicans, the Clantons Democrats. The Earps represented towns and cities and the westward march of civilization, the Clantons the rugged, wide-open frontier. It was a war to the death between two cultures utterly and mutually alien to one another.

And from where Macklin was sitting it was beginning to look as though the war was turning against them.

"What d'ya think Spence is doing here?" Berry asked. While not one of the Earps' inner circle—he was acquaintance rather than confidant—he knew as much as anyone in town did about the Earp-Cowboy feud. "Hey, mebee he came to see if'n you boys was here!"

Neither Earp replied, and their silence was as worrying as any answer could have been.

"Want me to go check him out, Wyatt?" Macklin asked. For the past several months, since just before the O.K. Corral gunfight, in fact, Macklin had been working for the Earps . . . pretending to be gunfighter Johnny Waco in the hopes that Ike Clanton, Curly Bill Brocius, and some of the other Cowboys would think twice about taking on the Earps.

The plan had never worked well. The Clanton-Brocius gang had forced a showdown at the O.K. Corral despite Macklin's presence. Evidently, the Cowboys had decided to strike back the only way they could . . . one at a time and from ambush. They'd damn near killed Virgil in December, and everyone knew that Wyatt and Morgan were next on their list.

In fact, there were five Earp brothers in all. James, the oldest, was partly infirm, due to a wound he'd received in the war. He worked at Jim Vogan's Bowling Alley on Allen Street. Warren, the youngest, had only recently arrived in Tombstone. He'd missed the O.K. fight completely, but his added gun had helped keep the wolves at bay since.

Wyatt seemed to consider Macklin's question. "Nah. It's just Pete by himself, and he's not going to try anything against all of us."

"Maybe we should check in on Warren," Morgan said. "He's over at the Oriental tonight, last I heard." Warren had a job there on an irregular basis as a faro dealer.

That was a thought, too. The Cowboys' grudge was with Virgil, Morgan, Wyatt, and Doc Holliday, and to a lesser extent with Earp supporters like Macklin and John Clum. But suppose they wanted to just hurt the Earps, and maybe deliver a message? Curly Bill Brocius and his bunch weren't above plugging Warren in the back just to get back at Wyatt and Morgan.

"They're not interested in Warren," Wyatt said. "Not if they can get at us direct."

"Ah," Morgan said, as the man in the black overcoat paid for his drink and walked out through the saloon's front door. "Spence is leaving."

"After only one drink?" Wyatt said. "That *is* suspicious."

"No joke, Wyatt. I think the son of a bitch is up to something."

Macklin thought that Morgan was right. Why had Spence come into Campbell & Hatch's for a single drink? Was he waiting for someone?

Or surreptitiously checking the back room to see who was there?

"Think I'll check out front," he said. He drained his glass and set it on a small table by his chair. Standing, he retrieved his coat from a peg on the wall next to the back door, then walked into the saloon, his boots clumping hollowly on narrow floorboards. A few men sitting at various tables nodded to him, or called out a friendly "Hey, Macklin!" or "How's it goin'?" as he passed.

Macklin was an accepted fixture around Tombstone now. He still remembered how much of an outsider, how *alien* he'd felt when he first came to town five months before. Being associated with the Earp faction didn't hurt. A fair number of townspeople here liked the Earps and what they were trying to do, and a good many more would be friendly just to get on the Earps' good side.

Of course, he had no friends among the Cowboy elements in town. Pete Spence, for instance. Or Frank Stillwell. Even Ike Clanton still turned up from time to time, though he'd been a lot quieter lately, ever since he'd begged for his life and run during the O.K. Corral shoot-out. Macklin had gotten used to checking the street before stepping outside, glancing over his shoulder if he walked down an alley . . . and making sure he never sat with his back to a door or open window. It was a part of life in this culture . . . and an important way of ensuring that life continued.

He stopped at the bar. "Hey, Charlie. Let me have my gun."

"Sure thing, Mac," the bartender said. He handed Macklin his leather and the .45 Colt Peacemaker he'd bought at Spangenberg's Gun Shop shortly after the O.K. Corral fight. "You leavin'?"

"Just for a second," Macklin replied, buckling on the leather and adjusting the hang of the pistol at his hip. "Gotta check on something."

Charlie's expression told Macklin that he knew what that "something" was. "Take care, Mac."

"Always do."

Passing through the bar, he pushed open the swinging doors and stepped out onto the wood-plank sidewalk on the north side of Allen Street, feeling the bite of a chill March evening. Tombstone was a lively town, especially at night, when the streets were lit up with lanterns in store- and saloon-front windows, and the evening was alive with shouts, laughter, and even good-natured gunfire once in a while. A long-standing ordinance required that everyone check his guns in town—you could hand them over at any bar or hotel and pick them up when you left—but the law wasn't enforced with any regularity or zest. Cow-boys—some members of the Cowboy gang, yes, but mostly just ranch hands and cattlemen—liked to come into town once in a while and do a little serious hallooing, and things could get pretty noisy when they celebrated a paycheck with a few rounds from their Colts.

Right now, though, the evening was relatively quiet. Loud laughter and the sounds of breaking glass floated from the brightly lit building to Macklin's right. Campbell & Hatch's was right next to the Alhambra Saloon, separated from it by a narrow alley opening onto Allen. Across the wide street were the lights and banners of the Grand Hotel, right next to I. Levy's Musical Instruments and Stationery and Watt & Tarbell's Undertaking Parlor. A few men were on the street, a few horses lashed to hitching rails.

Macklin didn't see any sign of Pete Spence, to either right or left. He might have ducked into one of the other buildings on Allen, but . . .

Suddenly worried, Macklin stepped around the corner of the Hatch saloon and looked down the alley. Nothing there, either, but this was one of the few directions Spence could have gone to have vanished so quickly. The alley, Macklin knew, led around behind both the Alhambra and the billiard hall. If Spence was going back there . . . if there were people already waiting back there . . .

He considered charging down the alley . . . but if he was wrong he would be wasting time, and if he was right he might still be too late. Instead, he whirled about and plunged back into Campbell and Hatch's Saloon, racing through the bar to the billiard hall in the back.

"Morgan!" he called. "Wyatt . . . !"

Morgan was standing with his back to the rear door, the one leading out to the back alley, dusting the end of his cue with chalk. Wyatt was still in his chair, tipped back against the wall, right next to George Berry. The other spectators to the game sat or stood about the room, eyes on Macklin as he entered. Bob Hatch was bent over the table, about to make a shot.

The clock on the wall stood at just past eleven.

The panes of glass on the back door exploded into the room then, a cloud of shards sparkling in the light of the oil lamps hanging from the ceiling as gunfire, sharp and staccato, cracked and boomed from the alley out back. Morgan lurched forward, caught in the spray of glass and lead, his hip slamming into the table, his back arching sharply, the pool cue spinning from his grasp. At the same instant, George Berry screamed and toppled from his chair, a shocking splash of blood staining the wallpaper at his back. Two bullet holes drilled the wall inches above Wyatt's head; the gunfighter lunged forward, partly seeking cover on the floor, partly reaching out to his brother, who was turning now, collapsing in a string-cut heap.

Macklin dropped to the floor as gunfire crashed and thundered for a nightmare second or two, as bullets splintered glass and wood alike. Then the gunfire ceased, as suddenly as it had begun. Rising, he yanked his pistol from its holster and bolted for the shattered door. Bob Hatch banged through the door first, stepping into the alley, staring into the night. "Thought I heard someone running that way," he said, pointing.

"Help Wyatt and Morg," Macklin said. "I'll find 'em."

But the alley was empty, with no sign of the attackers. A couple of partly smoked hand-rolled cigarettes on the ground showed where someone *might* have been waiting, and a tang of gunpowder still hung in the chilly air. A back door into the Alhambra was open; if they'd gone in there, he'd never be able to smoke them out. And the alleyway leading south to Allen Street was empty.

Furious, frustrated, Macklin let down the hammer on the revolver and shoved the weapon back in its holster.

Inside, Wyatt and several of the spectators were tending to Morgan. "I sent Luke for Doc Goodfellow," Bob Hatch said. "They should be back soon."

"Let's get him into one of the card rooms," Charlie the bartender suggested. "There're sofas in there."

Together, they eased Morgan into one of the side rooms reserved for private card-playing parties and laid him on a couch with floral-print cushions. His eyes were closed, and his breathing was ragged. There was a lot of blood from a nasty hole in his back, which one of the onlookers tried to plug with a wadded-up handkerchief. There might have been other wounds as well—Macklin couldn't tell—but that one hole alone square in the center of Morgan Earp's back looked damned bad.

And when the doctor entered a few moments later, it didn't take him long to reach the same conclusion. "I'm sorry, Wyatt," Doc Goodfellow said, rising and shaking his head. "His spine's broken. I'm afraid he's done for."

Others began arriving, crowding into the small room. Two more of Tombstone's doctors, Mathews and Millar, arrived and examined the wounded man but had no better prognosis. Jim Earp, looking gray and grim, arrived . . . followed by Virgil, leaning heavily on a cane, his left arm dangling uselessly at his side. Warren Earp came in, breathless and a bit wild-eyed, a few minutes later.

Macklin stepped back into the hall and watched, moved by the tableau of brothers bent over the dying man on the couch. Morgan's eyes opened for a moment, squinting against the lantern overhead. "The game's over," he said, the words strangling on the blood in his throat, and died.

Death was a constant shadow to life on the Western frontier. Unlike the images conjured by Western dime novelists, though, there was no glory in gunfire and sudden death, and very little bravery. Most battles were ambushes, a sniper from the shadows, bushwackers in the dark, the gunshot through the back, and not the standup quick-draw affairs beloved of such novelists as Ned Buntline.

And the pain, aching and real, remained with the loved ones who'd survived.

T W O

✧ 1 ✧

SARAH NEVERS HEARD THE RATTLE OF A KEY IN THE LOCK downstairs, the creak of the front door opening, the board-squeaking footsteps of someone quietly entering the house, and she reached for the double-barreled shotgun she always kept propped against the table next to her bed. Dressed in her nightgown, she swung her legs over the side of the bed, heart pounding as she dropped a wrap over her bare shoulders, snugged the tie tight at her waist, and stepped barefoot onto the hardwood floor. It took every bit of courage she had to pad across the half-light of her room to the door, unbolt it, and step into the shadow-haunted hallway beyond.

She knew with the rational part of her mind that who-ever had just let himself in had keys and probably be-longed there, but she took the gun with her, anyway.

It had to be Macklin—she prayed it was Macklin. But the terror remained with her, a hammering of her heart against her breastbone, a tight feeling at her throat, a dry-ness in the mouth. *Please let it be Mac. . . .*

It was. He was quietly tiptoeing up the stairs when she met him at the top landing. " 'Bout time you showed up," she whispered. Her house was the Sarah Nevers Boarding House, Rooms To Let, and there were boarders sleeping in two of the upstairs rooms. She didn't like it when Macklin came banging in long after hours. It disturbed the guests.

Besides, she worried about him. A lot.

"I wish you wouldn't point that thing at me," he said. "I'm not *that* late!"

She lowered the shotgun. "Are, too. It's past one." She'd heard the big grandfather clock downstairs chime a few minutes ago. "Where've you been?"

"Morgan Earp is dead," he said, by indirect way of an answer.

"Oh, God, no!"

Sarah didn't like the Earps . . . and never had. To her way of thinking, they were cold-blooded gunnies who dealt in death and pain, and the sooner their type killed themselves off, the better. She'd lost her husband to a stray bullet in a shootout on the streets of Tombstone a few years back, and for Sarah, the Earps had come to represent all that was wrong in the lawless, hell-bent-for-leather lunacy of six-guns and showdowns.

Still, the Earps were prominent men in Tombstone, and the crippling of one, the death of another, meant the lawless elements were gaining the upper hand. Besides, she didn't like hearing about *any* man's death . . . even an Earp's.

"Caught him from behind while he was shooting pool at Bob Hatch's place. I think they were trying to get Morgan and Wyatt both . . . and maybe me, too." Mac hesitated. "George Berry's dead."

"Oh, damn, *damn!*" she said, the expletive shocking from a woman's mouth. "No, not George, too!" She knew George Berry, a decent man, a good husband and a loving father. Certainly not a shootist like the Earps. Why did the good ones have to die, and for no reason at all except that they were in the wrong place at the wrong time?

Her face was wet as the news flung wide open the doors to memories of Curtis Nevers, dead from a stray bullet when two so-called shootists began blazing away at each other in the street outside the saloon where he was having a drink.

"I'm sorry, Sarah," Macklin said, and he sounded as though he meant it. He knew about Curtis, and about how much she missed him still.

He reached the top of the stairs, and Sarah took three barefooted steps and was in his arms. She cared for Macklin, cared for him a lot, even if he had been working for the Earps since last October, when he'd shown up, literally, on her front porch, hurt, unconscious, with no name but Macklin, and no memory at all of who he was or where he'd come from. Macklin wasn't like any of the other gunnies she'd known. He was sweet, gentle, and considerate.

And he'd come after her when that . . . that nightmare horror had taken her off into the hills west of town. She shuddered at the memory. Macklin tightened his hold around her. "It's okay, Sarah. It's okay now."

Together, they walked to his room at the end of the hall to the right at the top of the stairs. The hallway had been repapered, but there were still smudged spots on the ceiling plaster to remind her of the fire. Those . . . those horrible *things* . . .

Macklin had told her later that they were Kra'agh, that they were . . . were *people* of a sort, but from another world. Sarah couldn't even begin to think of them as people, as human beings. They were so different, so strange, she couldn't even remember what they looked like now. In her nightmares, they were little more than horribly confused knots of black and brown, with the flat heads of snakes, large-pupiled eyes that turned the blood cold, and misshapen bodies drawn from the blackest depths of a raving lunatic's brain-fevered visions. Usually, she thought of them simply as . . . as *things*, as animals, perhaps. At other times, she imagined they must have been demons from Hell, and then she tended to lock herself in her room with her shotgun, read her Bible, and pray.

Mostly, she tried not to remember at all, and mostly she succeeded.

The nightmares could be pretty bad, though. . . .

"You know, Sarah," Macklin said gently, sitting on the edge of his big brass four-poster bed, "it really might be best if you sold this place and moved on. I think there are too many memories for you here."

They'd had this discussion before, and more than once. "You know I'm not going to leave," she said. "Curtis put his heart and soul into this place, and I'm not giving it up, not if all the demons of Hell parade right here in front of me."

Besides, she thought. *You're still here, Mac. You think I'm going to leave, while you're still here . . . ?*

She wondered again if she was in love with him.

He was having some trouble getting his boots off, and she stooped to help pull them free.

"You don't have to do that."

"I want to. Let me help."

Rising again, she helped him remove his shirt. Lightly, her fingers brushed against that enigmatic disk of shiny black translucent material set low in his chest, at the bottom of his breastbone. He called it his Companion, and had told her it was supposed to talk to him . . . except that it was broken. It had been the sight of that disk, five months ago when he was brought in unconscious and she undressed him for bed, that first stirred an awakening wonder in her, and the knowledge that, whatever he was, Macklin was not like other men. The object tended to support his story that he was from another world, though she still wasn't sure how much of that she could swallow.

To hear Mac tell it, he wasn't sure how much he believed either, and that was reassuring, somehow. If some of the strange things he said were true, the world, the universe, was a much stranger place than she'd ever imagined.

It was a much more dangerous and unsettling place, too; she tried again not to think of the Kra'agh. If Mac didn't entirely believe the story—which had been passed on to him by that strange woman, Doris—then maybe she didn't need to believe it either.

It was much more comforting that way.

When she started to unbuckle his jeans, he stopped her with a gentle hand and pulled her to his side. "We've talked about this before," he said. "You know I can't stay here, that some day I'm going to have to leave."

She nodded. She was terribly aware of his closeness, of the mingled smells of boot leather, sweat, and man. "You have to go to Tucson, you said. But that's only seventy-five miles. You can do it in a day if you catch the train up at Benson."

"Sarah . . . if I go to Tucson, I might not be coming back. I might be going farther. A *lot* farther."

"As . . . as far as California?" She knew that that was not what he was talking about, but she couldn't bring herself to face the idea.

"Yes. A lot farther than California."

"But you could still . . . could still come back to Tombstone someday. If you wanted." Her eyes were filling with tears again, and she brushed at them angrily with the back of her hand. Damn it, she didn't want to show weakness. . . .

"If I can," he said. He shook his head. "But I don't know if I can ever come back here. They might not let me."

She leaned over and laid her head against his bare chest, her hand touching the black disk. Deep-buried rectangles of colored light flickered in its black crystal heart.

She always expected it to tick or buzz or whir like some clockwork contrivance, and was always a little surprised when she sensed nothing with her touch but his heartbeat.

"By they . . . do you mean the people you and that woman worked for?" She was never able to call Doris by her name. "Or the . . . animals?"

He sighed. "They're not animals. They're as smart as we are, and maybe a good bit smarter. They just think differently than we do."

She didn't want to think about the Kra'agh. Here, in the circle of Mac's arms, she was safe. She would *not* remember. . . .

"I don't know, Sarah. All I know is what Dorree . . . what *Doris* told me. Earth, this whole planet, is under the protection of something called the Associative. Part of what they're doing is protecting primitive worlds like Earth from predators such as the Kra'agh."

"Primitive!" She snorted. "You make it sound like we're wild Indians. Like Apaches."

"Maybe we are, to them." He shrugged. "There's another Associative Monitor, a kind of a spy, I guess, in Tucson. If I can reach him, give him a code phrase I've been taught, I'll be able to talk to my people. They'll send a ship, maybe, to pick me up."

"And that's the silliest thing I've ever heard. There's no ocean within three hundred miles of Tucson, unless you count the Gulf of California, down in Old Mexico!"

"An airship, Sarah. Maybe aethership would be a better word. A ship that can travel out in space, between the stars."

"I still . . . can't grasp that."

"I know. I have a lot of trouble with the idea myself."

"Then don't believe it."

"Sarah . . . I think I have to." He reached up and tapped the black disk on his chest. "There are a few things that say I *have* to believe it. Like this. Like Dorree. Like the

Kra'agh Hunters. If those things aren't true, then I'm just plain crazy. And that's a damned scary idea."

"You don't have to go. You don't have to do *anything* you don't want to!"

"I told Dorree I would try to get to Tucson. I promised her when I went back to find you." An unreadable expression passed over his face. His eyes looked troubled. "You know, I should have gone a long time ago . . . after the O.K. Corral fight. But, well . . . you'd been hurt, and I didn't want to leave you like that. And the Earps still needed me, wanted me to stay, especially after Virgil was hurt.

"But I have to admit it to myself, Sarah. I've been afraid of leaving Tombstone. I think I'm afraid of finding out who or what I might be. Afraid of finding out if this weird stuff that happened to us is real, or just some kind of bizarre dream, or maybe insanity."

"You told me last November you wanted to stay and learn about the people here."

"That was part of it, sure. With this amnesia, everything, even ordinary day-to-day things like eating a meal or taking a walk down the street, seemed so strange. Some things—like handling a gun—I kind of took to right off, you know? Like I knew how to use it, but just didn't remember. And languages. I've been finding I know lots of languages besides English . . . and I don't think English is my native tongue." He tapped the disk on his chest again. "Dorree said this is something called a computer, an intelligent computer, that can give me information, help me learn things, help me know things . . . but it was damaged in the crash. The connections are broken in places, so the only way it can talk to me now is in dreams or hunches. Well, I kind of had a hunch to stay put for a while. Maybe it was telling me that."

"You scare me when you talk that way, Mac."

"I don't mean to. I just want you to understand . . . I

don't belong here. And I'm going to have to leave, soon."

She tried changing tack. "I don't trust that Doris woman, you know. Not as far as I could throw her."

He smiled. "I know. But . . . she knew who I was. Was able to tell me things about where I came from, what I was doing here. And . . . I could remember bits and pieces of stuff with her in it, usually in my dreams. So I have to believe her. If I don't, everything I think I know is a madman's ravings." He reached out and stroked Sarah's cheek. "And the worst of it is, that would make you part of my ravings. I'd hate like hell to find out you weren't real, Sarah."

"I'm real enough, mister. Just give me a try if you don't believe it!"

"Oh, I believe you all right. But you know I can't settle down with you, get married or anything like that."

"I know, Mac. But I can dream, right?"

He drew her closer, arm tightening around her shoulder. "Sometimes I think our dreams are all we have left that's real."

✧ 2 ✧

THE DREAM USUALLY STARTED THE SAME EVERY TIME, though there were variations. He was in another . . . place, a place like the Earth he knew, except for the impossible city of blue crystal, and the vast, banded world, like a moon but encircled by glorious rings, suspended against a sky far thicker with stars than the night skies of Earth. He was not Macklin, but Ma'khleen, a primitive-worlds Monitor for the Associative. Dorree was there, dark-haired and impossibly beautiful, and they were partners, both in the mission they were about to embark on together, and in love.

Then he was in . . . another place, the control cabin of a spacecraft, and the dazzling, silver light of a full moon shone through the cockpit windows and viewscreens, dazzling, and the two of them were doing . . . something . . . something, *he couldn't remember what . . . but* they *were attacking . . . they were moving in for the kill. . . .*

"Maybe we can outrun them!" Dorree called.

"It's too late!" *he shouted, and the panic was a black cloud gnawing at his mind. "The base is gone! They must already be on Earth. . . ."*

"Target, bearing one-seven-one by plus-five-three! They've got a lock . . . !"

"Hang on! We might be able to lose them!"

"Range seven-five-one-one, closing!"

Stars wheeled past the cockpit, which was plunged into an eerie, instrument-lit darkness as the moon fell astern. Ahead, Earth hung suspended against the stars, a blue and white ornament, impossibly fragile and alone. . . .

"Ma'khleen," *she said.* "If the Monitor base is gone, if they have a fleet moving toward Earth . . . !"

"The primitives won't have a chance," *he replied, grim as death.* "But maybe we can—"

The explosion tore at them, hammering the ship. Air whistled into space, shrill and deadly. Ahead, the Earth rapidly expanded, filling the forward sky.

And then the second explosion took them, a thunderclap shattering creation. Clouds streaked past as they fell toward a wildly spinning world.

"Eject!" *he shouted.* "Eject! Eject!"

"Ma'khleen!" *she shrieked. . . .*

And then they were falling, out of control, spinning through a night sky, ejecting in flame and violence. . . .

And the next thing he remembered was awakening in the desert, on this savage world called Earth. There were confused memories of a face, the face of an old man helping him, and of a stagecoach on the dirt track in the desert.

And they were still after him, determined to hunt him down, no matter the cost.

"Ma'khleen . . . !"

✧ **3** ✧

HE AWOKE WITH A START, SWEAT DRENCHING HIS FACE and neck and chest, the bedclothes wringing wet. Groaning, he sat up.

It was early morning. Sunlight streamed through the window in his small bedroom. The smell of frying bacon, the sounds of laughter, the clinking of glasses and silverware, rose from the dining room downstairs.

Sarah had left his jeans on him, but placed his shirt neatly folded over the back of a chair. He reached for it, put it on, then retrieved his boots.

A few moments later, he entered the dining room. Business at the Sarah Nevers Boarding House had been slow lately, and there were only three other guests besides Macklin. All three sat at the table, discussing the news splashed across the front page of the Tombstone *Epitaph:* MORGAN EARP MURDERED!

Harry Fulbright had long been a regular at Sarah Nevers' place, a one-time miner who'd had his right arm crushed in a cave-in. He held the newspaper up in his good hand so Macklin could read the headline. "So! You hear about this?"

Macklin sat down, taking the neatly folded cloth napkin from beside his plate and placing it in his lap. Sarah ran what she was pleased to call a *genteel* boarding house. "I was there, Harry."

"Well, yup. So you were. Says so, right here. You see who done it?"

"Nope."

"It was the Cowboy gang, of course," Roger McAllister said. He was a lawyer only recently arrived from New

York City, with hopes of setting up a practice here in Tombstone. He'd been staying at the Nevers boarding house until he could afford a place of his own. "Trying to get back at the Earps and their friends!"

"Yeah, it looks like your friends the Earps are in real trouble now, eh, Macklin?" Fulbright said. He'd never had much love for the Earps . . . or the Clanton-Brocius gang either, for that matter. A lot of people in town thought both factions were troublemakers, and lived for the day when both would depart for good, leaving the decent and God-fearing citizens of Tombstone in peace. "Two down, four to go, if'n you count Holliday!"

"Way I heerd it, the Cowboys ain't interested in Jim or Warren," John Biscayne said. He was a thickly be-whiskered drummer for a dry goods firm back East, stopping off in Tombstone for a week on his way to Los Angeles, or so he claimed. "So I guess it's more like two down, two to go, huh?"

"Question is," Harry said, looking narrowly at Macklin, "are Clanton and his bunch gonna be satisfied just plantin' the Earps and Doc Holliday? Or will they be evenin' the score with some of the Earps' friends?"

"You just watch your tongue, Harry Fulbright," Sarah said, entering from the kitchen with a plate of still-sizzling bacon. She dropped the plate onto a cast-iron trivet on the table with an angry clank. "You got no call goin' on like that!"

"I didn't mean nothin' by it, ma'am. But the fact is, the Cowboys is after blood since the O.K. Corral fight." He waved at Macklin with the blunt stub-end of his right arm. "Heh! You ever think about maybe takin' a vacation somewheres else until this all blows over?"

"A long trip," McAllister said darkly, "for your health."

The front bell sounded. Sarah looked flustered. "Now who could that be?"

"You want me to get it?" Macklin asked.

"No, no. You go on and eat. Bacon's gettin' cold." She untied her apron as she left the dining room, heading for the front hall.

"Seriously, Macklin," Fulbright said when she'd gone. "My cousin Ned, over at the Tombstone Livery 'n' Feed, said he'd heard Pete Spence and Frank Stillwell and some of the rest of the Cowboy gang talking. Stuff like how they won't rest until all the Earps and all the people who stood by 'em are dead. Face facts. There's just too many of them, and not enough of you!"

"You know," Biscayne said, looking at Macklin with bright interest, "they say you was at the O.K. Corral, too, that day."

"I got there late," Macklin lied. "I didn't see what happened."

In fact, moments before the fight he'd learned that Ike Clanton and his friends were setting up a deliberate confrontation with the Earps, one that would move the Earps into position for hidden gunmen to take them down by rifle fire from a nearby stable barn. Macklin had gone to the barn while the Earps and Holliday tried to disarm the Cowboys in front of the corral. There'd been a Cowboy gang member up there, okay, unconscious . . . and a Kra'agh disguised as another Cowboy. Macklin had wounded the creature and it fled into the hills west of Tombstone, where he tracked it down and killed it.

The man in the barn, a kid named Jake Thurston, was hopelessly insane when he came to, babbling about hideous monsters who looked and talked like men. . . .

Later, Macklin had discussed what had happened with Wyatt. He'd had to, since he'd been under suspicion at the time for the death that morning of another Kra'agh victim, Doc Shea.

Macklin didn't think Wyatt quite believed the tale, and he didn't blame the man one bit. Sarah's story had supported his, however . . . and there was the matter of those strange, H-shaped footprints Virgil had seen in the ashes of a burned-down farmhouse on the outskirts of Tombstone, and all those butchered dogs in town.

Macklin's help in the barn behind the O.K. Corral had cemented his relationship with the Earps, and the charges in the Shea murder had been dropped. Virgil had asked him to keep on working with them as a hired gun, known variously as John Macklin or Johnny Waco.

But it was also decided to downplay his role in the shootout, the "street fight," as Wyatt called it. It was best for all concerned if tales of weird, nightmare monsters were kept quiet, to keep from panicking the town . . . and also to keep the Earps and their supporters from becoming laughingstocks. Monsters that somehow disguised themselves as men? Nonsense!

"Mr. Macklin?" Sarah said, coming back into the room. She looked worried. "You have . . . a visitor."

Who the hell would be looking for him here? He dropped his napkin on the table. "Excuse me, gentlemen."

Wyatt Earp was waiting for him in the front parlor, his hat in his hands. The face above the shaggy, drooping mustache looked gray and drawn, and there were heavy circles beneath the eyes. He was wearing the same dark suit he'd been wearing at Bob Hatch's place last night, and looked as though he hadn't gotten a bit of sleep.

Macklin carefully ignored the dark stains on Wyatt's gray vest, and the carefully shuttered pain behind those dangerous eyes.

"Sorry to intrude, Macklin," Wyatt said. He turned his flat-crowned hat in his hands. "Wanted to tell you, though . . . we're putting Virg and his wife and Jim on the train to California tomorrow . . . and we're sending Morg along to be buried back home." The Earps' parents lived in Colton, California now.

"Okay. By 'we,' you mean you and Warren?"

"And Holliday, and a few others. We're going to see them as far as Tucson."

"Oh?"

"Just to see that they're safe, the first part of the trip." He turned his flat-brimmed hat in his hands as he spoke. "Talked to Marietta Spence this morning. Had her swear out a deposition at the courthouse."

Marietta was Pete Spence's Indian wife. They had a small shack on the west side of town, on Fremont Street north of the Mexican quarter.

"You know, Pete never treated her well," Wyatt went on. "Beat her something awful. She told us that he'd threatened to kill her if she ever talked about what she knew about the Bisbee stage robbery, and a lot of other things. But she told us this morning, right enough."

"What'd she have to say?"

"She told them that Morgan was killed by Spence, Frank Stillwell, a woodcutter named Florentino Cruz, Indian Charlie and another half-breed she didn't know, and a German named Freis."

"You don't say?

"I do say. According to Marietta, Pete up and ran for the Mexican border early this morning. And Indian Charlie surrendered to Behan, which kind of puts him out of our reach, right now. But she says that Frank Stillwell and Ike Clanton are both in Tucson."

There was a dark light in Earp's eyes, a reflection of a carefully controlled, murderous fury, feeding on the pain there. "Doc and Warren and a few of the boys and I are going to take him down. We wondered if you wanted to come along."

So . . . there it was. His chance to go to Tucson. He wondered if he dared.

Face it, Macklin, he thought. *You've been running scared, not willing to even look at what you have to do. If you don't go now, you might as well bury everything*

Dorree told you, forget about the stars, and make a home for yourself right here in Tombstone.

But he already had a home in Tombstone. People who knew him. A girl who cared for him. Did he even *want* to leave?

"Something else," Earp added. "Some dogs've been killed in Tucson. Gutted."

"Oh, damn." The monsters again, the alien Kra'agh. Dogs and horses didn't like their smell. Apparently, dogs went berserk, and quite a few had been sliced open in a casually hideous fashion just before the O.K. Corral fight. Macklin thought the Kra'agh were killing them when the animals threatened to give them away. Wyatt accepted the theory without saying whether he believed it or not . . . but he was passing on the news now because he knew Macklin believed it.

Kra'agh in Tucson? That couldn't be good.

"What do you say, Macklin?" Earp prompted. "Are you in or out?"

Macklin nodded. He wasn't entirely sure why. He just knew he had to do this. "Count me in," he said.

He heard a muffled sob at his back, and turned in time to see Sarah, who'd just entered the front hall and was standing in the doorway to the front parlor. She pressed the back of her hand against her mouth, then whirled and fled.

And he knew he wouldn't be able to find the words to make it right with her.

THREE

◆ **1** ◆

THE DLAADTHMA CIRCLED, WHEELING SO HIGH ABOVE THE human town that from the ground it was no more than a black speck, a buzzard circling lazily in the bright March sky.

From a distance, it looked like a buzzard . . . but it was not. Leathery bat wings stretched three meters, catching the rising thermals. Clawed feet, slightly webbed, were tucked up into the gray fur shrouding the elongated body. It was headless, but two large eyes set far apart in the being's shoulders provided a crispness of resolution that could make out the gleam of sweat on the brows of the humans half a kilometer below. By nature, the dlaadthma was a nocturnal being; those eyes possessed retinas that cast back the light in baleful, twin orange glows, giving it excellent vision even by starlight. But the Masters had sent it aloft in the glare of this alien sunrise, and its eyes worked well enough, now, even at this high level of illumination.

It had no choice in the matter, of course. The Masters had come to the dlaadthmas' world many cycles ago, and now all dlaadthmas existed solely to serve them. Most of the life native to their homeworld had been exterminated for the Masters' pleasure and feeding, but a few species, judged useful, had been preserved . . . though genetic manipulation had reshaped them in improbable ways. The dlaadthma's eyes, for instance, worked now in bright daylight, where the creature's ancestors would have been blinded. The brain had been redesigned in subtle ways, making the aerial being at the same time less intelligent, less free-spirited, more tractable, but with a far sharper memory. An embedded technological device—the dlaadthma had never been technic beings, had never even known the making of fire—allowed the creature to transmit what it was seeing to its waiting Masters.

The Masters used them on alien worlds such as this, as scouts.

And what this dlaadthma was seeing below would be of interest to them.

❖ **2** ❖

MACKLIN FELT AN EERIE PRICKLING AT THE BACK OF HIS neck, and looked up. It was early in the morning, a couple of hours past daybreak, and the sky was a bright, deep blue with only a few wisps of high cirrus clouds to mar its otherwise infinite and empty depths.

A lone buzzard, a tiny, shapeless spot, wheeled and circled at the zenith, almost as though it knew there was death here in the street so far below.

He stood off to the side on the dusty Tombstone street, his hat in his hands as Wyatt and Warren Earp, Doc Holliday, and three other men carefully, reverently, slid the pinewood coffin bearing Morgan Earp's body into the back of the hearse. Hundreds of townspeople stood on the boardwalks to either side of Allen Street, paying their final respects to the second-youngest of the Earps, the man known as the hothead within the Earp fraternity, the man most people had simply known would die young, if the gossip of the past two days was any indication.

Virgil Earp stood at Macklin's left, leaning heavily on a cane, his ruined arm hanging at his side. Next to him was Allie, his wife. On Macklin's right was one of Tombstone's foremost citizens, John Clum, the town's mayor, editor of the Tombstone *Epitaph,* and an ardent supporter of the Earps.

"Damned shame," Clum said, a hard murmur beneath his breath. "A crying damned shame."

"What's gonna happen now?" Kate Elder said. "Are the Cowboys gonna take over things again?" The woman, "Big-nosed Kate" as she was known, was a prostitute—a "soiled dove" in the parlance of the locals, and also Doc Holliday's mistress. They weren't together any longer, not since she'd let herself be pressured by Behan and his cronies into giving evidence against Doc last year . . . but they were still seen together from time to time, enough to set tongues wagging and eyes to winking.

"Not likely," Jim Earp said nearby. "Wyatt and Warren are just clearing the decks for action, as they'd say in the Navy. I'd wager you ain't seen nothing yet!"

The city fire bell tolled, a single, clear, heart-tugging note. The bells had tolled all day the day before, while Morgan's body had lain in flower-bedecked state in the lobby of the Cosmopolitan Hotel. It rang again now as a final send-off.

The coffin was loaded. Wyatt and Doc clambered into a waiting buggy. Virgil helped Allie aboard another buggy, then climbed up with her, while Jim Earp and Warren took a third. With a rumble, the hearse began moving forward, followed by the procession of horse-drawn buggies. Macklin walked over to the hitching rail where his placid chestnut mare, Molly, waited patiently. Freeing the reins, he swung up into the saddle, wondering as he settled back whether he would be able to walk tonight. Nearby, two more escorts—Sherman McMasters and "Turkey Creek"

Jack Johnson—were already mounted, with Winchester rifles prominently displayed across their saddles. Together,
they walked their horses after the buggies, eyes alert on the
gathered crowd, and the buildings behind them. If the
Clanton-Brocius Cowboy gang wanted to try picking off
another Earp, this might be the place for it.

But the town remained quiet, save for the crunch of
gravel, the clop of horseshoes on hard-packed earth, and
the steady tolling of the bell. The procession moved
slowly past the Allen Street entrance to the O.K. Corral,
site of the "street fight" of the previous October, and on
through the Mexican Quarter to the west without incident.

The Cowboys, evidently, weren't about to dare a move
against all of the Earps together, especially when they had
their escort with them. But everyone knew the gang would
try again.

The thought made Macklin wonder about the Kra'agh.
The alien Hunters had been determined to destroy any
Associative Monitors on this world—at least, that was
what Dorree had told him. Especially after he'd killed one
and wounded another during the events surrounding the
O.K. Corral fight, he knew they would try for him again.
According to Dorree, the Kra'agh were relentless, mer-
ciless, and driven by a cold-blooded determination to
eliminate anything they saw as a threat.

Macklin took another look up into the blue depths of
the sky.

The buzzard was still there, circling.

✧ **3** ✧

*THE IMAGE OF THE MAN OTHERS KNEW AS ROWDY BRICE
hesitated at the entrance to the human structure. Behind
the fiction of its* gah-*projected camouflage, the Kra'agh
Hunter known as* Kehleh-Dr'kwegh, *Eater of Living
Hearts, tasted the late afternoon air with flicking scent-*

tongues. Its senses were fully extended, vision, smell, hearing, infrared, emotional reception, and magnetic and electrical field detection all stretched to their utmost, questing ahead and all around for any sign of ambush. It could taste the electrical fields of Deathstalker inside, could smell the other Kra'agh among the mingled smells of hay and rotting wood and the bodily excretions of the four-legged prey animals the locals called horses.

Inside, the light was dim, cut to a pale, dust-filtered twilight falling through the spaces between the rough-hewn boards that made up the walls of the building, which it had recently learned was called a barn.

The barn was empty, save for the scurryings of furry fear-squeakers . . . minor life forms not worthy of the attention of a Kra'agh Hunter. There were horses outside, in the corral beneath the big, hand-lettered sign that read Logan's Stable, *but the dirt-floored interior was empty . . . except for the dark emotion-leakings of Deathstalker.*

Movement stirred in the corner as Eater entered, with a rasping hiss of scales and fur, of uncoiling neck and unfolding feeder arms. Foreleg slasherclaws gleamed in the half-light, matching the cold-gold reptilian glitter of the eyes.

"Droo'kah! Droo'keh!" *Deathstalker said, its formal greeting a rasping hiss punctuated by the clatter of hard-edged mouth parts.*

"Droo'kah! Droo'keh, Chahh dukregh!" *Eater replied in the same voice, before shifting to English.* "It is good of you to come, Blood-taster."

"Our agents have reported that the prey has finally left the human hive-center called Tombstone," *Deathstalker said, switching also to English. Kra'agh vocal cords were not well suited to the language, and it was important to keep in practice.* "Unfortunately, it is still closely protected by the well-armed prey-creatures called Earps."

"We have the objective under constant observation. There has been no sign of the prey as yet."

"The patience of the Hunt. Our scouts report that the prey has arrived in this area. It is only a matter of time before it approaches the ambush site in order to communicate with the Associative Monitor."

Eater's feeder arms twisted behind the gah-projection image, a gesture of concern and displeasure. "It is dangerous allowing the Monitor to live while we operate in this area. It could discover our operations."

"It will be dealt with at the same time we take the prey. Have there been any unforeseen difficulties with the infiltration?"

"None, Deathstalker. The prey-animals known as Ike Clanton and Bill Brocius have accepted me as a member of the gang. I can sense no suspicions on their part that Rowdy Brice has been patterned." It paused. "I wonder, though, if it would not be more efficient to pattern the leaders rather than the lesser herd-members. If we replaced Ike Clanton, we could control the gang's activities directly."

"Perhaps. But we would also run the risk of someone detecting the replacement. Our command of local idiom may be less than perfect, and gah-projections do not provide perfect camouflage at close range or in bright light. For now, it is better to pattern gang members who are less prominent than the leaders, and remain out of view as much as possible."

"As you command, Deathstalker." Behind the electronically projected image of the patterned human, Eater made the habit-driven k'grekch-gesture of deference and respect. It allowed itself a small claw-twist of irony, however, one unseen by the other Kra'agh. Deathstalker might be dominant here, leader of the Hunt, Taster of Blood . . . but it was well known throughout the advance Kra'agh fleet that Deathstalker had allowed itself to be *trapped and badly wounded by its prey-beast, some sixteen* ch'graach-ngah *ago. Why Deathstalker had been allowed to remain in command of the scouting expedition after such a humiliation was unknown. Possibly the Blood-Taster had been grooming the Fleet Commander's mouthparts lately to curry favor.*

Or . . . more likely . . . perhaps it had retained power simply by virtue of knowing this planet and its food beasts. Its understanding of the semi-sentient life forms on this primitive world was certainly impressive.

Eater began to turn away . . . then staggered to the side as Deathstalker struck a savage blow across its side with one foreleg. The slasherclaw was retracted, as ritual demanded, or Eater's flank would have been laid open from foreleg to braincase, but the attack was powerful enough to bring Eater to its foreknees, slasherclaws scrabbling ineffectually at the dirt.

"You will address a Blood-Taster with proper deference," Deathstalker told it.

"Yes, Blood-Taster." Eater didn't pretend ignorance of its offense . . . though it did wonder how Deathstalker had sensed that ironic claw-twist. Deathstalker's cha-sense must be unusually sharp for it to read Eater through its gah-*projection. Extending its snaky neck, it dropped its head to the position of the subordinate. "My kill is yours for first taste."*

"Keep that in mind," Deathstalker replied. "We must retain discipline if we are to survive this world. The near-sentients are primitive, but they can be as dangerous as ghraelleth *at high suns."*

"I will remember, Blood-Taster."

"Maintain your watch over the ambush zone," Deathstalker said, the incident apparently forgotten. "The prey comes soon."

"You are leader of the Hunt, Blood-Taster." This time,

Eater's gesture was straightforward, carrying only respect.

But perhaps it was just as well that Deathstalker could not read its thoughts.

⁕ **4** ⁕

MACKLIN LAY BACK IN THE STIFFLY UPRIGHT SEAT OF THE railway coach, eyes closed, feeling the sway of the odd vehicle as it clackety-clacked along the rails. The sun had gone down moments before, setting the western sky ablaze with reds and oranges and purples, a fantastic spectacle of color and cloud shapes as entrancing, he thought, as the green, star-clotted sky above the city of blue light that he saw so often in his dreams.

He thought he remembered vehicles something like this one from those dreams . . . but those flew, magnetically levitated through gold-glowing hoops, with inertial damping fields that blocked out the lurches, bumps, and swaying from side to side as they hurtled above a landscape of light and crystal.

Inertial damping fields? He shook his head in wry bemusement. Another concept leaking into his conscious mind from his damaged Companion? Or a fragment of a dream? He couldn't tell . . . and it was possible that there was no distinction between the two.

This world's far more primitive technology relied on enclosed, wheeled carts strung together in chains drawn along paired, steel rails by steam-powered vehicles called locomotives . . . impressive, noisy beasts nevertheless woefully underpowered considering their size. *Trains*, the giant machines were called.

Still, for all its faults and discomforts, the train was faster and infinitely more comfortable than any of the alternative modes of available transport, which included several types of animal-drawn carts and coaches, or riding on horseback. Macklin had learned how to ride months ago. In five months of practice, he still hadn't gotten the hang of spending hours in the saddle without ending up saddle sore and blistered.

Yes, the train was much preferable for long journeys.

The procession of buggies, hearse, and horsemen had reached Benson, twenty-three miles northwest of Tombstone, by afternoon. After a three-hour wait at the Benson station, they'd loaded the casket aboard the westbound train, boarded one of the coach cars, and enjoyed the next two hours in relative comfort as the train chugged and clacked its way across the fifty-some miles of open desert between Benson and Tucson. The Earp party had the coach to themselves. Wyatt, Holliday, and Macklin occupied two facing seats on the left side of the car, while Warren, Virgil, Jim, and Allie took the benches across the aisle. Johnson and McMasters had the seats behind Macklin. There were lots of empty seats left in the coach, but other passengers entering the car at Tombstone had taken one look at the grim-faced men and lone woman and hastily went on to the next car.

They were nearly all the way to Tucson when Doc Holliday removed his hat from over his eyes and sat up straighter in the seat opposite Macklin's. "Pity about Pete Spence gettin' away to Mexico," he said. He started coughing then, letting go with a deep, rasping hack that stained his already soiled handkerchief with blood when he brought it away from his lips.

"We'll get him," Wyatt promised. "Pete Spence is a dead man. But we'll get Stillwell and Ike Clanton in Tucson."

The train coach gave a lurch and swayed alarmingly from side to side, as a piercing shriek scratched the night air. Macklin felt the car slowing. "Now what?" Holliday rasped.

"We're stoppin'," Turkey Creek Johnson said from the

seat behind. He had his face pressed against the window, trying to see ahead.

"Think it's a trap, Wyatt?" Warren asked from across the aisle.

"Hard to say," Wyatt replied. "Lots of reasons we could be stopping."

After a moment, the car shuddered to a halt. Macklin drew his .45 and checked the ring of cartridges in the cylinder. The Earps did the same, including Virgil, awkward with his crippled arm.

"I see a light outside," McMasters said. "Couple guys on horseback. One's got a lantern. Other has a railroad signal flag."

"Could be a holdup," Turkey Creek said. "That, or they're after *us*. . . ."

"Easy does it," Wyatt warned. "I doubt they'd try to take us here, all at once. Not when they've got to come through those narrow doors one at a time." He indicated the doors at either end of the coach with a nod. Still, he shifted his jacket so his holstered pistol was easily accessible, and he moved the rifle he was carrying from the floor to his lap.

"Yeah," Holliday said. He was holding a shotgun, the muzzle almost negligently pointed toward the door at the front of the coach. "Would *you* want to be the first one to knock and come on through?"

A moment later, that door opened, and a lean man in a dusty overcoat stepped through. A badge flashed at his breast.

"Joe!" Virgil Earp said, startled. "What the hell are you doing here?"

"Hello, Virgil," the man said, peering about the car.

"It's okay, boys," Virgil said. "This is a friend of mine."

"Glad I found you. Wyatt Earp? Is he here?"

"Here I am."

"There you are. I'm Joseph Evans, Deputy United States Marshal. Sorry to flag you boys down, but I thought you ought to know."

"Know what?"

"That Frank Stillwell, Indian Charlie, and Ike Clanton are all in Tucson, and they know you're coming. They've received a couple of telegrams from Tombstone today, one right after your train woulda left. They could be waitin' for ya."

"Appreciate the warning," Warren said.

"How long they been in Tucson?" Wyatt wanted to know.

"Indian Charlie, Stillwell, and Clanton, they've been here a few days. They're in Tucson giving depositions on the Bisbee stage robbery to a grand jury."

"I'll just bet they are," Doc cackled. "Lyin' through their teeth is nearer the mark."

"What are you boys doing in Tucson, anyway?" the deputy marshal asked.

Wyatt nodded toward James, Virgil, and Allie across the aisle. "Seeing them out of Tombstone. Our parents are living in Colton, out in California. They're going out to stay with them, for a spell. That's where they'll bury Morgan."

"I see. You ain't figuring on settling old scores in Tucson, are you?"

"We'll protect ourselves," Warren put in. He patted the shotgun he was holding. "If the Cowboys come after us, you'd better know we're gonna protect ourselves!"

Evans gave a tight smile. "Well, now, no one's sayin' you can't look after yourselves. But it's kind of a funny coincidence that Stillwell, Clanton, and Indian Charlie are all here, just when you boys come into town."

"Are we supposed to turn our lives inside out trying to avoid Clanton and his bunch?" Wyatt said easily. "There's just one railway in these parts, and it runs through Tucson

and on to California. We can't help it if those people are
here."

"The fact that they're here is why we're all coming
along," Warren said. "We *don't* want any trouble."

"Okay, boys. No one said you did. In fact, if we hear
that Clanton or his bunch tried to start something with
you, we'll probably just happen to be lookin' the other
way while you deal with things."

"They'll be discreet, Joseph," Virgil said. "Wyatt and
Warren and the boys'll just see to it we're safe and on
our way, and then they'll turn around and head straight
back to Tombstone. Isn't that right, boys?"

The others chorused grunts of assent.

"That's fine. We just don't want any trouble in Tucson.
You people can do what you want in Tombstone, but we
don't want your war up here."

"There won't be any trouble, Deputy," Wyatt said.

"Glad to hear it, boys." Evans touched the brim of his
hat. "Gentlemen. Ma'am. Sorry to have delayed you. And
boys, I'm real sorry to hear about Morgan. You all take
care, now."

Evans left the car and, moments later, the train started
moving again, slowly, with a jolt that rattled their teeth,
then faster and faster.

"What he said," Holliday pointed out as they gathered
speed, "kinda confirms what they're saying back in Tombstone."

"What's that?"

"That Frank Stillwell was seen in Tucson Sunday
morning, less'n ten hours after Morg was shot. If that's
true, he couldn't of had a hand in what happened."

Macklin watched Wyatt's attention shift to the seat
across the aisle, where Jim was talking quietly to Virgil,
while Allie sat next to the window, silently staring out
into the evening light. "We know the sons of bitches that
got Morgan," Wyatt said in a low and ice-deadly

voice. "Stillwell and Clanton were in on it, even if they weren't actually there. And if we don't stop them now, and stop them hard, they're going to pick us off, one by one."

"I know that," Holliday said. He grinned, then coughed into the handkerchief again. "S'cuse me. I know that and you know that. Trouble is, could you convince a jury of it? Juries can be a bit backward about things like that, y'know."

"Which is why neither Stillwell or Clanton are going to live to stand trial," Wyatt said.

Macklin looked away, studying the night-shrouded landscape out the window. Sparks from the locomotive up ahead flashed and swirled through the darkness, like myriad orange shooting stars.

In five months, Macklin had learned a lot about the concept known as "justice" on this world, or at least justice as it was practiced in this region of the planet. After the gunfight at the O.K. Corral, Wyatt Earp had been put on trial for the murders of Billy Clanton and Frank and Tom McLaury. Morgan and Virgil Earp and Doc Holliday had all been wounded in the fight and not indicted; Virgil had been a federal marshal attempting to disarm the Clantons and McLaurys. The arresting officer was Tombstone's sheriff, Johnny Behan, who'd sided more than once with the Clantons in the long and intensely personal feud leading up to the fight.

Wyatt had been acquitted, of course. The judge and jury were all Tombstone citizens, most of whom favored what the Earps claimed to be trying to do—break the power of the Clanton gang in Cochise County once and for all. Virgil Earp had been relieved of his town marshal badge by the city council in a closed meeting, but everyone involved seemed to agree that Billy Clanton and the McLaurys had gotten what was coming to them.

"Justice," it seemed, had very little to do with impartiality or fairness. Sarah Nevers had long claimed that the Earps and Holliday were cold-blooded killers, as vicious, as unsavory, as lacking in morals and common refinement as the Clanton gang had ever been. She hadn't been quite so outspoken since Macklin had been working for them, but he knew she still felt that way.

Macklin could not remember anything about the culture or the legal system he'd grown up with, presumably on that world in his dreams with the green sky and two orange suns. But he could read English—a gift, apparently, of the mechanism embedded in his chest and brain—and he'd devoured Sarah Nevers' library in the boarding house's front parlor, including several decent histories of the United States of America. He knew the ideals of the nation that included the Arizona Territory, and the history of its legal system. He knew about concepts like trial by jury and arrest warrants.

And he knew that what Wyatt Earp was proposing to do to Frank Stillwell was diametrically opposed to those ideals.

And yet . . . Macklin knew the realities of life in Arizona. Five months of living in Tombstone had taught him things the history books had never mentioned.

Like the fact that the law often couldn't protect those who couldn't protect themselves. Like the fact that the ultimate legal authority was often a .45 caliber bullet or a load of shotgun pellets discharged at point-blank range.

Like the fact that the human representatives of law and order were themselves often corrupt. Johnny Behan had been the Earps' enemy from the beginning, and he was Tombstone's sheriff. Pete Spence and Frank Stillwell both had been Behan's deputies until they were implicated in the robbery of the Benson stage last September. The Earps had arrested them, Behan had contrived to set them free . . . and the arena was so muddied now with charges and countercharges that the two might never be brought to trial.

Macklin knew what Wyatt was thinking. Rely on the normal turnings of the legal system, and the men who'd crippled Virgil and murdered poor Morgan would get away clean. Worse, the other Earps, Doc Holliday, and anyone else who'd helped the Earp faction might soon find themselves at the wrong end of a shotgun some dark night in a Tombstone street or saloon or theater.

Survival in this war might well depend on getting them before they could strike again.

Macklin still wasn't sure how he felt about it. If what Dorree had told him was true, none of this was his fight or his concern anyway. The Associative Monitors were on Earth to keep an eye on the planet as a whole and try to protect it from predator races like the Kra'agh . . . not to get involved in the petty squabbles of primitive locals.

But in his amnesia, he knew these people a lot better than he knew Dorree or any of the far-off citizens of the Associative. The Earps, Holliday, Sarah Nevers . . . they'd offered shelter, help, and work when he'd needed it. They were his friends and, in a way, his family.

He would stand by them, no matter what.

"Tucson!" the conductor cried, entering through the rear coach door and making his way down the aisle of the coach. He was a portly man in a blue uniform, a heavy silver chain swaying at his belly. "Tucson, next stop."

Macklin felt the train lurch and squeal as the locomotive rounded the final mountain curve and began slowing again as it came down into Tucson.

Moments later, the train chugged and puffed to a gradual halt, and passengers began descending from the other cars onto the platform. "Let us go first," Wyatt told Virgil. Leading the way, he took Doc, Macklin, Johnson, and McMasters outside, leaving Warren with the others. "Fan out," Wyatt said. "Keep your eyes open for anyone who looks suspicious, not just Stillwell or Clanton. Remember, they have a lot of friends in this town."

Macklin quartered the south side of the platform, checking a baggage shed and a small restaurant that served passengers waiting for the train. It was nearly full dark now, and the only light came from the surrounding buildings, and from the headlamps on the locomotives. There were several in the rail yard next to the station, two of them, the train from Benson and another one, fired up and belching steam in great, filthy, hissing clouds. Hell, an army could have been hidden in those shadows waiting to ambush them, and he'd never know it.

Ahead, the locomotive that had just brought them from Benson had drawn up beneath a round, wooden tower and was taking on water from the tank. Steam blasted from the locomotive's undercarriage. A shadow moved against the boiling white smoke.

Something stirred in Macklin . . . warning, presentiment, he wasn't sure what, but he drew his Colt and stepped forward.

The shadow twisted and appeared to grow, silhouette of a monstrous shape out of sheerest nightmare.

Kra'agh!

Tightening his grip on his revolver, Macklin hurried forward. . . .

FOUR

FRANK STILLWELL DIDN'T LIKE THIS, NOT ONE LITTLE BIT. This whole scheme of Ike Clanton's had gone entirely too far.

He stood in the gathering dusk just outside the pool of light spilling from the Tucson Southern Pacific depot, drawing hard on a hand-rolled cigarette. Steam shrilled from the big locomotive that had just pulled into the station. Passengers were beginning to alight, shadows moving behind the billowing, gaslit clouds of steam.

He was nervous. Hell, he was *scared*, and wished he'd never gotten involved in this. He was beginning to wonder if killing the Earps was worth the risk.

Oh, he hated the Earps, all right, hated them and everything they claimed to stand for . . . towns and civilization and progress. Pah! The Tombstone Law and Order League? A bunch of pantywaist, hymn-singing hypocrites bent on crowding out the free range, throwing up buildings and fences everywhere, and putting an end to the cattle industry. Towns? Good for three things only: letting off some steam with liquor, cards, and women; a place to buy supplies and grub; and a market where you could sell

a few head—"beeves" in the easy slang of the cattleman—
and make a few hard-earned dollars.

Ever since they'd arrived in Tombstone, the Earps—
and Doc Holliday, their consumptive shadow—had been
pushing, pushing, *pushing* for a fight, trying to break the
Cowboys' long-time hold on the county. The way Frank
had heard it from Ike Clanton, they'd finally forced the
issue at the O.K. Corral last October 26 and gunned down
both McLaurys and Ike's brother, Billy, in cold blood.
Hell, to hear Ike tell it, some of them hadn't even been
armed.

Frank Stillwell had been one of the men who'd evened
the score a bit two months later by ambushing Virg Earp
from the unfinished recesses of the Palace Saloon. He'd
been here in Tucson the other night when Morgan was
gunned down, but he'd known it was going to happen.
He and Pete Spence, Karl Freis, Ike Clanton, Rowdy
Brice, and Indian Charlie had all planned the thing together right here in Tucson, in Frank's hotel room. The
Earps were damned bloody-handed murderers, and de-
served whatever they got, and the sooner the better so far
as he was concerned.

But . . . damn it all, Rowdy Brice just wasn't himself
lately. Something about the old Clanton-gang cowhand
was just plain wrong, though Frank couldn't put his finger
on it. Partly it was his manner. Rowdy'd always been a
kind of happy-go-lucky guy, cheerful and good-natured,
at least when he wasn't drunk. Now it was like he was
on a mean drunk all the time, and he hadn't touched a
drop of the stuff in weeks.

And as for that German fellow, Freis . . . he was just
as bad, worse, maybe, with his fragmented English. And
neither one seemed to like the light anymore. Creepy,
that's what it was. Creepy as hell.

Only a handful of passengers got off . . . eight or ten,
perhaps, most of them men. Frank's eyes narrowed as he

tried to make out faces in the uncertain light. Yeah . . . that one, the short guy with a big, droopy mustache . . . that was John Holliday, without a doubt. And he was talking with a big man, neatly dressed in a flat-crowned hat and black coat. It might be Wyatt. But where were the others?

Three other men had stepped off the train with Holliday, though they immediately dispersed into the night. Frank decided they must be part of the Earp party . . . hired bodyguards, maybe, or shooters from the Earps' inner circle. They would be checking for a possible reception committee. He would have to be damned careful.

He inhaled on his cigarette, the tip glowing bright orange as he dragged it down almost to his lips, then flicked it away, a spark against the night. Turning, he glanced back at Ike Clanton, who was leaning against the wall of a shed, watching the passengers disembark. Ike met his eye, and grinned and nodded, as if to say, *We got 'em now.*

Frank scowled and turned back to watch the platform. He wasn't sure that having Ike at his back was all that reassuring, just now. Young, a bit wild, and saddled with a hell of a temper, Ike had a mouth as big as the open range. He was a bully and a braggart, and the word going around Tombstone these days was that when the Earps opened fire on the Clantons and the McLaurys in the O.K. Corral, Ike had turned yellow. Ike Clanton, damn it all, had provoked the fight in the first place and been telling everyone in town how he was going to shoot the Earp brothers down, but according to the stories, he'd grabbed Wyatt Earp's coat, begged for his life, claimed he wasn't armed, then fled through the nearby photography studio of Camillus Fly.

Frank wasn't sure how much credence to give those stories, but he had the unpleasant feeling that they rang true. Clanton was a real fireball when it came to big talk,

but Frank had never seen him actually stand up to anybody, leastwise not without six or eight of the boys at his
back, and a hefty advantage in numbers and weapons.

He was almost glad that Brice and Freis were out here,
too. *Almost* . . .

A shadow moved among shadows, and Frank caught a
faint, unpleasant whiff of sulfur. The hairs on the back of
his neck prickled erect.

"That iss one of them, *ja*?" asked Freis.

"Can't quite tell," Frank said. "I think it might be Wyatt."

"Kill him . . ."

"Jesus, Freis," Frank said. "Hold your horses! There
are two more Earps on that train, and three guys movin'
around who might be hired guns. *And* Holliday! We gotta
be damned careful with this. We're outnumbered, here!
We can't take 'em all out at once!"

"One iss following Rowdy Brice," Freis said, emotionless. He might have been discussing the weather.

How the hell did he know that? "Yeah? Where?"

"On the far side of the train. Ve vill draw the bodyguards away, my friends and I. You can then kill the
Earps without interference."

"You guys have that all figured out, or what? Who
made *you* the boss?" Frank didn't like the way that Brice
and Freis were taking over lately, telling the rest of the
gang what to do. He glanced back at Clanton, who
shrugged and looked away. Damn it all, Clanton had been
angling to lead the gang for months, despite the fact that
Curly Bill Brocius had been the unspoken head of the
Cowboys ever since old Neumann Clanton had been bushwacked by Mexicans the previous summer. It would be
kind of nice if the son of a bitch showed some leadership
now . . . but for the past couple of months, he'd been con-
tent to follow the lead of Rowdy Brice and this damned
foreigner.

No, he didn't like it at all.

He resisted the urge to light another cigarette. Instead, he focused on the train platform, where more people were getting off the train. Yeah . . . two, no, three more men, neatly and expensively dressed, their facial hair so identical they were damned near mirror images of one another. The one leaning heavily on the cane would be Virg, the woman at his side his wife, Allie. That young one was Warren, the older, graying one James.

All of the surviving Earps in one nice, neat package. Frank's right hand brushed the grip of his Colt, riding in its holster at his hip. It wouldn't do to start blasting away, though. The gang really had no interest at all in James or in Allie . . . or in Warren, for that matter. It was important, though, that Holliday and the three Earps who'd humiliated the Cowboys and gunned down three of their number in cold blood be killed. Wyatt was by far the most dangerous. He would be first.

Virgil, James, and Allie were leaving the platform now, walking into the depot eatery. Holliday, Wyatt, and two bodyguards remained on the platform, standing in the light in a way that almost invited attack. Were they holding rifles or shotguns? Frank couldn't tell.

He looked around to check on Freis, and swore softly under his breath. The German was gone, melted away into the night without a sound.

Why did he have the feeling that Brice and Freis were using the rest of them somehow, manipulating them for purposes of their own?

"C'mon, Ike," Frank said. "Let's see if we can get a little closer. Ike?"

He looked around and swore again, louder this time. Ike Clanton was gone, too, the yellow-bellied coward. The hell with it. If he could get close enough for a shot without risking return fire from those guns, it was worth the chance.

Grimly determined to have it out with the Earps once and for all, with or without Clanton, Frank started forward.

✧ 2 ✧

MACKLIN BLINKED, TRYING TO SEE THROUGH THE STEAM still hissing from the locomotive's undercarriage. The nightmare shape was gone. Had he really seen it? Colt tight in the wet grip of his hand, he moved carefully forward, keeping to the shadows beneath the water tower, walking toward the rear of the locomotive on its right side, opposite the platform. He was aware that light spilling from the depot and the brightly lighted windows of the train's passenger cars could backlight him through the steam as they had the Kra'agh a moment before, making him a perfect target.

What were the Kra'agh Hunters doing here? When he'd first met them, shortly after his arrival on this primitive world, two of them that he knew of had been infiltrating the Clanton-Brocius Cowboy gang; the shootout at the O.K. Corral had been a setup to give one of the monsters a shot at the Earps, a plot that Macklin had only just managed to disrupt.

Were they after him, an amnesiac offworlder stranded on Earth? Or were they still trying to kill the Earps for reasons of their own?

Macklin didn't know. All he could say for certain was that the Kra'agh were up to no good, and that if he didn't watch himself, he was going to end up very, very dead.

He wondered if he should double back and warn the Earps, then decided to press on. He had to locate the alien horror, know where it was and what it was doing before he could do anything like formulate a plan.

He did wish he was carrying one of the long arms the Earp party had brought along, a rifle or shotgun. He'd learned from experience that handguns, even a rugged man-stopper like the Colt .45, weren't all that effective against a Kra'agh, unless you could plant a couple of rounds solidly into the hump on their shoulders, where they kept their brain.

Heart hammering, his senses extended in a hyperaware embracing of the darkness around him, Macklin continued his pursuit.

✧ 3 ✧

EATER EXTENDED ITS ELECTRONICALLY ENHANCED SENSES into the night, reaching for the human it knew was following it. A prickling in the sensitive patch of feathery scales on its chest, at the base of its snaky neck . . . a sense of direction and rough distance . . . yes, the prey was following. . . .

A little farther now, away from the glare of lights and into the privacy of the night.

The Kra'agh had evolved over millions of cycles as hunters, creatures superbly adapted and attuned to the needs of the hunt. Pre-sentient Kra'agh had developed the skill of projecting a psychic field about their bodies that suggested other shapes . . . a rock, say, or the folds and tendrils of a harmless ychjaariv *plant. In recent cycles, as they reached out beyond the sulfurously teeming atmosphere of their own world, they'd learned how to capture, amplify, and project the* gah, *allowing them to take on the quite solid-seeming illusion of other life forms as camouflage.*

By using a patternmaker driven into a creature's living brain, that creature could be captured for later use, from its outward appearance right down to its language and thoughts. The food beast that had called itself Rowdy Brice had been patterned in this fashion, when Eater had encountered the creature, its mind numbed by chemicals, in a dark alley behind a drinking place in Tucson.

The camouflage, unfortunately, was not perfect. It never was. Sustained through holographic projection from the microelectronics embedded in the harness that Eater wore, the illusion did not hold up well in strong light, and the Kra'agh had no control over the shadows it cast.

Eater was concerned about the prey, and its abilities. The Kra'agh had survived and prospered because they did not underestimate their prey, and maintained hard and accurate impressions of their capabilities both in flight, defense, and attack. The prey that called itself Macklin on this world was an enigma, almost certainly one of the meddling Associative Monitors, and therefore possessing dangerous hardware, including artificially intelligent implants that gave it some truly impressive abilities to retrieve and manipulate data, as well as communicate with other Monitors and perhaps also to serve as weapons. The Hunters would have to approach Macklin very carefully indeed; it had already demonstrated its ability to outwit and outfight a pair of Hunters. That fact alone was enough to give one pause.

Eater felt the thrill of rha'akashj . . . *the blood-quickening of a confrontation with dangerous prey. The trick was to pretend to be the hunted, drawing the prey ever deeper into the trap set for it.*

It wouldn't be much longer now. . . .

◇ **4** ◇

MACKLIN KNEW HE WAS STALKING A KRA'AGH, AND HE knew, too, that unless he was damned lucky and managed to place a couple of shots into the massive, bony hump behind the creature's forequarters, his Colt wasn't up to the task. The nightmare things were tough. He'd fought more than one in close-quarters battle, and he knew from experience just how hard it was to kill them.

But he also knew that he had to face the monster. If what Doris—no, Dorree—had said was right, the Kra'agh were here at least in part because of him. They knew he was an Associative Monitor, and feared that he'd be able to communicate what he knew to the Associative.

Dorree. He wished she was here to tell him what was going on. And he wondered if he would believe her if she did.

Oh, he trusted the Associative woman, all right. The woman who claimed to be his partner monitor had shown up in town shortly after his arrival the previous October, and managed to tell him some of what he'd been so desperate to learn. The crash of their ship out in the desert had left him with amnesia . . . and also damaged the small machine—she'd called it a *Companion*—embedded in his chest and, she claimed, inside his skull. He could only take her word for who and what he was, and what he was supposed to be doing here. Unfortunately, she was gone— evacuated by her offworld friends—and he was again alone on this world, at least for the moment.

Dorree had told him much about his life, that part of his life, at any rate, that lay behind the wall of darkness blocking him from his own past, from his own memory of self. He'd clung to her words, revelations of other worlds, other ways. She was the only one on this world who knew . . .

But now she was gone, taken away by one of those spacecraft she'd spoken of. And the fragments of memory that remained . . . how could he ever reconstruct an entire life from such scattered shreds and tatters as he possessed now?

How could he face the monsters in the night, when he didn't even know with any certainty who he was or why he was here?

He heard a noise to his left, and spun . . .

✦ 5 ✦

FRANK STILLWELL HEARD A NOISE . . . A SCRAPING SOUND, like leather on stone, followed by the crunch of gravel from heavy but carefully placed footsteps. He'd been making his way forward along the line of train cars, hoping to get close enough to fire a shot at the Earps still waiting on the passenger platform. Damn, where was Ike . . . or Brice and Freis, for that matter? Why did he have the feeling he'd been left out here dangling in the breeze?

He suppressed an urge to pull his gun. If the Earps spotted him first with a gun in his hand, he was a dead man. No, he needed to get close and get the drop on them, preferably from a good hiding place. Turning, he stared at the light behind him, shrouded now in swirling steam from the locomotive as it took on fresh water from the tower. He saw a shadow there, black behind the steam, only a few yards away. . . .

For a long second or two, Frank tried to make sense of the shadow's shape. At first he thought it was a man on horseback, but then he realized it looked more like one of those man-horse centaurs from Greek mythology . . . a four legged beast, yes—but the stance was all wrong for a horse—with a shaggy hump above the shoulders. He could make nothing at all of the thing's forequarters, though, a misshapen nightmare, a blackness drifting toward him out of the night.

The shadow stepped closer, the steam parting. Karl Freis was there, looking at Frank with cold eyes . . . and the shadow twisting in the steam cloud behind him was still monstrous, a misshapen, impossible *thing* straight from a Hell-born nightmare.

Frank screamed . . . or tried to. The sound caught in his throat and emerged as a sharp bark of surprise and terror. He stumbled back a step, then turned and started to run, boots crunching loudly on the cinders beside the track.

"Frank, vait!" Freis called, but Frank Stillwell was beyond reason now, his heart pounding so hard it felt like it was going to tear itself from his chest, his breath coming in ragged, shallow gasps. Air . . . he couldn't get enough air . . . and the panic shrieked and gibbered in his skull like a host of howling lost souls. Running wildly, he stepped onto the tracks in front of the stationary locomotive, and for a second the glare of the headlight bathed him in its harsh yellow spill. He had to hide! Had to find some place away from the light and the steam, away from that *thing* . . .

He kept running, fleeing the light.

"Hold it, Frank!" a sharp voice called. A human voice. He veered toward the sound. Three men, shadows themselves, stood on the railway roadbed. "Stop right there!"

He kept running, unheeding, unhearing, desperate for the sight of a human face. The plan, the ambush were forgotten now. All he wanted was the safety of human company.

Wyatt Earp and Warren Earp raised their rifles, Doc Holliday his shotgun. "Stop right there, Frank!" Holliday snapped.

"Wyatt!" Frank yelled. Suddenly, he realized his danger. Frank Stillwell was fast with a gun, and a good shot, but they had the drop on him already, and his Colt was still riding in its holster. He knew it was too late, but his hand dropped to the pistol's grip . . .

A fusillade of gunfire thundered above the hiss of the steaming locomotive, muzzle flashes stabbing the night. Buckshot and rifle balls tore through Frank's body, hurling him back, a bloody torn rag limp on the railbed.

✧ 6 ✧

MACKLIN HEARD THE GUNFIRE, A RIPPLING CRACKLE IN the darkness at his back . . . at least six or seven shots, it sounded like . . . the heavy *boom* of rifle and shotgun fire.

He stopped, hesitating as if at the brink of a precipice. The shadow he'd been following had led him some distance from the rail yard, into a deserted maze of cattle pens and storage sheds, and suddenly he felt as though he'd been deliberately led there.

Why? An ambush staged for him? Or a means of separating him from the Earps so someone could ambush them? He didn't know, and right now he didn't care. Either way, he was out here alone dancing to someone else's music, and he knew he had to get back to the Earps *now*, whether it was to cover their backs, or to get them to cover his.

Ahead, a path led between two slat fences, opening onto a street on the outskirts of Tucson proper. On the far side of the street, a pool of light cast by a single gas lantern hanging above a storefront illuminated the wooden boardwalk and a hand-painted sign: Apache Slim's Dry Goods and Mining Supplies.

Macklin's heart raced. Apache Slim? That was the name Dorree had told him to look for in Tucson, the name of the Associative Monitor who would be able to help him get off this world and back to his home, wherever that was.

But . . . something just wasn't right. Gunfire behind him. The Earps needed him. And ahead . . . something was wrong, a shadow waiting for him to step into that pool of light. He could feel it.

Five months before, the last time he'd seen Dorree, she'd been up in the mountains west of Tombstone, hurt, and awaiting the arrival of an Associative ship that was to have taken both of them home. Macklin had elected to stay long enough to kill the Kra'agh Hunter he'd tracked to that place, the Hunter that had taken Sarah. Dorree had given him some advice.

Trust your instincts, she'd said. *Your implant's con-*

nections have been damaged, but the AI is still trying to leak information to you through your right brain. Through emotions. Through feelings and intuition. Listen *to it.*

Was his implant, the black disk embedded in his chest that Dorree called an "artificial intelligence," trying to tell him something now through his instincts?

Or was he just allowing the night and his own fears to spook him?

No matter. He knew that if he stepped into that circle of light up ahead, something bad was going to happen. He would have to come back, but later, on *his* terms.

Besides, it looked like the dry goods store was closed up tight. Apache Slim must have already locked up and gone home for the night. Macklin decided to come back in the morning.

Pistol still drawn, he turned away and hurried back toward the train station.

✧ 7 ✧

IN THE DARKNESS OF AN ALLEY TO THE LEFT OF APACHE Slim's store, Deathstalker vented a low, disappointed hiss, and allowed itself to relax from the spring-ready crouch it had been holding for many droks. *The prey had been so close, so* very *close. He'd been able to taste its blood upon the evening air.*

No matter. The creature would return, seeking the Associative Monitor that occupied this place. And when it did . . .

FIVE

"YOU CAN RIDE WITH US ANYTIME, MACKLIN," WYATT said, extending his hand. As always, his eyes were as cold, hard, and pale as blue diamond, glittering in the light spilling from the headlamp of the slowing locomotive.

Gravely, Macklin shook Wyatt's hand. With a drawn-out chuff and hiss, the locomotive shushed to a stop. McMasters and Warren climbed aboard and began speaking with the conductor.

They were a long way from civilization now. Hours before, they'd made their way out beyond the Tucson city limits, where McMasters had used a lantern to flag down a train bound for Contention. With Virgil, James, and Allie now safely on the train to California with Morgan's body, Wyatt, Warren, Holliday, and the other two bodyguards planned to ride to Contention, where they would hire horses for the return to Tombstone.

"Don't reckon we'll be in Tombstone for long," Holliday said to Macklin. "I'd advise you not to show your face around there either, for a spell. Anyone who seen you riding out with us might put your face together with Stillwell's death."

"Where will you be going?" Macklin asked.

"Not sure, yet," Wyatt said. "We still have unfinished business with some of those people." The way he said it chilled Macklin's blood. Frank Stillwell, he knew, wouldn't be the last of the Cowboys to feel the Earps' thirst for vengeance.

"Take care of yourselves," Macklin told them.

"Don't you worry about that," Holliday said, grinning. "We always do. You watch your back, too. There's folks about who don't think too kindly of us, or the company we keep!" He started coughing then, plucking a bloody handkerchief from his pocket and holding it to his mouth. Wyatt helped Doc clamber up onto the train as the locomotive began chuffing slowly forward once again.

Macklin watched as the train pulled out, a line of yellow-lit windows dwindling into the darkness, the sparks from the engine's smokestack flaring like tiny red stars on the night.

And then he was all alone.

In a way, Macklin was glad to be free of the Earps. Their feud with the Clanton-Brocius Cowboy gang might have genuinely started as a bid to civilize the wild town of Tombstone, but lately it had turned into something else, something darker and less subject to reason. The world would be well rid of the men who'd murdered Morgan and crippled Virgil . . . but now there was something lurking behind Wyatt's eyes that was as ruthless and cold, as tempered-steel hard as anything those murderers could conjure, and Macklin wanted no part of it.

In the night, a coyote howled a mournful salute to the first-quarter moon as it sank gently behind the rugged silhouette of the Tucson Mountains in the west.

Macklin turned and started walking back toward the lights of Tucson.

✧ **2** ✧

George "Apache Slim" Flannigan was up well before dawn. His sentry had chirped twice, alerting his Companion, and the second time it happened he'd decided it
wasn't worth it to go back to bed again. From the look
of things, Hunters were gathering nearby again, and last
night they'd once more tested the invisible defenses protecting the store. They knew he was here, and knew that
he knew about them. The question of the moment was
how much longer he had before they tried something more
than a tentative probing of his security system.

How much longer before the probes stopped and outright invasion began?

Taking a seat at the large rolltop desk in his bedroom,
he pressed a concealed button that opened the cover with
a thin whine of motors. Inside, a monitor screen lit up as
a touch-panel control board began to come to life.

A Kra'agh Hunter is still outside, the voice of his
Companion whispered in his mind, speaking G'tai.

"Attempting to penetrate the perimeter defenses?"

No. It continues to . . . simply watch.

The screen cleared, showing a view from one of some
hundreds of insect-sized robot sentinels crawling or flying
about Tucson and its environs. The scene was of the street
outside, of a man slouched against the wall of a building
in a narrow alley, watching the storefront. He appeared to
be a typical human, a cowboy in a flat-brimmed hat, vest
and shirt, jeans, and worn leather boots.

The image was overlaid, however, by a faint, blue-
glowing shadow, an aura of sorts showing the outline of
a much larger, bulkier creature heavily veiled by the swirling electronic illusion of a *gah*-projection field.

*The same one that's been outside for the past two
weeks*. There was a pause in the AI's mind-linked voice,
an uncharacteristic hesitation. *It occurs to me that the*

Kra'agh may be using us as bait. There is the matter of the missing Taled *observer.*

"It's been five months, now. He's probably been caught and killed already."

Possibly, but I tend to doubt it.

"Why?"

For one thing, he—or his Companion, rather—carries information the Kra'agh would have used against us. Information such as the code to penetrate a Monitor station's defensive screens. I also expect there would have been at least an attempt to pattern him and use him against us.

"If the survivor of a ship crash was wandering around loose, with no access to advanced technology, no electronic defenses, the Kra'agh would have snapped him up long ago . . . and they would have destroyed this outpost shortly afterward. It's more likely that he was killed in such a way that the enemy was unable to tap his Companion's memories." Apache Slim shrugged. "Or that his Companion's memories were damaged and useless. Dorree indicated that there'd been damage, that the survivor doesn't even remember who or what he is."

Dorree has not given up hope, as of her last message. Neither should we.

Slim frowned. The thought of giving up had not occurred to him. "I was not planning on it," he told the AI machine implanted in his head and breastbone. "Any more than I plan on surrendering this outpost to the Kra'agh."

The observer mission to this barbaric world was a sacred trust. Three centuries ago, as the people of Earth measured the passing cycles, a human community on the verge of extinction had been rescued by G'tai ships, snatched from the planet and taken to the world of Shanidar, the world they now called home.

The human inhabitants of Shanidar numbered now in the tens of thousands. Most had never heard of Earth, save as one place among many in the download feeds dealing with history, culture, and the philosophy of Mind. Few of those who remembered even cared; the Associative was a sprawling collision of galactic cultures—some three hundred thousand of them at last count—sparkling gems of civilization and high technology scattered across the glow of the Great Spiral. There were millions of worlds like Earth, worlds of life and burgeoning intelligence, worlds of promise. . . .

And the vast majority would become extinct before they even learned to leave the surfaces of their worlds. Many would destroy themselves in war, or die more slowly under the assault of self-destructive philosophies or technologies; others would fall victim to the blind and manic lurchings of an uncaring universe—to newly evolved plagues, to impacts by asteroids and comets, to the detonations of novae, to the onset of glacial planetary epochs. Saddest, perhaps, were those worlds overwhelmed by neighbors centuries or millennia in advance of them. Not every technic species in the Galaxy subscribed to the Associative's philosophies of noninterference and voluntary association. There were predator species loose within the star-swarms of the Galaxy, species originally driven by evolutionary pressures to be faster, smarter, meaner, and more vicious than their competitors on their homeworlds . . . pressures which had carried over into their dealings with the species of other worlds once they broke free of their home star systems.

There were thousands of such predator species, scattered across the Galaxy from the Core to the outermost fringes of the spiral arms. The Kra'agh were among the worst.

Slim's fingertips danced across the clear hard plastic of his touchscreen board, bringing up on the screen the communicator format. Tapping in the code for the nearest on-line Associative relay, he began calling.

"*Cha meth, cha meth,*" he said, speaking G'tai. "*Taled neh vero kah. Elan eh'vash grelet'dtha.*"

For answer, he received nothing but a cascade of snow across his display screen, and the hiss of static from his speakers. A sharp, screeching whine, rising and falling, overlaid the static. He was being deliberately jammed.

With the destruction of the Monitor advance base on Earth's moon five months earlier, and the elimination of the logistical depot and research station on Mars at the same time, only the observer bases on Earth itself were left in-system . . . and Slim had no way of knowing how many of the other outposts were still up and running. For all he knew, he was the last vestige of Associative presence left on this world.

"*Cha meth. Taled neh vero kah. Elan eh'vash grelet'dtha.*"

The Associative Monitor Corps had been created to watch over primitive, pre-starflight worlds. Slim—his G'tai name, his *real* name, was Thlana'ghahan, which he'd reshaped into "Flannigan" as his role-name during his stay on Earth—took his deployment to Earth with a seriousness bordering on the grim. He actually looked a bit Irish at that, with pale, freckled skin and blond hair. A descendant of the English colonists of Roanoke, he had no Indian blood in him; the locals here in Tucson had given him the incongruous Apache-Slim moniker a few years ago when he'd insisted that Apaches in town be treated like human beings.

As a Monitor, he wasn't supposed to interfere in the politics or social customs of the locals, but Slim also had to live with himself. The aboriginal population of this area, he was convinced, was on its way to extinction, victim of invading peoples with better technology and a low tolerance for ways, customs, and beliefs different from their own.

There was grim irony in that. Every human on Earth

was about to experience the same sort of invasion. The Kra'agh had exactly zero tolerance for *any* culture or species other than their own.

And Earth's myriad cultures were doomed, unless the Associative intervened.

The trouble was, Earth was an out-of-the-way backwater, far from the bright center of galactic politics. The Kra'agh Grand Fleet had destroyed Associative Monitor bases on Earth's moon and on the fourth planet out from the Sun, and blockaded the entire system. Apache Slim hadn't been able to get through to the Associative interstellar communications relay for weeks now. He was cut off, isolated on this barbaric planet, with no way at all to call for help.

Dorree had made it offworld five months ago. Maybe she would be able to get the Associative Council to organize a fleet and come break the Kra'agh blockade . . . and maybe not. It could well be that Earth simply wasn't worth the trouble of saving.

No matter. Slim was one of those handful of Shanidar humans who believed that Earth and its squabbling, noisome, superstitious, primitive population should be saved, if only because the planet was the birthworld of humanity. Those humans who'd been born and raised on Shanidar had been civilized by the G'tai; perhaps, one day, the rest of humanity could enjoy the benefits of civilization as well. . . .

But first, the Kra'agh would have to be stopped, or there would be no humanity left to civilize, other than the tiny colony on Shanidar.

He just wished he knew how to break their jamming to make contact with the G'tai scout vessels circling the outskirts of this system.

And he wished, too, that he knew if he was in fact facing the Hunter invaders alone.

❖ **3** ❖

MACKLIN HAD ARRIVED BACK IN TUCSON IN THE EARLY
hours of the morning—far too late for respectable people
to be renting a room for the night. Instead, he checked in
at Carlos's Saloon, still open, still lively with boisterous
cowhands and miners finding interesting ways to lose the
last of dwindling reserves of cash. A quarter bought
Macklin a small room in the back and a mattress stuffed
with straw, tucked in among piles of lumber, crates, and
barrels. The rats were annoying, but left him alone after
he nailed one with a well-aimed boot.

He was awakened at daylight by the bartender who'd
sold him the room, and a tall, familiar-looking man. It
took Macklin a moment to remember where he'd seen him
before . . . on the train last night, as they'd been coming
into Tucson.

"Marshal Evans," Macklin said, sitting up and rubbing
the grit from his eyes. "What can I do for you?"

"Sorry to wake you, mister, but I've got some questions for you."

"Okay." He started pulling on his boots. He had to
retrieve the left one from the other side of the room, where
he'd thrown it at the rat.

Evans watched him with eyes that gave away nothing.
"You came in with the Earps and Holliday last night,
didn't you?"

"That's right." There was no sense in making a secret
of that. He'd already agreed with Wyatt that if he was
questioned, he would tell everything he knew. Not that
there was much to tell.

"What's your name?"

"John Macklin."

"From Tombstone?"

"Used to be. Guess I'm just moving through."

"Going where?"

"Well, here, for a start. Need to find someone."

"Who?"

"I just know he's called Apache Slim."

"Slim? Will he vouch for you?"

"I doubt it. We haven't met. But I was told to look him up."

"For what purpose?"

"He has some information. Why are you asking me all this, Marshal? Am I in trouble?"

"Well, that all depends. Were you with the Earps last night at the train station?"

"Got off the train with them. We were checking around for those people you warned us about . . . you know, make sure there wasn't an ambush. Virg had his wife with him, you know. We didn't want any trouble."

"Hm. And was there an ambush?"

"I don't really know. I know I was off on the other side of the train yard when I heard gunfire. I hurried back to see if they needed me. Met up with Wyatt and Warren, and they said there'd been some trouble, but it was okay now."

"Yeah? What happened after that?"

"After Virg, James, and Allie finished their dinners at the station restaurant, we put them on the train for California. Wyatt, Warren, Holliday, Johnson and McMasters all headed out into the desert to flag down a train headed to Contention. I walked out with 'em, said good-bye, and that was the end of it."

"How come you stayed behind?"

"Like I said. I have business with Apache Slim."

"You know Frank Stillwell?"

"Heard of him."

"You know he's dead?"

"No. Is he?"

"Shot six times. Four rifle balls and two loads of buckshot. He was shot real close, too. Powder burns on his skin and clothing. And he never even had a chance to draw his gun."

"Somehow, Marshal," Macklin said wearily, "I'm not surprised."

"Yeah? Why not?"

"Because this damned feud between the Cowboy gang and the Earps just keeps going on and on. Where's it going to end?"

"You think the Earps deliberately gunned Stillwell down?"

Macklin thought about it. "I don't think so. I know Wyatt's a cold son of a bitch, and he was convinced Frank Stillwell had a hand in Morgan's murder. But he was more concerned last night about someone taking a shot at Virg as he left town. We were here to escort Virgil and James Earp out of town, not hunt down bad guys."

"Did you know that Frank Stillwell was real fast with a gun?"

"No. Didn't know the man, myself."

"He was *fast* . . . and damned good with a gun. He used to be an Indian scout with the Army. But the poor son of a bitch didn't have a chance to draw on his killers. Did you know that witnesses saw Frank in town Sunday, the day after Morgan was killed? He couldn't have been in Tombstone at eleven the night before, not and gotten himself all the way here to Tucson."

"If you say so."

"You have a gun, Macklin?"

"Just this." He reached over to a pile of meal bags and picked up his belt and holster, handing it to Evans.

Evans drew the Colt, broke open the chamber to count the rounds inside, then held the weapon to his nose and sniffed. "This your only piece?"

"That's it."

"You carry a rifle? Or a shotgun?"

"Nope. Why, you think I killed Stillwell?"

I think your friends did. There were witnesses, and they saw all five of them in the rail yard last night. And Wyatt, Warren, and Holliday were all seen close to where Stillwell was shot."

"Am I under arrest?"

Evans seemed to consider the possibility. "No," he said finally. "But you are a material witness, so I'm ordering you not to leave town. There's going to be an investigation, and you're going to be asked to give testimony." He slipped the Colt back into the holster. "And I'll keep this for now."

Macklin's eyes widened. "Marshall, Stillwell's got a lot of friends, from what I hear. I'd rather not be out on the streets unarmed.

"Tucson's a law-abiding town, Macklin. I don't know how you do it in Tombstone, but we have gun laws here. You're supposed to check your gun soon as you come into town. I'll just take care of checking it for you. You can have it back after the inquest."

Macklin scowled. There was a similar ordinance in Tombstone. Not that it was rigorously enforced, as the recent body count proved. If the law in Tucson was equally lax when it came to the gun laws, he could be a dead man. Not only would Frank Stillwell's friends be gunning for him, there was still the much deadlier problem of the Kra'agh Hunters he knew to be in the area.

"When's the inquest going to be?"

"Don't know, yet. Have to talk to the judge. Things are pretty backed up at the courthouse, though. Stillwell was here in town to answer some questions for an inquest into the Bisbee stage robbery last year."

"That was six months ago!"

"Yeah, well, I doubt it'll be that long." Evans grinned and touched the brim of his hat. "So, you have a nice stay in Tucson, Macklin, hear?" He walked out the door, taking Macklin's gun belt and revolver with him.

Macklin wasn't sure what he was going to do without a gun, but he knew he couldn't stay here in Carlos's back room. He needed to find Apache Slim. He was remembering the wicked little weapon Dorree had carried, a slender device that loosed a beam of incendiary light that caused whatever it touched to burst into flames. If the Associative Monitor had weapons like that, perhaps he could get one. He'd already been thinking along those lines, in fact. A Colt revolver would be a chancy weapon at best in a one-on-one with a Kra'agh, since he would need a couple of good, clean shots at the creature's heavily bone-armored hump.

Or perhaps Slim would just be able to whisk him off this confusing and troubled rock in one of those sleek flying craft he'd seen in the desert . . . and in his oft-repeated dreams.

Another quarter bought him a shave and a bath at the barber's next door. He was careful about preserving his modesty in the big metal tub behind the curtains, though; he didn't like having to explain to people about the dollar-sized disk of black, hard, slightly flexible material embedded in his chest. Clean and fresh-faced then, though his clothes were still trail-worn and dusty, he set out for Apache Slim's Dry Goods and Mining Supplies.

It was high time, he decided, to meet the gentleman Dorree had once told him was an Associative Monitor working in disguise on the planet Earth.

Tucson was a busy town, with more life and more bustle than Tombstone. It was a town well on the way to becoming a city, with two- and three-story buildings, many of stone, adobe, or brick. Wagons rattled down the broad, dirt streets, people strolled the boardwalks, men on horseback paced their animals along the dusty thoroughfare. A number of men in blue tunics were in evidence; though details of their garb differed—they wore a bewildering variety of headgear, from kepis to broad, floppy-brimmed hats—something about the look of their tunics and the insignia on their sleeves told Macklin that these were military personnel in uniform. He searched his faulty memory for some indication of what soldiers would be doing here, but could recover nothing. It seemed self-evident, though, that these soldiers must be part of some military force or encampment close by Tucson.

He wondered why they were there. Soldiers suggested . . . war.

Then he put the pieces together. Apaches . . .

There'd been plenty of rumors lately in Tombstone about Apache raids on outlying settlements or traveling parties. The Earps had made the wagon trip to Benson with plenty of armed men as escort at least as much because of the possibility of attack by hostile natives as because of the chance of ambush by the Clanton-Brocius Cowboy gang.

Macklin had some memories—vague and fuzzy, but different in tone and shape from the memories he retained of strange and otherworldly dreams—of seeing someone in the desert, shortly after his amnesia-clouded arrival on this world. A man had pulled him to safety, then left him beside a dirt road where he'd been picked up by the occupants of a stagecoach. The man, he'd later guessed based on conversations with Sarah Nevers and Doc Holliday and others in Tombstone, had been a native, an Indian or "Injun" as the locals called them, and quite probably an Apache at that.

The fact that the only Indian Macklin had met so far had been a benefactor kept him from sharing the rather blunt and sometimes bloody opinions of most of the good citizens of Tombstone about the local natives.

But he'd also learned to keep his mouth shut on the topic. If he wanted to maintain the respect of the town's citizens, he'd found that it was better not to find anything good to say about the Indians, *especially* the Apache.

The street outside Apache Slim's Dry Goods and Mining Supplies didn't feel nearly as sinister as it had the night before. Macklin stood on the boardwalk for a moment, getting his bearings. There was the storefront . . . and there was the alley that had felt so menacing. Across the street were the storage sheds and cattle pens and, beyond, the rail yard. A couple of old-timer types were slouched in straight-backed chairs on the boardwalk outside the store, watching as he approached. Three patient-looking horses were tied to the hitching rail, and a wagon drawn by two horses waited nearby. A boy, perhaps twelve years old, sat with the reins. Slim's was busy, it looked like . . . or at least attracted more than its share of loiterers.

He spent a moment studying the windows overlooking this part of the street. He still felt uneasy, as though he were being watched. Kra'agh? Or something else?

Feeling suddenly naked and vulnerable in the bright morning sunlight, Macklin hurried inside the store.

S I X

STEPPING FROM THE OVEN HEAT ON THE STREET INTO THE cool shade of the store was like a step into another world. As his eyes adjusted to the relative darkness, Macklin became aware of crates, boxes, barrels, and counters. Saddles hung in bulky ranks across the ceiling, and shelves were high-piled with everything from tobacco and cornmeal to lanterns and shovels, from boots and riding tack to plug chewing tobacco and hats. A man with an apron and a handlebar mustache was on the far side of the counter between the ornate green-brass cash register and a set of scales.

Four men were on the customer side of the counter. One wore the blue tunic that Macklin had decided was a military uniform of some sort, while the others, evidently, were civilians. All were bearded in various fashions and degrees of neatness.

The man behind the counter looked up at Macklin as he walked in. "With ya in a minute," he said.

"No hurry," Macklin replied. He stopped to study the array of merchandise displayed on one of the shelves, as the conversation he'd interrupted resumed.

"So there been any trouble up there before last week?" the soldier asked.

"Nah," one of the three other customers said. He wore a checked red shirt, jeans caked with dried mud, and a scraggly beard that reached to mid-chest. "Lots of smokes, but that's jes' usual. But then it got kinda quiet, like."

"The lull before the storm," one of the other civilian customers said. He was small and dapper, with a neatly groomed and waxed goatee, the kind known as an "imperial." He wore a long, dark coat and a string tie that gave him a prosperous look, and carried a gold-headed cane. He appeared to be in his late fifties, or perhaps his sixties.

"Exactly!" the first man exclaimed. "Damn, but you got a way with words, Ned!"

The goateed man smiled. "It's my job, after all. Go on, Tom. What happened next?"

"Not much t'tell, really." Tom shrugged. "Last Saturday, th' damned savages jes' started a-boilin' out of the rocks, it seemed like."

"Apaches?" the man behind the counter asked. He was walking back and forth along the back-wall shelves, pulling down various small items as he referred to a piece of paper in his hand, and placing them on the countertop.

"Hell, how should I know? Injuns is Injuns, I guess." Tom's eyes narrowed thoughtfully, and his cheek bulged. He had something in his mouth, and was working at it around the words. "Come t'think on it, yeah, I 'spect they was. Dirty, filthy critters. Like animals, y'know? And I reckon the 'Paches is the only hostiles 'round these parts now."

"They were Apaches," the third civilian said. He had a hard, no-nonsense look about him, and Macklin noticed that he was wearing a revolver, whatever the town ordinances might have to say about it. "Chiricahua, to be precise."

"That's awfully far west for Chiricahua," the soldier said. "You sure?"

"I'm sure. My guess is that they were part of that bunch that bolted from the San Carlos Reservation a few months back."

"I thought they all headed for Mexico," the clerk said.

"Not all," the soldier replied. "We've been getting a lot of reports at the fort. There're a couple of bands loose in the hills. If they keep up the horse-stealing and ambushes, we're going to have to go up and root 'em out, I expect."

"So what do you think they wanted from Apache Peak?" the goateed man asked.

"What do th' damned, thievin' savages ever want?" Tom said. "Horses. Guns. Our women. And us dead. We fixed 'em good, though. Managed t' git ourselves back to the 'dobe, barred th' door, and waited till they come up by th' corral. Then we opened up from inside." He turned his head suddenly and loosed a stream of black liquid at a brass receptacle on the floor with fair accuracy. "Nailed two of 'em, too. After that, they run for it. No stomach fer a standup fight."

"Damned redskins," the man behind the counter said. "We'd be best off if every last one of 'em was hunted down and killed!"

"Well, mebee we can take a first step in that direction," Tom said with a wink. "Know what I mean. Ol' Nate, him an' some of the boys is puttin' together a little surprise for those savages that they won't forget!"

"Any of your people get hurt in the attack last week?" the dapper man asked.

"Jes' Fred Clancy," the hard man said. "He took an arrow through the fleshy part of his arm. That was up by the mine workings, when they first attacked. Got it cleaned up and bandaged okay, and he's going to be all right."

"That's good," the clerk said. "Was wondering why he didn't come down with you folks for supplies this month."

"Oh, he come down with us, okay," Tom said. "We left him at Doc Pardoe's up th' street, to have th' wound looked at and th' bandage changed."

"Well, it could've been a lot worse," the clerk said, taking down a shovel from a hook on the wall and laying it beside the rest of the items on the counter. "Okay, we got everything on your list here. Anything else?"

"That should do it."

"Okay . . . well . . . the total comes to twenty-eight dollars, fifteen."

"I think we can manage that, all right," Tom said. He pulled out a pouch, and with a flourish spilled a cascade of coins onto the countertop. With one grimy forefinger, he scooted a pair of big twenty-dollar gold pieces across the counter, then scooped the rest back into the bag.

"Damn it, Tom," the hard man said. He threw a suspicious glance at Macklin. "Told you not to flash 'em like that."

"Where's the fun a' that? Keep th' change, Jeb."

Jeb grinned. "You boys're doin' all right up there, I take it."

"You could say that," Tom replied with a cackle. "Shoot, Dan," he added, looking at the hard man. "The claim is ours, all nice an' legal. What's it matter?"

"What matters," the soldier said, "is if you boys manage to start a silver rush up there. You know the Apaches aren't going to take kindly to a lot more white men going up into their hills."

"*Our* hills," Tom said, putting the bulging pouch away. "Our hills, fair an' square! An' we're gonna make Apache Peak the biggest damned name in silver mines in these parts! Bigger 'n the Comstock, even! An' we're all gonna be *rich*!"

"God *damn* it, Tom!" Dan snapped, shooting another dark look at Macklin. "Hold your tongue!"

Macklin chuckled. "Don't worry, mister," he said. "I'm not out to jump your claim."

"Maybe you're not," Dan replied slowly, "and then again, maybe we don't know you from Adam. Haven't seen you around these parts."

"Just came to town last night," Macklin said.

The dapper man turned and looked at Macklin with interest. "By any chance did you come in by the west-bound evening train?"

"Sure did."

"You wouldn't happen to know about the murder of a man named Frank Stillwell, would you?"

"I know it happened," Macklin said. "Not much more than that."

"He was found shot dead on the tracks in a welter of blood. Shot ten times."

"According to Marshal Evans, it was only six times," Macklin replied. He wondered what a welter was.

"They're saying that Wyatt Earp was on that train," the man said.

"Now, Ned," Jeb said, a twinkle in his eye. "You can't believe all those wild stories they tell over at the Granada, y'know!"

"As a matter of fact," Macklin said, "Wyatt Earp *was* on that train. And Virgil and Warren, and James, too."

Ned's eyes grew wide. "And . . . and Doc Holliday?"

"Yup. And Sherman McMasters and Turkey Creek Johnson."

"Don't care about them. How do you know all this, Mister . . . Mister . . ."

"Macklin. John Macklin. Happens I was with their party. They were seeing James and Virgil and Virgil's wife off to California, along with the body of Morgan Earp."

"I heard about Morgan," Ned said. "It made the papers all over. That was too damned bad. So . . . is Wyatt still here? Where's he staying?"

"I'm afraid not. He and Warren and the others all headed back to Tombstone late last night. Why, you know him?"

Ned laughed. "No, but I'd sure like to!"

Jeb laughed. "Better keep your stories straight there, Ned. What about Dodge City?"

Ned made a face. "You boys know that was just a story for the newspapers! Ain't a word of truth in it!"

Jeb wiggled a large thumb in Ned's direction. "This here's a celebrity, Mr. Macklin. A gen-u-wine big-time author from the East Coast! Edward Zane Carroll Judson. But he goes by the name of Colonel Ned Buntline. You might've heard of him?"

Macklin shook his head. "Sorry. I'm afraid not."

"Where you been, mister?" The soldier laughed. "This here's the King of the Dime Novels hisself! *The Scouts of the Plains*? *The Comanche's Dream*? *Maud Granger: How I Saved her Life*? All those dime novels about Wild Bill Hickok and Buffalo Bill Cody? Colonel Buntline here is maybe the most popular author in the United States of America. His books are damned popular around the barracks, anyway, I can tell you!"

"Well, I haven't had time to read very much lately," Macklin said, accepting Buntline's hand and shaking it. "But it's a pleasure to meet you."

Buntline's grip was weak, and the man didn't look well. There was something sickly about the pale skin and the way he carried himself, but there was a spark of humor and sharp wit in his eyes. "Dang! I'm sorry to hear I missed meeting Wyatt Earp!"

"Well, I'm sure he would have liked to meet you, Colonel," Macklin lied. Wyatt was an intensely private man, and though he wasn't above looking for some free publicity in the newspapers, he probably wouldn't have cared to meet the novelist.

"Was he here to take down Frank Stillwell?"

"Like I said, he was escorting his brother's body this far, on the way to California. I didn't see what happened to Stillwell." Macklin cocked his head to one side. Ned Buntline looked . . . worn out was the best phrase he could think of to describe the man. And Jeb had said he was from the East Coast. "So . . . what brings you out here, Colonel?"

Buntline coughed. "Boredom, mostly. That and knowing I don't have many years left in this world. I've been writing for a good many years now—over four hundred novels, you know. I've done some traveling, but, well, it's been the Wild West that's provided me with my best stories, my most thrilling plots. I thought I'd come out here for a few months and kind of soak up the local color. Maybe meet some of the heroic men I've been writing about."

"Like Wyatt Earp?"

"He's one. I've met a good many already, over the years. William Cody? I was the one who gave him the name Buffalo Bill, you know. I actually got him to star in my stage-play production of *The Scouts of the Plains*, in Chicago a few years back. You might have heard of it? . . ."

Macklin shook his head. "Afraid not."

"A spectacular play, if I say so myself, though the critics were *not* kind."

"The story's goin' around that the Colonel here presented a Colt .45 with a twelve-inch barrel to Wyatt Earp, Bat Masterson, and some other famous lawmen in Dodge City a few years back," Jeb said. "The Buntline Special, it was called. Had a wooden case for a holster that could be screwed on as a stock, turning it into a carbine, slick as you please. And now the Colonel says it was all a lie, that there never was such a wonderful gun! I'm really hurt!"

"Well, you must remember I'm paid to tell lies," Buntline said with a smile. "Even though that one didn't happen to be mine. Still, it's a pleasant conceit. I might give some thought to the idea when I get back to my Eagle's Nest. . . ."

Macklin turned to face Jeb behind the counter. Buntline seemed pleasant enough, but he was talkative and his grandiose manner of speech that indicated that he possessed an enormous ego or that he was a showman . . . and likely both. Macklin hoped to extricate himself by turning to the business at hand. "So . . . are you Apache Slim?" he asked.

"Nope. Jeb McNulty." His eyes narrowed. "What do you want with Slim?"

"I was told to look him up when I came to Tucson."

"Yeah? By who?"

Macklin considered the question. "Doris," he replied. That was the name Dorree used on this world, and if she knew Slim, perhaps she knew this man. "She said he might be able to help me get some information."

"Yeah? Well, Slim ain't here," Jeb told him.

Macklin felt pretty sure that Jeb was lying, but he knew he wouldn't get anywhere badgering the man. "When will he be back?"

"Hard t'say. He don't talk much with strangers, though."

" 'Cept for his pals, the Apaches," Dan said. "Them he talks to!"

"Is that how he got his name?" Macklin asked.

"The 'Paches are kind of a sore point, 'round these parts," Tom said. "Gov'mint keeps tryin' t'put them on the reservation up at San Carlos, and they keep a-wanderin' off and killin' decent folk. They're wild. Ya can't tame 'em. Y'ask me, every 'Pache male that leaves the reservation oughta be hung, and that's a fact!"

"So how does Apache Slim fit into this?" Macklin asked. "Is he an Apache?"

Jeb and Tom both laughed. "Not hardly!" Jeb said. "But he caused kind of a stir during the Camp Grant affair."

"Camp Grant? What's that?"

"An Army camp about fifty miles north of here," the soldier said, "at the mouth of the Arivaipa River." He made a face. "There was some . . . trouble there, about ten years back."

"Trouble, he says!" Tom laughed. "No trouble! The damned Army wasn't doin' its job, so some decent folks who were sick of 'Pache atrocities took matters on themselves and settled things."

The soldier looked at him evenly. "Forty-eight Mexicans, ninety-eight Papago Indians and six Anglos snuck into a camp of Arivaipa Apaches before dawn. They butchered eight men and a hundred and ten women and children, using clubs and knives and, later on, guns. They kidnapped twenty-eight papooses. A number of the squaws were raped. There was one survivor, an Arivaipa woman, and she was so terrified they couldn't get her to testify at the trial."

"They was all found innocent!"

"The jury deliberated all of twenty minutes," the soldier told Macklin. "It was a put-up job. The fact was, the Arivaipas were peaceful. They'd asked to come in. Most of the men were out hunting."

"Says you!" Tom flared. "If the Army had been takin' care of things the way they was supposed ta—"

"What was Apache Slim's involvement?" Macklin wanted to know.

"He stood up for the Injuns, is what," Tom said. "Told folks he thought they got a raw deal! Some folks hereabouts thought he was a traitor!"

"Including you?" he asked Jeb.

"What, me? Of course not! First off, he's my boss and he's a good guy. And anyway, the way I figure it, a man's entitled to his own opinion, even if it does sound a mite loco. Right?"

"Well, thinking them 'Paches's got *rights*, same as a white man, is more'n a mite loco," Tom said. "But ol' Slim, he's all right. I been buyin' from him for years, now." He patted the top of a kerosene lantern, one of the items Jeb had piled up on the counter. "Best prices on mining supplies in town. Better'n down in Bisbee or Tombstone, even. That's why we come down here every month, even though it's a further drive."

Macklin considered this, giving nothing away with his expression. He'd encountered this kind of prejudice before, and he knew that arguing about it wasn't going to change a thing.

He'd learned a lot in the five months he'd been stranded on this world. There were a number of tribes of relatively primitive peoples in this region of the Southwest—Papago, Navajo, Comanche, Hopi, Zuni, Yavapai. By far the most troublesome, though, throughout the entire stretch of desert and mountain from New Mexico to central Arizona and down into the northern reaches of Old Mexico, were the Apache.

He wondered why people hated them so much. Hatred he could understand just fine . . . but most white men seemed to think of the Apache as some sort of loathsome animal, vicious, filthy, unpredictable . . . and deadly. Most seemed to feel that extermination was the only answer— out and out genocide. Macklin couldn't help wondering what the Apache thought of the whites.

"So, stranger," Jeb said, picking up on an earlier thread of the conversation, "whatcha want with Apache Slim, anyway?"

"I need to talk to him. And the sooner the better. How long is he going to be out of town?"

"Didn't say he was out of town," Jeb replied. "I 'spect I can pass on a message for you."

Macklin thought about that. He wasn't sure he trusted these people, but they were human, and the man behind the counter worked here and must know Apache Slim. Maybe Slim had to be careful because the Kra'agh might be about.

On the other hand . . . the Kra'agh could alter their appearance. Macklin didn't know how they did it, exactly— some sort of projection from a device they wore, according to Dorree, which could make them look like people or animals they'd killed and "patterned." They could also camouflage themselves as inanimate objects, like a rock.

The effect didn't work all that well in bright light, or when the Kra'agh was trying to handle something complex, like a rifle. In direct sunlight, it was possible to see the real Hunter behind the illusion, and their shadows were dead giveaways. That seemed to be the reason they preferred the night.

He didn't think any of these men were Kra'agh Hunters. True, the light inside the store wasn't all that good . . . but there was also a smell he associated with the Hunters, a kind of burnt-sulfur, rotten-egg stink, faint but unmistakable. All he smelled now were the mingled aromas of the store—sawdust and tobacco, leather and oil. And Ned Buntline's handshake had been real enough.

"Okay," Macklin said at last. "Tell him that Doris sent me, and that I was supposed to tell him '*Taled* One-three-three.' "

"What the hell's that? An address?"

"Kind of. Just tell him, will you?" He fished a silver dollar from his jeans pocket, and tossed it to the clerk. "It's important."

The man snatched the spinning dollar out of the air

and made it disappear. "You gonna be around town, then?"

"Sure am."

"Where you staying?"

"I don't have a place yet. Where would you recommend?"

"The Tucson Hacienda's a decent place," Buntline said. "That's where I'm lodging, and I know they have rooms available."

"Much obliged. Where is it?"

"A few blocks from here. I can take you. Ten dollars a week . . . and that includes breakfast."

Macklin frowned. "Looks like I'm going to need to see about getting myself a job." He looked at Jeb. "You wouldn't need someone to help out around here, would you?"

Jeb shook his head. " 'Fraid not. You can take it up with Slim, of course, but we have a couple of boys who help with the stock, and so on."

"Tell me something, Macklin," asked the quiet man they'd called Dan. "You claim you were with the Earp party. Doing what?"

How much to tell? Macklin decided that the short story was best. "You might've heard there's been a lot of trouble in Tombstone. The Earps—Virgil was the town marshal until after the O.K. Corral fight—were cleaning out a gang that called themselves the Cowboys."

"Ike Clanton," Dan said. "Curly Bill Brocius. The McLaurys. Billy the Kid Claiborne. Yeah, we've heard of them."

"Wyatt hired me as an extra gun, is all," Macklin said. "To kind of even up the numbers a bit."

"You any good?"

"What?"

"With a gun. Can you hit what you shoot at?"

"I do okay." He let the understated words speak for

themselves. In fact, it was his speed with a gun that had convinced the Earps and Doc Holliday to hire him to pass himself off as Johnny Waco, a gunman with a dangerous rep.

Macklin's problem was that he still didn't understand just how he'd learned to handle a revolver as well as he did. Dorree had explained, once, that he had a lot of highly specialized training stored inside his Companion, the AI embedded in his chest and brain, but he couldn't imagine how such a thing could work.

"You have anyone who can vouch for you?" Dan continued. "I mean, you say you know the Earps. . . ."

Macklin shrugged. "Well, the Earps aren't in Tucson anymore, but I imagine you could wire them in Tombstone. Or . . . you could ask John Clum. He's the mayor of Tombstone, and also the editor of their newspaper. He's a close friend and supporter of the Earps, and he knows I was with them. Or you could talk to Sarah Nevers. She runs the boarding house on Toughnut Street where I was staying." Of course, Sarah had a low opinion of all "shootists," and of the Earps in particular, but she would tell the truth as she saw it, no matter what.

Dan had pulled a small notebook with a well-worn leather cover from his jacket pocket and been making some entries with the stub of a pencil. He closed the notebook and returned it to his pocket. "I'll tell you what, Macklin," he said. "How would you like to sign on with our outfit?"

"And what outfit is that?"

"The Apache Peak Mining Company. We have a consortium going, based here in Tucson, with a good, solid claim about fifty miles southeast of here."

Macklin's eyes narrowed as he tried to picture it on a map. "Back toward Tombstone?"

"We's northwest of Tombstone," Tom put in. "About twenty, twenty-five miles. Like I say, we come here for supplies because it's cheaper. Besides, we haven't wanted t' cross paths with the likes of the damned Clanton gang."

"You *don't* need to draw the gentleman a map, Tom," Dan said, his voice low. "He ain't with us yet!"

"Shoot, everybody knows the claim is up there," Tom said with a shrug. He cackled. "*Findin'* it, though, that's another matter altogether!"

Macklin grinned. Dan's mistrust of potential claim-jumpers bordered on the paranoid. "So what do you want me for?" he asked.

"We need guns. Lots of 'em. There's a band of wild Apaches up that way that doesn't want us up there. They attacked us a few days ago, and we figure they'll be back."

Macklin glanced at the soldier. "Isn't that the Army's job?"

"We're not getting that much cooperation from the Army, lately," Dan said.

The soldier shrugged. "We can't be everywhere, Dan. And, frankly, Apache Peak's not really in Fort Lowell's patrol territory. That's down toward Fort Huachuca." He looked away. "In any case, you guys might not be the injured party here."

"See?" Dan said. "See? Just like at Camp Grant! The Army backs the damned redskins! That claim is *ours*, filed right here at the government claims office in Tucson! Got a judge's name on it and everything, all right, proper, and legal! And no band of thieving, ragged, scarecrow Apaches are going to scare us off of our rightful claim!"

"Well, we got a right to protect ourselves, *and* our property," Tom said. "And if you're who and what you claim to be, Macklin, you can help! Pay's two dollars a day, and if you prove yourself and make yourself useful, maybe in six months we can cut you in for a share or two."

"Sounds good," Macklin said. "But I won't lie to you.

I've been told I have to stay here in town. They want me to tell them what I know about Frank Stillwell's death."

"We can fix that. Long as they know where you are, they won't care. But let me send a couple of telegrams first, and then we'll talk again. You'll be staying at the Hacienda, then?"

"I reckon so."

"I'll be in touch." He extended a hand and Macklin took it. "Name's Dan Granger."

As Macklin stepped back into the midmorning sunlight outside, a couple of teenaged boys were already loading the waiting wagon with bags and crates of supplies. Ned Buntline joined him, limping slightly as he leaned on his cane. He pulled a cigar from a breast pocket, cut the end, then stuck it in his mouth without lighting it. "So," the writer said, "let me walk you over to the Hacienda."

"I appreciate your kindness, Mr. Buntline."

"Call me Ned. And it's I who should thank you."

"Oh? For what?"

"I can always smell a story, my boy. Always. And you fairly reek of action, adventure, and daring . . . of far horizons and rescued damsels and high stakes. You've ridden with the likes of Wyatt Earp and Doc Holliday. For that reason alone I would want to pick your brains . . . but I sense that there's more to you. A lot more. And I would be much obliged if you would tell me your story."

"I'm not sure I can do that, Ned." Macklin smiled. "To start with, I don't think you would believe a word I said."

"Just try me."

"There's also the problem that, well, I was in a crash . . . uh, in an accident last year. Couldn't remember a thing, not even my own name. I still don't remember much, though I've had some people helping me fill in a few of the gaps. But to be honest, I'm not really sure how much of it *I* believe! It doesn't feel . . . real, somehow.

It's like it all happened to someone else, and doesn't connect with me at all."

"Ha! I knew it! A man of mystery. There is a story here, I'm certain of that much. Maybe if you tell me what you know, we can fill in a few more of those gaps. As for believing . . . well, hey! I'm paid to tell lies, and to make them believable. It's called 'suspension of disbelief.' You might let *me* be the judge about whether something is believable or not!"

"Let me think about that, okay?"

"Fair enough. And I can tell you a bit about myself, just so everything is on the square." He took Macklin's elbow, steering him to the right. "Come, my boy. The hotel is this way. Did you know that once I was actually strung up by a lynch mob? Hung by the neck, God's own truth! That was back in 1846, after I had this run-in with a jealous husband. You see, it was like this . . ."

As they started stepping along the planks of the boardwalk, Macklin shivered, and stopped. He looked back over his shoulder, across the street, up at the empty windows of the surrounding buildings, and finally into the crystalline blue depths of the sky, where a solitary bird of some sort—a hawk or a buzzard—was making lazy circles at the zenith.

He had the damnedest feeling that he was being watched.

The feeling pursued him, unshakable, all the way to the hotel.

❖ 2 ❖

DEATHSTALKER RELAXED, ALLOWING THE DLAADTHMA'S *thoughts to flood its own mind. One of the creatures below, clearly, was the prey. The trouble was, it had just left the native hut where the Associative Monitor that called itself Apache Slim kept its listening post. Had*

Macklin communicated with Slim? There was no way to tell.

But Deathstalker did recognize that the time to act had come at last. Attempts to lure the prey into a trap had failed. Now they would use direct action.

And they would strike tonight.

SEVEN

✧ 1 ✧

IN THE COURSE OF THAT DAY, MACKLIN LEARNED FAR more about the adventurous life of Colonel Ned Buntline than he really cared to know. Buntline seemed to enjoy talking about himself at length. If hc rcally wanted to interview Macklin about his life, he had a strange way of going about it.

By the time the pair entered the Granada Bar on Main Street late that afternoon, Macklin had heard all about how Buntline had gone to sea as a cabin boy at the age of fourteen, how he'd then entered the Navy and served as a midshipman for five years . . . and how his first story, a true tale about the disappearance of a roast pig from the captain's table, had gotten him in so much trouble with the man that he'd had to resign from the service. That had been the first appearance of the pseudonym Ned Buntline, a name taken from the line attached to the bottom of a square-rigged sail.

Macklin had learned about a bewildering array of Buntline's novels—*The Last Days of Calleo, Doomed City of Sin, A Visit to Lafitte, Running the Blockade of the Last War, Love's Desperation, The President's Only*

Daughter, The Red Revenger. He'd learned that Buntline had created whole dictionaries of new words and expressions. In his popular *Mysteries and Miseries of New York*, Ned had introduced such varied expressions as "blowout" for a party or feast, "coppers" for policemen, "kid" for a little thief, "lifting" for stealing, "swell" for gentleman, "square" for honest, and "swig" for a drink. Only William Shakespeare, Buntline contended grandly, had added more to the English language.

He'd been active in politics, creating a reform party back in the 1850's devoted to preserving America and American jobs from foreigners—especially the Irish and all Catholics. He'd even created the party's name—the Know-Nothings.

He'd served as a scout with the New York Mounted Rifles for fourteen months during the American Civil War, and that was where he'd picked up the honorary rank of "Colonel." He was a friend of Buffalo Bill, and had given him his nickname. He was a devotee of guns and had a large collection at "The Eagle's Nest," his home near Stamford. He'd been married seven times, loved the life of adventure . . . but lately had been slowing down under the crippling effects of gout and sciatica. This trip to the West, to meet some of the adventurers he so admired, was, he claimed, likely the last of his travels.

All of this and more, Macklin learned in the day he spent with Buntline, who was pleasant enough as a companion, if a bit egoistic. "I found that to make a living I must write trash for the masses," he told Macklin grandly as they entered the bar. "After all, he who endeavors to write for the critical few and do his genius justice will go hungry if he has no other means of support. Is it not so?"

"Uh . . . I suppose." Macklin looked about the bar, as if searching for a way out. Buntline's author's ego was entertaining in small doses, but wearing after the first few hours. The man seemed obsessed by the fact that he'd made his fame and fortune writing dime novels—pure action and adventure—instead of the serious literary works he was convinced were his true calling. True, he had introduced Macklin to Mrs. Collins, who ran the hotel, and vouched for his character, for which he was grateful, but . . . "Look, excuse me for a second, will you? I see someone I have to talk to. Alone."

"Right you are, m'boy," Buntline replied cheerfully. "I'll get us something to swig and meet you at that table in the back."

"Right."

The Granada was similar to the dozens of saloons Macklin had seen in Tombstone, wood-floored and smoky, with a pot-bellied stove in the back and a massive wooden bar tenanted by a line of men nursing drinks and telling stories. There were cowhands and miners, business-suited men and guys in clay-smeared dungarees . . . and even a few "soiled doves," prostitutes plying their age-old trade. The large painting hanging behind the bar, for a change, was not a naked woman, but a crude, somewhat garish depiction of a battle between blue-coated soldiers and hordes of red-skinned savages. From the looks of things, the soldiers were getting the worst of the deal, though a carpet of dead Indians covered the grassy hillside around them. Only a few troopers were left standing or kneeling, each in an appropriately heroic pose, led by a golden-haired man in buckskins at the center, who blazed away at the oncoming foe with a six-gun in each hand.

After a glance, however, Macklin plowed ahead through the crowd, aiming for a table near the front window. The soldier he'd seen at Slim's earlier that morning was there, sitting with two friends, a bottle of whiskey, and three glasses on the round tale between them. The man looked up as Macklin approached.

"Well, well. Mr. Macklin, was it?"

"Still is. Got a moment?"

The soldier exchanged a look with his friends. Macklin knew he was intruding, but the chance to get away from Ned Buntline, at least for a few moments, was too good to pass up. "I reckon. Pull up a chair."

"Thanks. Say, I never did get your name this morning."

"Sergeant Sam Donovan." He nodded at the others. "Corporal Sawyer, Sergeant McMurray. What can we do for you?"

"I need to find out the story—the *true* story—about the Apaches. I've heard all sorts of things lately . . . and, frankly, what you said over at Slim's was the first time I'd heard someone who sounded like they were on the Indians' side. *Every* story has two sides, at the very least. I wanted to know what yours was."

Donovan looked surprised. "I'm . . . flattered that you want my opinion. But most people's minds are already made up when it comes to the Indians, and especially the Apache. Why isn't yours?"

Macklin shrugged. "I'm new in these parts, Sergeant. I haven't heard much . . . outside of what bloodthirsty savages they are, and I have some trouble believing that any human being could be that downright evil."

McMurray laughed. "You don't know the Apaches very well!"

"Shaddup, Mac," Donovan said. "You don't know what you're talking about."

"The hell I don't!" He tossed back the last of the golden liquid in his glass. "But you always was a strange one, Sam."

"Dissension in the ranks?"

"Tom here lost a buddy to the Apache a couple years back. The *slow* way, if you know what I mean. So you can imagine he doesn't exactly feel charitable towards 'em."

Macklin wasn't sure he wanted to know what "the slow

way" was, but he could guess. The expression on Mc-
Murray's face told him a lot.

"So what can you tell me about the Apaches?"

Donovan leaned back in his chair. "What do you want
to know? And more to the point, I guess, why?"

"You heard that guy with the mining company offer
me a job this morning. I guess mostly I'd like to know
what I'm getting into. Is it really just a matter of protecting their property and people? Or is there something else
I should know about the situation?"

"I'll give you credit, mister," Donovan said. "Most
white men wouldn't even think of asking a question like
that. But you're right. There are two sides of it. Dan
Granger and his bunch are begging for trouble if you ask
me. And you're six kinds of idiot if you get messed up
in it. Sorry . . . but you did ask."

"Yes, I did. What's the whole story?"

"It's a pretty big topic. What do you know about the
Apache already?"

"Well, I know that most of the people—the white
men—I've talked to in the five months I've been here
either hate or fear the Apaches, and usually both. Back in
Tombstone, the Earps hated the Clantons and vice versa
. . . but this is something quite different. 'Filthy, thieving,
murdering savages' was one of the gentler descriptions I
heard back in Tombstone, and that was from a kindly old
woman who was a school teacher in town. She told me
her husband was killed during Cochise's uprising in the
1860's. She didn't tell me much more than that, but she
was mighty bitter." He looked at McMurray, who stared
back, eyes hard, fists clenched. He heard the echo of Donovan's words. *The* slow *way, if you know what I mean.*

Donovan nodded. "No one much likes the Apache, and
that's a fact. They came into this region from somewhere
up north eight, maybe nine hundred years ago, which
makes them relative newcomers. They live by preying on

their neighbors. Always have. They have no friends among the other Indians in the area either. You know, the name Apache isn't even the name they call themselves. It's a Hopi word, and it means 'enemy.' So that'll give you an idea! Their word for themselves is *N'de* or *N'dee*, which just means 'the People.' They call us *Indaa*, at least when they're being polite. Means 'white-eyes.' "

"You speak the language?"

"A little. But you have to be born Apache to really know the language, or them." He took a swallow from his glass. "Anyway, when the Spanish took this area over back in the sixteen, seventeen hundreds, they inherited the problem, and before long they found themselves in a constant, low-grade war with a people superbly adapted to life in the mountains, scrub plain, and desert. You know, I've actually seen Apaches still wearing bits and pieces of old Spanish armor and I know one who carried an ancient Spanish arquebus. Things must have been taken from some poor *conquistador* and been handed down within the band for generations.

"Then the Anglos—us—moved in. For a while, the Apaches thought we were going to help them fight the Mexicans, and when we wouldn't go along, they started raiding us as well. They're pretty good at playing both sides of the fence, fighting one and making peace with the other, 'cause they know neither the Mexicans nor the Americans are supposed to cross the border in between.

"We don't often catch them in big battles. They move in small bands, and they prefer to ambush travelers, raid isolated farms, steal livestock, stuff like that."

"They're cowards," McMurray put in.

"No, they're not," Donovan shot back. "They fight a different kind of war than we do, is all."

"Yeah, bushwacking and murdering and then running away without standing up to a fair fight!"

"The British redcoats probably said the same thing

about us after Concord," Donovan said, a shadow of a smile crossing his face. He looked at Macklin. "Fact of the matter is, the Apache might just be the toughest, best damned warriors on this continent, and maybe in all of history. They can go anywhere in that hell of mountain, rock, and sand, cover fifty miles in a day, find water in a desert that would choke a scorpion, blend into the undergrowth like they were a part of it. They signal one another with puffs of smoke that can be seen clear to the horizon . . . or with rocks arranged beside the path in a kind of code, so they always know you're coming, how many of you there are, and how well you're armed."

"And if you ask me," McMurray put in, "every damned one of them savages oughta be taken out and hung. There won't be peace in Arizona Territory until the Apaches are dead or gone, every last one of 'em."

Macklin didn't comment. He'd heard the sentiment often enough in Tombstone. While he couldn't remember anything about his own past or training, he found himself immediately suspicious of any argument concerning them-and-us, with "them" as the embodiment of pure, barbarian evil, and "us" as blameless, wholesome, and good. From what he'd seen so far, the Anglos of Tombstone were fully capable of some pretty savage acts. The Apaches, clearly, represented a different culture than the Americans did, and possessed a more primitive technology, but that of itself didn't make them evil.

People were people, he thought . . . and the Apaches were as human as any of the finely dressed and educated citizens of Tombstone or Tucson, however much the Americans he'd spoken with might resent the comparison.

"We all know what you think, Tom," Donovan said. He sounded tired. "Me, I have to live with myself. I still remember those bodies at Camp Grant."

"You were there?" Macklin asked.

"I was there. I was a corporal with the detachment that

went out from Camp Grant that morning and found them."
He made a face. "Those bastards from Tucson were off
celebrating someplace. Left those bodies to rot in the sun.
Damn it, a hundred and eighteen bodies, and only eight
of them were men! And we call *them* savages?"

"Wasn't the first time," the quiet soldier between Donovan and McMurray said. "Won't be the last."

"Well, damn it all, Ben, what would you feel like if
someone with better weapons and a taste for slaughter
came along and decided we didn't belong here? Someone,
maybe a few hundred years further along, with guns that
make our Sharps and Winchesters look about as modern
as an Apache war lance? Put yourself in their moccasins,
for God's sake!"

Macklin started at that. Donovan could not possibly
know that the Kra'agh were exactly that, a predator species technically far in advance of the dominant cultures
of this planet, and who planned on turning this world into
a kind of free range for raising food beasts—like humans.

"So," Macklin said carefully, hoping to shift the subject to safer ground. "Are you saying that Granger and
his people are in the wrong? Is their mine on Apache
land?"

"Well, 'Apache land' is kind of a funny idea to begin
with. They don't really believe you *can* own land, any
more than a man can own the air around him. Besides
that, the Apaches hereabouts have all been officially re-
located to the reservation up at San Carlos. The only Indians off the reservation now are the rogues, the ones who
won't come in, or who got tired of reservation life and
went back to the old ways.

"But, well, there are places that are important to them.
Holy ground, you might say. The Chiricahuas that the
Apache Peak Mining Company is tangling with have a
special place up in those hills, and they don't want us
white-eyes mucking about back there."

"Why is the place so special?"

"I can't say I understand Apache religion, but I know they believe in a bunch of spirit people—not quite gods, but more than humans, anyway—they call *gan*, or *ga he*, mountain people. They live up in the high places with the Apache gods, the mountain spirits that bring thunder and lightning. Places like Apache Peak are sacred to 'em, the place where the mountain spirits live. Us moving in . . . well, it'd be like someone getting mineral rights to the nave at Notre Dame and sinking a shaft."

"No wonder they attacked the miners."

"Can't say I blame them much myself . . . but around here, high-grade silver talks a hell of a lot louder than any native traditions about spooks or mountain spirits. It's easy to find a judge who'll sign the deeds and transfer rights . . . and the hell with what a bunch of dirty, thieving redskin savages who shouldn't even be there have to say about things."

"I see." Macklin crossed his arms and leaned back, the chair creaking beneath him. Damn, he needed the job, but he didn't like the idea of siding with the mining consortium people when it sounded like the folks they were fighting were the aggrieved party. "Well, I appreciate your telling me all of this. Thanks for talking. You've given me something to think about." He stood to leave.

Donovan glanced past Macklin's shoulder. "How do you like Ned Buntline?"

Macklin grinned. "Persistent fellow. Nice enough, but he does love to talk."

"If he's a real colonel, I'll eat my horse, tack and all. But he seems all right. Just don't let him talk you into one of his wild adventures. Life out here is considerably different than it's painted in his dime novels."

"I'll keep that in mind."

"One more thing, Macklin."

"Yes?"

"Don't sell your soul out here. You'll find yourself shortchanged, every time."

Macklin read the look in Donovan's eyes, and saw a hopelessness there that burned Macklin like fire. The man, he decided, had sold his own soul several times over, and was trying to warn him. Of what? Macklin had the impression that Donovan genuinely admired the Indians, especially the Apaches, but he was caught in a web of orders, duty, and responsibility that put him on the side of forces that would inevitably destroy the native cultures.

As inevitably as the Kra'agh would destroy all the cultures of Earth.

Damn it, he had to make contact with Apache Slim. More than his own rescue depended on it. The Kra'agh had to be stopped.

It wasn't too late for the Americans.

For the people known as the N'de, however, outnumbered and outgunned by a vastly superior and hostile culture, he had the feeling that it was already too late.

✧ 2 ✧

THEY WOULD HAVE TO DO THIS THE HARD WAY.

Deathstalker and the other Kra'agh in its hunting pod had been watching for many cycles, unwilling to make a move that would precipitate Associative interference on this primitive world. The human called Macklin, however, was a serious threat to Kra'agh plans, since it had already interfered with the Hunters' activities on this world and might well have additional strategic information from the now-destroyed Associative base on the planet's moon.

They would deal with Macklin later, but the human called Apache Slim had to be taken out of the Hunt now, before Kra'agh plans could be compromised. It was in its dwelling now, upstairs, above the dry goods store.

Deathstalker gave a signal, and it, Eater, and Flesh-

ripper emerged from the shadows cloaking the alley and flowed swiftly and silently across the broad, dirt street. They appeared to be denizens of the planet, three cowboys in jeans, leather vests, and broad-brimmed hats, but the shadows cast on the street behind them by a gas-flame streetlight shifted in vast, grotesque shapes that were in no way human.

The sun had long since set, but Tucson was still brightly lit and noisy. The tinkle of pianos, the raucous bark of laughter and shouted, good-natured insults floated from the windows and batwing doors of a dozen bars up and down Main Street. A cowboy, brain poisoned by the alcohol it had consumed, lay sprawled in the alleyway next to Apache Slim's Dry Goods and Mining Supplies, making loud, wet, rattling sounds through its open mouth. Deathstalker stepped past the unconscious form with an inner sneer; creatures that deliberately embraced chemical comas and oblivion had no right to survive, other than as objects for the Hunters' sustenance and entertainment. Humans were troublesome, but should pose no serious challenge to the Kra'agh invasion fleet when it arrived. Only the Associative, with its bizarrely contrasurvival idiocies about ethics and the inherent value of Mind, threatened Kra'agh plans for this sector and this world.

Wooden steps on the outside of the building led from the alley to an upper-floor apartment. "Stohl chat!" Eater said, snapping warning. Its field detector had registered the faint pulse of flowing electrons and gently twisted magnetic fields . . . impossibilities for this technically primitive culture.

The three paused at the bottom of the stairs as Eater manipulated a device on its harness. With a sharp snap and the stink of ozone, an electrical circuit overloaded and failed. Eater signaled All Clear, and they ascended the steps rapidly. The stairway creaked ominously—Kra'agh massed considerably more than most humans, whatever *they might look like behind the shroud of a* gah-*projection—but they reached the door at the landing on the top of the stairway in seconds.*

They were taking a terrible chance. It would have been better to leave the Monitor watch stations intact. To actually take one down would warn other Associative outposts that the Kra'agh were openly on the move, and that might well trigger the defensive response the Kra'agh scouts on Earth had been warned to avoid.

But if Macklin had made contact with the local Monitor . . . or if it was about to, the station had to be taken down.

Eater disabled a second electronic device warding the doorway. Deathstalker held the thermal claw against the primitive, mechanical lock, gaze averted as heat, visible to its infrared-sensitive vision, flared in momentary brilliance. Brass ran like water . . . and then with a snap the lock parted and the door swung open.

Deathstalker slipped the claw back into its harness to recharge as it stepped through the door. The creature calling itself Apache Slim was here; Deathstalker could taste its scent heavy on the still and musty air. The Hunter drew a beamer; it wanted to keep Apache Slim alive, at least for the time being, but it would incinerate the Associative Monitor if it had to. At its back, Eater edged into the room, beamer in one of its feeder hands.

The outer room was darkened, but harsh light spilled through the crack of a closed door beyond. The intruders' electronically heightened senses could pick up the words being spoken in the next room. "Ch'vannah! Ch'vannah! N'gan shav erit groneyth!" The words were G'tai. The prey was calling for help.

Ahead, on either side of the door, sentry floaters rose from concealment, metallic spheres unevenly patterned in black and white with glittering lenses like crystal eyes.

Eater fired its beamer, blue light searing vision, sparks

dancing from the stricken robot sentinel. A thread of ruby light flared from the remaining sentry, clawing at Death-stalker's protective fields. Deathstalker returned fire, shattering the floater in a dazzle of cerulean light.

Deathstalker's illusion of a human cowboy failed, the gah-*projector in its harness damaged. Huge and centaur-like, the Kra'agh Hunter plunged forward, shattering the closed door, smashing into the room beyond heedless now of the danger of Monitor weaponry.*

Apache Slim crouched behind the corner of a massive rolltop desk next to a four-poster bed. The light was not the gas lamp or candlelight common to this culture's technology, but glared from a monitor screen alive with white static. The creature's shirt was off, and scars showed purple on its pale skin. It was human, but the black plastic shininess of an AI implant gleamed in the center of its chest, betraying its Monitor status. It had known they were coming for it, and was ready; blue-white light stabbed at the door from a power gun clenched in one hand.

The beam brushed Deathstalker's head, burning one of its feeder arms. The Kra'agh threw back its head and shrieked in pain, rage, and battle lust.

Eater and Fleshripper fired together, their beams raking the desk in blossoming flame and splintering wood. Deathstalker flowed across the floor as quickly as a striking hual'tchka, *reaching out and slapping the Monitor's weapon aside before it could thumb the firing button. The power gun clattered across the wooden floorboards as the Hunter's feeder arms closed on the prey's arms, lifting it bodily from the floor. The human gave one sharp scream, broken short when Deathstalker cracked the side of its skull with the beamer's blunt muzzle. The Hunter was careful with the blow, and surgically precise. Humans were appallingly fragile, and tended to come apart if you handled them too roughly.*

The Monitor lived, its breathing a throaty gurgle, its eyes unfocused. Deathstalker lowered the creature to the floor, holstered the beamer, and pulled the patternmaker from its harness. Positioning the probe's needle-slim point above the unconscious human's optical organs, it drove the device through skin and bone with a sharp, satisfying crunch. Engaging the receivers and main memory, ignoring the mounting flames against the wall, Deathstalker let the creature's thoughts and memories cascade through the device and into its own mind.

Deathstalker tensed at the inrushing flow of discordant, alien thoughts. . . .

✧ 3 ✧

MACKLIN WAS BEGINNING TO WONDER HOW TO GET RID of Colonel Ned Buntline.

The man was agreeable enough, a pleasant, witty, and highly intelligent companion, but he seemed to have attached himself to Macklin and now refused to be dislodged. They'd spent much of the afternoon at the Granada, sitting at a table and talking. Late in the afternoon, they'd made one trip together back to Apache Slim's, learned that Slim still wasn't available, and then they'd gone to the New Orleans Restaurant for dinner . . . a steak dinner that Buntline grandiosely insisted on paying for over Macklin's protestations.

By the time they at long last began walking back to the hotel, Macklin had consumed enough beers to have a very pleasant buzz going in his head. His steps were a bit unsteady, and he felt queasy. Ned Buntline was, if anything, worse off. He was leaning heavily against Macklin in an attempt to stand more or less upright. The hotel, at this point, seemed like a very long way down the street.

A noisy commotion rang through the town at their backs. Turning, they observed what seemed to be a fire several blocks back. Macklin could see the Tucson Volunteer Fire Brigade swinging into action, with hand-pushed pumper carts and lines of men with buckets.

"Wa's burning?" Buntline wanted to know, squinting at the glow in the distance.

"Dunno," Macklin replied. "Wanna go see?"

"Nah. Too far. I'm fer bed."

"Yeah . . ."

"Macklin . . ."

He turned at the name, called from the shadows cloaking the mouth of a side street. A shadow moved there, huge and monstrous . . . and Macklin felt the first pricklings of sharp, fast-rising fear. Then the shadows coalesced. A human form stood before them, dimly seen in the wavering light of a street lamp.

"S'allright," Buntline said. "John Macklin? Meet Apache Slim."

Macklin's eyes widened. The man before him didn't look like what he'd expected of the Associative Monitor, old, white-haired, and pale.

"Macklin," Slim said again, stepping closer. There was something in his hand . . . but it seemed blurred somehow, and oddly held. Macklin breathed in, and caught the brimstone stink of sulfur. For just an instant, the image of Apache Slim wavered, then flickered . . . revealing a monstrous centaur form with writhing arms like black snakes on its head, and razor-edged slasher claws on its forearms. . . .

Ned Buntline screamed. . . .

EIGHT

❖ 1 ❖

THE BUZZING EFFECTS OF THE BEER DRAINED FROM MACK-lin's system as though a plug had been pulled. Adrenaline flooded his body. His hand dropped to his gun . . . and too late he remembered that the deputy marshal had taken his gun from him that morning.

The creature lunged, fast as a striking snake. Macklin leaped to the left, fell, landed on his shoulder and rolled in the dusty street. The Kra'agh spun, following him, its shadowy, monstrous mass fading again to invisibility behind the hazy form of Apache Slim.

"Shoot, Ned!" Macklin yelled, letting the roll take him to his feet. "Shoot!"

Buntline appeared dazed, standing in the street . . . but Macklin's shout seemed to galvanize him. He drew his Colt, aimed it uncertainly in a two-handed grip, then squeezed off three fast shots.

The creature screamed, a piercing shriek accompanied by a stronger whiff of sulfur as it emptied its lungs in the night air. A bolt of blue-white light snapped from the darkness of another alley, across the street, crackling through the air inches above Macklin's head with a breath of dry heat trailing in its wake. The bolt hit the side of a building with a flash and an explosion of hot splinters, and both Macklin and Buntline dropped to the street, rolling for cover.

Their Kra'agh attacker was gone, and no further beamer fire snapped from the alley. Slowly, Macklin rose. A few splatters of milky white liquid lay in the dust nearby, slowly absorbing into the ground. Ned had hit the creature at least once. He doubted, though, that the wound would discourage the Hunter for long.

Buntline stood up, his revolver still clutched in both hands. "You okay, Macklin?"

"Yeah. I think so."

"What in the great blue thunder of the beyond was *that*?"

"That, Colonel Buntline, was a Hunter."

"A . . . a bounty hunter?" Ned's gun hand sagged, until the Colt was hanging loose at his side, muzzle pointed at the street. His voice trembled with a barely suppressed terror. "No. I mean, the thing wasn't human!"

"It's a Hunter, and it's after me. I've tangled with the likes of it before." He looked at the writer with new respect. "That was pretty good shooting. Thanks." Stooping, he studied a track in the slightly damp dirt of the street near the blue-white blood, an H-shaped mark unlike the footprint of any creature native to Earth.

"It was . . . it was . . . it was . . ."

"Not human. No, you're right. If my information is correct, it is a being—a *person* as smart as you or I, even if it doesn't look like us—from another planet so far distant from here that even light takes thousands of years to cross the gulf from there to here."

Slowly, Buntline holstered his pistol. Other people were spilling into the street now, emptying the Granada and several other bars. Deputy Marshal Evans was there, thumbs tucked into his gun belt. "Who fired those shots?" he demanded.

"I did," Buntline said.

"What's the damned idea? Tucson is a civilized place. We don't take kindly to hallooing in this city."

"We were, we were attacked . . ." Buntline seemed dazed. He met the marshal's eyes for the first time. "We were attacked. Out of that alley."

"Yeah? By who?"

"By Apache . . ." He stopped. "I-I'm not sure."

"What, Apaches?" someone in the crowd said. "Apaches here in Tucson?"

"No," Macklin said. "It looked like Apache Slim at first. It wasn't, though."

"You should have checked that gun," Evans told Buntline. Then he frowned. "Of course, then we might not be having this conversation. Did you get him?"

"Yes. I mean . . . no. I don't know."

"It might have been wounded, Marshal," Macklin put in. "But it was moving pretty fast. I don't think you'll catch it."

Evans frowned at Macklin. "What do you mean by 'it'?"

Macklin shrugged. "Him, then. We didn't see . . . whoever it was very well."

Evans looked him up and down. "You say the guy looked like Apache Slim?"

"That's right. The . . . light was kind of bad, though."

"Have to be. Y'see, I just came from Slim's. He's dead."

Macklin's eyes widened, the words jolting him like an electric shock. "Dead!"

"Someone broke in down there. Looks like they tried to set fire to the place. The bucket brigade's still over there, putting out the embers."

One of the townspeople, a lanky man in a knee-length

black coat, was examining the wall of the building, a doctor's office, where the Kra'agh shot had struck. By the light of a nearby street lamp, it looked as if someone had hit the dry wood with a sledge hammer, but the edges were warped and blackened by intense heat. Smoke curled away from the hole like steam in damp air. "Shoot, it looks like someone tried to set fire to Doc Pardoe's place, too. What the hell? Was they using *artillery*?"

"Something like that." Macklin looked at Evans. "Marshal . . . right now my life in this town isn't worth two cents. I'll be happy to fill out any sworn statement, sign any document you want, but I'm leaving here before those . . . *people* try to get me again."

"Where do you want to go?"

"I have a job offer at a mining camp out in the hills, someplace. If I can go there, maybe they'll come after me. Maybe I can lose them. If you don't let me go, though, they're going to keep trying until they kill me. And the bad news for you is, they may kill some other people while they're trying. They're not very . . . discriminating."

Evans rubbed his chin. "Well, I don't know . . ."

"It's either that, or you let me go armed. And you might want to call in the Army's help as well. These people are dangerous."

"You keep talking about 'these people.' Who are they?" Evans straightened, standing taller, his glare dangerous. "This is the Brocius-Clanton Cowboy gang, isn't it?" Before Macklin could reply, he went on. "We do *not* want the Earp-Clanton feud spreading over here to Tucson. Not in my town!"

"The feud wasn't my doing, Marshal. I worked for the Earps, yeah, and I suppose some of the Clantons would like to kill me, too. But this . . ." Macklin waved at the smoldering hole in the doctor's office. "All I can say is that I think some of these people work with the Clanton gang, at least sometimes. One of them was at the rail yard last night, when Stillwell was killed, I'm pretty sure."

"You have any names?"

"No." How could he tell Evans that the Kra'agh Hunters could perfectly mimic anyone they'd been able to capture and imprint upon the workings of the devices they employed to project camouflage illusions?

"If 'these people,' as you call them, aren't regular parts of the Cowboy gang, why do they want you?"

"I honestly don't know." That was a far safer answer than an explanation of Macklin's otherworldly origins and the fact that they feared he might warn the humans of an impending Kra'agh invasion.

Not that such a warning would do any good. Right now, if what Dorree had told him was true, only all-out military intervention by the Associative would save this planet.

"I think," Evans said, eyeing him narrowly, "that you know a lot more than you're letting on. I'm thinking that a cell in the city jail might be the safest place for you."

"It wouldn't do any good, Marshal. They'd get me, one way or another." He cocked his head to the side. "How much help can I be at your inquest if I'm dead?"

Evans appeared to come to a decision. "C'mon," he said. "Let's get off the street."

"Where you taking him, Marshal?" Buntline wanted to know.

"Back to my office. You come along, too, Colonel. I want to hear this story from both of you."

"Come to think of it," Buntline said, "so would I." He shook his head ruefully. "I've never written anything as wild or as exciting as *this*!"

✧ **2** ✧

*D*EATHSTALKER *QUIVERED AT FLESHRIPPER'S TOUCH, AS THE other Kra'agh Hunter plied the wound in its flank with a*

*needle beam. They were within the dark and musty con-
fines of a barn on the outskirts of Tucson, an unused
structure on the point of tumbling down, rarely visited by
the natives. A deft flick of Fleshripper's feeder arm, and
the lead projectile, coated with milk-white blood and tis-
sue, dropped into a tin plate with a clink.*

*It shuddered, savoring the ecstasy of pain. Kra'agh
enjoyed pain—whether their own or that of their victims—
with an intensity that was almost orgasmic with its as-
surance that the sufferer lived. Its pleasure was tempered,
however, by powerful survival instincts that left it feeling
weak, even helpless, in the wake of an injury such as this,
a sensation that Deathstalker detested.*

*"Enjoy," Fleshripper said quietly. It was using a
sealer now, closing the gaping wound in Deathstalker's
leg. "Imagine the pain you will draw from your prey when
you take it."*

*Deathstalker closed one feeder hand in agreement, not
trusting itself to speak. Macklin would die with a terrible,
delicious slowness as Deathstalker drained its soul.*

*Eater of Living Hearts rested on a bale of dry straw
nearby, watching the bloody proceedings. "I still do not
understand," it said, "why you do not wish to simply kill
the Macklin-creature. I could have burned it down tonight, and ended the problem forever."*

*"Because it is worth nothing to us dead," Deathstalker
said, its voice a harsh croak. "We need to know what it
knows."*

*Eater's feeder arms spread, digits peeling back in a
gesture that meant "Why?" It then added, its voice carrying a hint of amusement, "It is clear by now that these
primitives can offer no resistance to our fleet. I understand why you were ordered to track and kill the two
Associative agents who escaped our destruction of their
base on this planet's moon. There was initial fear that
they would give warning of our presence, and plans for*

invasion. But the humans cannot possibly stop us with their pitifully inadequate technology. As for the Associative Monitors here, they presumably are aware of our presence, if not the extent of our plans. And that means the Associative knows we are interested in the planet and its resources." It gestured with the feeder arms again, a shrug this time. "If they have not moved against us by now, it is unlikely that they will. They don't care about backward, uninhabited worlds such as this."

"The question," Deathstalker said, "is whether the Associative views this world as 'uninhabited.' They have members of the dominant species of the planet trained to serve as Monitors, remember, and may consider them intelligent, at least after a fashion. And the one called Macklin seems . . . unusually t'scha'klehh.*" The Kra'agh word meant, very roughly, survival of the fittest, and might even have translated well as "Darwinian," had the Hunters ever heard of that human scientist. Within the context of Kra'agh philosophy and conditioning, it was a term of high praise indeed.*

"It was lucky, to be sure," Fleshripper said.

"The prey's luck should never be underestimated," Deathstalker agreed. "And this one exhibits something more than luck. I want to know *it, to know it completely."*

The word Deathstalker used for "know" was agh'nrek, *and meant both to understand, and literally to devour . . . a favorite Kra'agh pun.*

"Then this is not blood-obsession?" Eater asked. It did not sound convinced.

"No. I have the blood trail, but am not blinded by the taste." Deathstalker knew that reply to be bordering on untruth, but kept its voice steady. The human Macklin had more than once been a setback to Deathstalker's plans, had more than once humiliated it by escaping its traps and even by besting it in open fight. And more . . . those defeats violated Chahh kkit, *the Blood Law that declared*

the Hunter was not the hunted. Those violations burned hot, deep within Deathstalker's soul.

No matter. Deathstalker could still think of the problem with cold rationality. That was all that mattered.

"But what can you learn by devouring this one creature?" Eater asked. "It is only prey."

"What it knows of us, what the Associative knows of us, and our plans. Why this world is important to the Associative . . . if it is. How the creature Macklin was able to defeat us, to defeat me. *I suspect strongly that Macklin is more than what it appears to be. I want to know what that is." The word, again, was* agh'nrek.

"It knows we hunt it here." Fleshripper observed, replacing the medical instruments in a harness pouch. "It will flee."

"And we will find it," Deathstalker replied. "We have the blood trail. We will run it down and take it, pattern its soul, and feed on its pain as it slowly dies."

Eater's principle feeder hand closed in a Kra'agh gesture of assent. "Kkre!" Perfect agreement.

"Droo'kah!" Fleshripper said. "Droo'keh!" The phrase, roughly, meant "Good hunting, good eating."

"If the rest of the prey-beasts of this world are half as challenging as Macklin," Deathstalker said, "this will be a rich hunting world indeed!"

And both of the others agreed.

✧ 3 ✧

"I'LL TELL YOU WHAT I'M GOING TO DO, MACKLIN," Evans said slowly. He tipped his chair precariously back, his boots crossed on his desk top. They were back in the U.S. federal marshal's office, on Congress Street, close to the center of town. "Not sure this is a good idea, but I'm going to let you go."

"I appreciate that."

"Not half as much as I appreciate it, Macklin, believe me. Unfortunate incidents seem to happen around you, son. People die. I don't want you in my town, understand me?"

"I think I do."

Setting the chair down on all four legs with a thump, he reached out, picked up a sheet of paper from the top of his desk, and slid it across to Macklin. "I'm going to have you fill out a written deposition. Everything you can tell me about Frank Stillwell and what you know about his death, and the attack on you tonight. You'll swear to it, sign it, and leave it with me. And that doesn't get you off the hook if I want you to testify in court. You'll tell me where you're going to be, so I can come find you if I need to. Deal?"

Macklin considered this. If Evans knew where he was, and the Kra'agh took him, they would know where he was as well. Still, if this was his only way out of town without causing a posse to come after him . . .

"Deal." Macklin reached for a pencil on Evans's desk and began writing.

"You, too, Colonel Buntline," Evans said, producing another sheet of paper.

"I don't know anything about Stillwell's death," Buntline pointed out.

"No, but I want everything you know about the attack tonight, in writing. There's going to be an inquest into Apache Slim's death too, you know. And I have a feeling that's connected with what happened to you two tonight."

Macklin stared at Buntline, who stared back, eyebrows raised.

"I believe the marshal wants to know," Macklin said, "just what you can vouch for. Not what you think you may or may not have seen, but what you *know*."

"Don't coach him, Macklin," Evans warned. "I want your separate testimonies."

"I know," Macklin said. "It's just that things were pretty confused on the street tonight. Neither of us is real sure of what we saw, right, Ned?"

"You got that right. It all happened . . . kind of sudden."

"I mean," Macklin said, pushing ahead, "that we *thought* we saw Apache Slim kind of lunging at me, and he had a gun in his hand . . . but then we realized it wasn't him at all. I shouted at Ned to shoot, because I wasn't armed, and he did. I—"

"God damn it, Macklin!" Evans snapped. "You just tell your own story right there on that paper, and let Colonel Buntline tell his own! You two aren't supposed to work your story out together ahead of time!"

"No, sir. Of course not. I just thought he was confused about what you wanted."

The two men spent nearly an hour then, filling several sheets with their stories. Evans scowled as he read the statements, but then swore both men under oath, took their signatures, and signed the documents himself.

"Now get out of here, Macklin," he said. "I want you out of my town by noon tomorrow. And if any more citizens of Tucson are killed under mysterious circumstances, or burned, or attacked, I just might know who to talk to about it!"

Much later, Macklin sat with Ned Buntline on the front porch of the Hacienda, leaning back in a rocking chair as he studied the sparse traffic on Franklin Street. He was watching for signs that they'd been followed or were under observation, but so far had seen none.

"I must say," Buntline said after a while, "that what I wrote in that deposition was some of my better fiction."

"And a good thing, too. You know they would have thought we were crazy if we told them what we saw."

"Oh, I'd already seen that angle, Macklin, believe me. I wrote merely that your attacker looked like Apache

Slim, and that he was armed. If I'd tried to describe that
. . . that horror . . ." He closed his eyes and shook his
head. "Macklin, I'm beginning to think I am mad. What
was it we saw?"

"I told you."

"Yes, you did. But you didn't tell me the reality of it.
There is a thing in fiction called suspension of disbelief.
Your story . . . of beings like us, but different, from a
world of another sun . . . a star, in fact, in the night
sky . . ." He sighed. "It beggars belief. I find that my
imagination simply isn't large enough to take hold of such
ideas."

"It would make an exciting story."

"Assuming I could make my readers believe it. How
can I do that, when I don't believe it myself?"

Macklin smiled. "You think I'm crazy, then?"

"It's simpler to believe you mad—and myself infected,
somehow, by your madness, than it is to believe so wild
and impossible a story!" He shook his head again. "And
yet, I know I saw a nightmare on legs. God, what was it?
That such a horror could exist in God's perfect creation . . ."

"God's creation . . . the universe . . . is full of life,"
Macklin said softly. "Some of it far stranger than what
you saw tonight."

"Hmm. You don't look old enough . . . but by any
chance do you remember the Great Moon Hoax?"

"Can't say that I do."

"It was in 1835. I was only twelve when it was published. A man named Richard Locke ran a series of articles in the *New York Sun*, though it was claimed they were
reprinted from the *Edinburgh Journal of Science* . . .
which doesn't even exist. They were supposedly written
by Sir John Herschel, a well-known astronomer, using a
new telescope of revolutionary design at the Cape of
Good Hope.

"Now, supposedly, Herschel was looking through this telescope of his and seeing oceans on the moon . . . beaches, forests, bison, goats, flocks of birds, cities . . . and *people*. People four feet tall with wings and all covered with short, glossy fur, but otherwise not so different from you and me. It all turned out to be a hoax in the end, but for quite a while it had people talking. Such an idea! People living on the moon!"

Macklin was puzzled. "If the stories weren't true, why were they printed?" His only experience with newspapers so far was John Clum's Tombstone *Epitaph*, which insisted it printed only the truth.

Buntline gave him an odd look. "Where have *you* been living? The moon, maybe?"

Macklin chuckled. Though he couldn't remember it directly, Dorree had told him that they'd been at a Monitor base on Earth's moon until shortly before it had been destroyed by a Kra'agh sneak attack. They'd been aboard a spacecraft bound for Earth when the attack had taken place.

Flying people on the moon indeed . . .

"It simply doesn't seem to be in the best interests for a newspaper, which depends on the trust of its readers, to print what are obviously lies. What would be the point?"

Buntline snorted. "Circulation, of course."

"Circulation?"

"Those moon-man articles ran for about three weeks. The *Sun*'s circulation hit fifteen thousand the first day the story ran on page two. By the end, when they were running stories about the discovery of an enormous temple with a roof that looked like solid gold, they were pushing twenty thousand, and the *Sun* had the largest circulation of any paper in the world. Rival editors were going nuts trying to catch up, and some even claimed they had access to the *real* source of the articles, and reprinted them as their own. A bunch of scientists from Yale packed up and headed for New York to inspect the original articles." He stopped and chuckled. "No less a writer than Edgar Allan Poe complained later that he'd stopped working on the second part of "The Unparalleled Adventure of One Hans Pfall" because he felt he'd been outdone by the events of the real world! There was even a missionary society in Springfield, Massachusetts determined to send missionaries to the moon to convert the bat men to Christianity, and bring them the benefits of civilization."

Macklin blinked. "Civilization? If they had cities, temples with roofs of gold . . . doesn't that count for civilization?"

"Not in Christian missionary society circles, evidently. Remember, these bat men *didn't wear clothes*! Actually, what amuses me is that they were determined to send their missionaries to the moon in the first place. I wish them well purchasing the tickets!" He sighed. "Perhaps they expected to be transported to the celestial mission fields in the hand of God."

"Weren't people upset to find out they'd been duped?"

Buntline chuckled. "Oh, those Yale professors were a bit miffed, I should imagine. And the publishers of rival newspapers who'd lifted the *Sun*'s stories and passed them on as their own, I think they must have been talking about putting together an impromptu lynch mob. But most people? They loved it! It brightened their day, gave them something to wonder about." He sighed, staring off into the night. "If I could figure out how to put the same sort of thing into one of my novels, I swear I would. Something new, more exciting than sea romances or tales of the Wild West frontier. A romance set against the wilds of the moon? The oceans of Jupiter? I dunno. Maybe I need to believe that the story could be real before I can write it."

Macklin wondered what it would take to convince him. He'd actually seen a being from another world this evening—and not one of those improbable bat men from the newspaper hoax—and he seemed to be walling off that part of his mind that experienced it. What he'd seen *couldn't* be real, and so it wasn't. . . .

And this from a man who, by his own account, at least, was one of the most brilliantly imaginative people on the planet.

"Okay, so what's your point?"

"Only that folks seemed awfully ready to believe in monstrous people living on other worlds. Maybe they still are. Life on other worlds! Such an absurd notion!"

"You saw some of it today, Ned."

Buntline sobered. "Did I?"

"You saw a Hunter. It wasn't anything native to this world, was it?"

"No, not if my eyes were on the level." He took a deep, shuddering breath, then turned to stare at Macklin. "I knew you had a story in you, mister."

"Do you believe it?"

"Yes. Yes, I have to believe that. *Have* to, because if I don't, I have to believe that I'm losing my mind."

Interesting. Maybe Buntline's mind *was* flexible enough to wrap around the idea of life on other worlds.

"There aren't cities or golden temples or bat men on the moon, Ned," Macklin said after a long silence. "But there are other worlds, and other peoples. And some of them are powerful enough that they could send *their* missionaries *here* to convert and civilize *you*."

" 'You?' "

"Pardon?"

"You said 'civilize you,' not 'civilize *us*.' Are you one of these people from another planet?"

"Yes."

"Goddamn it all to hell. . . ."

Macklin chuckled. "Well, you wanted my story . . ."

"Yes, damn your eyes! And I can't tell it, because it's

too unbelievable. People would accuse me of a hoax more incredible than the *Sun*'s Moon Hoax, not fiction. . . . Fiction, above all, must be *believable*!"

"And life can be stranger than the strangest fiction."

"True."

"So . . . what are you going to do, Ned? You want to come to Apache Peak with me'?"

The writer held up a hand, shaking it as though saying good-bye. "Oh, no! Trying the mining life might be good for the likes of Sam Clemens or Wyatt Earp, but it's not for me, not at my age. I'll stay here, for another week or two, anyway, before returning to Stamford. I will continue my writing . . . and try very hard to forget that there are such horrors abroad in this universe."

"Suppose the Hunters know you now. They might have gotten a pretty good look at you. They might try to get you, to find out where I am."

Buntline looked startled. "Ah. I hadn't thought of that. I, um, may leave Tucson earlier than anticipated. There's a train heading East due in at the station tomorrow."

"I doubt that you'll have cause for worry," Macklin told him. "I suspect they have other ways of finding me, and that they will follow me to the mountains. But . . . be careful, will you? Keep a pistol with you always, and don't go out at night alone."

Buntline looked up at the stars, shining cold in a black velvet sky, and shivered. "My friend, I don't think I shall ever be able to go out at night alone again. Damn you, I used to *like* the stars. . . ."

Egoist and self-promoter Ned Buntline might be, but Macklin liked the man, and knew he would miss him.

NINE

✧ 1 ✧

THERE WAS NO SIGN OF THE OTHERWORLDLY ATTACKERS
by the light of the new day, and Macklin went down to
the train station and purchased a ticket for Benson. Deputy
Marshal Evans saw him off at the platform.

"I'm still not sure I'm doing the right thing, Macklin,"
he said, handing him his Colt and leather. "I have a feeling you know a lot more about all of this than you're
letting on. But, well, any friend of the Earps . . ."

He let the sentiment trail off, and Macklin remembered
that Evans had been the one to come out and warn the
Earps while they were still aboard the train that Stillwell
and Clanton were in town. He wondered how Evans
squared his friendship with the notorious gunmen—apparently he and Virgil went back a ways—and the need
to perform his duty. Everyone in Tucson knew by now
that the Earps and Holliday had killed Frank Stillwell, and
the rumor going around was that Stillwell, a fast man with
a gun, hadn't even been able to draw.

It looked now like there was going to be a murder trial.

"So, you're going to go work for the Apache Peak
Consortium?"

"I reckon." He still wasn't happy about it, but he had to get out of Tucson, and Apache Peak sounded like a good place to stay and work while he got his bearings. With Apache Slim dead, Macklin knew no one on this world who could help him contact the Associative off-worlders. He was alone and cut off, and needed to do some hard thinking about his next move.

His first need, though, was simply to survive.

"You know how to get up there?"

"I talked with Tom Crittenden and Dan Granger yesterday," Macklin said. "I guess I checked out okay, because they want me to go to work for 'em. They told me how to find the place."

Evans nodded.

"Crittenden and some of the others usually come in to Tucson for supplies, every month or so, even though Benson's a lot closer." He smiled. "They like it that way, to keep out of sight of the Clanton-Brocius bunch. Besides, most of the businessmen who are funding the venture are here in Tucson.

"So you know how to keep me informed of your whereabouts, right? I got your depositions, all right, but it might be we're going to want to talk to you in person about what happened to Stillwell. *And* Apache Slim."

"I'll keep in touch, Marshal. Thanks."

"Don't thank me, Macklin. Just take your goddamned bounty-hunter friends with you, before you burn down my town."

Somehow, the Kra'agh Hunters had evolved into bounty hunters after Macklin's scalp. He wondered just what Ned Buntline had written in his deposition that had fostered that idea. Bounty hunters suggested that Macklin was a wanted man with a price on his head. What did a deputy federal marshal think of that?

No matter. He was free to go to Apache Peak, and that was all that counted.

Ned Buntline also boarded the train at Tucson, and the two rode together in the same coach. Buntline seemed subdued, however, and distant, and he appeared not to have gotten much sleep. Macklin wondered how badly his encounter the night before had shaken him, and how well he was going to be able to recover.

"I feel like Edgar Allan Poe," the writer said at one point. "I may never be able to write again . . . not about adventure, anyhow. When I can't even write about reality." He put his face in his hands. "And Poe died mad. . . ."

"You're not crazy, Ned."

"I hope not." He sighed. " 'They who dream by day are cognizant of many things which escape the dreamers by night.' " The words were spoken softly and with measured cadence, as though he were quoting something. " 'In their grey visions, they obtain glimpses of eternity, and thrill, in their awakening, to find that they have been on the verge of the great secret. In snatches, they learn of the wisdom which is of good, and more of that mere knowledge which is of evil.' "

"What was that?"

" 'Mesmeric Revelation,' " Buntline replied. "Poe. I was up much of the night reading him, you know. I have a deeper respect for his melancholy now." He closed his eyes and shuddered. "I wish I could forget *my* glimpse of the knowledge of evil. . . ."

They shook hands and said good-bye when the train pulled into Benson. Macklin got off at the station, watched the train chugging off into the east beneath its puffing, billowing clouds of spark-shot smoke, then turned to the business of finding transport for the rest of the trip to Apache Peak.

There was no regular coach or stage connection to the place. He ended up using very nearly the last of his money buying a horse—an old and somewhat sagging roan with a white snip around its left nostril—plus tack, a couple of canteens, and a Winchester rifle with a hundred rounds of ammunition.

Apache Peak was just thirteen miles south of Benson, highest of the Whetstone Mountains which ran north and south along the west side of the San Pedro River Valley. He rode south through sagebrush and rocky desert, where long-vanished rivers had carved the landscape into bizarrely twisted and convoluted vistas of arroyos, mesas, and fantastically graven towers of red and yellow sandstone. In places, saguaro cacti rose like eldritch sentinels on the road, arms upraised.

Ahead and on his right, the mountains rose purple beneath a brassy sky. Apache Peak, he'd learned, rose about three thousand feet above the surrounding terrain. At the lower elevations, it was all desert and mesquite; as he started to climb higher, though, sage and cactus gave way to pine trees, and the air grew distinctly chilly. There were still patches of snow, he saw, tucked in among the boulders and crevasses where the early spring sunshine wasn't able to penetrate.

It wasn't hard to find the wagon road leading south out of Benson, heading due south toward Fort Huachuca. Crittenden had drawn him a crude map yesterday, showing the town of Apache Peak nestled beneath the shadow of East Peak, the northeasternmost sentinel of the upthrust Whetstones. A side road cutting off to the right and angling sharply up into the pine woods was the turning Tom had described to him as the way to the town.

He hadn't walked his horse very far along the road, however, when he heard the sudden crack of gunfire, coming from just ahead.

A second shot rang out, and a third. Macklin yanked his Winchester from the saddle case, cocked the lever to chamber a .44-40 round, and slid from his saddle. Tethering his horse's reins to a fallen branch, he moved forward slowly, working his way into a boulder-strewn area overlooking a deep gully hemmed in by trees.

The gunfire continued to bark and thunder, and now he could hear harsh, braying yells, whoops, and screams. At first, he'd thought he might have encountered hunters shooting at game, but this sounded more like a full-scale battle. He wanted to move carefully until he knew just who was fighting whom . . . and why.

Crawling to the top of a large, flat boulder hanging out above the gully, he could see an encampment of some sort to the west . . . five or six rounded, domelike structures constructed of slender branches bent and fastened together at the middle, and covered over with blankets or other pieces of cloth. The gunfire was coming from the camp, where a number of men were riding back and forth on horseback, or dashing through the smoke in a swirl of confusion, noise, and shooting.

Five figures were running down the gully just below Macklin's vantage point, two women and three children. The kids were nearly naked, save for breech clouts; the women wore what looked like blankets and buckskin, and one carried a basket made of woven reeds or sticks.

Before the fleeing group had gone more than a few hundred feet from the embattled camp, however, a pair of horsemen wheeled out of the other end of the gully, from the east. They were big men, Anglos, wearing broad-brimmed hats, buckskins, and boots. One carried a Winchester, the other a Colt pistol. "Whoa, there, ladies!" the man with the rifle yelled. "Where you squaws think you're goin'?"

One of the women screamed. The other shouted something at the children, who scattered toward the steep embankments of the gully. The man with the pistol took aim and fired, sending a bullet shrieking off a half-buried boulder.

Macklin started, and rose to his knees, furious. The

Anglo with the rifle took aim and fired, the big weapon's hollow boom echoing up the gully. The shot caught one of the kids, a boy of perhaps ten or eleven, from behind, exploding half of his head in a vivid splash of scarlet and crumpling his body into a rag doll heap.

The rifleman took aim again . . .

"No!" Macklin screamed. He brought his own rifle to his shoulder, aiming at the gunman, squeezing the trigger, then cranking the lever quickly to chamber another round. He fired again, cocked, and fired . . .

The rifleman twisted in his saddle as the horse shrilled and reared, his face grimacing with pain as he dropped his weapon. The gunman with the pistol looked up at Macklin, snapped off a wild, ricocheting shot that screamed harmlessly into the forest, then spurred his mount and galloped away back down the gully. The rifleman followed, but more slowly, his horse barely under control as he leaned far over, head against the animal's neck.

One of the women was kneeling above the body of the dead boy. The other stared up at Macklin, mouth open. He waved with one hand, pointing sharply up the gully and into the forest. "That way!" he shouted. "Run! Get away!"

The woman stared, uncertain, and Macklin had the feeling she didn't speak English. Damn . . . what to do? Gunfire and screams continued to emerge from the camp, where mounted Anglos were now using torches to set fire to the crude, cloth-covered huts.

Macklin sensed movement at his back, and turned.

Three men stood a few feet from him, at the edge of the overhanging boulder. One held a lance with a sharp iron point; the other two held rifles, aimed at his chest. They wore a mismatched collection of rags, colorful shirts, buckskin, and one had on a blue tunic identical to the one worn by Sergeant Donovan. They wore hats and beadwork, and their faces, sharply chiseled, deeply bronzed, gave nothing away. They must have moved with incredible stealth to get so close to Macklin without him hearing their approach.

"*Indaa!*" one snarled, gesturing with the muzzle of his rifle.

Macklin spread his arms. "Sorry, I don't understand you," he said.

Then one who had spoken moved forward then, swiftly, knocking Macklin's Winchester aside with the muzzle of his rifle, then snapping the weapon up, bringing the butt around to slam into the side of Macklin's head.

Pain and darkness exploded, enveloping Macklin. He was dimly aware of lying on his back on the boulder as hands grabbed at his clothing.

Then he was aware of nothing at all.

✧ 2 ✧

THE SUN HAD LONG SINCE SET, AND NA-A-CHA HAD GONE to his place of prayer, a boulder outcropping high up on the side of the mountain. From here, by day, he could look east and down, into the valley of the San Pedro. He often came here, to pray, to think, to try to plan for a future that with each day seemed more in doubt.

The sky overhead was as deep and bottomless a black as Na-a-cha had ever seen it, the stars set like gleaming crystal shards flung by the double handful across the face of Night. He was watching for another of the Moving Stars, the brilliant lights that occasionally violated the sanctity of the unchanging heavens, and seemed to foretell great events on Earth.

He desperately needed a sign.

His hands worked as he thought, shaping the *keshe ya ha*, the wooden staff which would symbolize long life in the Sunrise Ceremony, scheduled to begin tomorrow night. It was a walking cane made from an oak branch, stripped of bark so that it was white, the crook of the handle held in place by a rawhide thong. Once, Na-a-cha had been naive enough to think that politics were the domain of the *Indaa*, the white men. Lately, though, with his authority as a *diyi* of the People all but openly challenged, he realized that political maneuvering, character assassination, betrayal, deceit . . . all of these things and more were human things, and not the domain of the *Indaa* alone.

Black Wind was consolidating his power. He had proclaimed that Na-a-cha was old, that he should relinquish his position now as medicine man of the band, that his visions of the mountain *gan* were false visions, and evil.

And now, Black Wind had directly challenged Na-a-cha by accusing Tze-go-juni, his sister's daughter, of witchcraft. If she was judged guilty and condemned, Na-a-cha's powers, and his authority within the band, would be seen by all to be empty. If the band's chief had only been a strong man . . . but Shoz-pesh, still recovering from the savage effects of the burning sickness he'd suffered the previous summer, continued to vacillate, unable to make up his mind. Tze-go-juni's indictment might well tip the balance of power within the band in Black Wind's favor.

The band would never accept as *diyi* a man whose sister's daughter had been put to death for witchcraft.

He turned, and his old eyes watered as he stared down the mountain at a particular patch of blackness. It was invisible from here, lost in pine and boulder, but the *Indaa* camp encroaching on sacred ground was there, perhaps five miles down the slope, as the white eyes measured distance.

The Anglo attack this afternoon had been yet another of the escalating series of strikes and counterstrikes between the two peoples vying for control of this mountain. Four people had died, including Klah-ni-a-chi's son. The

Anglos had shown no mercy, and it was nothing short of a miracle that most of the People had been able to escape, fleeing through terrain impossible for the *Indaa*, while the warriors covered their retreat.

This latest atrocity left Na-a-cha in an impossible situation. For years now, he'd been calling for peace with the Anglos. They were too strong, too numerous, too well-armed for the N'de ever to have a chance of stopping the onrushing horde . . . like the boiling, deadly, all-consuming cascade of a flash flood thundering down an arroyo in the spring. Yet he also insisted that his vision of five moons ago was a true vision, that the mountain *gan* had let him see them as they truly were, and that the vision had been confirmation that the Chokonen band should stay here on the holy mountain.

The young men of the band wanted to lash out . . . to kill the Anglos or to join others of the People who had already fled south across the line into Old Mexico. To flee was to abandon the holy mountain to the Anglo invaders, and admit that his vision was false; to stand and fight was to die, and that meant his vision was false as well. Where was the middle path, the path of peace? Of life? Of a true vision?

Na-a-cha tried to pray, and could not. He'd tried to enter again *chidin-bi-kungua*, the House of Spirits, and could not. He'd tried to reach within himself for power, and found only the stifling pressure within his chest, clamping down on heart and spirit.

He was so worried about Tze-go-juni. Nothing else seemed to matter but her life.

And yet he could see no honorable course that would save her. To intervene would make it appear that he was using his position as *diyi* to save a relative's life, a blatant abuse of power. To do nothing meant she might be found guilty . . . and then she would burn.

And Black Wind would win, either way.

Spirits . . . ga he . . . *show me the path! Show me!*

Standing, setting the staff aside, he took a pinch of *hoddentin* from the buckskin pouch on his belt, and offered it to the east . . . followed by another to the south, the west, the north, the zenith of the sky, the earth.

A falling star flicked across Night, flaring briefly, and vanishing. Na-a-cha heard the scrape of soft leather on stone, and turned.

"Father *Diyi?*" a voice called from the darkness. It was Gochi, one of the older boys. "They said to tell you we have an Anglo captive! They have him in Big Rock Shelter! Black Wind says . . . I'm sorry, I do not want to be rude, but Black Wind says you are to come now!"

"Ah." Na-a-cha thought a moment. He'd heard a captive had been taken in the fight. That was always good. The captive might be useful as a hostage, for bargaining with the other white eyes.

That Black Wind had sent the message addressed as a command was not so good. In N'de society, one person never told another what to do directly, or expressed any phrase in a way that could be perceived as an order. White eyes did that, but not the People.

Again, his rival put him in an impossible situation. If he came, he would come at Black Wind's command. If he stayed away, he would be excluding himself from what might be of terrible import to the band.

"I come," he said at last. "But in my own time. Tell Black Wind that Na-a-cha knows the meaning of courtesy and respect when visiting the *chidin-bi-kungua.*"

"Yes, Father *Diyi.*" Gochi withdrew. Na-a-cha heard the clatter of loose rock as the boy hurried down the mountainside.

Na-a-cha waited as silence settled again across the mountain. A white-eyes captive! Was this the answer to his prayer? The news had arrived just at the moment he'd asked, just as the star had fallen.

He searched the night sky a moment more, but it was star-filled only, with no signs, no portents.

Na-a-cha picked up the staff and rose from his seat then, thanked the spirits, and began to follow Gochi. He was, frankly, impatient to see what the warriors had brought with them from the fight this day, and if Black Wind wanted to make something of his obedience to command, that was at Black Wind's peril.

It was more important to Na-a-cha that he learn what the spirits had brought him.

✦ 3 ✦

MACKLIN STRUGGLED BACK TO PAIN-FLECKED CONSCIOUSness, not sure where he was. It was dark—so dark that at first he wondered if he'd lost his sight. Then he became aware of a faint red-orange flicker in his peripheral vision. Turning his head—carefully! It hurt!—he saw a small fire, a glow against water-smoothed rock, and shapes and shadows that could only be a number of people. He was in a cave . . . no, not quite a cave, but a rock shelter, tucked away in a hollow beneath a monolithic block of sandstone that blotted out most of the sky.

He tried to sit up, and found his hands uncomfortably bound at his back, his ankles tied together as well. He was lying on a stone ledge beneath a low-hanging outcropping of rock, so low he could not sit up without hitting his head.

That he'd been captured was obvious. That his captors were Apaches was a fair guess, based on what he'd learned of them both during his months in Tombstone, and while talking with Sergeant Donovan in Tucson. The right side of his face felt swollen and crusted over with something—probably blood—and it hurt to open his mouth or move his head.

If half the stories he'd heard about the Apaches and

their treatment of captives were anywhere near the truth, he was in for a lot more pain than this. Some of the people in Tombstone had taken what had sounded like pure delight in regaling one another with tales of Apache savagery, viciousness, and fiendish joy in torturing their prisoners. He remembered Sergeant Tom McMurray in Tucson and the talk about his friend who'd died slowly at their hands.

He felt the terror building. Macklin didn't consider himself to be a particularly brave man, but he'd been in tight spots and he'd held his own. The waiting, usually, was the worst part. So he would wait, and see what happened. There was nothing else he could do, in any case.

A shadow blotted out the fire as someone moved close beside him. He tensed, trying to penetrate the darkness with eyes blurred by dried blood and pain. A hand touched his face, surprisingly gentle. It helped him lift his head. The opening of a canteen was pressed against his lips, and he eagerly, gratefully, accepted the offered water.

"Thank you," he said, his voice a croak. He squinted, trying to see. The shadow gradually resolved itself into a woman, a young woman, quite pretty, wearing a fringed buckskin shirt, with necklaces made of strung-together beads and a couple of small, round mirrors. Beads and bits of shell were worked into her hair. She said nothing, but turned away and used some of the water from the canteen to moisten a piece of cloth, which she used to sponge the cut on his head.

A voice, a man's voice, barked something sharp. The woman drew back, then rose and left Macklin's side. A man, tall, hard-muscled and bare-chested, with painted marks on his face, pushed close, staring down at Macklin. Steel glinted in the firelight, a knife in his hand, held just above Macklin's breast.

Macklin tensed, expecting to be stabbed. . . .

"*Ne!*" another voice called. The man turned, barking a

query. The other voice replied, and for several moments Macklin listened helplessly to what was obviously an argument. The knife was withdrawn, the argument continued.

Macklin, battling pain and dizziness, tried to concentrate on the words. It was as if he could almost understand them. Dorree had told him that his Companion, among its other capablities, could translate unknown languages and weave them into his existing memories in such a way that he should be able to learn a new language far more quickly and thoroughly than would otherwise be possible. The problem was, as always, that his Companion was damaged, losing its connections with the left side of his brain, the part that handled language and word meanings.

If the Companion was listening to this exchange, it must be drawing correlations between sounds and actions, beginning to build a vocabulary and grammar, perhaps even beginning to translate . . . but to Macklin, the words all were nonsense sounds, harsh, somewhat guttural, but with an underlying musicality that tugged at the edges of comprehension.

He wondered if the reason the words seemed almost intelligible was because his Companion was somehow implanting them within his subconscious, or in the right-side, feeling and emotional part of his brain. Since the crash that had stranded Macklin on this world, his only communication with his Companion had been through dreams, and occasional flashes of insight, of feeling. Might he be able to learn this language by intuition alone, *feeling* the meaning for each word?

Most likely, the Companion hadn't heard enough yet to allow it to translate anything. It couldn't assign meaning to unknown words without *something* to go on. The process, even if the Companion's links to his brain had been damaged, would at best take weeks.

As the argument went on, another shape replaced the

others, a man sitting down at Macklin's side. "Boy," a
deep voice said by his ear, "Ah mus' say, you be in a
heap a' trouble, white man, an' no mistake!"

The words were English, strangely accented, but un-
derstandable. Macklin blinked, staring at this man, who
appeared to be wearing the fragments of a uniform. A
golden object—a bugle, Macklin thought, though he'd
never seen the instrument before—was hanging around
his neck like an oversized talisman.

And the man had the blackest face, the blackest skin
he had ever seen.

Macklin had seen Negroes in Tombstone. There
weren't many of them, but a few had drifted west to Arizona in search of better wages and a better life. He didn't
know much about them, save that most people in Tombstone either ignored them or looked down on them, for
reasons that Macklin did not understand. "Who . . . are
you?" Macklin managed to say.

"Well, now, mebee that ain't none of yo' business,
white man. Afo' I tell you nuthin', I'd kinda like t'know
who you are, an' why yo' here."

"My name is Macklin. I was looking for a town called
Apache Peak when I heard what sounded like a fight."

"If'n yo' wid de 'Pache Peak folk, yo' in fo' a really
bad time. Wouldn't say nuthin' 'bout that, if'n I was you."

"Thank you." Macklin nodded toward the others, who
were gathered now by the fire. "These are Apaches?"

"Dey Chokonen of de People, white man. An' so am
I. I'se Tzit-dijin. Dat be my name wid da People. Mean
'Black Man,' which is what I is."

"I'm glad to meet you, Tzit-dijin," Macklin said, making a fair stab at the pronunciation. "I don't speak the
language yet. Can you help me translate what they're saying?"

"Don't know if I cares enough t' help you, white man.

Ain't like I got kind thoughts about you o' de other massuhs, know what I mean?"

Massuhs . . . masters? Macklin knew little about the
culture he'd been stranded in, though the books in Sarah
Nevers' library had been helpful. There'd been one book,
a history of the United States, that had helped him make
some sense of what people were talking about when they
mentioned "The War." The American Civil War, he gathered, had been fought just twenty years ago, and one of
the causes of that war had been the slavery of men with
black skin like Tzit-dijin.

"The . . . the Civil War was over a long time ago,"
Macklin said. "You're a free man, now."

"Free?" Tzit-dijin's eyes flashed, very bright in the dim
light. "Free to starve, you mean! Free t'get beaten up o'
mebee hung if'n the white men think I'se gettin' uppity."
He hesitated, as though deciding whether to say more.
"An' me, I'se jes' plain uppity, you better belicve it! I
jined the Army in '62, jined th' Fifty-fourth Massachusetts Volunteer Infantry, in fact. Fought at Fort Wagner
where half ob de Fifty-fourth was killed or wounded in
jes' that one fight!" He held up his right arm, and by the
firelight, Macklin could make out a savagely puckered
scar, beginning near the elbow and reaching clear to the
wrist. "Ah almos' lost my arm, but Ah got better.

"Den, after de War, Ah goes lookin' fo' work, but they
ain't no work, not for the likes o' me. So's I light out for
de West, an' jine the cavalry. Dey got de special cavalry
fo' black folks like me. Dey called dem 'buffalo soldiers.'
But, you know what? Things ain't no different. In fact,
de's worse. De buffalo soldiers, dey always get de dirty
end o' de stick. Dey get old guns, when there's any guns
at all, an' dey get old clothes and old boots, if dey get
'em at all, and de food, what dey feed us you can't hardly
even call food at all.

"So's, one fine day, I jes' said, 'Why's Ah keepin' on

dancin' to de white man's fiddle? I left, figurin' to go
down Mexico way, where dey don't care what color yo'
skin is, long as yo' can work. An', 'long de way, I met
up wid de 'Paches. Thought I was a dead man at first, but
de 'Paches, dey's okay. Dey don't know what t'make of
my skin, so's dey don't kill me right off. First time ever
Ah was happy 'bout de color of my skin. An' when Ah
treats 'em fair, an' tells 'em how black folk is treated,
why, dey treats me fair right back, an' dey don't care what
color my skin be. So's Ah jined 'em."

"So . . . you're helping the Apaches now, against your
own people?"

"Not 'gainst *my* people, white man. 'Gainst the white
man, an' why not? De Army, dey use tame 'Paches fo'
scouts 'gainst their own folk. I figure dis jes' be fair, me
helpin' de 'Paches. Fair's fair, know what Ah mean?"

Macklin digested this. Anglo society, he was beginning
to realize, tended to focus on itself as the measure of all
societies, had for centuries enslaved others, and even now
was only slowly beginning to redress the old wrongs. And
at that, they still treated blacks and Indians alike as infe-
rior beings, *things* to be avoided, used, or exterminated.

"You must hate white people a lot," Macklin said.

"Ah ain't got no lub fo' white folks, mistuh. No lub at
all! Das why Ah say Ah ain't all dat interested in helpin'
you."

"I understand."

The man's eyes widened. "No, white man. Ah don't
think you understand at *all!*"

One of the other voices in the rock shelter called
sharply, and Tzit-dijin turned and stood up. He spoke for
a moment with the others, and Macklin noted his Apache
words, fluent and liquid. To his ears, there was no accent
at all, and he wondered why the man's English was so
distorted.

After a moment, Tzit-dijin returned to Macklin's side.

"You better get ready, white man, 'cause de *diyi* is here."

"*Diyi?*"

"Dat's 'medicine man' to you. He not de chief, but he's plenty powerful. Mebee he decide how you gwine die!"

Another man was approaching Macklin now . . . a very old man, stooped and with eyes and mouth all but lost in a thick web of wrinkles in his sun-bronzed face. He wore a white bandanna tied about his forehead, and a green pendant on a leather thong.

He leaned close, staring into Macklin's face. Then his eyes opened wide, so wide that Macklin thought for a moment he was in pain. "You!" the medicine man shouted.

And then the Apache drew a knife and reached for Macklin's chest. . . .

T E N

THE OLD MAN GRABBED THE FRONT OF MACKLIN'S SHIRT, slashing at the material until he had exposed his chest . . . and the enigmatic black disk set into the bottom of Macklin's breastbone. The Apache drew back then, as others gathered around closely, talking excitedly among themselves.

"You are the one," the old man said, looking hard into Macklin's eyes. The sharp eyes, the beak of a nose, made him think of a bird of prey. "You are the one I found in the desert, five moons ago."

"I . . . remember," Macklin said.

The memory was fuzzy; he'd been semiconscious at the time, dazed and hurt, moments after the crash of his life pod not far from Tombstone on an October night in 1881. But he remembered being carried head-down on the back of a horse, remembered gentle hands pulling him from the saddle, of a voice, *this* man's voice, saying "You stay. Wait here. No move. Soon, your people come."

Macklin had been left lying next to a road. Before long, a stagecoach had found him there, and taken him on board. That had been where he'd met Doc Holliday, and Sarah Nevers.

"I find you after two stars fall," the old man went on. "And afterward, three, maybe four days, I see *ga he*. Big medicine. Powerful medicine. Much *hoddentin*."

This man might very well have saved his life. It sounded as though he'd actually seen the crash of two life pods, one his, the other Dorree's. Macklin didn't know what a *ga he* was, but the old man obviously was attaching tremendous importance to it.

Swiftly, the old man rolled Macklin onto his side and slit through the rawhide thongs binding his wrists. Another snick, and his feet were free. One of the other Apaches, the one who'd threatened Macklin earlier, said something with dark intonations.

The old man replied, sharp and to the point. Macklin wished he could understand. He could *almost* make out the words. . . .

"Do not move swiftly," the man said. "You are injured."

He helped Macklin sit up, watching to see that he didn't hit his head on the rock overhang. Macklin fought down a wave of dizziness, then sat on the ledge, massaging his wrists, working the feeling back into his fingers. He shivered. The air was cool, but he suspected that he'd been in shock. He felt cold, as well as weak.

"The fire is warm," his host said. Macklin took that as an invitation to sit by the fire, but he noticed the other Apaches moved away as he took a seat on a flat rock. One of the women, however, brought him one of his canteens. Macklin looked up at her. She was attractive, in a sharp-lined, hawkish way, but the tip of her nose, and the fleshy part around her left nostril, had been cut away, leaving her with an ugly, gaping hole above her mouth. She seemed to sense the direction of Macklin's gaze and drew back again into the shadows, modestly covering the scarred disfigurement with her hand.

He wondered what had happened to her. A bullet wound?

He drank, then offered the canteen to the old man, who refused it with a single shake of his head. Tzin-dijin sat with them.

"This be Na-a-cha," the former soldier said after a time. "It's bad luck fo' an Indian t'give his own name, but someone else can."

Macklin looked at Tzit-dijin. "Tell him my name is Macklin."

"This fella says his name is Macklin."

"Macklin," Na-a-cha said, a grave acknowledgment. He indicated two women near the wall of the rock shelter with a nod of his head. "These two women say you save them during attack today. They say you shoot white eyes who shoot Klah-ni-a-chi's boy, drive him off. Why you do that? Why you fight for N'de against your own people?"

Macklin thought for a moment. "I kind of stumbled into that fight by accident," he said. "But it was pretty clear that those women and kids were trying to get away. They weren't armed, and those two men were going to shoot them down. The boy *was* shot down. It wasn't right."

"You not with white eyes who attack *gowaa* . . . our camp?"

"No."

"That what women say, but . . . they are only women."

"Women are people."

Na-a-cha didn't reply to that.

"You a funny kind o' white man," Tzit-dijin commented. "You think 'Paches and women are *people*?" He laughed and slapped his knee. "Ha! Mebee black men too?"

"I wish to hear what this white eyes has to say," Na-a-cha said quietly. Tzit-dijin immediately fell silent.

Macklin had the feeling that he was on trial. And . . . why not? Apaches and Negroes, two groups long persecuted by the whites. They had no reason to love him. No wonder they saw him as the enemy.

"What I think," he said slowly, "is that not all of the N'de are the same."

Na-a-cha's eyes widened slightly at Macklin's use of the Apache's word for themselves. "This is true," he said after a time. "White eyes tend to think all Apache the same, all *Indian* the same. But there are Chokonen. The Chihinne, who are called Red Paint People because of the color clay they put on face. Nednhi. Bedonkohes. White eyes call all these Chiricahua. And besides, are Tonto, White Mountain, Coyotero, many other. All *Apache*." He spat the final word. "White eyes see no difference."

"Not all white eyes think that way," Macklin said. "But what I meant was . . . you, Na-a-cha, are not the same as that man." He pointed at the big man who'd first threatened him. "And he is different from that one." He pointed at another man, chosen randomly. "As he is from him . . . or him. Do you think the same as Klah-ni-a-chi? Do you think the same as Tzit-dijin?"

"*That* one," Na-a-cha said, indicating Tzit-dijin with a nod, "is not N'de."

"Hey!" the black man said. "What you mean by that?"

"*Indee k'ego nadaagoldehe,*" Na-a-cha said gently, with a smile.

Obviously, he'd spoken the words in his own tongue to hide them from Macklin, but something about the cadence, the context . . .

"Tzit-dijin may *play* at being *N'de*," Macklin said, "but his heart is in the right place. *Ne?*"

The reaction in Na-a-cha was almost explosive. He started back from the fire, rising to his knees, staring at

Macklin as if seeing him for the first time. "You . . . you speak *indee bi yati*?"

Macklin shook his head slowly. "Very little. But I'm learning. And I want to learn more."

"Very few white eyes take trouble to learn our tongue," Na-a-cha said. "Tzit-dijin, he learn. Take him five year, maybe six, but he learn good. White eyes too *k'ago* . . . too much higher. They, how to say? *Des aa des ii* . . . they look down on the People, look down on everyone they think be lower."

"Do *all* white eyes think that way?"

The answer was a long time in coming. "Maybe not. I must think on this."

"I still want to know what you mean by me not bein' N'de," Tzit-dijin said.

"You were not *born* N'de," Na-a-cha said. "But you are brave warrior, and good friend."

"You can't be completely N'de," Macklin said with a smile. "You told me your own name."

Tzit-dijin blinked at that, and looked as though he was going to give an angry retort. Then he laughed. "Mebee yo' right, white man!"

"In the long run," Macklin said, "it doesn't matter so much what group we were born to. It's what each of us as an individual thinks and says and does. For my part, I'd rather not be judged by what other white eyes might do. Just as you're not responsible for what other N'de might have done."

"*Aa*," Na-a-cha said. "You speak truth." He studied Macklin for a long moment, his eyes bright with reflected firelight.

After a time, he reached into a buckskin pouch at his side and extracted a pinch of yellow powder. Chanting in a low, singsong litany, he sprinkled some on his own head, on his tongue, and on his chest. Taking another pinch, and reaching across the fire, he repeated the ritual on Macklin. When Macklin extended his tongue, as Na-a-cha had done, the powder tasted dry and slightly bitter.

A pinch of something else went into the fire. It spat and crackled there, exuding a warm, cloying scent rising with the smoke. Na-a-cha then produced a large gray and white feather, with which he began to make motions about Macklin's head and shoulders, all the while continuing the chant. Macklin sat quietly, listening and watching. That the old Chokonen Apache's chanting held religious significance was obvious. How Macklin should respond was less so, but it seemed right to simply remain passive and accept what was happening.

Strange. His vision seemed changed. Na-a-cha and the fire were still sharply in focus, but the other men and women, silently watching, seemed out of focus . . . distant, somehow.

Macklin wasn't sure yet what he thought of religion. There'd been the St. Paul Episcopal Church on Safford Street in Tombstone . . . and a Catholic church that was still being built. He'd gone to St. Paul's a time or two with Sarah Nevers, but the services had been alien, remote, and unfeeling. The singing had been enthusiastic, if not exactly melodious, but the talking part had droned on and on with references to ancient writings that seemed far removed indeed from the realities of day-to-day life in Tombstone.

As Na-a-cha brushed at Macklin's face with the feather, chanting all the while, he had the sense that as a religion, this one was far more immediate, based on feeling and on experience . . . on *mystic* experience, something welling up unbidden from within.

He wondered if there was anything to it.

Abruptly, Na-a-cha stopped chanting. He was leaning forward, staring deep into Macklin's eyes. Then he gave a small gasp, leaning back. "I see your *chidin*," he said. "Your spirit. You are not like other men."

Macklin waited.

"There are two spirits within you, yours . . . and another, a rider. But the other spirit, he is not speaking."

Could Na-a-cha sense, somehow, the artificial intelligence dwelling within the devices implanted in his body? How?

"I see you . . . flying . . . flying beneath an enormous moon."

Dream memory flooded Macklin's mind, memory of dazzlingly silver moonlight flooding the ship as they plunged out of heaven toward Earth.

"I see you falling between the worlds . . ."

Stars whirled past the stricken ship's viewports.

"I see stars, spinning . . ."

Earth, much nearer now, tilting crazily as they fell. . . .

"I see clouds, and sky." Na-a-cha looked into his eyes a long moment more. "You are not as other men. Your spirit is that of *itza-chu*, the eagle. You walk between the worlds."

Which, Macklin thought, was truer than Na-a-cha could possibly know. He took a deep breath, trying to clear his head, and felt suddenly dizzy. "What's in that smoke?"

"Only what you bring with you." Na-a-cha sprinkled more powder on Macklin's head. "I name you *Itza-chu-klego-na-ay*, which is Eagle of the Full Moon."

One of the other men shouted something, but Na-a-cha silenced him with a guttural rebuke. Several of the men stalked out then, obviously angry. Macklin had the feeling that he was a game piece in an unusually complex and possibly dangerous game.

What part, he wondered, did Moon Eagle have to play in the drama unfolding in this shelter?

✧ 2 ✧

IT WAS LATE. APACHE SLIM'S DRY GOODS AND MINING Supplies had been closed all day, of course, but Jeb McNulty was at work, going through the store's inventory and moving much of the merchandise to a nearby barn for safe storage. The fire in the apartment upstairs had not burned through to the store—the Tucson Volunteer Fire Brigade had responded quickly and managed to put the fire out before it could spread—but smoke had filled the back storeroom, and water had soaked through the ceiling. A good hundred bags or so of feed had been soaked through and were probably ruined, along with an unknown number of bolts of cloth, spools of yarn, and several cases of that newfangled dynamite stuff.

That last was particularly worrisome. Dynamite had been introduced into the United States perhaps fourteen years earlier, and was a hell of a lot safer for blasting purposes than black powder or nitrocgylcerin. Still, Jeb had heard that dynamite was nothing less than pure liquid nitro absorbed by a dry packing material. Supposedly, you could drop it, bang it, even whack it with a hammer and it wouldn't go off. Jeb wasn't sure he trusted the stuff, though. He'd also heard that if it was stored badly, the nitro could leak out again and make the sticks deadly to a touch. They said it was safe when wet, but damned if he was going to experiment to find out.

It might have been easier if the fire had reached the dynamite and blown the whole shebang up, store and all. He didn't like working as a clerk at the store, and when he'd heard the boss had been killed, he'd been tempted to walk away, maybe catch a train for California and a new life.

His wife, Bess, had urged him to pack up and leave, and to take her with him. She hated life in Tucson, hated the heat, hated the constant worry about attacks by wild Apaches, and she thought San Francisco a far more urbane, more cultured, more *civilized* place to live.

Jeb McNulty, though, was plagued by a conscience that nagged worse than his wife, and a relentless work ethic born of poor Scots transplanted to Appalachia a century before. He'd agreed to take on running the store so the boss, Apache Slim, could do whatever it was he did all day and far into the night upstairs behind locked doors. Slim had taken him into his confidence, letting him see some of the inventions he was working on, things that buzzed and glowed and gave off unearthly light, and once Jeb had seen a moving picture of light up there.

That had damned near scared him away for good. It smacked of magic and black arts, though Slim had explained that what he was looking at was simply a refinement of the telephone invented by Mr. Bell a few years before.

Jeb McNulty had never seen a telephone, and didn't want to. In the end, he'd decided that Slim knew what he was tinkering with, and that he, Jeb, didn't want to know more than he had to. The work was hard but the pay was good. If he left for San Francisco like Bess wanted, what would he do? Open up a dry goods store of his own?

No, better to stick with it and see it through. He didn't know what would happen to the place now that the owner was dead. If there was a will, he didn't know anything about it, or who the heirs were. For the time being, he would keep on working, until the money gave out or he was told to leave, whichever happened first.

And that meant he had to save as much as he could from the water, even if it meant working all night. Stooping, he picked up a water-sogged case of dynamite and gingerly carried it toward the back door. The barn was across a small, empty lot, thirty feet away. The sky was dark, but there was light enough to see by. He'd hung a kerosene lantern up on a hook beside the barn door, which cast enough light for him to see his feet and not trip over something on the way.

As he entered the barn, though, he stopped. Something wasn't right. There was a foul odor in the air, something sharper than the old stink of manure, horses, and rotting hay in the back. It smelled like brimstone or poorly burned black powder . . . or maybe like rotten eggs.

He sensed someone else in the barn with him. "Hello?" he called. Jeb McNulty was no coward. He'd been a kid when he'd joined the Georgia Militia, and he'd been wounded at Sharpsburg. He liked to say he'd never run away from a fight in his life, but right then, right there, in a midnight-black barn, he came as close to taking to his heels as he ever had in his life. Someone had broken in and killed the boss last night and damned near burned the place to the ground. That someone could still be hanging around.

He sensed movement to his left, and whirled, still clutching the dynamite. He was unarmed; at the moment, he wasn't thinking of the case of high explosives in his hands as a weapon. He'd forgotten he was even holding it.

There was a slithery hiss, much closer now. He turned and looked up at a shape just barely visible in the dim haze of light filtering through the open barn door from the lantern outside. He actually didn't see very much—a monstrous body as large as a small pony on squat legs; an upper body like a man's, but with horribly clawed arms and a crisscross of leather straps, like a harness of some sort; a head like a snake's, broad and flat and mounted on a slender neck; slender arms like black branches growing out of the head; eyes that looked like they were burning into his soul.

Jeb dropped the dynamite from nerveless fingers. The case smashed open, spilling the red tubes, but there was no explosion. Like they'd said, dynamite was safe when wet.

Clawed forearms snapped forward, grasping Jeb by the arms and sides and lifting him bodily from the dirt floor. He opened his mouth to scream . . . but one of the branch arms was holding something like a silver pencil, and the nightmare horror holding him brought the point of the device down hard, driving it squarely into the center of McNulty's forehead.

He heard the crunch of splintering bone. Pain exploded through his head, a terrible, wrenching, burning pain that seemed to be flooding up through his body and into his eyes.

The last thing he was consciously aware of were the golden eyes of his inhuman killer, of a buzz of something like garbled words or thoughts flooding into his brain, of the sense that he was falling, somehow becoming lost inside the horror's bottomless eyes. . . .

✧ 3 ✧

DEATHSTALKER FED ON THE MIND OF WHAT HAD BEEN JEB McNulty, momentarily losing itself in the prey-beast's pain and gibbering, insane terror. It opened the gates of its soulcatcher, patterning the fast-firing flicker of impulses cascading through the creature's nervous system, following them, replicating and storing them until the impulses were too faint and random to constitute anything more than simple bioelectric noise.

And when Jeb McNulty was dead, the Kra'agh could still hear the creature shrieking within its mind, and savor the raw terror lingering there.

Deathstalker tasted the night. There were no other humans nearby, and so it could afford to eat. It had wanted to eat the body of Apache Slim the night before, but the fire started by the quick, sharp gunfight had brought hu-

mans running in large numbers. Deathstalker, Fleshrip-per, and Eater of Living Hearts had been forced to flee, leaving the body behind. Deathstalker hadn't even been able to obtain all of the information it wanted from Apache Slim's mind. It still didn't know if Slim had made direct contact with Macklin yet, or what it had been able to communicate to Associative Monitors lurking offworld.

That was unfortunate, and the main reason that Deathstalker had returned to this place. It was possible that McNulty knew of Slim's movements, plans, and con-tacts.

As it ate the body, tearing large chunks off and swal-lowing them, bloody and whole, Deathstalker reviewed the information trapped in McNulty's mind when it had died. It did know Macklin; it had a clear image of the prey in its memory. Better, it remembered parts of a con-versation, where Macklin had expressed interest in going to a place called Apache Peak, seeking work.

McNulty had known nothing else of import. It knew little of Apache Slim's operations, and wasn't even aware that the Associative Monitor was an offworlder.

But now the Kra'agh Hunters had a place to start look-ing. Deathstalker had been pretty sure that Macklin fled the town. He could no longer taste the prey's essence in the area, and Macklin had already proven itself elusive when it knew it was being hunted.

It wouldn't escape the Hunters at Apache Peak, though. If Deathstalker could have smiled, it would have. The Hunters knew the geographical area called Apache Peak. Deathstalker had hidden its ship not far from there.

Macklin had just sealed its own doom.

❖ **4** ❖

"THERE AROSE THEN AMONG THE COYOTERO PEOPLE A powerful medicine man named Noh-ka-del-klin-ay. One time, he go to East, meet with white eyes *nantan*, Anglo President Grant. Wear medal around neck, say 'On Earth Peace, good Will toward Men, 1871.' "

Na-a-cha sat by the fire, rocking slightly as he related the story. The other Chokonen had lost some of their fear of Macklin, it seemed, and drawn closer as well . . . all but a few, who had joined the big Apache called Black Wind and left, their bearing and manner radiating disgust. "Noh-ka-del-klin-ay teach us new dances and new rituals. He promise that our dead warriors would live again. At first, he say they rise and join us to drive the white eyes away. After time, dead warriors, dead chiefs, not appear. Noh-ka-del-klin-ay, he say dead chiefs tell him they not come back until all white eyes be driven away."

Convenient, Macklin thought. But he said nothing, let his expression give nothing away.

"The white eyes, they become much worried. Many N'de scouts in their army leave, go back to people. Others talk among themselves, say this country belong N'de, not white eyes.

"One day, one warrior approach Noh-ka-del-klin-ay after dancing. He say, 'Show us what to do! Call upon the great leaders, ask them what we should do to drive white eyes away!'

"So Noh-ka-del-klin-ay and three of closest followers, they go to top of mesa. They fast. They pray. 'Come to us,' we call. 'Come show us what to do.' "

Macklin didn't comment on the use of the word *we*. He'd had the impression, as Na-a-cha told him of the history of white-N'de relations, that most of it was an eyewitness account.

"And then there appear to us a vision. Three great ones rise from ground, but no higher than knees. They like shadows at first, but then we see clear. 'Why do you call us back?' the great ones asked. 'We not want to come back. The buffalo are gone. The white eyes are everywhere where once our people walked free. Why do you call us back?'

" 'But tell us what we must do,' we cried, begging them.

"And then the great ones begin to turn to shadow again, and sink away into ground. 'Live at peace with white man,' we hear them say. 'Live at peace and let us rest.'

"We all hear this. We talk about it. We go back to others, in big camp. Many come from far away to hear Noh-ka-del-klin-ay's words, learn his dances. We tell them what we see, what great ones say.

"Right away, there is fight over what great ones say. Many men, many young warriors, say great ones mean we must drive all white eyes out of N'de lands, because that is only way we ever live in peace with them. Things get worse, then. Much fighting with words. Much anger. Some say great ones mean this. Some say they mean other thing. Very few think great ones mean what they say . . . *live in peace with white eyes*."

"Then, one day eight moons ago, soldiers come to great camp at Cibecue Creek. They come, say to Noh-ka-del-klin-ay, 'You come with us. You prisoner. If you no do bad thing, you go free soon. But dances must stop, ritual must stop. You come.'

"Noh-ka-del-klin-ay come. Little way on, soldiers make camp. They followed by many N'de, many painted for war, but there is much confusion. No one want to attack. Then, shooting begin.

"One soldier, he watching Noh-ka-del-klin-ay, told not to let him get away. When shooting start, he shoot Noh-ka-del-klin-ay. Noh-ka-del-klin-ay only wounded. He try to crawl away, but soldiers, they shoot him again and again, but he still only wounded. Noh-ka-del-klin-ay's spirit strong, cannot be killed by white eyes' bullets. One soldier kill him finally with axe. Many soldiers, many

N'de, die in fight, then at Cibecue Creek. Much trouble, after. Many N'de living on reservations, they leave, go south. One is Go-yath-lay, He Who Yawns, who white eyes call Geronimo.

"Many of Chokonen band go with Go-yath-lay to Mexico. They say there can be no peace with white eyes, ever. Some, though, stay here. We come to this mountain to be close to *ga he*, the *gan* mountain spirits. We hope they guide us, show us how to live in peace with white eyes."

"And have they?"

"It is . . . difficult to hear their words."

"Have you ever seen these mountain spirits?"

"Oh, yes. I see. I see sometimes with spirit vision. I see also"—he pointed to his face—"with these eyes, in this world. Five moons ago, I am in mountains west of place you call Tombstone, not so far from here. This not long after Noh-ka-del-klin-ay killed, after Go-yath-lay leave reservation and go south." He cocked his head to one side, studying Macklin closely. "This very soon after I find you in desert. I see mountain spirit in true form."

That piqued Macklin's curiosity. Na-a-cha seemed to be differentiating between what he saw in real life, and what he experienced in the spirit world. The two appeared to be equally real, perceivable places to the Apache medicine man.

And, Macklin thought wryly, *that very well might be the case.*

"Can you describe this true form to me?"

Na-a-cha picked up a twig lying beside the fire, reached down, and scratched some lines in the dirt. "Some of this not for white eyes. Is for the People only. But I can show some. Our people, our dancers, since old time make selves look like mountain spirits for some dances, some ceremonies. Everyone, they know dancers just men, but they take place of real mountain spirit. They wear mask, wear headdress, like this."

The image he scratched into the dirt was crude, but recognizable as a man wearing a tall cylindrical mask or headpiece. There were no features on the mask, but from either side grew a large L-shaped branch extending straight out to the side, then turning to point straight up. Smaller arms branched from the main body, making them look a little like arms held high. "These arms on head, like horns. They represent *ittinde*, the lightning. These pieces of wood hang down . . . so. They click and bang as dancer walks, represent thunder.

"This *gan* dancer," Na-a-cha said. He began sketching again. "Mountain spirit I see look like this in head, but different body, like mountain lion. Have hump, like buffalo. Have four legs, so. Have body like man, with two arms, so. Have head like *gan* dancer, with arms . . . so . . ."

Macklin felt a chill prickle at the base of his neck as the sketch took shape. The creature Na-a-cha was drawing was a fair representation of a Kra'agh. The centauroid body with the odd hump above the forelegs was too close to the mark to be coincidence.

Na-a-cha had seen a Kra'agh, somewhere in these mountains. More to the point, he'd seen one and *lived*. Interesting.

Macklin wondered if the *gan*-dancer costumes were based on sightings of Kra'agh, or if the resemblance—the lightning-horned heads of the dancers with the slender feeder arms of the Kra'agh—was coincidence.

Coincidence, most likely. If "old time" meant what he thought it did, the N'de had been imitating mountain spirits in ceremonial dances for a lot longer than the five months or so since the Hunters had arrived in Arizona Territory.

"I've seen these mountain spirits as well," Macklin said. He wondered how much he could tell Na-a-cha. If he said the Kra'agh were enemies and not to be trusted, the assumption would be that they were enemies of the white eyes . . . and friends, therefore, of the N'de. Macklin very much doubted that that was true.

"Then, perhaps Itza-chu-klego-na-ay is favored of the mountain spirits," Na-a-cha said. "Perhaps Itza-chu-klego-na-ay is a messenger to us from the mountain spirits. You came from the sky. You are marked"—he pointed at Macklin's chest—"by the gods. This I thought when first I saw you, Moon Eagle."

"I have seen the mountain spirits," Macklin continued, "but not as friends. They have tried to kill me several times."

Na-a-cha considered this. "That is not good. Still, you have much *hoddentin* . . . much power. Perhaps there are different kinds of mountain spirits, as there are different kinds of men."

"It could be that these mountain spirits," Macklin replied, "hate all men, and want to kill us all."

"This I do not believe." Na-a-cha appeared lost in thought for a moment. Finally, he said, "Moon Eagle. If you truly believe that the N'de are men, no different, no lower than white eyes, you can help us. If you believe N'de should live in peace with white eyes, you can help us."

"How?"

"We have wished for long time to talk with white eyes of place called Apache Peak. They no want to talk. They only dig for silver, and want N'de gone."

"And what do the N'de want?"

The old man glanced about the rock shelter, as though taking it all in. "The highest part of this mountain is holy. It is a place of the mountain *ga he*, a place of visions, a place of powerful medicine. It is not a place for the white eyes."

Macklin remembered the conversation with the miners in Tucson. "I'm afraid," he said, "that they're not going to listen to me any more than they would listen to you. They think they've found silver on this mountain. They're going to want to stay and mine it."

Na-a-cha sighed. "True. But you talk to them, maybe, get them to listen. We are *only* savages, *only* Apaches, in their eyes. Some of young men in band . . . and Black Wind, who would be medicine man of Chokonen, they say, fight white eyes. Kill them, drive them from the holy mountain. Black Wind, he want to attack town of Apache Peak, kill all white eyes. But I know if we kill white eyes, more white eyes will come, and more, and more, and they will fight until all Chokonen dead.

"Some of Chokonen band want peace. This is big mountain. We live on mountain, white eyes live on mountain. We share. You could tell white eyes this, tell them we want peace."

"They's gonna want you back on the reservation," Tzit-dijin pointed out. "And *I* ain't got no reservation to go back to! It's the noose o' the firing squad for me, if'n they catch me!"

"Then it be best if you go to Mexico. But first, we see if Moon Eagle can get white eyes of Apache Peak to agree."

"What can you offer them as a guarantee?" Macklin asked. "They're not going to trust you, you know."

"We will honor our word," Na-a-cha said stiffly, "if *they* will. We will promise not to attack the town, not to kill all white eyes. They may look for silver. If they promise to let us stay on this mountain, and stay away from our sacred places."

"There are some white eyes," Macklin said quietly, "who would never agree to that."

"As there are some N'de who will never choose peace. But there are some who would. Those who would must talk."

"And the ones like Black Wind, who want to attack the town?"

"I am *diyi* of this band, a medicine man. I am not *nantan*, not chief . . . but I have some power. They will listen to me."

"I wish you better luck than I'm likely to have. I can't promise anything, Na-a-cha, but I'll try."

"We do not understand the white eyes wanting so many rocks . . . the gold and silver. Tell them they can have silver near Apache Peak, but the high places belong to us."

"All I can do is try," Macklin said.

"All I ask is that you try, Moon Eagle." Na-a-cha smiled for the first time. "You may be our one hope."

If that was the case, Macklin reflected, it was a damned slim hope indeed.

⋄ 5 ⋄

BLACK WIND CROUCHED ON THE BOULDER TOP, WRAPPED in darkness. Two others crouched with him. The mountain peak showed vast and black, a jagged outline against the starlight. Somewhere in the night, an owl hooted, and one of the men shivered at the mournful cry.

"An omen!"

The N'de dreaded owls, which they thought of as embodiments of the ghosts of the dead. To see an owl, to hear its call, meant that someone close was about to die . . . or that some other misfortune would soon strike the band. A dead owl left in a tree was a sign to others to stay away, that the area ahead was cursed.

"It is *her*," Black Wind said. "I saw an owl on her wickiup three nights ago, and knew then that she was a witch. It is she who has brought the Anglos to our mountain. It is she who caused the camp to be attacked this morning. And now she has brought this Anglo into our midst, and bewitched our *diyi*. She must be dealt with!"

"But if she is a witch," Running Bird protested, "she could kill us! This is not the proper way to do this!"

"If we accuse her in public," Black Wind explained, "Na-a-cha will see to it that she is protected." He closed one fist, shaking it slowly. "I believe she is the power behind Na-a-cha. If we take her, if we kill her as a witch, his power will be broken. And *my* words will be heard."

Jiminez, the half-breed, nodded. "She is a *bruja*. I have seen this. But you must protect us from her powers, Black Wind."

He gestured at the medicine bags both of them wore. "I have worked the medicine. You will be protected by the mountain spirits themselves. If you do not let her speak, you will be safe."

"The mountain spirits," Running Bird said, shaking his head. "Old Na-a-cha is always talking about the mountain spirit he met in the flesh. If he is such good friends with them, why should they protect us?"

"The mountain spirits," Black Wind said with the cold-edged grin of the cynic, "protect those who are strongest. And in this, *we* are the strong ones."

"We will do this," Jiminez said. "But in return, you will help us. You will protect us from the witch's power. You will protect us from Na-a-cha's vengeance. And you will make us men of importance in the band, when you are sole *diyi*."

"That is our agreement," Black Wind said.

Jiminez and Running Bird were newcomers to the band. They were not even Chokonen, but members of the White Mountain Apache, refugees from the reservation at San Carlos. They had approached the band several months before, seeking refuge, and Black Wind had taken them in. They were not wholly trusted by the others, even yet. But Black Wind saw in them an opportunity.

Black Wind had been preparing for this for a long time.

He'd been hoping to wait until Shoz-pesh, the old *nantan*, died, because he'd supported Na-a-cha's position with the band, and accepted him as a lightning shaman. With Shoz-pesh dead, Black Wind would be able to sweep Na-a-cha aside, and become the Chokonen band's lone *diyi* . . . and perhaps the new *nantan* as well

The attack this morning and, far more, the arrival of the white eyes called Macklin, had provided him with an opportunity, however, an opportunity too powerful to pass up.

In the lore of the N'de, one could not kill a snake within the camp. To do so could bring terrible misfortune on the band. There was no prohibition, however, against getting outsiders to kill the snake, or drive it away.

Jiminez and Running Bird were about to kill a snake . . . the witch Tze-go-juni. She *was* a witch; Black Wind was certain of that . . . although he'd made up the story about the owl on her wickiup. With her dead, Na-a-cha's power would be broken. He would not have his niece to support him with her magic. More telling, her death would leave the old man broken.

And the rest of the band, then, would follow Black Wind.

And that would be just the beginning, as he began the campaign that would take back this entire land from the white eyes. . . .

ELEVEN

✧ 1 ✧

"I LEAD!" DEATHSTALKER RAISED ITSELF ONTO HIND LEGS, *gaining height, and the strength of position. "The prey is mine!"*

"Your leadership is flawed!" Eater of Living Hearts hissed in reply. The two confronted one another in the dusty shadows of the abandoned barn. "The prey has escaped! And questions will be asked about the destruction of the human dwelling place, and the death of Apache Slim!"

"The prey has not escaped. We know where it has gone. We need only pick up its blood trail, and follow. We must proceed with caution!"

"You risk everything with your fears!"

It was a rare thing for Kra'agh to confront one another with open hostility. As a predatory hunter species, they'd long ago learned to sublimate such hostility into ritual, form, and show. It was that, or face the specter of self-destruction. The inhibitions against violence against their own kind were deep, so deep they were scarcely recognized for what they were.

With a rasping hiss, Deathstalker lunged, head for-

ward and down, jaws gaping, then closing on Eater's sinuous neck. The jaws locked, the savage fangs held just short of ripping scaled flesh. Eater twisted, hard, its own jaws closing on Deathstalker's throat. Feeder arms grappled, straining, squeezing. For a small eternity then, the two Hunters remained there, barely moving, locked in a death embrace.

Slowly . . . slowly . . . Eater relaxed its grip. Its jaws gaped, and it sagged in Deathstalker's grasp. "My blood," it said, the words a gurgled wheeze, "is yours."

Deathstalker opened its mouth then, releasing the defeated Hunter. It had proved itself the stronger, for now.

"It is dangerous to hunt our prey within the human hive. The chance is too great for discovery. The creature called Macklin is exceedingly dangerous. It knows of us, and has defeated us in combat before. It must be approached with extreme caution.

"And more important still, we must remember just how weak, how vulnerable we are in the face of human numbers. There are a scant handful of us, against some thousands of humans in this one region alone. If we are discovered by the general population now, before our plans show blood, we are doomed. Is this clear?"

"It is . . . clear."

"Macklin has fled this city. Thanks to the memories of Jeb McNulty, we know where it has gone. We will follow it. We will kill and pattern other lone humans in the area until we learn precisely where Macklin is now. Then we will take it. Is this clear?"

A feeder hand closed, a gesture of assent. "It is clear."

"Then do not challenge my leadership of the Hunt. What I do, I do for the Kra'agh, to win this world and its resources for the Fleet. Now . . . follow!"

"Kkre!" The word meant "Deathgrasp," and indicated complete—if perhaps unwilling—agreement.

"Good. Now follow. We must find blood trail!"

✧ **2** ✧

THEY GAVE MACKLIN BACK HIS HORSE AND GEAR, AND one of the young men of the band led him on foot down the mountain, along winding trails descending through narrow passages among the rocks, thick forests of pine and juniper, and out at last onto level ground in the foothills along the eastern slopes of the Whetstone Mountains.

"You will be welcome on your return, Itza-chu-klego-na-ay," the *diyi* said quietly. "We will watch for you."

"You're sure I'll be back?"

"You will be back," the old man said, looking north, in the direction of the town. "You will find no place *there*."

He reined his horse northward and set off at a walking pace. His N'de guide vanished into the brush as silently, as completely, as the vanishing of a dream.

The Whetstones were a collection of mountains and rugged hills shouldering into the sky west of the San Pedro Valley. The mountain of Apache Peak was by far the tallest, towering a good thousand feet or more over the lower peaks, purple and brooding. South was the sharp-pointed tangle of Granite Peak; north, the stubbier eminence of Haystack Mountain.

Macklin's guide had led him to the head of a deep and twisty canyon—Guindani Canyon, according to Critten-den's crude map—which ran southeast from the central fastnesses of the Whetstones, past the southern flanks of East Peak, and opened at last on the rolling barrenness of the San Pedro Valley.

As he rode—and sometimes the terrain became rough enough that he had to dismount and lead his horse by the reins—Macklin continued working his problem, no, *problems*, about in his head. If he did have an artificial intelligence locked up inside somewhere, he damned sure needed its help now.

Item. He was alone, cut off as no one else had ever been, with no way to contact his people, no way to get back to his home.

Item. There were some very smart and nasty folks looking for him, and they were not going to let up until they had him. The Kra'agh struck him as basically bullies and cowards, relying on their camouflage skills and the cover of darkness to lay traps and ambushes and to close in on their prey slowly, and so far he'd been able to stay a step or two ahead of them. But they'd gotten Apache Slim, and sooner or later they would get him.

Item. If Na-a-cha's scratchings in the dirt meant anything, there were Kra'agh right here, on this mountain. It might even be their local base of operations, and he'd managed to deliver himself to their front door. All that could be said about *that* as a plan of operations was that it had the advantage of being unexpected.

It was ironic, actually. He'd been thinking that the Kra'agh might follow him here, and leave Tucson alone. He hadn't thought of the possibility that they were already here.

Item. Na-a-cha thought the Kra-agh were gods of some kind . . . and the *diyi* didn't want to leave the mountains where they'd been seen. In fact, he wanted Macklin to convince the local white miners that they could all *share* the mountain, an idea that was not exactly going to thrill the whites.

Item. In the middle of all of this, Macklin still faced the fundamental problem of survival on this world. He needed money for food and a place to stay, and that meant he needed a job. So far, the one career choice that seemed to have commended itself to him was that of a shootist . . . a hired gun.

It was an impossible problem. Unless he wanted to go Tzit-dijin's route and join the Chokonen, he needed to stay on the good side of the whites in the area. He had an idea that Tom Crittenden and his bunch weren't going to keep their job offer open once he started talking about peace with the Apaches.

He emerged from the canyon mouth on a bluff overlooking the broad, brown plain of the San Pedro. *That* way, invisible among the low, purple-brown hills toward the southeast about twenty miles distant, lay the town of Tombstone. He could go back there, he knew. Wyatt, Warren, and Doc Holliday were still there, at least for the time being, though Frank Stillwell's death might put them on the move soon for more hospitable climes. He was pretty sure he could stay on with them, no matter where they ended up moving.

Damn it, it was tempting. He could just ride away, leaving the Whetstone Mountains behind him. And yet . . .

Turning in the saddle, he looked up at the brooding cliffs and fastnesses, the forest-blanketed slopes at his back. If the Kra'agh were up there, somewhere . . .

What could he, one amnesiac man, do about such nightmare invaders? Warning the locals wouldn't do much good, even if he was believed. He'd talked to enough people to know that humans, in this area, at any rate, had little concept of the possibility of other worlds or other peoples among the stars. Ned Buntline's story about the Great Moon Hoax almost fifty years before suggested that people could be made to believe . . . but belief itself wasn't going to stop the invasion.

He needed to reach the Monitors . . . the Associative peacekeepers offworld that Dorree had told him about. And he had no idea how to do that. He didn't even know if there were other Monitors on Earth, now that Apache Slim was dead, and if there were, he didn't know how to find them.

He continued to stare at the mountains behind him, their upper peaks red and brown against piercing blue in the golden morning light. If somehow the Kra'agh could be made to reveal themselves. Or . . . he knew they had ships, a way for Macklin to get offworld and reach the Associative.

He had no idea how to pilot such a craft, but perhaps . . .

But what decided him was the knowledge that Na-a-cha's people were up there, close enough to the Kra'agh to see them occasionally, high up among those peaks. They were in terrible danger.

And, he *had* promised to help them negotiate with the white men.

He had to at least try.

Tempting as Tombstone was at the moment, he reined his horse around to the north, and started walking along the bluff toward the eastern slopes of East Peak, close beside the rocky tumbledowns and boulder-strewn depths of Guindani Canyon.

He found the town less than an hour later . . . a ramshackle, dusty place not nearly so prepossessing as the mountain it had been named for. Almost lost amid boulders and sagebrush, it consisted of a dozen makeshift structures that looked as though they would fall down in a stiff gust of wind, a scattering of tents and makeshift lean-tos, and a single squat, whitewashed adobe building two stories high. A sign outside the edge of town proclaimed it to be Apache Peak, population 158, and private property, trespassers will be shot.

As Macklin rode into town, he saw few signs of life— dogs asleep in the hot morning sun, some horses and pack mules tied to hitching rails, and one old-timer seemingly asleep on a crate in front of the adobe building, which squatted in the town's center like a tiny, sullen imitation of the mountain to the south. A large hand-painted sign above the adobe's door bore the legend: Apache Peak Mining Company. Apparently the consortium of businessmen who'd funded this venture also ran the town. At least, they had the only substantial building.

There was none of the stolid permanence of Tucson, none of the buzzing entrepreneurial excitement of Tombstone. Apache Peak had a temporary look, a few buildings thrown up almost overnight . . . buildings which a few years from now might have vanished back into the sand and gravel as though they'd never existed at all.

Unless, of course, they really had managed to strike it rich. Tombstone had become a permanent fixture on the southeastern Arizona landscape virtually overnight with the proving of the Schieffelin claim.

Interesting. Tom Crittenden had all but openly claimed they *had* struck it big at Apache Peak, despite his friend's paranoia. But this didn't look like a mining town; it didn't even look alive.

Maybe, he decided as he walked his horse up to the adobe building, fear of the Apaches had put a lid on things.

"Hold it right there, stranger," a voice said, coming from overhead. Macklin looked up, and saw a man in a leather vest aiming a double-barreled shotgun at him from the building's roof, which was flat, and had a low wall around the outside like the battlements of a small and crumbling fortress. "Who are you, and what do you want?"

"Name's Macklin," he replied, careful to keep his hands easily visible on the pommel of his saddle. "Tom Crittenden hired me."

The old-timer on the crate in front of the building nudged his floppy-brimmed hat back off his face. Macklin noticed that he was wearing two pistols in belts crossed over his hips, and had a Winchester rifle close to hand.

"Did he, now?" the old man said, before squirting a jet of black liquid into the dust of the street. "Well, you get down off that horse an' come on inside."

"Watch him, Joe," the voice called from above. "Is he carryin'?"

"Yup. But he don't look so tough. I reckon I can handle him."

As Macklin tethered his roan to the hitching post outside the adobe, two more men came out of the building and stood there, watching him narrowly, saying nothing, their hands never far from the grips of their holstered revolvers. Both wore expressions mingling suspicion with outright hostility. If this was typical of the hospitality offered by the citizens of Apache Peak, Macklin thought, it was no wonder the place seemed dead.

"Gimme your gun," one said.

"And you are . . . ?"

"Smethers," the taller of the two men said. He wore a plain black suit and string tie, almost as though he were consciously imitating the Earps. "I'm sheriff here. Now gimme the gun."

For the third time in two days, Macklin surrendered his pistol. He'd gotten it back both from Evans and from the Indians, but these two didn't look nearly that generous.

"Tom Crittenden ain't here," the second man said. "But he did say someone named Macklin was coming out here. C'mon."

Macklin had expected to be taken into the main building, but they led him instead to the next building up Apache Peak's single broad, dusty street. The board nailed to a post outside read El Camino Real. Macklin had picked up Spanish enough during his months in Tombstone to know that meant The Royal Road. What he couldn't tell was whether the grandiose name was a joke, or an expression of desperate hope.

The ambiance inside wasn't nearly so prosperous-looking as the Oriental in Tombstone, or Carlos's Saloon in Tucson. The bar was a long table, the floor was dirt.

A dozen men sat on rickety chairs or crates or barrels, drinking vile-smelling brew dispensed by a mustachioed man behind the table in a dirty white apron.

Macklin saw one lone woman in the place, a plain-faced girl in a checkered gown, seated on a cowboy's lap. The man had one arm around her shoulders, the other clamped possessively over her breast. The woman's expression was one of detached boredom.

A prostitute, most likely, a "soiled dove" in the gently euphemistic language of the region.

There was one decent table in the place, and that was set far back at the end of the low, narrow room. Two men were seated there in expensive-looking clothes, half-full glasses and an ornate bottle labeled "Fay-Mus Whiskey" before them. Both had their gaze steady on Macklin as his escort led him to the back of the room.

"So," one of the men, ponderously fat, with a three-piece suit and a long, heavy gold watch chain across his belly, said around the well-chewed end of a cigar. "What have we got here?"

"He just rode in, Your Honor," Pete Smethers said.

"Yeah?" The other man looked Macklin over. "Who are you, mister, and what do you want in Apache Peak?"

"The name's John Macklin. Tom Crittenden hired me day before yesterday, up in Tucson. But I'm beginning to think you people don't care for newcomers around here."

"Watch your mouth, fella," Smethers snapped. "This here's Vic Norden, the mayor of this here town. And Hizzoner, there"—he nodded at the fat man—"is Big Nate Thornton, the justice of the peace. So mind your manners!"

"Now, Sheriff, let the fellow alone. He didn't know any better." Thornton studied him a moment longer. "Tom told me you might be coming down here, Macklin. Said you used to work for the Earps."

"That's right."

"Any good with a gun?" Norden asked.

"I've been working for the Earps since last October."

"Huh. That's a decent enough recommendation. And Tom said you checked out, when he telegraphed Tombstone." He stroked his chin, thoughtful.

"Mr. Crittenden said you needed help with the Apaches hereabouts."

"That's the damned truth," Norden said. He was as lean and wiry as Thornton was fat, with a drooping blond mustache and a well-tailored suit. "We've had nothing but trouble with them red sons of bitches since we moved in here." He grinned unpleasantly.

"I reckon we taught 'em a thing or two yesterday, though," Thornton said. "Hit one of their camps, up on the north side of the mountain, and we hit it hard!"

"Not that that'll drive the rest off, Nate," Norden said skeptically.

"No, no, I don't expect it will. But it'll make 'em think before they try tackling this town. And if we kill enough of 'em, the rest will get tired of it and move away." He chuckled. "Maybe down Mexico way. Let the greasers deal with 'em!"

Smethers laughed. "Y'know, it was General Sherman hisself who said that we fought a war with Mexico a few years back to take this country away from 'em . . . and we was gonna have to fight another war to make 'em take it back!"

"Hell, we bought this part from them," Norden said. "The Gadsden Purchase, remember? Maybe if we pay them . . ."

"Now, now, boys," Thornton said. "This land has been good to us. And it's going to be much better." He folded his hands across his belly and leaned back in his chair, cocking an eye at Macklin. "Well, fella, if Tom Crittenden vouches for you, you're all right. And if you worked for the Earps, you're even better. We'll put you on the payroll right off, say . . . twenty-five a week. Course, you're gonna have to swear an oath not to reveal what you know about this place."

"I'll swear any kind of an oath you want," Macklin said. "But it still all comes down to whether you want to trust me or not."

"Raise your right hand."

"I beg your pardon?"

"Raise your right hand," Thornton repeated. "Don't have no Bible, but I reckon it's binding when the oath is administered by a justice of the peace. Now, repeat after me: 'I, John Macklin, do hereby swear in front of God and these here witnesses not to ever breathe a word about what I hear and see in and around the town of Apache Peak . . . so help me God.' "

Macklin repeated the phrase, with a bit of prompting along the way from the others. He wondered, though, how seriously they could be taking all of this. Their own people—he was thinking of Tom Crittenden in town the other day—were a pretty loose-tongued lot, and if Jeb McNulty was any indication, plenty of people in Tucson already knew about the consortium's operations here.

"Okay," Thornton said. "Breathe a word and you'll be hit with contempt of court so fast your head will spin. Fact is, we need men to help us protect our claim, but we have to be damned careful about word getting out to the wrong parties."

"Especially parties named Clanton," Norden added.

"True, true," Thornton said. "Mostly, they're just interested in picking up cattle on the Mexican side of the line and selling 'em over in Charleston. But rumor of a good silver strike is a lot more'n what it takes to bring out the greedy in folks."

"You're afraid of a silver rush, I take it?"

Norden and Thornton exchanged glances. "Shoot," Thornton said. "He took the oath."

"He's gotta know sometime."

"Well, y'see," Thornton said, "it's like this. A feller came up here out of Tombstone about two years back, name of Josiah Bennett. Story is, he struck it big, I mean *really* big. Found silver somewhere up on the high slopes somewhere between Apache Peak and East Peak, with ore that proved out absolutely top grade, with a little gold thrown in for good measure.

"Me and Mr. Norden here, and a few others, agreed to back him. He established his claim, took some folks up there with him, and started mining. They kept the location real secret, 'cause the Clantons were running high and wide just then. Hell, the Earps, too. Just because a feller wears a badge doesn't mean he's above strong-arming a bit of the profits for himself . . . or maybe arranging a little accident for you and a change of the names on the claim. The mine proved profitable, real profitable. At the end, there were forty men up here, and they were sending down freight wagons filled with absolutely top-quality ore.

"But last year they all disappeared. None of 'em was ever seen again. Just . . . gone. We figure the Apaches got 'em, poor devils."

"Nate here put together a party to go up and find the Bennett Mine," Norden continued. "Trouble was, the people who knew just where it was were all dead. The description on the deed filed in Tucson isn't all that explicit, you see . . . for obvious reasons.

"Well, to make a long story short, the expedition didn't come back either. Another party was formed up, and they tangled with Apaches not too far from here. Three men were killed. Another who got captured was found later. The bastards had skinned his face and arms and legs and turned him loose in the desert."

"That," Thornton put in, "was when we decided to stake another claim right here, in the Whetstone foothills.

Built this town from scratch, out of investments made by myself and the other owners of the Apache Peak Consortium. But the point is to find the lost Bennett Mine, not start a new one, because it looks like old Josiah Bennett found himself the mother lode."

"We have been doing some mining hereabouts, of course," Norden added. "Got a small shaft going northwest of here, up against East Peak."

"Right. We've found enough silver to know we're damned close . . . and to keep our operations going. But the Bennett Mine is still up there, somewhere, and with silver so pure and so rich, and with so danged much of it, it's going to make the Comstock Lode look like a hole full of cow patties. Apache Peak, Arizona is going to be the next Virginia City, you mark my words!"

Damn. The way Thornton and Norden were talking, the lost Bennett Mine must be somewhere way up in the Whetstones. Macklin had a feeling he knew what had become of those vanished expeditions . . . and the explanation had nothing to do with Apaches.

"Point is," Smethers said, "we're still losing people who go up in those hills looking for the mine. For a while, we thought we might have some competition, maybe from the Clanton-Brocius boys. They still operate through this area, you know, from Benson clear down to the border, and they'd be real interested in knowing about a lost mine up here."

"That's why we have to be secretive about this, Mr. Macklin," Norden added. "We can't let any of this get out."

"What I heard," Macklin said, "was that you mostly needed help against the Apaches."

"True enough," Smethers said. "If we could just find out what they want . . ."

"You can't negotiate with savages," Norden snapped.

"What they want," Macklin put in, "is to have a sacred

part of the mountains set apart for themselves. But they are willing to strike a deal with you, so that both them and you share the mountains in peace."

Norden's eyes narrowed to dangerous slits. "How do you know that?"

"I was with them last night," Macklin said, in matter-of-fact reply. "Their medicine man, Na-a-cha asked me to talk to you about it."

A half-dozen other men were gathering about the table, drifting over to within earshot. Macklin's admission raised a sudden murmuring stir of conversation. One man, Macklin saw with a jolt of recognition, had his arm wrapped in bandages and hanging in a sling. It was the man with the rifle that Macklin had shot the day before. Macklin hadn't expected this.

The guy didn't seem to recognize him, though.

Next to him was the woman Macklin had noticed when he entered the bar. "You should listen to him, Nate," she told Thornton. "This sounds like the first good news we've had here in a couple of months!"

"Now, Cissy, you stay out of this," Thornton said. "This is man talk."

"*Man* talk?" she sneered. "I don't see nothing here but boys playing king of the mountain!"

"Shut up, girl," someone in the crowd called.

"Aw, let her talk," said another.

"I'm just sayin'," Cissy continued, looking around at the men gathered there, "that this fella seems to be giving us a chance to live in peace, without always havin' to watch our backs. Ain't that worth somethin'?"

"We don't know this man," someone said.

"What *I'd* like t'know is how you walk into an Apache camp and walk out again alive," the injured man demanded.

"Actually, I was captured by them," Macklin said. "Some of them don't have any love for white eyes, that's true . . . but the medicine man wants peace for the whole band."

Another man peered closely at Macklin. He looked familiar . . .

"Wait a second! I seen this guy at the Injun camp yesterday! Up on a boulder above the gully! I think he's the one who shot Fred!"

"What the hell?" Thornton demanded.

"The deuce you say!" Fred, the man with the sling, exploded.

"What do you say, Fred?" Smethers asked. "Is this the guy who plugged you during the battle?"

"I . . . I'm not sure."

"Yes, I shot him," Macklin said, his voice low and edged with just a shiver of deadliness. The room went silent, except for one half-whispered "Son of a bitch!"

"He'd just shot a kid in the back of the head," Macklin continued. "He was about to shoot another, the same way. It didn't look like a battle to me. It looked more like murder."

"Nits make lice," Fred spat.

"Oh, very *nice*," Macklin said, his voice dripping with venom. "You're one of those people who favors wiping them *all* out—men, women, and kids?"

"Is that true, Fred?" Thornton wanted to know. "That attack was supposed to go after their braves!"

"This guy don't know what he's talkin' about," Fred said. "But if he's the one who bushwacked me, I want him arrested! A man's got *rights*, ya know!"

"We don't want any massacres up here," Norden warned. "We don't want the Army involved!"

"I say we string him up!" someone in the crowd shouted.

"Yeah, hang the sonofabitch!"

"Indian lover!"

"Get him! Get some rope!"

Someone grabbed Macklin by his shirt. Turning smoothly, Macklin brought his arms together, between his attacker's arms, and thrust upward, hard and sharp, breaking the hold. Someone else grabbed his arm . . . and Macklin's free hand caught the fellow's wrist and bent it back, eliciting a squeal of pain.

Somewhere in his amnesiac past, Macklin had been trained in unarmed combat; the moves and reactions were still there, even if he couldn't remember learning them. Or . . . maybe they'd been fed to him, like the languages he knew.

It didn't matter . . . and there were too many of them crowding close, grabbing him, striking him. He brought his knee up, and a bearded miner grunted and dropped to the dirt floor, clutching himself.

"Tie him up!"

"String him up!"

"Hangin's too good for a goddamn Apache-lover!" someone yelled.

"Just a goddamn minute!" Smethers bellowed. His pistol was out, and as the crowd continued to shout and demand that Macklin be hung, he pulled the trigger. The flash in the dimly lit saloon was startling, the crack of the gunshot louder still. The ringing silence following the shot seemed louder than the cries for blood a moment before.

"*I'm* the law in this camp," Smethers yelled into the stunned quiet, "and there ain't gonna be no hangings, or nothing else like it! Now back down, all of you!"

The man who'd recognized him pointed a grimy finger at Macklin, his hand trembling with fury. "That man is a *renegade*, Sheriff! Probably just like the Comancheros in Texas! Raping, thieving, murdering bastards! He's probably in tight with the Apaches! Probably was gonna set things up so they'd come in when our guard was down and murder us all!"

"I heard of renegades runnin' with the Indians," another man said. "They're worse than the redskins, 'cause they *knows* better and don't care!"

"Just simmer down, all of you!" Smethers yelled. His hand closed on Macklin's upper arm, and he started steering him through the mob and toward the door, stepping across the incapacitated miner on the floor. Macklin, relaxed, catlike, let himself be guided, watching for another attack.

"You're dead, mister!" Fred yelled after him, pointing with his good hand. "You hear me? You are *dead*!"

Macklin paused to look back at Thornton and Norden. "Under the circumstances," he said, "I think I'd better not take that job. But . . . you have a way open to you for peace with the Apaches. If you don't take it, it's your fault what happens after, not theirs!"

"Get him outa here, Sheriff!" Norden shouted.

"C'mon, Sheriff! Give him to us!"

"Yeah! We'll take care of him!"

"I got a rope right here!"

"Hang him!"

Smethers shoved Macklin ahead and out the door, into the bright Arizona midday sun.

"That," Macklin told Smethers as he was led across the street, "could have gone better."

"Shut up," the sheriff replied. "You're not out of this yet!"

Macklin heard the angry shouts follow them as they headed for a tent across the street from the adobe . . . a flimsy canvas structure with a hand-lettered sign out front reading *Sheriff*.

Behind them, the mob was growing, and getting louder.

TWELVE

◇ **1** ◇

THE SHERIFF LED MACKLIN TO THE BACK OF THE TENT, made him turn around, and began tying his wrists together at his back. Being tied up, Macklin decided, was becoming an unfortunate and extremely unpleasant habit.

"Sorry to do this to you," Smethers told him, "but up to now, Apache Peak hasn't needed much in the way of a real jail. If someone gets drunk and disorderly, why, we just tie him to a tree outside until he sobers up. But I think we'd better keep you in here, out of sight."

"That crowd out there doesn't sound too pleased."

"That they aren't." Smethers shook his head. "Damn it all, mister! Why'd you have to blurt that stuff out in front of everybody?"

"Maybe because I thought people would listen to reason, in a reasonable way?"

Smethers grunted. "You want reasonable, don't talk to these folks. All they care about is silver . . . and knocking down anyone who gets in their way."

"Like the Apaches."

"Especially the Apaches. Sit down. Feet together." Smethers picked up another length of rope and began tying Macklin's ankles. The rope work wasn't as snug as what the Apaches had done to him, and Macklin thought he might be able to work himself free, given the time.

The question was whether he would have that time.

"What they're doing can't be legal, Sheriff," Macklin said. "Raiding Indian encampments? Shooting kids? Sounds like what happened at Camp Grant a few years ago."

"So? Ain't no crime to kill Indians!" He finished tying Macklin's feet, and sighed. "But, you're right. After Camp Grant, there was a real hue and cry around here. Came close to having martial law established. Thornton and Norden don't want that. They don't want the Army anywhere near this place. They're damned fools for not taking you up on that offer of yours. 'Course, they'd be damned fools for trusting the Apaches, so I guess they just can't win."

"From what I've heard, it's not usually the Indians who break their word."

"Yeah, well, there is that. But you gotta understand, the Apaches are *bad*, the most savage Indians on the continent. What they do to their captives . . . what they did to that man of Thornton's they captured . . ." He was tying Macklin's wrists to his ankles with a short length of rope, now, leaving him on his side with his legs pulled up, unable to stand or hobble.

"I didn't see any evidence of that when they had me up in the mountains."

"You were really there? With them?"

"Yes, I was."

"And you walked away. Mister, you are just about the luckiest man I've ever heard tell of."

Macklin cocked an ear at the crowd noises outside. Someone was haranguing the rest, though Macklin couldn't make out the words. "I'm beginning to think I used up my luck with the Apaches."

"Don't worry." He licked dry lips. "You're under my protection now."

"I appreciate that, Sheriff." But how much protection could one man offer, against what sounded now like a large and very angry mob? From the tone of the voices, they were trying to work themselves up enough to take matters into their own hands. Bravery, it seemed, came in numbers and noise.

"I'll go out and try to talk some sense into them. You just stay put."

"So . . . what's going to happen to me, Sheriff? I mean, assuming they don't hang me?"

"Nobody's going to hang you." Smethers sagged back against the board stretched between two barrels which served him as a desk. "You'll stay here until I can arrange transportation back to Tucson. Won't do no good having a trial here. Wouldn't be able to find twelve jurors who weren't already set to convict you."

"What am I charged with?"

"Assault and attempted murder to begin with. Hell, you admitted to shooting Fred! Hardly need a jury to tell us you're guilty."

"I shot him to stop him from killing a child."

"Well, we'll have to let the jury decide the rights and wrongs of that."

"I have a better idea. You can let me go."

"Nope. That would be more than my life was worth. Besides, I swore an oath to uphold the law, and by God that's what I'm going to do!" He ducked his head as he pushed through the tent flap, and was gone, leaving Macklin with his thoughts.

Macklin had seen frontier justice at work more than once; Frank Stillwell's assassination was a case in point. If they thought you were guilty and your crime was heinous enough in their eyes, they hardly needed to stop for the formality of a trial. He needed to get out of here.

First, though, he needed to get out of the ropes, and he quickly found that that was going to be no easy task.

It had been plain bad luck that one of the people he'd shot at had recognized him. At that range, all that the two men in the gully should have seen of him was a silhouette atop the boulder. Maybe . . . maybe he could convince the jury that he hadn't been trying to kill the guy, only wound him.

No. When Macklin thought back to the moment, to the sight of that Indian boy's head coming apart, he knew he'd been trying to kill the boy's murderer, nothing less, and he wouldn't try to claim otherwise.

Hours passed. Macklin made no more progress against the knots, so after a time he gave up, opting to conserve his strength and watch for an opening. Smethers would have to let him up and out once in a while, for sanitary reasons if no other. Damn it, where was he?

His arms and legs were beginning to cramp, when the tent flap was pushed aside and someone came in.

He'd been expecting Sheriff Smethers, but it was the woman they'd called Cissy, holding a tin plate and cup. "Brought you some grub, mister," she said. "Can you sit up?"

Macklin squirmed around to a sitting position, his knees pressed up against his chest. "Can you untie me?"

She shook her head. Her hair was dark brown, and gathered into a bun. Her eyes were very green . . . but with a trace of terrible, unresolved pain somewhere deep inside. "No! But I can feed you this way." She knelt beside him. The plate was piled high with beans mixed with rice, which she began spooning up for him. "Open up."

"Pretty good service for a town jail," he said, swallowing.

She snorted. "Ain't no town. It's a filthy no-account pigsty mining camp. And you can see this ain't no jail."

"Look, this would be easier if you could untie me."

"Oh, gosh, mister. I *can't*! Sheriff Smethers would have my hide!"

"Even if I promise to be good?"

"Not even then." She offered him another spoonful.

"Well, I had to ask. My arms are getting damned sore."

"I'm sorry about that, but the sheriff, he said I wasn't to touch those ropes."

"Where is the sheriff, anyway? He went out to talk to the mob, but I haven't heard anything for some time."

"They're all over inside the Camino Real, having a powwow."

"Oh? About what?"

"You, mostly. Open up." He took the bite, and she added, "He had to offer to buy 'em all drinks to get them off the street."

"So what's the consensus?"

"I think they're just trying to decide what to do with you. The sheriff, he wants to turn you loose 'cause you ain't really done nothing, but Big Nate and Mayor Norden, they're afraid you're gonna blab what you know about the town and the silver and everything. And a lot of the miners, they're just mad 'cause you winged Fred Gorham yesterday. I don't know who you are, mister, or why you came here, but you done stirred up a real hornet's nest, comin' in here, shooting Fred like that and then saying the Apaches want to make peace."

"Your friends here don't seem real inclined to talk peace."

"No, sir. They ain't. There's been too much bloodshed already. On *both* sides. Too much for live-and-let-live, or forgive and forget, you know?"

Macklin thought about the angry Chokonen he'd seen, Black Wind. He had a feeling *that* one was no more eager to make peace with the white eyes than the white eyes wanted to make peace with him.

"So . . . what's your name, anyway?"

"Cecilia Colburn, but everyone calls me Cissy." She brushed a lank strand of dark hair back from her eyes. She was, Macklin thought, in her thirties, though it was hard to tell, her face was so dirty.

"Nice to meet you, Cissy. I'm John Macklin."

"Uh, charmed, I'm sure." She spooned up some more rice and beans. "Were you really with the Apaches?"

"Sure was. They weren't nearly as vicious and savage as everyone says."

"Well, they're not as vicious and savage as some white men I've known, and that's a fact!"

"They want peace with you. What I don't understand is why you pcoplc don't want pcacc, too."

"Some of us do. I *hate* the killing. The not knowing when you wake up each morning whether you're gonna see an Apache war party outside your tent. My . . . my parents were Quakers. I 'spose a lot of what they tried to tcach mc didn't take so good, but I *do* know that killing is wrong!" She looked around, as though checking for unseen listeners. "Mister?" She laid one slim hand on his knee. "If . . . if you could get away from here . . . No. Let me ask you: How much money you have?"

He smiled sadly, assuming she was trying to drum up some business for herself. "Sorry. I'm afraid I can't—"

"No, no, you don't understand. I want to come with you."

"Come with me? Why?"

"Because I've been stuck in this damned camp since they opened it, trying to make enough money to get back home and never being able to put aside more than five or ten dollars at a time."

"Oh? Where's home?"

"Philadelphia."

"That's a long way from here. How'd you get all the way out to Arizona?"

"Long story."

He shrugged with tied arms. "I have plenty of time, it seems."

"Well, I left Philly to meet my husband, in Dodge City. I'd applied to one of those heart-and-hand correspondence newspapers, you know? He saw my picture and wrote to me, and after a while we decided to get married, only when I got to Kansas, it turned out he'd up and married someone else and moved to California."

"Ah. And there you were, stranded in Kansas, without a return ticket, is that it?"

"That's just the way it was, sir. I tried to get work, but the only place that would have me was a saloon . . . the Long Branch? You heard of it? So I worked there for a year, then kind of drifted west, still trying to get together enough money for that ticket."

"Seems to me you were drifting in the wrong direction, Cissy. Philadelphia is east, not further west."

"Well to tell the truth, I kind of met up with a cowboy in Dodge, and he married me, and we moved to Tucson, only then he left me." Her mouth hardened with an unpleasant memory. "Ran off with a saloon girl and took with him a whole seventy-five dollars that I'd saved up in Dodge."

"I'm sorry."

She shrugged. "I ain't afraid of work, Mr. Macklin. I worked as a laundress at Fort Lowell for a while after that, but then Congress passed a law that said us girls weren't allowed to work on the post anymore. I ended up working on my back in a crib in the hog farm outside the gate."

Macklin was following the unspoken part of her story . . . barely, thanks to some stories he'd heard from Sarah Nevers back in Tombstone. Sarah had strongly disapproved of "street nymphs" and "soiled doves," and her stories had always carried a certain moralistic slant to them, but Macklin had learned a lot. Saloon girls often ended up working as prostitutes. For a desperate woman with no money, it was often the only way to survive. Sometimes, they ended up marrying one of their customers, but those were usually marriages of convenience, which might last for a week or less.

For a long time, women had lived on Army posts as laundresses . . . but their unofficial duties had extended beyond washing linen and underwear. Since 1878, though, women had been forced to live off-post, in rundown sin-strip districts called "hog farms."

Young and pretty and talented women might avoid all that by working in the more fashionable parlor houses of the larger towns and cities, and Sarah had said that some of them earned as much as $230 a month . . . twice the income of a bank clerk, a bricklayer, or a salesman. Their dream, always, seemed to be to save up enough money to buy new clothes and move to another city, where they could step off the stage a "respectable widow," and leave behind forever the sordid world of red-light districts, filthy bedrooms in the back of dingy saloons, and two-room shacks, called "cribs," at the poor end of town. Sarah, Macklin recalled, had lived in dread that some might assume she was hiding such a past when, in fact, she really was the widow of a man accidentally caught in the crossfire of a saloon shootout.

Cissy, though, was at a dead-end, unable to charge enough money—or attract enough customers—for her to escape this squalid trap.

"I don't think you would want to come with me, Cissy," Macklin said gently. "Between the Apaches and your neighbors out there, I'm not a real healthy person to know just now. But . . . can't you ride up to Tucson with the freight wagon some day? Maybe you could get a job there, start saving again . . ."

"But I couldn't get any farther than Tucson, and that's not far enough! I have *got* to get out of this town, mister.

You could take me. I can be *real* nice to you, and I could make myself useful, and I won't be no trouble. I promise!"

Behind her eagerness, Macklin sensed a deeper, darker undercurrent of fear. No, not fear . . . it was terror.

Why was she so afraid?

"I don't have much money, Cissy . . . and even if I get out of this, I still have . . . business to attend to, up on the mountain."

Her eyes widened at that.

"Are you afraid of the Apaches, Cissy? Or . . . no. You're afraid of something else. The men in Apache Peak?"

"No, most of them are okay. I admit, I ain't got no reason to trust men, right now, but most of these guys are okay. And . . . and I liked you right off, just lookin' at you. You look like the kind of guy who wouldn't hurt a woman, wouldn't abandon her at the train depot. The situation, being trapped like this, that's pretty bad, but being just about the only woman in a camp full of men does have some advantages." She smiled, but her lip was trembling. "Some of them, they look after me, almost like fathers."

"So . . . what are you afraid of?"

"It's that mountain, Mr. Macklin. That terrible mountain. There's something bad up there. Something *evil*."

"Oh?" That piqued his interest. "Have you seen something?"

"Some nights, real late, when I don't have no more clients but I'm not ready to sleep yet, I come outside . . . and there's this . . . this *glow* up there. A kind of blue-white light up near the top, like nothing natural I ever seen. Big Nate, he was in Alaska, once, and he told me it's just northern lights, but I seen northern lights in Pennsylvania, and this wasn't *nothing* like that." The words were tumbling out now, faster and faster. "And sometimes, sometimes you can hear these . . . these *things*, horrible things, shrieking. The men in the camp, they say it's just mountain lions, but I can see how afraid they are, beneath the words, like they don't really believe that, and are just sayin' it to feel better.

"Lots of nights, you can look up at that mountain and see these real, real bright stars up there, only . . . only they're moving. Swooping around like birds, but glowing real bright. And sometimes I've seen something like a really huge bird circling overhead, only it's like no bird I've ever seen, huge and black and no head, and with wings like knives and no tail.

"And there was this one time . . . I saw . . ." Her voice trailed off, and he saw the terror in her eyes, brighter, stronger than ever.

"What, Cissy? What did you see?"

"Well, I was out for a walk at the edge of town, and I got to feeling like something was watching me, you know? And I thought maybe it was Indians, but I looked and saw this . . . this horrible *thing*, like a demon out of Hell, just standing under the trees, staring at me."

"What did it look like?"

"I can't begin to describe it. It was . . . I don't know. It was like a horse, kind of, on four legs, but with arms, too, and a head and neck like a snake, and something like horns on its head. I couldn't get a real close look, you see. It was pretty far away, off near the tree line, and while I was looking at it, trying to decide whether to run or scream, it kind of faded away and vanished, right in front of my eyes. I've never seen anything like it! Whatever it was, it was horrible and I still have nightmares sometimes, just thinking about it. When it looked at me, I could *feel* it staring at me, cold and knowing, like, sort of like it was measuring me somehow.

"And, you know what, Mr. Macklin? I don't think no Apaches got those men who disappeared, like they say.

And lots of the people in the camp, they don't think it was Indians neither."

"What do you think the thing was?"

"I dunno. A demon. Ghosts? Maybe the mountain's haunted. All I know is, I don't want no part of it! I want to get away, far, far away, and live a normal life and get married and have kids—"

She stopped abruptly. There were tears in her eyes, and the hand holding a last spoonful of rice was trembling slightly. She fed him the rice, then looked away. "I've asked some of the men to take me away from here, but they all just laugh and say that I'm being foolish. They don't want me to talk to other people about this place, of course. And they all say that if I hang on just a little longer, they'll find the lost Bennett Mine, and then I'll be richer than I can imagine. Well, I've hung on a long, long time, Mr. Macklin, and I am sick to death of this town and these people and that mountain and this wretched, desert country! I want to go back East where I can be civilized again.

"I'm twenty-four, Mr. Macklin. It ain't too late to start over, is it?"

"No. No, Cissy, I don't think it's too late at all." He wished he could help her, but he didn't see any way of doing so without exposing her to considerable danger. "I'm afraid you can't come with me." Her face fell, and he pushed ahead. "It's just too dangerous."

"I ain't afraid of danger, and I ain't afraid of work!"

"I know. But, you see, one of the reasons I'm here is to stop that thing you saw in the woods—it, and others like it."

Her eyes got much larger at that, and she leaned back a little, as though trying to move away. "I . . . I have the feeling those things are pure evil, Mr. Macklin."

"They are . . . well, they're monsters. I wouldn't feel

right about putting you in a position where you might run into one up close.

"But if you could help me get away, I'll promise to try to come back and see that you get to another town. It might not be farther than Tombstone . . . but I know people there who might be able to help you." He was thinking of Sarah, especially. She might hate the idea of soiled doves, but she had a big heart and would do anything to help a *person*. She knew what it was to struggle.

"Would you? Would you really?"

"I promise," he told her as solemnly as he could. "I know you don't trust men, but I'll do what I can, I swear it."

She reached out and squeezed his shoulder. "I believe you. I really do."

"Of course . . . I have to get away from here first."

"Well, I promised not to touch those knots. I *can't* let you go, Mr. Macklin. You understand, don't you?" She stood suddenly, with a rustle of gingham.

He felt the disappointment crashing down. He'd thought . . . "Yes. Yes, I understand."

Holding the now-empty tin plate in one hand, Cissy suddenly squatted, reaching with her free hand beneath her skirts. Something flashed in the light as she tugged it from her boot. Then, with a little gasp, she turned and fled through the tent flap.

A small knife, a boot dagger, lay on the tent's canvas floor.

Macklin smiled. No one could prove that she hadn't dropped the blade by accident, or that he'd managed to get it from her, somehow, without her knowing.

Smart girl . . .

Wriggling around, he picked up the knife and drove it, point down, through the canvas floor and into the ground, anchoring it. Then he began sawing at the ropes on his wrists.

✧ 2 ✧

Tze-go-juni left the rock shelter in the early afternoon, making her way down a steep and tortuous path.
She needed to collect some chokeberry root for the ceremony planned for the following night, and she knew
where some of it was growing, in an arroyo not far from
the mouth of the cave.

The entire band was preparing for Rain Blossom's
Sunrise Ceremony tomorrow. Of all the dances and rituals
of Apache lore, the Sunrise Ceremony, also called Gift of
a Changing Woman, was the most important. It was done
each time a girl reached the age at which she became a
woman, and now it was Rain Blossom's time.

There had been considerable discussion in the camps,
late at night around the fires. Because of the trouble with
the white eyes, it might be better to delay the ceremony
. . . or even to travel elsewhere.

But . . . where? Scouts returning from across the line to
the south reported that there was trouble with the Mexicans. Go-yath-lay had attacked several villages, stealing
cattle and horses and killing Mexican soldiers. There was
no peace there.

Where else, then? Back across the valley of the San
Pedro, past the white eyes great-camp called Tombstone
to the Dragoon or Chiricahua Mountains? That was the
traditional home of the Chokonen, the homeland of Cochise and Go-yath-lay. But a movement of so large a
band—almost one hundred men, women, and children—
across lands so heavily settled by the white eyes invited
disaster.

As for postponing the ceremony, that would be to deny
to themselves who and what they were. Would the Chokonen allow the white eyes with their greed and anger
and hatred to dictate what they should be, how they
should act? It would be better to die.

And so, the decision had been made. The band would hold the Sunrise Ceremony here, close by the sacred mountain heights, and they would hold it beginning tomorrow night and going on into the next day. Na-a-cha's attempt to make peace with the white eyes of Apache Peak was at least partly aimed at securing a respite from the constant raids and skirmishes and alarms, so that the ceremony could be held without interruption.

And if the white eyes refused to make peace, if that strange white eyes with the black moon-circle in his chest failed to convince them, well, the ceremony would be held with men watching all of the approaches . . . and when the ceremony was complete, Black Wind and his faction would have their way, and the young men would paint their faces and descend upon the Anglo town, kill every white eyes they could find, and burn the place to the ground.

After that, they would have to leave these mountains, because the Anglo soldiers would never rest until the band of People who'd done this thing was hunted down and exterminated.

Violence . . . giving birth to violence, a cycle old as Moon, and apparently never ending.

A shrill keening rose from the *gowaa* set up just below the mouth of the cave, a handful of dome-shaped wickiups and a single "squaw cooler," or *ramada*, where other women were making tortilla cakes on flat stones. The screeching was coming from a small puppy being tortured to death by three boys, while Na-u-kuzze, Great Bear, looked on with amusement and approval.

It was a part of every Apache boy's warrior-training, a way to become hardened, to show no mercy to one's enemies. These three had built a small fire and were holding the dog above it, their laughter at times drowning out the animal's cries.

She sighed, and hurried on. It was wrong to question *dikohe*, the wisdom of the People, much of which had been painfully learned over many, many generations, and much of which had been handed down by the spirit-*gan* in the dawn times. Still, did anyone ever win with raid and counterraid, attack and attack in return, murder and vengeance, death and retribution?

There had to be a better way. But Tze-go-juni could not think what it might be. It made no sense to leave others in peace, when they refused the same courtesy to you.

Sometimes, she felt like an outsider, an enemy, within her own band.

"Tze-go-juni? Are you all right?"

Maria had come with her, carrying the basket for the roots, and was following along behind. Tze-go-juni realized that she'd let herself be distracted by the dying puppy, and was not paying attention to where she was going. It was a dangerous trait, one that Tze-go-juni wished she could cast out into the darkness.

"Sorry, Maria. I was just . . . thinking."

The older woman was her closest friend . . . perhaps because she, herself, was an outsider within the band. Maria had been kidnapped and raised by the Mexicans when she was a child, and not managed to escape and return to her own people until five summers ago. Though she'd immediately abandoned the Catholic religion forced on her by her former owners, she'd kept her Christian name.

Unlike Tze-go-juni, she was married. Part of her nose was missing because her husband had cut it off, in accordance with N'de practice, when she'd been found with another man.

Life with the People could be hard . . . especially if you were a woman.

They passed another *gowaa*—there were a number of encampments scattered about the general area of the rock shelter. Ever since the attack on the outlying encampment yesterday, the band had been pulling together in one place, finding safety in numbers, and defensibility in the rugged terrain in the heart of the mountains the white eyes called Whetstones.

Past a tangle of borders where men sat with rifles, watching the southern approaches to the encampments, the path descended sharply in a series of switchbacks, opening at last in a gully partly blocked by ancient landslides and tumbledown sandstone boulders. Century plants grew here—the people cut strips from them to make mescal—as well as a profusion of chokeberry plants. Tze-go-juni selected one of these last and started toward it.

"Tze-go-juni!" Maria screamed.

She turned . . . too late. Someone tackled her from behind, driving her hard full-length against the rough, grainy surface of a boulder, smashing the breath from her lungs. Strong hands clutched at her arms and legs; one clamped down over her mouth, the fingers pinching her nose shut. Unable to breathe, she thrashed in the brutal embrace, rasping the skin of her face against the rough sandstone wall in an attempt to dislodge the hand.

She heard Maria scream again, then heard the scream change to a grunt of surprise and pain. Hands stuffed something soft deep into her mouth, then tied a rawhide strip about her head, gagging her. Other hands wrenched her arms behind her back, binding her wrists with rawhide . . . and then her ankles.

The hand pinching her nostrils was suddenly gone, and she fought to gulp down a lungful of sweet, precious air . . . but in the next instant, a burlap bag was pulled down over her head and tied off around her neck. The stench within the bag was overpowering, and between the sack, the gag, the ties around her throat, and her terror-fueled gasping, she was rapidly suffocating.

She was barely clinging to consciousness as one of her captors struck her a savage blow across the head, scooped her up, slung her over his shoulder, and started down the gully. She thought she could hear Maria screaming in the distance, but with the terrible roaring of her own blood in her ears, she wasn't sure.

Tze-go-juni was pretty certain she lost consciousness then. She was aware of fighting her way back to awareness through black pain and dizziness, finding herself slung head-down across the back of a pony, remembered feeling the lurching, ambling gait of the animal as it was led down the gully at a pace dangerous over such broken ground.

She felt unconsciousness closing on her, as suffocating as the bag enveloping her. She refused to give in . . . refused . . .

But before too long, she simply could not keep fighting, and the darkness won.

THIRTEEN

❖ 1 ❖

Something was happening near the native camp.

Deathstalker had been watching the natives carefully for some weeks now. It was aware of the enmity between them and the more technologically advanced humans, who maintained an encampment of their own not far away.

The Kra'agh had watched both groups of humans closely. The primitives, who called themselves N'de, had been here when the Kra'agh set up their base on the highest of these mountain peaks some eight eights of ngh'droks *ago, living in a number of semimobile encampments, or in several of the caves that riddled the rocky hills and uplands. The more advanced humans, who called themselves Americans or Anglos or whites or men or a variety of other names, had settled in one of their primitive social-group clusters and stayed there . . . though some of their number had made explorations into the mountains. Most of those had been taken, for information and for food.*

Through the eyes of a circling dlaadthma, *Deathstalker had watched a number of the Americans set an ambush around one outlying native encampment, moving in by stealth and attacking with their primitive firearms.*

Though Deathstalker's triple hearts had beat faster with excitement as it watched the carnage, the fighting also increased its disgust for the inhabitants of this world. Kra'agh might disagree with one another, might even engage in the mock-combat of sserazh'n, *but physically attacking another Kra'agh outside of the ritual constraints of the Authority of the Claw was almost literally unthinkable.*

Filthy barbarian savages . . . !

And so, Deathstalker had watched with considerable interest, and revulsion, as it observed two natives of the subtype known as female stalked by two males. Here was a case of fighting among the humans carried out within a single tiny band.

The attack evidently had been carried out in order to capture one of the females. From far overhead, the dlaadthma circled, watching the males as they carried the captive female to another part of the mountains. Deathstalker was interested in the captured creature's fate. Did the males want it for information? Or possibly for sexual activity?

The phenomenon called sex was still being studied by the drevech'narred, *the caste of Kra'agh scientist-observers. Kra'agh themselves were hermaphroditic, exchanging genetic material with other adults in dander brushed from their skin, shedding wild larval young, called* dlik, *from beneath certain specialized scales on their bodies. Sex, as an emotion, as a drive, was an alien concept, observed on many worlds but never comprehended.*

But they had noted that sex was important to these creatures, and was occasionally engaged in without the mutual consent of both creatures. Perhaps that was what was happening here.

Deathstalker focused its mind, instructing the dlaadthma to move in closer.

*Any information which would improve understanding
of these creatures and their way of thinking was valuable.*

✧ 2 ✧

MACKLIN DUCKED LOW AND RAN.

Once free of the ropes, he'd used Cissy's knife to slit
a hole through the back of the tent and wriggle through.
There were trees about fifty yards away, close against the
base of some sheer red cliffs shouldering skyward in a
series of uneven steps. If he could make it to their shelter
without being seen . . .

And then what? The question pricked at the back of
his mind even as he ran for safety. His guns had been
taken from him. His horse was still tied up in front of the
adobe building. If he could make it up Guindani Canyon,
he might be able to find the Apache who'd led him down
from the encampment in the hills, *if* the man was waiting
for him, *if* he could make the two-and-a-half mile trek up
the broken, boulder-strewn floor of the canyon in gathering darkness, *if* the good citizens of Apache Peak didn't
decide to form up a posse and come run him down.

The only other option was to try to make it to Tombstone . . . twenty miles to the southeast. Or Benson, a bit
less than twenty miles to the north. On foot, over rough
ground, he could expect to reach either destination in . . .
what? Twelve hours? Or more like fifteen?

He had no water, either. And he'd lost his hat when
the Apaches captured him the day before. Once he'd ridden across ten or fifteen miles of this country without a
hat, and regretted it. Trying to cover twice that distance
on foot by day, bareheaded and without water, was a great
way to end up dead.

He reached the trees and dropped to the earth, hugging
the ground as he stared back at the squalid collection of
tents and shacks called Apache Peak. No sign of alarm or

pursuit. The lookout atop the adobe must not have—

He heard a yell, and saw several men trotting out of the adobe's front door, some making for their horses, others standing, shouting, and pointing. His escape had been noticed by the lookout after all.

The cliffs at his back were unscalable, not without ropes and climbing gear better than his bare hands. He could make his way south, toward the canyon's mouth . . . or north. Norden had said something about a small mine that way, northwest of the town and against East Peak, the diggings the town had been running in order to keep going until they found the real mine, the Bennett Mine.

If they put together a posse, they would check the canyon first. The lookout had seen him coming from that direction this morning, and would assume that he was going to try to make it back to the Indian camp. At the mine there would be . . . opportunities. A chance to find a horse, maybe . . . and a gun. The only alternative he could think of was to stay put until sundown, and then try sneaking back into town to get his horse and some weapons. If he did that, he would still have to get out of town unseen, and the mining company's security was just a little too tough for him to count on being able to pull that off.

He would go north, toward the Apache Peak mine, and quickly, before the townspeople decided to send a detachment up there to warn the miners, just in case.

Staying flat on his belly, he worked his way back into the trees that cloaked the lower part of the cliffs, then turned and started following the cliff face toward the north.

Damn. He wished he had a horse.

⋄ **3** ⋄

AGAIN, TZE-GO-JUNI SWAM BACK TO A PAIN-SHOT CONsciousness. Head down, the blood was rushing to her face.

Her nose was plugged, making every attempted breath an agony of not quite enough. She'd become used to the stink of the burlap bag; all she was concerned about was getting enough air to stay alive.

She'd tried to keep track of where they were taking her by sensing the changes in direction as they led the pony across the mountains by various twisting paths, but before long she was hopelessly lost, would have been lost, she thought, even if she'd not repeatedly lost consciousness.

Eventually, though, they'd arrived *here*, wherever here was, dragging her from the horse and dumping her unceremoniously on the hard ground. She'd tried rolling away, but stopped when her back came up hard against a boulder. She lay there, chest heaving as she struggled for each breath, waiting for whatever was going to happen next.

But nothing happened, and minutes dragged on and on, until she thought she must have lain there for hours. She was able to breathe a little better now, but she was weak and dizzy and nauseated. If she vomited, she knew she could easily choke to death, and she had to concentrate to keep her tortured stomach quiet. Once, she heard her captors talking together in low, nervous tones nearby. She didn't learn much, though it was clear that they were actually afraid of her.

And well they should be. She was a witch, after all, with power over animals, sickness, and men. She had visited the *chidin-bi-kungua*, and she had seen the mountain *gan* with her inner eyes.

This had to be something involving Black Wind and his plotting against her uncle, she decided. Nothing else made sense. She was aware that some of the members of the band knew that she worked medicine. Some, including Maria, even called her *bruja*, the Spanish word for "witch," to her face.

That by itself meant nothing. In Apache belief, anyone could work magic. The question was how that magic was applied. The band's *diyi*, or medicine man, was expected to work various kinds of magic, to ensure success in battle or the hunt, to bring good fortune, to divine the ways of the mountain spirits. Some people worked magic on their own, a practice frowned upon, but not forbidden. After all, everyone carried, at the very least, a small buckskin bag of *hoddentin* for purification and to appease spirits, and knew how to call upon the spirits in any perilous undertaking.

Trouble arose if a person used magic against someone else, however . . . to make them sick, to bring misfortune. The Apache believed that all death came as a result of injury, of sickness, or of witchcraft. For the People, there was no such thing as death from old age. The fact that a witch could kill someone with the proper words and ritual gave them power and respect, in Apache eyes.

But a witch was not considered bad unless he or she *did* kill. That was what defined witchcraft as a bad thing, in Chokonen eyes, and it could be a very serious matter indeed. A witch who had brought death to a band had to be killed, and killed in a very particular way.

The thought of what awaited her brought new life to Tze-go-juni and she struggled hard against the ropes and the stifling bag over her head, but won nothing but a curse and another ringing blow across the back of her head which left her stunned and bleeding. She stiffened as she felt hands groping her, checking her bonds, and she braced herself for rape . . . but nothing more happened. Satisfied that she couldn't get free, her captors ignored her again.

After that, however, she heard them breaking sticks and branches, and the panic boiled up from within, a frantic, writhing, pleading *no*.

They were going to burn her . . . burn her to death

slowly the way those children had been burning the puppy.

And there was not a thing in the world that she could do to stop them.

✧ 4 ✧

THE SUN HAD LONG AGO VANISHED BEHIND THE WHET-stone Mountains, sending their shadows stretching far down into the San Pedro Valley. It was still light, however, with a clear blue sky given depth by a few scattered horsetail cirrus clouds high overhead.

North from the town of Apache Peak, a ridge of blocky, sandstone hills appeared to have broken off from the main body of the Whetstones, forming a narrow valley. Macklin didn't like the idea of getting himself trapped in a dead end, but from what he could see of the cliffsides below East Peak, there might be a way up and over the barrier farther on. He kept moving.

Moving slowly and keeping under cover when he could, Macklin eventually reached the rocky ground above the Apache Peak Mine, which appeared to be nothing more than a crude tunnel cut into an earthen bank, braced by timbers and surrounded by crates, barrels, digging tools, and a couple of wagons. A hand-lettered sign on a plank nailed to a tree stump warned off trespassers, while two armed sentries patrolled the remuda of some twenty horses tied to a long rope stretched between two trees. Another guard stood outside the mine entrance, and Macklin wondered if there were others, posted among the rocks on the surrounding hillsides. The ones he could see all carried rifles, with pistols holstered at their hips.

The number of horses visible gave him a rough idea of the number of men present. Most must be underground right now. The only ones visible at the moment were the guards, and three men picking through a small wagon full of rocks . . . apparently separating the silver ore by hand. Most of the mines Macklin had seen in and around Tombstone were either vertical shafts or hillside tunnels like this one, but with railroad tracks carrying ore cars. These diggings looked a lot more primitive and less permanent, as if the miners hadn't cared to put that much cost or effort into the endeavor.

Well, that fit with what he'd been told. Norden and Thornton wanted to find the lost Bennett Mine and recover their losses there, not start a whole new mine.

He studied the layout of the place for a long time, lying flat on his belly atop a sandstone boulder as the shadows grew slowly deeper, darkening toward twilight. One guard he might have been able to handle barehanded, if he managed to sneak up behind him. Two . . . he wasn't so sure. Besides, the horses were in clear view of the miners working the ore wagon. He didn't see how he could get down there and at the horses without someone seeing him and giving the alarm.

He'd decided that the only way he was going to be able to get close was to wait for it to get fully dark. Then he noticed a lone figure approaching on horseback from the south—a rider, he thought, from the town, come to warn of his escape.

As the rider grew closer, however, Macklin could see that it was a woman. Her face was lost in the shadow beneath a broad-brimmed man's hat, but there weren't that many women in Apache Peak. He was pretty sure it was Cissy. What's more, she was riding *his* horse, the roan with the broad white snip around the left nostril.

As he watched, she stopped short of the camp, and seemed to be studying the rocks and scrub brush around her with particular care. When one of the remuda guards called to her, though, she eased the roan into a walk again and approached.

Macklin was already working his way closer, slipping

down off his boulder-top perch and crawling through the underbrush toward the little copse of trees where the camp horses were tethered.

"Hey, boys!" he heard her call out. "You seen anything of that guy Macklin?"

"Mack who?" one guard asked. Apparently, the mine crew had not been warned of his escape. Both men leaned their rifles against a tree and walked out to meet her.

"Guy who rode into town this morning. A stranger. You seen him?"

"Nah," the other guard said, coming up to take her reins. "Ain't seen nobody all afternoon, 'ceptin' you, sweetie. You come up here to keep us entertained?"

"Well, that depends. What do you boys find entertaining?"

"I kind of like the man's clothing," he replied, eyeing the blue jeans Cissy was wearing. Women wearing men's clothing was not unheard of in the West, especially when they had to ride astride, but it was unusual enough to draw comment.

Macklin emerged from the shadows and underbrush at the men's backs. Both guards were close to Cissy now, one holding her bridle, the other positioning himself to help her down, and both were completely preoccupied with her. As Macklin took a step forward, his eyes locked with Cissy's, above the men's heads. Until that moment, Macklin hadn't been entirely certain whether she was here to help or spread the warning, but he caught the flicker of an eyelid, the slightest of nods, and knew that she'd come looking for him . . . and brought along his horse and Winchester in the bargain.

"We could do a little dancin'," one guard said. "Joe, here, has his harmonica!"

"I'm sure a couple of big, strong hands like you two will be able to think of *something*!" She leaned forward in the saddle, giving both men a generous view down the front of her shirt, which had the top three buttons undone. "Help me down?"

"Why sure, li'l darlin'!" The man closest to Cissy reached up to take her into his arms. Macklin broke into a run, covering the last few feet swiftly and almost silently.

The guard holding Cissy's bridle heard or sensed something, and started to turn, but as he did so, Macklin's elbow slammed into the side of his head, knocking him backward. The roan was an old and placid animal, but the sudden excitement made it shy. Cissy fell heavily into the other guard's arms just as he realized that something was wrong. He turned, almost dropping Cissy, who squealed. Macklin caught him full in the face with the heel of his hand, then kicked his knees from behind, driving him to the ground. Cissy fell on top of him, legs flailing.

Macklin spun and took down the first man with two more hard blows to the head. Another spin and drop, and the man on the ground thrashed once, then lay still.

He helped Cissy get to her feet. "Is this a rescue?" he asked.

"Sure is. I looked *everywhere* for you! But I figured at last you'd come here, instead of trying to go back up Guindani Canyon, 'cause that's where the sheriff and his posse are right now."

"Smart thinking." He looked toward the mine entrance, where the third guard was lounging against an upright timber, lighting a cigarette. The miners at the ore wagon were absorbed in their work. So far, the events at the remuda had gone unnoticed, but that state of affairs couldn't last for long. "But we need two horses."

"What's wrong with one of these?"

There was no choice, really. Macklin had lived long enough in Tombstone, though, to know that horse thieves were considered the very worst, the very lowest of all criminals. After all, ranch hands and drovers couldn't work without a horse, and stealing one was tantamount to stealing their career.

Most of the horses on the tie line were without saddles, but a few still had their tack. Macklin selected one of these, a chestnut with a blaze on its face and one white stocking. Holding its bridle, he pulled Cissy's knife from his boot and slashed through the rope securing the entire string.

"What are you doing that for?" Cissy asked.

"So they don't follow us," Macklin replied. "We're going to have enough problems without that. Get those guns."

Cissy unfastened the gun belts from both unconscious guards and slung them over the neck of her horse, then grabbed one of the Winchesters leaning against the tree and a bandoleer of .44-40 ammo and tossed them to Macklin.

Macklin swung into the saddle, reining back the chestnut as Cissy climbed onto the roan. Someone shouted in the distance.

"Heyah!" Macklin cried, waving his arm. The riderless horses started, milled, then began running in every direction. His new Apache friends, he thought wryly, would thank him for this.

"Let's ride!" he called, and the two spurred their mounts into an easy, loping gallop, clattering across the open ground toward the north. A gunshot banged after them, and another . . . but in moments they were well out of range.

They rode for nearly an hour, circling East Peak around toward the west. Once out from behind the Whetstones, they could see the sun again, huge and red, dropping slowly toward a horizon piled high with distant purple and white clouds. Finally, though, as the last bright sliver of the sun vanished, lighting up the sky in a glorious blaze of reds and greens and lavender, Macklin and Cissy reined up their horses.

There'd been no sign of pursuit.

Macklin pointed north. "Okay," he said. "Benson is that way, about seven or eight miles. If you keep heading north, sooner or later you'll cross the Southern Pacific Railway tracks, and they'll lead you into town."

"Why, Mr. Macklin," she said, cocking an eyebrow. "Are you trying to ditch me so soon?"

"Not ditch you, Cissy. But get you on the way to safety." He shook his head. "You *don't* want to go where I'm going."

"Why not?"

"Because my only friends out here are the Apaches . . . and because I have to find that monster you said you saw. There are a bunch of them out here in these mountains, and they're up to some definite no good. Not to mention the fact that Smethers and his posse will be after us."

"And do you think they won't come after me in Benson? I don't have enough money to my name to get farther than, I don't know, Dodge City, maybe. *If* I can outride Smethers' men, which I doubt. I think I'll be safer with you."

"Damn it, Cissy—"

"You just go ahead and cuss all you want to, Mr. Macklin. You're the best thing that's come my way in eight years, and I'm not letting you get away. Now, if you want to come with me to Benson . . ."

"Cissy, I can't. There's too much at stake!" How he wished he could say yes!

She nodded. "You want the truth? I've been thinking I was crazy ever since I saw that thing in the woods. Now, you come along and tell me the thing is real, that I'm not crazy. I want to see it. I want to know what the hell it is."

"Believe me, Cissy. You don't want to know." He

looked back the way they'd come, wondering if they were being followed yet. *"Please* go!"

"You can ride on without me," she said, stubborn. "But I'll follow you. Wouldn't it be easier just to accept the inevitable and let me come along?" She reached out and touched his arm. "Like I said this afternoon, I can be very useful. . . ."

Macklin sighed. He knew there was no way to argue with her.

For a moment, he wondered if it wouldn't be better for him to give up now, and go with her to Benson. They could sell both horses there, and their tack, and realize enough to get them tickets to Dodge City, or maybe even St. Louis. And from there . . .

But, no. Those *things* were in the mountains, and they were here at least partly because of him. They represented a terrible and terrifying threat to the people of this world, people who didn't even suspect the danger they now faced. He didn't know if he could do anything, but, damn it to hell, he was going to try.

"Okay," he said at last. "But you'll do what I say, when I say it."

"Of course, Mr. Macklin." She dimpled. "You're the boss!"

Somehow, he didn't trust the way she said that.

✧ 5 ✧

THEY PULLED THE BURLAP BAG OFF HER HEAD, AND SHE squeezed her eyes shut as the sudden light assaulted her eyes. It took Tze-go-juni a moment to realize it was, in fact, twilight, so accustomed had her eyes become to the dark.

At least she could see her captors now—Running Bird, Jumps Far, and the half-breed, Jiminez. All White Mountain people, newcomers to the band. All of them of Black Wind's circle.

She could also breathe again, though the gag still stifled her mouth. She grunted at the men standing over her, raising her chin, asking wordlessly to be released.

Jiminez reached down, fumbling with the rawhide strap at the back of her head, but Running Bird punched him hard in the arm. "No!" he said. "Fool! Do you *want* her to witch you?"

"Is she really a witch?" Jumps Far asked. He was bent over, hands on knees, staring at her as if she were some kind of bizarre, improbable animal.

"Of course she is," Running Bird snapped. "We've all seen her working her medicine. But Black Wind saw the owl on her wickiup. And she brought down the attack upon our *gowaa* yesterday."

She grunted and *mmphed* at them through the gag, trying to deny that she had brought any misfortune on the band, but the men ignored her.

"So," Jiminez said. "How will we do it?"

"That tree," Running Bird said, pointing. "Get the rope."

A long, horsehair rope was tossed over one of the tree's lower branches, about nine feet off the ground. Then Jiminez advanced on her, grabbing her legs. "Take her."

She struggled, but the three men picked her up and hauled her to the tree. They went about the operation in a precise and businesslike fashion. First they stripped off her long buckskin skirt. There was no licentiousness behind the act; they simply didn't want it to fall over her head, catch fire, and hasten the process or, worse, trap the smoke around her head and suffocate her too soon. Jiminez used his knife to cut off her fringed jacket, the thong with her bag of *hoddentin* worn about her neck, and her long black braids as well, again so they wouldn't catch fire and kill her too quickly.

Jumps Far tied the end of the hanging rope around the rawhide lashing at her ankles, and then the three of them hauled her up by the rope, until she was dangling upside down, head about three feet off the ground.

She twisted and struggled, trying to free her hands, which were still bound, trying to kick free, trying just to *see* as she swung back and forth, turning at the end of the rope. Terror pounded behind her breastbone, and burned at the back of her throat. The world, upside down now, swayed in dizzying arcs as she continued to swing and turn. The rawhide was cutting painfully into her feet as it took her body's full weight. The blood rushed to her head, and she was again having trouble breathing through the congestion.

The men watched her for a moment, eyes very large. No doubt they were thinking that if she was going to do something unexpected, something magical, it would be now. She couldn't tell if they were disappointed or simply afraid as she continued to swing helplessly back and forth.

"*Vamanos*," Jiminez said, and then he repeated the word in Apache. "Let's go."

They arranged a pile of sticks and small branches on the ground directly beneath her head. Then Jiminez used flint and a small bar of steel to strike sparks into some dry shavings scraped from a branch, and blew on them gently until they kindled into a bright flame. Moments passed, as Tze-go-juni craned her neck sharply back, staring down into the growing fire. She felt the first blast of hot air shimmering past her face, smelled the smoke, and writhed in terrified anticipation of the first real pain.

Very slowly, the men added a few more sticks to the blaze, and Tze-go-juni gave a gag-muffled scream. To deal with an evil witch in Apache tradition, the captive had to be burned slowly. The longer it took him or her to die, the more painful the dying, the less likely it was that the witch's ghost could return to bring vengeance to the executioners. If these three knew what they were doing, they should be able to keep her alive all night, and possibly well into tomorrow.

The smoke grew thicker and eagerly she tried gulping it down through her nose. If she could lose consciousness in the smoke . . .

But the men waved their hands, dispersing the cloud. There would be no release for her *that* way.

"*Gun-ju-li, chil-jilt, si-chi-zi, gun-ju-li, inzayu, injan-ale* . . ." she prayed behind her gag, the ancient words of supplication to the powers of the night taking on a new and more urgent meaning. "Be good, O Night; Twilight be good; do not let me die. . . ."

Flames crackled two feet below her scalp, as smoke curled around her head, choking her. The men were careful not to let the flames rise too high, though, or grow too hot. The pain was bad, searing the skin of her scalp and forehead . . . but it was bearable.

At least so far. She knew it was going to get a lot worse.

She thought about the puppy back in the camp, and sobbed in pain, fear, and helplessness.

✧ 6 ✧

DEATHSTALKER WAS HORRIFIED.

Once, many cycles ago, it had watched the scorching of an entire world, as the Kra'agh fleet exterminated a race of food beasts that had proven intractable. But that had been one species against another, in a situation where genocide was necessary to Kra'agh survival. Survival meant the pitting of one species against another in a struggle that frequently ended with the extinction of one in order that the other might survive.

But these humans . . .

Deathstalker was pretty sure the males were planning

to eat the female. Although Kra'agh preferred their food alive, they knew that others, including the humans, preferred their food cooked before they ate it. A strange trait ... but necessary, perhaps, if local parasites or microorganisms were killed by heat. It could think of no other reason for tying the female by its feet and hanging it over a small fire to roast.

Enough! Deathstalker needed to question some of the primitive humans, to see if they had seen Macklin. These would do. They were off by themselves, in an isolated canyon well away from the others. They would do perfectly.

The cannibalistic monsters ... !

FOURTEEN

✦ 1 ✦

DEATHSTALKER TOOK A FLYER FROM THE KRA'AGH BASE TO the spot pinpointed by the dlaadthma, homing on the signal transmitted by the creature wheeling far above the tree, the fire, and the three humans watching a fourth slowly die. Fleshripper and Eater of Living Hearts went with it, crowded into the cramped compartment. In moments, the craft was descending toward the lone spot of firelight in the darkness of the mountainside.

✦ 2 ✦

JIMINEZ ADDED ANOTHER BRANCH TO THE CRACKLING FIRE and the flames momentarily danced higher. The witch writhed and twisted, doubling her body to escape the fire's touch. She was trying to set herself to swinging, again, to avoid the worst of the heat, but Jumps Far and Running Bird jabbed at her with branches, stopping the swing and positioning her again above the fire. She continued to bend up at the waist, though, holding herself out of the blaze, but they could tell she was beginning to weaken. Before long, the heat would start to cook her brain and she would become delirious. It might be time to damp the fire a bit, to make sure she lasted until the morning.

Odd. She was . . . humming something. Jiminez leaned closer, trying to hear. At first, the witch had been screaming into the gag, but for the past half hour or so, she'd been saying something . . . no, *chanting* something. The words were unrecognizable, of course, but they carried a strange, almost hypnotic cadence.

Fear pricked at the back of Jiminez's neck. What was the witch doing, anyway? He leaned even closer, trying to see. Her face was blackened with smoke, and there were angry blisters on her face, shoulders, and upper body. Her hair was scorched, her eyebrows nearly burned away. Her eyes were squeezed shut, but he could see her mouth working through the gag, could hear the rhythmic cadence of muffled words.

Could it be she was working a spell? Could she work a spell, even if she couldn't get the words out clearly? Jiminez knew little of magic. Like any Apache, he knew how to use *hoddentin* to greet the sun or the night, how to purify, how to pray . . . but this, this was something beyond ordinary experience.

The witch's eyes snapped open, as though she'd felt him watching, and through the shimmering rise of heated air, she stared directly at him with a black and horrifying glare of pure hate.

Jiminez gasped and moved back. The witch closed her eyes again, still holding herself rigidly bent double, murmuring the cadenced intonations once more . . . louder and more urgently. Wildly, then, Jiminez turned and reached for his gun, fumbling with the hammer.

"What are you doing?" Running Bird demanded.

"She is trying to put a spell on us!" Jiminez raised the rifle. He would end this *now* . . .

"No!" Running Bird shouted. "This must be done properly!"

"Stop!" Jumps Far added. "She can't hurt us! Black Wind promised us this!"

Jiminez snorted. "Black Wind promised! He is not here. Facing *that* . . . !"

As he turned, pointing at the witch, he saw something stepping out of the night beyond the fire . . . something unspeakably horrible . . . indescribably *other* . . .

Jiminez shrieked in fear and despair. . . .

✧ **3** ✧

"GUN-JU-LI, CHIL-JILT, SI-CHI-ZI, GUN-JU-LI, INZAYU, INJAN-ale . . ." Tze-go-juni continued chanting, drawing power from the familiar rhythm of the words. "Be good to me, O Night, and do not let me die."

When she'd felt Jiminez looking at her, and seen the growing fear in his eyes, she realized that he, that all of them, were afraid of her, afraid that her chant was working some terrible medicine against them. She began grunting the chant louder, then. Why not? It was her only means of striking back and, just possibly, they would panic and she would find a way to escape.

At the very least, one of them might decide to kill her, releasing her from the slow torment of the flames.

Then she heard Jiminez shriek.

She opened her eyes, twisting in order to look around her. It was almost impossible to see anything. Her eyes were tearing and burning from the smoke, everything was upside down, and the glow of the fire had robbed her of her night vision. But it seemed to her that something was moving at the edge of the fire's circle of light, a wavering, shifting something, larger than a man, lost in shadow.

A gunshot rang out, and she heard a throaty, gurgling hiss. She sensed something moving, though she couldn't see it. She had only the impression of bulk, something as big as a small pony, moving rapidly past the fire.

She twisted again, trying to see. There was another shape . . . and another, a third. They'd ringed the fire, surrounding the men by the tree. She had a moment's tear-blurred glimpse of Running Bird in the grasp of . . . of *something*, a monster with four legs like a horse, but arms as well, and a snake-necked head with gold-bronze eyes as cold as the heart of a rattlesnake. Black, twisting arms like crooked branches on the sides of its head gripped something like a metal spike. It lifted Running Bird, his feet kicking well above the ground, and then drove the spike into his head just between and above his eyes.

Running Bird's arms and legs spasmed horribly, then continued to move, feebly, as the monster's flat head moved as close to its victim's face as a kiss.

He was still screaming. . . .

❖ 4 ❖

*D*EATHSTALKER *HELD THE CREATURE CLOSE WITH ITS* *slasher arms, savoring the sharp, singing bite of its howl-ing terror. The Hunter was hungry, had not eaten in sev-eral sixty-fours of* droks, *but it needed information now more than food. Gripping the creature's head with three of its feeder hands, it held the patternmaker, embedded between and above the human's wide-staring optic or-gans, with the fourth opening the flow of sensations, im-pressions, emotions, and memory from the dying food beast to Deathstalker's soulcatcher.*

Most of what came through for the space of several triple-heart beats was simple, pure, gibbering terror, and Deathstalker let the emotion wash through its being like a cleansing wave, eliciting the release of a host of fight-or-flight hormones within Deathstalker's body chemistry.

It felt wonderfully, savagely good, like the gush of hot blood at the inevitable conclusion of a victorious Hunt. . . .

But coming through beneath the fear and the rasping throb of pain was more useful information. Deathstalker saw within the dying human's mind the face of another human, the one called Macklin.

✧ **5** ✧

TZE-GO-JUNI LOOKED AROUND, HELPLESS, NOT KNOWING whether to know joy or terror. All three of her captors had been taken. Jiminez had been lifted from the ground, his rifle smashed from his hands. Screaming, Jumps Far turned and dashed for the safety of the night, but the third monster turned with the grace of a striking mountain lion, a silvery-black device in one of the branch-hands of its flat head. She had the impression that it was some kind of firearm even though it looked nothing like the pistols with which she was familiar. An instant later, a blue-white bolt of lightning crackled through the night air, striking Jumps Far in midstride and tumbling him to the earth. He lay face down at the edge of the firelight, smoke curling from the gaping, char-edged crater in his back.

The creature with Jiminez was finished with him. Lifting him high, it drew back one of its large, lower arms, a glistening, sickle-shaped claw gleaming by the light of the fire's embers, then disemboweled him with a single swift, groin-to-chest slash.

It tossed Jiminez in a bloody, mewling heap at the base of the tree.

She was aware now of the cold, ice-gaze of two of the beasts as she twisted and turned beneath the branch. The third was doing . . . *something* to Running Bird, holding him, with that brass-colored spike planted bloodily between his eyes.

Her heart pounded. She *wanted* to believe that she'd just been rescued. She'd been praying, after all, and with unusual fervor, and these three spirit-creatures had materialized out of the night and dispatched her tormentors in a few stark seconds of blood and terror.

But as she met their inhuman eyes, she realized that she didn't feel *safe* at all. . . .

✧ 6 ✧

DEATHSTALKER DRANK THE HUMAN'S SOUL, AND WITH IT its memories.

Blood taste! Success! The human Macklin had been at the N'de camp by the rock overhang high up on the slopes of the highest of the nearby mountains only one of this world's revolutions ago. If the creature was not there now, it would be soon.

The Kra'agh could see the human in Running Bird's thoughts, injured, but alive. The black disk of its Monitor AI was clearly visible in the N'de's memories; they'd been impressed by that, and thought it was a sign that Macklin was a spirit-being of some sort.

After twice losing Macklin in the human city, Death-stalker was going to take no chances. It would have the N'de themselves deliver the prey.

"Tcha'l graad!" The prey waits.

And the Kra'agh would be ready to take it.

Joyfully, it sucked the man's mind and soul dry; then, retrieving the patternmaker, it unhinged its lower jaw and gulped down the still hot and quivering body whole.

✧ 7 ✧

AS HORROR PILED UPON HORROR, TZE-GO-JUNI SQUEEZED her eyes shut . . . but she could not shut out the screams and pleas and gurgles of the dying men. When she opened her eyes again, it was to see one of the beasts eating Running Bird, swallowing him head first and gulping him down whole. She could actually follow the swelling in the creature's long throat as her former captor slid from its upraised jaws toward its monstrously misshapen body.

Something grabbed her from behind. . . .

✧ **8** ✧

As FLESHRIPPER LIFTED THE HEAD AND FOREQUARTERS OF the dangling food beast, turning them upright for closer inspection, Deathstalker, with a final, satisfying ripple of belly muscles, finished swallowing the creature Running Bird, then turned to examine the human hanging head-down from a branch.

What, it wondered, had been intended? Humans, gro-tesquely, liked to char their food before they ate it, and all Deathstalker could imagine was that the three males had been in the process of cooking the female before eating it.

Deathstalker had walked many worlds, had hunted and devoured numerous food beasts, some of them of fairly impressive intelligence and native cunning. It knew of species that devoured their own kind, some ritually, some in warfare, others to control their own numbers. There were some that ate their own young to cull the weak from the strong, and some so blood-lusting, hungry, and stupid they ate whatever was within reach.

From the Kra'agh perspective, few things were as re-pulsive. The thought that humans were cannibalistic served to knock them down several points in Death-stalker's opinion of them. Not only were they stupid, they wallowed in foul eating habits as well.

Deathstalker moved close, staring into the human's op-tic organs. It was still alive, though trembling violently with shock and ill usage. It stared back at Deathstalker, the spirit behind the gaze mingling deep pain and fear with . . . something else. Defiance? Or simple acquies-

cence, a willingness to surrender to the fate allotted the weak overcome by the strong?

Deathstalker was about to reach for its patternmaker. The creature was enjoying great pain, and the Hunter wanted to sample it.

But then the creature gurgled behind the hide strip covering its food-and-speech orifice, struggled a bit, then slumped in Fleshripper's grasp. Deathstalker reached out with one feeder hand and pried open the covering of one optic organ. The creature was unconscious.

Deathstalker had witnessed this behavior in other humans. In times of extreme stress or terrible pain, they actually lost consciousness . . . one of the most contrasurvival traits Deathstalker had ever witnessed in any prey species. Comatose, they were no fun at all . . . presenting no challenge, and no spicy taste of fear or pain to the bland struggles of their minds.

No matter. Deathstalker had eaten well already, and there was work to do. One more human, more or less, scarcely mattered, and there would be others to savor, and soon. Besides, the life force in this one was weak, lost in a long and losing struggle against its bonds, its captors, and its pain. Humans did not appear to understand how to enjoy pain as a means of embracing life. They fought it, and in fighting, weakened and died, or else escaped in the oblivion of unconsciousness. This one, Deathstalker could tell simply by looking at it, was already deep in shock, and would not survive much longer.

"Leave it," it told Fleshripper. "It will soon be dead."

Besides, Deathstalker was already eagerly anticipating the taste of Macklin's fear, pain, and flesh. . . .

✧ 9 ✧

TZE-GO-JUNI HAD TREMBLED VIOLENTLY AS ONE OF THE creatures lifted her head and shoulders with one cold, clawed, withered-branch of a hand. It twisted her up and up until her head was almost upright again. One of the other monsters had approached, and she found herself staring into bottomless, cat-slit eyes of bronze, gold, and obsidian black. She felt the brutal impact of the thing's gaze, felt its cunning, its cold intelligence. She tried to scream, but the thing seemed to drink her will and her strength, and she felt herself tumbling into darkness.

She awakened some time later. She was still hanging head-down, but the fire had dwindled to a patch of hot coals, the rising heat uncomfortable, but no longer searing her flesh. She could hear Jiminez still making wet, whimpering sounds at the base of the tree, but couldn't see him.

There was no sign at all of the monsters.

What, within the broad and loving reach of Usen, Earth Mother, *were* those horrible things? The Apache universe was filled with endless arrays of spirits, gods, and demons, but she knew of none matching the hideous shapes she'd just seen. For a time, she wondered if perhaps the burning was continuing, that her brain had manufactured nightmare images born of flame and torture, that she was going mad and seeing phantoms of her own agony-twisted brain.

But . . . no. The night around her was quiet now, and very real. She still felt the pain of her burns, the bite of the rawhide around her ankles as it held her weight, still smelled the rich cottonwood smoke and felt the rising heat of the embers, still heard Jiminez mewling as he died and the throbbing of her heartbeat in her ears. This was real.

The monsters had been real.

Somewhere in the darkness, an owl called. She struggled against the blackness that threatened yet again to close around her . . . desperately trying to hold the night at bay.

In the end, she failed, and her pain was swallowed once more in unconsciousness.

✧ **10** ✧

MACKLIN AND CISSY KEPT RIDING UP INTO THE WHET-stones despite the fall of night. At first, they'd just been trying to put distance between themselves and any possible pursuit, but after a while, Macklin continued pushing in the hope of finding one of the Apaches from Na-a-cha's band. His guide had said they would be watching for him. Where were they?

They'd been riding for nearly two hours over increasingly difficult ground when Macklin had heard something, far off . . . a scream, he thought. He reined in his chestnut and raised his hand, ordering a halt. A gunshot sounded, the muffled report echoing off the surrounding cliffs. It sounded like it had come from . . . *that* direction. From the south.

He spurred his mount ahead again, trying to move more quickly now, even though there was a danger that his horse could step in a hole in the darkness and break a leg. Screams and gunshots in the night. He didn't know what was gong on, but he had to get there, and quickly.

Before long, the screams had died away, but the riders had been led this far to a broad, flat gully descending the western flank of East Peak, and it seemed to be leading them straight toward the estimated source of the sounds. They kept moving.

The landscape lit up around them. Cissy gasped, and Macklin's horse shied and whinnied. Macklin felt his heart beating faster as he looked up at an incredibly brilliant star hanging in the sky above the mountains ahead, brighter than any star he'd seen. And . . . it was moving, drifting against the starry backdrop, descending gently toward the black, skyward thrust of Apache Peak.

The light seemed to melt into the mountainside, and vanish.

Kra'agh. Macklin was certain of it. The alien base must

be well up toward the top of Apache Peak itself.

The light's proximity to the screams and shots could not be coincidence.

Ten minutes farther on, Macklin reined up again. There was a faint, reddish glow coming from just ahead. It looked like a campfire. Dismounting, he handed the reins to Cissy and signed to her to stay put. Pulling one of the Winchesters from its saddle holster, he checked to make sure it was loaded, then started cautiously forward.

The campsite was a scene of horror.

One of the books in Sarah Nevers' library, by a man named Dante Alighieri, had described a mythical Hell composed of seven circles, each more horrible than the last. Nowhere in that book had a Hell like this one been described.

Blood was everywhere, soaking the ground, black by the red firelight. One Apache lay face down, his back horribly burned, revealing a hole punched through ribs and spine deep into his body. Another lay by the tree, broken-bodied, gut-slashed, his intestines spilled on the ground. Both were quite dead.

And above the glowing embers of a dead fire, a young woman had been hung up by her heels, naked, her hands tied at her back, her hair and face terribly burned. She appeared to be dead . . . but when he touched a fingertip to the angle of her jaw, he felt the fluttering throb of a pulse.

He heard a gasp at his back. Cissy had disobeyed orders and approached the fire, and stood there now, white-faced at the sight and smell of the slaughterhouse gore. "Quickly," he said. "Help me. She's still alive."

He kicked the embers out from beneath her head, then raised her head and shoulders, taking the weight off her ankles. Cissy reached high with her knife and, with a couple of slashes, cut through the rope, dropping the woman into Macklin's arms.

They laid the woman down on a blanket, and covered her with her buckskin skirt, which Cissy found in a heap nearby. Macklin cut the rawhide strip around her head and pulled off the gag, cut the thongs on her wrists and ankles, then took one of the canteens and poured splashes of water over her face. As the smoke-blacking washed away, his eyes widened. "I know her!" he exclaimed.

"Who is she?"

"Her name . . ." He searched for the name. He'd heard it once, at the Apache camp. Yes! Intuition welling up from the intelligent machine within him provided a fragment of memory . . . and a translation. "Her name is Tzego-juni. It means 'Pretty Mouth,' I think. She took care of me in the Apache camp, when they had me prisoner. I think she's related to Na-a-cha, the old *diyi* of the local band."

"Why would they do something like that to one of their own people?" Cissy asked, eyes wide. "I mean, I've heard stories about Apaches torturing white men . . . and women. But never their own kind!"

Macklin glanced past her, at the savaged corpse lying beneath the tree on which she'd been hung. He was pretty sure he'd seen that one, too, the Apache with the blue cavalryman's tunic, back in the rock shelter as well. He'd been one of the angry ones . . . one of the men who'd stormed out with Black Wind after Na-a-cha had given Macklin his new name.

The blue tunic had been ripped wide open, along with the man's lower torso. Somehow, that didn't look like the work of other Apaches.

And the other one, lying dead with a charred hole in his back. The Apaches had no weapons capable of doing *that*.

"It might not have been the Apaches," he said. "Those other two were killed by the Hunters, creatures like the one you saw in the forest."

Cissy seemed to be making an effort to keep her voice from shaking. "You . . . you really weren't just telling a tall one, were you? When you talked about those Hunters from the stars."

"No. I wish I had been. But they're real, and they're terribly dangerous."

And, he thought to himself, *they're here*.

"What do they want?"

He sighed. "I'm not entirely sure." Dorree had told him a little about the Kra'agh, but not enough. Not enough by far. "I think they want us for food, but it's more than that. A person who told me about them, once, said they want to turn all of Earth into a kind of game preserve. They really are hunters . . . but it's more than just food they're after. Our fear, maybe. Our pain. Our . . . our *despair*. I don't know them well enough to say, or know what they get out of it."

"I've got some ointment in a bag," Cissy said. "Brought it along for sunburn, if we were going to be out in the desert. But I guess it'll work on her burns just as well."

"What's in it?"

"Just some turpentine, sweet oil, and beeswax. It's what's recommended for burns."

Macklin had less than complete confidence in the medical practices and understanding of the people of this world. Though he could remember nothing about his former life, or the medical technology he might have been exposed to there, the Companion embedded in his chest suggested that that technology was formidable indeed. Some of the medical knowledge, so-called, of the inhabitants of the Arizona Territory ranged from laughable to outright deadly.

But oil and wax would at least help keep Tze-go-juni's burns from drying out, and might help prevent infection. Simply as an emollient, it sounded as though it would do less harm than good.

"Okay. Get it."

"Wish I had some laudanum. She's going to need it when she wakes up."

Cissy returned to her horse and fished around in the saddlebag for a moment, returning with small tin. "Ain't much in here, I'm afraid."

"It'll have to do."

He held the woman as Cissy smeared some of the ointment on the worst of the blisters on her scalp, forehead, ears, and shoulders. She stirred during the ministrations, moaning slightly. Macklin touched the side of her face, avoiding the angry blisters. Her skin was clammy, as cold as a fish and slightly moist. Some inner, unbidden part of Macklin recognized the condition as traumatic shock. It could kill her.

"Drag that log over here," he told Cissy. "And see if you can find some more clothing or blankets or anything. We've got to keep her warm."

"They was just burning her over a slow fire, and she needs to be kept warm?"

"Just do it!"

There was pathetically little he could do to help the woman, save treat her for shock. He thought that if she could wake up enough to be given something to drink— she was probably terribly dehydrated after her ordeal— she would be okay.

After a time, he left Cissy to stay with her, and walked about the clearing. He used some of the firewood carefully stacked nearby to rekindle the fire, this time for warmth instead of torture. By its light, he was able to make out some odd-looking tracks pressed down in the dirt . . . H-shaped marks unlike the prints of any Earth creature with which Macklin was familiar.

But he'd seen marks like that before, proof positive that Kra'agh had been here.

"John?" Cissy called. "I think she's coming around!"

He reached her side just as she moaned, opened her eyes, then started violently. She screamed a single, sharp, guttural word.

"Easy!" Macklin said. "Take it easy! You're safe now! Tze-go-juni? You're safe!"

Her eyes focused slowly on Macklin's face. She was shaking hard. "Ma-kleen?" Then, with more vigor, "*Itza-chu-klego-na-ay!*"

"Yes. Yes, it's Moon Eagle."

She began speaking rapidly in her dialect of the People's tongue. Macklin found he could pick up a word or a feeling here and there, but she was speaking far too quickly for him to be sure of the message.

He didn't need to speak Apache, however, to know what she was saying. She was terrified. She'd seen something horrible.

And she was afraid they were coming back.

Macklin knew exactly how she felt.

FIFTEEN

◆ **1** ◆

THEY DECIDED TO TRY TO GET TZE-GO-JUNI BACK TO HER camp the next afternoon. After a night of rest, she seemed well enough to sit on horseback; Macklin had her sit astride the chestnut and led her up the mountain paths, with Cissy riding behind. She'd donned her long skirt, but went bare above the waist with a casually practical lack of modesty. The burns on her back and shoulders were simply too painful to cover with her buckskin jacket.

Tze-go-juni spoke very little English, and Macklin's Apache was considerably less than proficient. Both Tze-go-juni and Cissy spoke Spanish, however—a side benefit, as Cissy explained it, of her line of work—and their conversations that morning had been three-way roundtable affairs, with ideas communicated in a bizarre mix of all three languages.

The Indian woman had managed to convey, in this way, that it had been other Apaches, a faction following the one named Black Wind, who'd abducted her and tried to burn her as a witch. Macklin wasn't sure he followed her reasoning, but it sounded as though she was convinced that the attack had been politically motivated . . . and somehow directed against her uncle, the band's medicine man. The upside-down burning, she explained, was the People's traditional means of dealing with evil witches.

That news was unsettling, because it meant the strife within the Apache band had escalated a level or two . . . and raised the possibility of an Apache attack on the way to the shelter.

Worse, though, was her broken, at times incoherent description of the Kra'agh attack. "*Posiblemente*," she said in Spanish, translated by Cissy, "*soy una bruja maligna en verdad*."

"Perhaps I really am an evil witch."

Macklin had trouble following her narrative; she seemed to think that she was responsible for summoning the creatures. According to Tze-go-juni, she had been praying to the night, and the night had given her three monsters which had utterly destroyed her tormenters.

"But they just left you there," Macklin protested. "They killed the others, and they left you hanging over the fire!"

"The . . . the things I summoned," she replied, "were evil incarnate."

Maligna encarnada, she'd called them. A good enough description, Macklin thought, for beings determined to drive humankind to extinction.

An interesting parallel, too. The Anglos had been systematically slaughtering vast herds of creatures called buffalo on this continent; Buffalo Bill Cody had won his nickname by leading such hunts. There were military men who advocated slaughtering all of the buffalo, as a means of controlling the Indians, who depended on them for food and much else.

Perhaps the Anglos were just another kind of Hunter. . . .

They had traveled for less than an hour toward the center of the Whetstones, when Tze-go-juni had swayed in the saddle and almost fallen. Macklin called a halt. The Apache woman was still desperately weak, and as the day grew hotter, the sun's heat seemed to leach what little strength remained in her abused and blistered body.

Macklin found a small rock shelter, an overhanging boulder casting a deep pool of shade beneath it, with plenty of rocks and trees all about to shield them from unfriendly eyes. He left Cissy to watch the Indian woman while he went out, scouting for Apaches, for water, for any sign of pursuit, for any sign of the monsters.

He saw a very strange-looking bird circling above Apache Peak, but nothing more.

Toward evening, as it grew cooler, Tze-go-juni appeared to be recovering. The last of Cissy's ointment was gone, but Tze-go-juni made a poultice for herself from certain leaves, which she carefully described so that Macklin could gather some, mashed up with water and the yellow powder she called *hoddentin*, and carried in a small buckskin bag which had been with her clothing. This dubious-looking yellow concoction was daubed on the worst of her blisters, and she seemed stronger after that. Food helped, also. Cissy had brought along some jerky from the mining camp, and Tze-go-juni ate several strips ravenously.

"We *must* reach the main camp within a few hours after sunset," she told them. "Black Wind wanted both me and my uncle out of the way. I think he means to use the Sunrise Ceremony to win power over the entire band."

"Sunrise Ceremony?" Macklin asked. He found that listening to Tze-go-juni's Spanish and Cissy's translations was rapidly feeding him Spanish of his own. His inner Companion apparently did serve as a ready conduit for new languages, given time and patience. "What's that?"

Tze-go-juni closed her eyes. "When a girl of the band reaches the age of womanhood, a special ceremony is held in her honor. The mountain *gan* descend from the heights and dance with her. It is the rite of Changing Woman, our most important hero. The entire band attends, and usually it is the *diyi*, the medicine man, who leads. If Black Wind wishes to become the band's medicine man, this would be the night to assert his power. My uncle loves me very much, and would be heartbroken to hear I had been killed as a witch. Black Wind would use his weakness to take power."

Macklin wasn't sure he followed the ins and outs of Apache-band politics, but he recognized Tze-go-juni's desperate, almost pleading, need to get back to her people quickly. He was pretty sure she was planning some sort of confrontation with Black Wind, whom she called *el brujo malo*, "the evil sorcerer."

Mountain *gan*. Na-a-cha had described those to Macklin . . . the men of the band dressed in elaborate head-dresses intended to represent the spirits who watched over the Apache peoples. Interesting. Tze-go-juni did not appear to be identifying the Kra'agh she'd seen with the *gan* of her people's religion, as Na-a-cha had. Perhaps when confronted by strangeness, people only saw what they wanted to see . . . or what they were most comfortable with.

"These spirits you saw are evil," he told her. "Only they're not spirits. They're flesh and blood. They can be hurt, and they can be killed. I know this, because I've fought them before."

Tze-go-juni's eyes widened at that. "But the mountain *gan*—"

"They are not *gan*. They go on four legs, not two. They are here to destroy all men. All *people* . . . yours, the N'de. And mine, the white eyes. And we must stop them."

Her look was cold, and he wondered if she thought he was trying to trick her into some sort of blasphemy against her gods. "Why us?"

"Because we're all there are. We're here. We know what they are and what they're trying to do. And nobody else does."

"I do not believe this," she said. "I *cannot* believe this. I prayed, they came. They are my night powers . . . even if they are evil."

Macklin thought a moment. "Tze-go-juni? Are you really evil? Did you try to destroy your people by calling the white eyes to the camp two days ago?"

She hesitated. "I . . . I did not call the white eyes."

"And yet they came. They destroyed that camp, and killed several of your people."

"Yes . . ."

"Are the white eyes evil?"

"Yes!" Then she blinked, looking at him. "Well . . . perhaps I do not know all white eyes that well."

"I am a white eyes. I am not evil. Do you believe this?"

It took her a few seconds to reply. "I . . . believe."

"Some white eyes are evil. The ones who attacked your camp. Some are good, like me, or like Cissy, here. Are all of the N'de good?"

"No," she said, and the word was low, a growl. Then she sighed. "I know what you are doing, Moon Eagle. And I know you are right. Some men are good, some are bad, and it doesn't really matter what band or group or race they belong to."

"Exactly right. And . . . can you believe that not all of the spirits' powers are good?"

"I *know* that is true."

"The *gan* who came last night. I don't think they came in response to your prayer. I think they just . . . came. Maybe they saw the fire and were curious. Maybe they were just hunting for information . . . or food.

"Now, I don't know about the N'de, how you do it, but I know good white eyes and I know some bad ones, and when the bad ones pretend to be good, the only way

I can sort them out is to wait and see how they act. True?"

"*Es verdad,*" she replied. "It is truth."

"If those monsters had taken you down, maybe tried to heal your burns, I'd be willing to admit that they were the good guys. Since they didn't, I have to assume they are *malo. Maligno mucho.*"

"*Si,*" she said after another long pause. "*Creo que si. Es la verdad.*"

"And you didn't summon them. They've been here for a long time, and they do what they want to. They don't obey people. They eat them. So stop thinking that they are your fault."

But she didn't answer that, and Macklin wondered if he was going to have as much trouble convincing the rest of her people.

Especially when some of them, at least, were not going to be all that pleased to see her alive . . . or him.

❖ 2 ❖

NA-A-CHA SAT TO THE SIDE, AMONG THE CLOSE-CROWDED spectators, watching as the Sunrise Ceremony began. A huge bonfire had been started in the center of a clearing below the rock shelter, and nearly everyone within the Chokonen band—everyone save a few guards posted around the camp for obvious reasons, and the *gan* dancers themselves—had gathered in a circle about the clearing.

This evening was only the preparation for the main ceremony, which would begin with the rising sun tomorrow. Rain Blossom had been closeted since sundown with her sponsor, Bright Pebble, who was Klah-ni-a-chi's sixty-four-year-old mother. During this time, her sponsor would have been telling her the story of Changing Woman and all about life, with advice on how to be happy, how to keep from being depressed or ground down by hardship. Most especially, Bright Pebble would have bestowed

upon her the thirty-two lightnings, powers that would sur-
round and protect her always.

Also at this time, the medicine men of the band would
visit her, each with a special skill or knowledge to impart
. . . knowledge of proper food, of the heart and soul, of
the body, of herbs.

And the head medicine man, meanwhile, would be preparing to be the ceremony's singer.

Na-a-cha had expected to sing Rain Blossom's Sunrise
Ceremony. The pain burned in his throat, and behind his
breastbone. *Poor Pretty Mouth! She was counting on me,
and I failed her . . . !*

He should have sent her away as soon as the rumors
and charges of evil witchcraft first surfaced. She'd been
a target . . . no, she'd been a rifle, conveniently aimed at
Na-a-cha's heart, and needing only one of the *diyi*'s enemies in the band to grasp the weapon and pull the trigger.

There was still hope. Black Wind's men had not returned today with news that his sister's daughter was
dead. Still . . . how could it be otherwise? Maria had told
everyone in the camp of how Black Wind's men had captured Tze-go-juni when they'd gone down to the arroyo
yesterday for chokeberry root.

And Black Wind had not denied it . . . though he'd not
accepted responsibility, either. "Your niece has brought
misfortune on the band, Na-a-cha," he said bluntly, and
with just a hint of a malevolent smile. "Can you blame
them if some here wanted to deal with her as tradition
demands?" Later, he'd appealed to the entire camp, pointing out that the spirits were displeased that Tze-go-juni
had been working bad medicine, and telling them how
he'd seen an owl perch upon her wickiup.

Shoz-pesh himself, *nantan* of the Chokonen band, had
asked Na-a-cha to step down as singer for Rain Blossom's
ceremony. Tze-go-juni's crime tainted all associated with
her. The Sunrise Ceremony was the most important of all

Apache rituals, and the leading singer had to be pure and without fault.

Na-a-cha had agreed. He had to, or else face the entire band and prove his niece's innocence. Besides, he knew that he was not without fault. His hatred for Black Wind was so great he could think of nothing else. If he tried to sing for Rain Blossom, he would offend the powers, and worse still would befall them all.

Of course, Black Wind had stepped in as singer, and was using his role to solidify his position as chief *diyi* of the band. Na-a-cha was helpless . . . and he feared for the future. Once Black Wind was confirmed as chief medicine man, he would almost certainly try to have Na-a-cha forced out of the band . . . or killed. He couldn't afford to have powerful enemies within the group, especially one hungering for revenge.

Na-a-cha wished that he were just thirty summers younger. . . .

While he'd been sitting on a log thinking dark thoughts, the drummers had been beating out a hypnotic rhythm, and singers had been chanting little-girl lullabies. Now, however, the singing and drumming accelerated, and expectancy swept through the throng of waiting Chokonen.

Then the drums fell silent, and with all the rest of the watching band, Na-a-cha turned and looked off into the darkness. He could hear the approach of the *gan* dancers now, the soft, singing click of the bits of wood dangling from their *iche-te*, their ceremonial headdresses.

The *gan* dancers impersonated the mountain *gan*, stood in for the mountain folk in most Chokonen ceremonies. There were four of them, entering the fire-lit clearing in a line, and followed by a fifth dancer covered in white powder—the clown.

The dancers representing the great mountain *gan* had been preparing for this for hours, out beyond the circle of the camp. Carefully painted by shamans or one another, all had to observe strict rules of behavior; any breach of the rules would be received by the powers as an insult, which might threaten the ceremony, or even the participants themselves. Each was individually painted, in patterns of black, white, brown, and yellow. They wore knee-high moccasins on their feet, and broad buckskin skirts held in place by belts decorated with brass tacks and silver conchos. Each carried two wands, pointed and two feet long, with blue lightning symbols painted along their lengths.

Most startling, though, were their *iche-te*. Their heads were completely covered in blackened buckskin hoods, with only tiny slits for their eyes and mouths. Pieces of abalone shell were attached to their foreheads, bouncing with their movements. The abalone was an incredibly tough and durable shell, and the decorations were intended to give endurance to the dancers.

Attached to the tops of their heads were the spreading horns of the costume, like antlers, extending straight out to the sides, then jutting straight up, with small, triangular points sticking out along the edges. Made from pieces of oak soaked in water, split, heated, and shaped, they were painted black, yellow, and green. Red was used only if the dancer was a witch. Turkey feathers attached in bunches symbolized the union of the *gan* impersonators with the true *gan* of the mountains.

The four entered the clearing and began dancing with slow, rhythmic motions, bending alternately far forward and far back, until their torsos were level with the ground. As they danced, they gestured with their wands in all directions, cleansing the sacred space. The clown, meanwhile, danced as well, but separately, sometimes threatening and chasing children among the watchers with mock attacks that sent them screaming with more delight than fear. Other times, he would make rude gestures, or lie on the ground and kick; his role in the ceremony was to remind the onlookers that, sometimes, humans do foolish things, even in the middle of solemn ritual. He wore nothing but moccasins, a breechcloth, and a black rawhide mask shaped to give him a long nose. He was a figure of fun, but in many ways he was the most powerful, the most dangerous of all the dancers, for he carried messages from the true *gan*, and served as a focus of their power.

Though *gan* dancers were a central part of many Apache ceremonies and dances, their appearance the night before the Sunrise Ceremony was mostly for entertainment. While the sacred ground did have to be ritually cleansed, the fact was that everyone loved watching the *gan* dancers, and the performers themselves took every opportunity they could to step into character.

As Na-a-cha watched the dancers, he thought again of their origins. In the days when the world was young, it was said, Giver-of-Life had brought the Apache up from the bowels of the Earth and set them in this country, where they were to conduct themselves properly, in harmony with nature, and caring for all living things. Sadly, though, the people had given in to temptation. Coyote had brought evil; as it was said, no bad thing was ever done except that Coyote did it first. The men of that distant time became corrupt.

And so Giver-of-Life had sent the *gan* as his emissaries, to discipline the wayward People, to teach them to live decently and to cure the sick, to govern fairly, to teach them how to plant and harvest, and how to discipline those who failed to please Giver-of-Life. The *gan* had terrible power, power to help or to hurt the People. Though at first the People, awed by the mighty *gan*, had lived better lives, soon they had weakened and again fallen to temptation.

And so the *gan* decided to abandon the unhappy People, and leave them to their fate. They were good spirits, however, and wished to hold out some help. They left pictures of themselves on the rocks outside certain caves, and on the inside walls of the caves as well. Then they vanished into the depths of the Earth, returning to the sacred mountains where the sun shone always, even when greed and envy and bitterness in the world below brought darkness upon the land.

The Apache, bitterly sorrowful with the *gan* departure, studied the drawings carefully and, in time, learned to copy the designs in the headdresses and garments of the dancers. The dances connected them with the true *gan*, and channcled powcr from the sacred mountains. In this way, the people could again live as Giver-of-Life had intended.

And so the traditions and the rituals and the dances had been passed down from generation to generation, ever since the far-off Time When the World was Young.

The drumming, the chanting by different singers, was increasing in tempo once again. At the preordained time, the *gan* dancers withdrew to the side, and the clearing, now spiritually cleansed, was silent again.

And then, the hanging cloth at the entrance to Rain Blossom's preparation wickiup was thrown back, and the girl stepped out into the camp's central clearing.

Rain Blossom, Na-u-kuzze's daughter, stood for a moment at the edge of the clearing, at once a small and hesitating child . . . and powerful, at least in promise. She wore a buckskin skirt which hung to her ankles, and a fringed and richly beaded buckskin shirt of ancient design, just like the one worn in the dawn time by Changing Woman. Around her neck she wore a thong with a short drinking tube and a pointed scratching stick, both painted yellow. Tribal lore held that if in the next three days she drank water without using the tube, her fingernails would grow long and bend back, distorted . . . while if she scratched herself in that period without using the stick, she would grow whiskers like a man.

A small eagle's-down feather adorned each of her shoulders, and another hung from her hair at the back of her head. The shoulder feathers would enable her to walk, dance, and run throughout the long ceremony to come and not grow tired. The feather on her head was her guide, and would be with her for the rest of her life . . . even after the physical feather was removed. On her forehead, dangling just above her eyes from her forelocks, was a small, circular bit of shiny abalone shell, concave side out.

In her right hand, Rain Blossom held the *keshe ya ha* . . . the hook-stick cane Na-a-cha had prepared for her the day before. It had been painted with yellow mud from a sacred riverbank site, and decorated with four ribbons, black, blue, yellow, and white, symbolizing the cardinal directions. No matter where she went after her dance was complete, some of those colors would be present, meaning that there would be someone to hear her, to watch over her, to guard her. Two golden eagle feathers were attached upright to the top of the stick, one with a white stone bead attached to its base, the other with a bit of turquoise. The feathers and beads would protect the girl against any hostile spirit-power, especially against power-induced sicknesses. Oriole feathers were tied between the eagle feathers; the oriole was a happy bird that minded its own business and was well-behaved, and the feathers would guarantee a pleasant disposition in the girl.

The gift of the *keshe ya ha* bestowed both protection and long life on the girl, and on everyone who witnessed her dance. She would carry it throughout the dance and, years from now, when she was old and bent, Rain Blossom would use the stick as a cane to support herself when she walked. There was a tremendous magic here within that one stripped and decorated branch, the magic of the maiden, becoming grown woman, and one day becoming crone.

Rain Blossom began dancing, as the lead singer sang of new beginnings and purity, of the great hero-goddess White Painted Woman, of power, and the sun.

I come to White Painted Woman,
By means of long life I come to her.
I come to her by means of her blessing,
I come to her by means of her good fortune,
I come to her by means of all her different fruits.
By means of the long life she bestows, I come to
    her.
By means of this holy truth she goes about.

I am about to sing this song of yours,
The song of long life.
Sun, I stand here on the earth with your song.
Moon, I have come with your song.

White Painted Woman's power emerges,
Her power for sleep.
White Painted Woman carries this girl;
She carries her through long life,
She carries her to good fortune,
She carries her to old age,
She bears her to peaceful sleep.

You have started out on the good earth;
You have started out with good moccasins;
With moccasin strings of the rainbow, you have
    started out.
With moccasin strings of the sun rays, you have
    started out.
In the midst of plenty you have started out.

Others danced with her, including very young children who watched her hand gestures with intense concentration. And attempted to copy them. During the dance, Rain Blossom's new name was *Saan Nabidegishe*, meaning "Old Woman Makes Gestures With Hands." The gestures helped mark her transition from a girl to a marriageable young woman.

Black Wind led the dance. As chief medicine man, as the chief shaman and singer for the rite, he wore no special costume, but he was in his glory nonetheless, smiling as he guided the line of dancers about the fire.

There would be no stopping him now.

And then, a scream sliced through the thump of drums and the singers' voices; shrill and etched in agony. All sound, all movement, stopped—a shocking blasphemy—as dancers and spectators alike stared into the night. The scream sounded again . . . long, dragging out into an agonized gurgle . . . and then silence.

The dance forgotten, the spectators began talking with one another. Some jumped to their feet, reaching for guns. "The white eyes!" one cried, and then they were all in motion, racing for their weapons. Rain Blossom stood in the center of the clearing, her large eyes dark with dismay as her ceremony, so long anticipated, dissolved in tatters about her.

Na-a-cha was too old to fight, and had no weapon except for his knife, so he rose and walked toward Rain Blossom, holding out an arm to comfort her. With so many people running this way and that, in all the confusion there was a danger that she would be trampled.

And then . . . and then Horror materialized out of the night . . . black shadows forming, shifting, and coalescing into firm yet somehow incomprehensible shapes.

Na-a-cha took an unsteady step backward as he stared once more at the being he'd first seen five moons before. So often in the days since, he'd wondered if the encounter had in fact been a dream, a meeting of spirit within the material world.

He saw the monster again, and knew that it was as real and as solid as himself, knew too as he stared into black-slitted gold-bronze eyes that this was a being both of high intelligence and terrible malevolence.

There were three of the things closing in on the clearing from three directions. Stands-Up-Tall raised his old Sharps carbine, and a blue-white lightning bolt from one of the beings burned him down. Another of the beasts swung one of its powerfully muscled forearms, an arm with a glistening black sickle of a claw, and slashed down a man and a woman who were trying to flee from its path.

Rain Blossom screamed; the nearest of the monsters was coming directly toward her.

"Get behind me!" Na-a-cha said. Somehow, he kept his voice firm as he invoked his own Powers. "Run! Swiftly, girl, run!"

But Rain Blossom was frozen fast, and the three beings were closing in from all sides. Another warrior died, shrieking in terror, pain, and despair, his back laid open from neck to buttocks. *Kliz-litzogue*, Yellow Snake, the lead *gan* dancer, confronted one of the weird beings, himself passing weird in costume and swaying *iche-te* head-dress and armed only with his two-foot lightning wands. The being confronting him paused only an instant, then cut him down with a vicious, clawed slash that left Yellow Snake shrieking in the dust.

Na-a-cha stepped forward. His left hand closed on the small pouch he wore around his neck, within which was a *gan* of another type, a small piece of carved wood called a *tzi-daltai*, painted with signs of his Powers and incised with images of lightning. He raised his right arm, palm out. "Halt, spirit!" he cried. Once before, he had faced one of these horrors, and it had turned away from him. Perhaps he had the power to—

The creature swung its forearm, striking Na-a-cha in the chest. Fortunately, the claw no more than scratched him, tearing his shirt and snapping the hide thong holding his *tzi-daltai*, but the strength of the blow lifted him from his feet and slammed him onto his back several yards away. Rain Blossom shrieked and kicked in her long skirt as the thing grabbed her and lifted her high above its immense rattlesnake's head.

"People!" the being called, in the N'de tongue. The voice was thick and liquid, almost gurgling and deeper than any human voice Na-a-cha had heard, but it was intelligible. "We will take this one to our place of safety on the mountain. You will bring to us at the place with the needle rock the human called Macklin, the one you have named Moon Eagle. Bring it alive and unarmed. Do this within three risings of the sun. If you do not, this one will die very, very slowly, and then its spirit and its body will be devoured. If you want it back, still alive and uneaten, give us Macklin!"

And then the monsters were fading back into the shadows, as the people wailed in fear and dismay.

And Na-a-cha slowly rose in the center of the clearing, fists clenched, tears streaming down his cheeks. Rain Blossom's *keshe ya ha* lay on the ground where she'd dropped it, and he picked it up. Its powers had done nothing to protect her.

He felt as though his gods, his very reason for staying alive, had just deserted him, becoming his sworn enemies.

His world was turned upside down, and he didn't know what to do next.

SIXTEEN

THEY SEEMED TO MATERIALIZE OUT OF THE NIGHT LIKE ghosts—grim, hard-faced Apache men who leaped from rocks and hiding places along the trail as silently as shadows. Macklin was on foot, leading Tze-go-juni astride his chestnut, when an Apache warrior, his lank black hair secured under a dirty bandanna, seemed to rise up out of the ground and knocked him down with a vicious swing of a rifle butt. Cissy screamed as three warriors grabbed her horse and dragged her down in a struggling flurry of kicking legs.

"No!" Tze-go-juni snapped, her voice a whipcrack in the night. Her upraised hand stopped the warriors reaching for her bridle as effectively as a brandished pistol. "They are friends!"

"Tze-go-juni!" one of the warriors cried. He took a step back. "You live . . . !"

"I live. These people saved me. Take us to the camp!"

"The camp has been . . . attacked." Macklin heard the fear in the man's voice, saw it, a glimmer only, in his eyes.

"My mother!" she said. "My uncle . . ."

"They are well. But four of our people were killed, and

others hurt." He hesitated. "And Rain Blossom was taken." He gave Macklin a hard look. "The monsters stole Rain Blossom!"

"Who did this?" Tze-go-juni asked. "The white eyes?"

"Devil-spirits." The man's control slipped, ever so slightly, and Macklin saw depths of horror reflected in those eyes. "Powerful, angry *gan*. I . . . I don't know what they were. But they demand *this* one in exchange for Rain Blossom."

Macklin felt hard hands grasping his arms and shoulders. He considered making a break for the shadowed underbrush, but knew it would be futile. There were at least eight well-armed Apache warriors surrounding them, and likely more hidden in the night round about.

Someone pulled the pistol from Macklin's holster. "We go. Now!"

They were led up a sharply switchbacking set of hillside trails, arriving at last at the encampment at the rock shelter. The place, Macklin thought, had all the frenzied emotion of an overturned beehive. A large bonfire in the center of the camp had mostly burned down, but still glowed enough to illuminate the camp. Macklin and Cissy were taken immediately to see the chief, an old man with a face deeply furrowed and cracked by age, care, and disease. The chief's name, Tze-go-juni told Macklin, was Shoz-pesh, Iron Bear. He'd been a powerful war leader in the time of Vittorio, a man to be honored and feared.

And then she saw Na-a-cha, his face lighting up, his arms open wide as Tze-go-juni ran to him with a glad cry.

Black Wind was there as well, in a red cloth shirt and baggy white trousers, holding a rifle and scowling as he watched Na-a-cha's reunion with his niece. She was speaking to him rapidly, gesturing at Macklin.

Black Wind raised the rifle and aimed it at Macklin. "Take him! Tie him!"

"No!" Tse-go-juni replied. She pointed at Black Wind. "That man is the enemy! He had me captured by his people and tried to have me killed, so that he could take over as *diyi* for the band! If any should be given to the devil-spirits, it is he!"

"But it is the white eyes Macklin they demand for the return of Rain Blossom," Black Wind said. "And if you are alive, you must be a witch in league with dark Powers!"

The old chief held up his hand. "Enough! Black Wind! You were leading the Sunrise Ceremony. For such evil to befall the band this night, your leadership must have been corrupt. I am thinking that you wanted the power that leadership would bestow too much."

Iron Bear spoke in Apache. A young man stood beside the chief, translating into English, but it was hard for him to keep up with Iron Bear's rapid barrage of guttural words.

Macklin, though, found he could understand a great deal of it, enough to get an idea of what was being said, at any rate, with details filled in by the translator. He could sense his own comprehension of the Apache language growing as he listened.

"I am sorry, Black Wind," the chief said, concluding his monologue, "that I let you sing for the ritual! You have brought a great darkness upon the band, and much pain!"

"I did not!" Black Wind shouted. He pointed at Macklin, hand trembling slightly with a barely suppressed rage. "There! The white eyes! *They* are the ones who bring evil to us, to our land, to our children! I have spoken to my own Powers, and they tell me that this is so! All we need to do is give them to the mountain *gan*, and the angry spirits will be satisfied!"

"Black Wind speaks a little too loudly, and with too much emotion," Na-a-cha said quietly. "He speaks like a man trying to prove something to himself, by forcing others to believe first."

"Your sister's daughter has bewitched you, old man! You no longer see clearly! It is time for you to step down! And *she*"—Black Wind pointed at Tze-go-juni—"should be burned as a bad witch!"

Macklin stepped forward. With a single motion, he ripped open the front of his shirt, revealing the ebon, silver-dollar-sized implant in his chest. The mystery of the disk was bound to give him an emotional advantage, and the sight brought an abrupt silence to the gathering.

"Is it permitted that I speak?" he asked, in Apache.

He didn't know how he knew. The words were simply . . . there, welling up from somewhere deep inside, *feeling* right, even though he wasn't sure from word to word what the *next* word would be.

A low-voiced murmur came from the watching crowd, some gasps of surprise, some angry looks, some fearful ones. Cissy stared at his chest with an emotion wavering between fear, surprise, and intense curiosity; she hadn't seen the implant before.

Na-a-cha raised a hand. "He is Moon Eagle, and he is our friend. Listen to him!"

Iron Bear nodded. "Speak, Moon Eagle." He shifted to English. "Speak your own language. I know your words."

"Well, to start with, you'd better just forget right now any idea of burning this woman," he said, switching back to English. It was good not to have to think about whether the words he was speaking were the right ones or not. Iron Bear's English seemed to be pretty good, and an interpreter stood by his side, whispering. "Na-a-cha told me the other evening that I walk between the worlds. That is truer than you people know. I have walked on the moon. I have lived on another world, another Earth, like this one, but so far away that its sun is one of the stars you see in the night sky. Na-a-cha can tell you how he found me, in a kind of ship that had fallen from the sky."

There was a temptation here to rely on the Apaches' superstitions and fears, to portray himself as a spirit or god—a *gan*—that should be listened to because it had great power. He resisted the urge. The Apaches were a primitive people in the technological sense, but they were not stupid. They seemed to have insights into people, relationships, spiritual ideas that the more technically proficient white eyes lacked or ignored. He told them he was from another world only to establish his spiritual credentials, as it were, then moved on.

"Despite this, I am a man, not a *gan*. I can be hurt, and I can be killed.

"These devil-spirits, strange as they look, are people, too, just like you. Just like me. Like me, they come from the stars. They are extremely powerful. Their weapons, their tools, are far better than anything you or the white eyes have. But they can be hurt and killed.

"These devil-spirits you've seen are enemies of mine. I can tell you from personal experience that they are evil . . . not just for my people, but for yours as well. If they succeed at what they are trying to do, humans, *all* humans, N'de and white eyes, will become slaves or food for them, creatures to be hunted down and destroyed the way you might hunt down a deer. You can't deal with beings like that, can't negotiate, can't make friends, because they're not working with the same picture of the world that you are. If they think you're an animal, well, they won't be able to deal with you in any other way. When you hunt deer, do you stop to talk to it, to ask it if it minds be killed, try to reason with it?"

"Yes," Iron Bear said. "We do. At least, we ask Usen, the Life-Giver, for permission to hunt his deer. But . . . I do not think this is what you mean. We are men, not deer."

"To the Kra'agh, which is what they call themselves,

you are deer. Their name for themselves, I'm told, means
Hunters. They consider all other peoples to be game for
their food and sport. They think—"

"No!" Black Wind stepped between Macklin and Iron
Bear, speaking Apache. "This white man lies! If evil and
misfortune have come upon the Chokonen people, it is
because of this white man and others like him, and because of the witch!"

"Black Wind's men tried to kill Tze-go-juni," Macklin
said. "The Kra'agh killed *them*, but they left Tze-go-juni
to die. I promise you, they are no friends of humans.

"As for Black Wind, he is mistaken. Tze-go-juni
brought no misfortune to this camp. The misfortune was
the greed, the bitterness, and the short-sighted ignorance
of the white men. *They* attacked your camp the other day,
not this woman."

"The white man calls me a liar!"

"No. I said you were mistaken, Black Wind."

"We will prove who is the liar here!" Black Wind
turned to face Iron Bear. "I demand to have our words
tested. Either he is right, or I am! We will fight to see
who speaks truly!"

There it was, then. Reason and rationality, apparently,
could only be carried so far. The Chokonen were a warrior
people, and something within Macklin told him that they
would attach great importance to a man's prowess and to
his success or failure as a warrior. If he were to back down
from Black Wind's challenge, he would lose whatever
rapport he'd been able to establish with the band so far.

"Moon Eagle!" Iron Bear said. "Will you fight to prove
your words?"

Macklin looked at Black Wind, measuring him. The
man was bigger than he was, and bulkier, more heavily
muscled. Macklin, on the other hand, had proven to himself on several occasions that he'd been trained, sometime
in his forgotten past, at hand-to-hand fighting techniques

which the humans of this world didn't seem to know.

It was worth the chance.

"I will fight."

The spectators exploded in shouts and catcalls above an undercurrent of murmured, excited conversation. Several braves, meanwhile, began marking off a circle in the clearing about ten yards across.

Tzit-dijin approached Macklin. "You know what th' hell you're doin', mister?"

"I think so. I'll knock him out, and maybe your people will listen to me, then."

"You don't understand, white eyes. This is to th' death." He pulled out a length of rawhide cord. "Gimme your left hand."

"Why?"

"The Chokonen take a right poor view of someone runnin' away."

He tied one end of the thong to Macklin's wrist, the other to Black Wind's left wrist, with perhaps eighteen inches of cord between them.

"You both know th' rules," Tzit-dijin continued, " 'cause there *ain't* no rules." He added something in Apache to Black Wind, who scowled at Macklin.

"I will carve that thing out of your chest, white eyes, and wear it as a talisman!" he snarled in English. "I will make a necklace with your fingers, and offer your skull to the crows to pick clean!"

Tzit-dijin walked away. Five yards to Macklin's right, he drew a knife, a heavy-bladed Bowie, and drove it, point down, into the dirt at the center of the circle. Shoz-pesh raised his hand, the crowd of spectators grew silent, and then the band's *nantan* dropped his arm.

Black Wind's fist came snapping in above their bound arms, as he tugged hard to pull Macklin forward and off-balance. Macklin caught the blow with his own right, tried to recover, and then dropped hard as Black Wind delivered a sweeping roundhouse kick to the back of his left knee. Black Wind dove for the knife, dragging Macklin through the dirt. The spectators yelled, some cheering, others just screaming.

Macklin hung onto the binding rawhide strip with both hands as he tried to slow Black Wind, but the Apache was strong, and he waded forward a step at a time. Macklin tried digging in with the toes of his boots, pulling back hard. Black Wind turned then, and swung his moccasin-clad foot toward Macklin's face.

Rolling to the side, Macklin grabbed the Apache's foot, twisting hard. The big man went down then, falling full length with a thud and a grunt, and rolling as Macklin continued to twist.

Macklin leaped to his feet, moving toward the knife. Black Wind grabbed his leg and pulled, tripping him. For a moment, the two men rolled together in a confusion of blows and flying dust. Black Wind used his greater mass and strength to flip Macklin over, get to his knees, and begin again to drag them both toward the waiting knife, now only a few feet away.

Macklin was at a disadvantage. He might have been trained in hand-to-hand fighting, but those moves and blows all depended on *balance* . . . and on having his hands free. With one hand tied, and with Black Wind tugging him this way and that unpredictably, he was finding it difficult to center himself for an effective blow.

He would have to take the initiative, make Black Wind fight on *his* terms, instead of simply reacting to the Apache's moves. Gathering his knees under himself, Macklin lunged forward and up, crashing into Black Wind's side, driving the Apache over and past the knife. The two men hit the ground in a confused tangle, rolled, then rose again.

Black Wind threw a punch and Macklin ducked and blocked, getting in two quick punches of his own. Then

Black Wind hit him with a face full of dirt, dust, and gravel, slung stingingly hard, and for a critical instant, Macklin was blind.

Macklin staggered back, while Black Wind spun around and dropped full-length on the ground, lunging for the knife with his right hand. When Macklin blinked his vision back, Black Wind had the blade and was coming at him.

Macklin sidestepped as Black Wind's knife hand slashed past him, missing him by inches. His knee came up, colliding savagely with Black Wind's groin. At the same time, his hand dropped to Black Wind's wrist, thumb finding a pressure point and bending the wrist back in one smooth motion until nerveless fingers opened, releasing the blade. Then Macklin kicked Black Wind's knees from behind, dropping him to the ground.

He tried to kick the knife away, but Black Wind simultaneously grabbed his ankle and tugged on the strap, pulling him off balance. As Macklin fell, landing on his back, Black Wind grabbed the knife again and leaped up, the silver blade flashing in the firelight as he raised it high.

Macklin met the charge with a boot planted in Black Wind's stomach; as the Apache's mass kept him lunging forward, Macklin used the man's inertia, picking him up on his boot and sending him sailing over his head.

The strap jerked Black Wind up short as Macklin snapped his left hand back, and the Apache landed face down with a hard, gut-slamming thud. He started to roll over, but Macklin was on top of him an instant later, slamming one booted foot across Black Wind's right wrist, pinning the hand with the knife, and his other knee into Black Wind's throat.

The Apache gasped and struggled. Macklin plucked the Bowie from his hand as the spectators shrieked and whooped. He hesitated, then flipped the knife end-for-end, and slammed the butt of the hilt hard into the side of

Black Wind's skull. Reversing the blade again, he snicked through the rawhide strap with one clean slice, and stood up, towering above the stunned Apache's sprawled body. If Black Wind had committed any crimes against his own people, it was up to them to judge and condemn him, not Macklin. On a more practical level, Black Wind had friends, lots of them, and Macklin didn't want to add them to his list of enemies.

"Does this prove my words are true?" he demanded of Iron Bear.

The old *nantan*'s mouth pursed, then spread in a crooked smile. "No," he said. "It proves you are the better fighter, or the luckier one. And we need both good fighters and lucky ones if the devil-spirits are against us."

"Then you need Black Wind as well." He handed the knife, hilt first, to Tzit-dijin. "I will not kill him."

He thought Na-a-cha looked disappointed at that. Perhaps the medicine man thought that Black Wind would still pose a threat to his niece.

"And what do you intend to do about these Hunters, Moon Eagle?" Iron Bear asked him.

"Find them," Macklin replied. "Attack them. Destroy them if I can." He paused. "Will you help? They are *your* enemies, as well as mine."

Iron Bear frowned. "We will need to talk of this in Council. I believe we can tell you where to find them, however."

That got Macklin's attention. "Yes?"

"There is a place," Na-a-cha said, "partway up the tallest of these mountains, on the western face. It is where the white men dug their first caves in search of the white metal. We have seen the devil-spirits' stars entering and leaving that place."

The lost Bennett Mine.

"The white men might be able to help us," Macklin said, thoughtful. "Especially if you let them have that . . .

cave." He spread his hands. "That cave is why they are here, what they are looking for. They may join us against the Kra'agh, if you let them have the silver."

"The high places are *ours*," Iron Bear said. "They are for us and our *gan*. Not for the white eyes."

"Perhaps," Na-a-cha said, "the events of this night tell us the *gan* have forsaken these mountains after all. Perhaps the only *gan* here are the evil *gan*, these Hunters of Moon Eagle."

"It was you who counseled us to stay in these mountains, Na-a-cha, and not join our people in Mexico."

"Perhaps I was wrong. I thought these *gan* were here to help us." He sighed. "Last summer, Noh-ka-del-klin-ay told us how the dead would return. First, he said the dead would return and help us take back our lands. Then he told us the dead were being held down by the white eyes, that they could not return until the white eyes were driven away. He promised that bullets would not hurt us, if we followed his ceremonics and danced his dances. He told us that he would not be killed . . . and later he told us that if he was killed, he would come back to lead us.

"That was seven moons ago. Noh-ka-del-klin-ay was killed by the white eyes at Cibecue. He has not returned. The dead have not returned. *It was a false vision.*

"I think now that I had a false vision as well. I did not understand what I saw, when I saw the mountain *gan* five moons ago. I did not realize that what I saw . . . was evil.

"I believe what Tze-go-juni has told me. I believe what Moon Eagle says. We must help him in any way that we can to destroy these demons, even if it means helping the white eyes as well. As Moon Eagle says, these Hunters from the stars are enemies of all men. It is necessary for all men to fight them."

"No!"

Everyone turned. Black Wind was on his feet again, though just barely. Fresh blood smeared the side of his head and dripped down his chin, where Macklin had hit him with the knife hilt.

"Be silent, Black Wind," Iron Bear said. "You have no more say here."

"You anger the true *gan*," Na-a-cha added, "by using our ceremonies . . . and our *people*, to create new power for yourself."

"The white eyes are the true enemies!" Black Wind shouted. "We will not ally with them!"

"If what Moon Eagle says is true," Iron Bear said, "then the devil-spirits are a threat to us and the white eyes. We must help the white eyes to help ourselves."

"Some of us will never join the white eyes!" Black Wind leaned forward, wavering a little from side to side as he pointed at Macklin. "This white eyes will make you surrender your souls to the white men! They will keep coming, in greater and greater numbers, until there is no land left anywhere for the People! No game! No mountains! No *gan*! I have seen this in a vision, and it is a true vision!"

"Black Wind," Na-a-cha said. "You must listen—"

"No! I will *not* listen! And neither will the white-eye soldiers, when I am finished! There can be no peace with the whites! There will be no peace with them, ever and ever!" Turning sharply, he stalked out of the circle of firelight. Macklin heard him calling to others, heard the rustle as other men began leaving the crowd sitting in the darkness outside the fire. First in ones and twos, then in larger groups, young men began filtering out from among the spectators.

"Na-a-cha!" Macklin called. "Where are they going?"

The old man seemed to sag a bit. "They are Black Wind's men. His friends. Arivaipa and White Mountain Apache, many of them, driven out by the whites, and bitter toward them. I fear he means to strike the white eyes, and soon."

"We must stop them!"

"How?" Na-a-cha appeared to have aged many years since Macklin had talked with him a few days before. "Would you have Apache fight Apache?"

"That has already happened," a warrior sitting nearby said. Not all of the fighting men, it seemed, had joined Black Wind. "The Anglos use Apache scouts when they hunt us."

"But this would be different."

"How?"

In moments, the entire crowd was arguing. Macklin stepped forward, holding up his hands. "Wait, people. Wait! *Let me speak!*"

The camp fell silent, save for the crackle of the fire.

"Is Black Wind doing what I think he's doing? Is he going to attack the white mining camp?"

"Them . . . or the Anglo soldiers at Fort Huachuca," the warrior said. "One way or another, he will start a war."

"Black Wind is not foolish enough to attack the soldiers at the fort," Iron Bear said. "His force numbers forty, perhaps forty-five. But he could attack the town with that number . . . or the cave nearby where the white eyes dig for silver."

"Which one, do you think?" Macklin asked. It would help a lot if they could guess Black Wind's strategy.

"The town," Na-a-cha said after a moment's thought. "There are more men at the mine than at the town during the day. There is more to be taken from the town, as booty."

"And," Iron Bear added, "with the town burned, the men at the mine will have no place to go. They will have to leave, and Black Wind will have won his battle."

"If Black Wind destroys a white eyes town," another warrior pointed out, "then the white soldiers will never rest until the last of us are tracked down and destroyed."

"We need the soldiers to help, if we can get them," Macklin said. "Where are they?"

"The nearest are at Fort Huachuca," Na-a-cha said. "A four-hour ride south. There are many more at Fort Lowell, near the town they call Tucson, but that is much further away."

"Will Black Wind attack them tonight?"

"No," Iron Bear said. "We do not fight battles at night, unless there is no other choice." He frowned. "Do we really need the soldiers? How many devil-spirits are there?"

"I don't know," Macklin replied. "Even one is terribly powerful and very hard to kill."

"Their weapons throw lightning," someone said.

"Three attacked the camp this evening," Iron Bear said, "to carry off Rain Blossom."

"Three attacked Jiminez and the others who'd captured me," Tze-go-juni said.

"One night, several days ago," Na-a-cha added, "as I was praying for a sign in the hills, I saw three moving stars in the sky, like those we have seen sometimes above this mountain. I believe we are dealing with three Star Hunters."

"That's a good guess,' Macklin said, "though I wouldn't want to put too much faith in it. There could be others we haven't seen. And even if there are only three, I don't know if all of the men of this camp would be enough . . . especially if Black Wind has taken some with him."

"We have *two* problems, then," Na-a-cha said. "We must stop Black Wind, if we can, from attacking the white eyes. And we must assemble as large a force as possible to fight the Hunters and rescue Rain Blossom."

"How can we fight to rescue the girl?" someone in the crowd demanded, speaking Apache. Macklin found he could understand the language now almost perfectly. "The spirit-devils command the lightnings! That alone proves they are powerful *gan*! We *cannot* fight them!"

"I've been thinking about that," Macklin said in English. "It's pretty clear you're going to have to give them what they want."

"John!" Cissy exclaimed.

He shrugged. "No other way. I'm going to have to be bait. But for that to work, we're going to need a real strong force ready to jump on them as soon as Rain Blossom is safe. Otherwise, I become a trophy hanging on their wall."

"These are strange days, indeed," Na-a-cha said, "when N'de join with white eyes to fight spirit-devils from the stars."

"Two problems," Macklin said. "Stopping Black Wind and getting back Rain Blossom. Maybe we can solve them both at once. If we warn the town, and the soldiers at that fort down south . . . perhaps we can get them both to send people here to help us."

"The white eyes would never help us!" one warrior, whose name was Hawk-Takes-Prey, shouted.

"They would," Macklin said quietly, "if you tell them the location of that silver mine they've been hunting for."

There was disagreement about that, some unpleasant grumbling and not a few angry outbursts. Warning the white-eye soldiers of Black Wind's threat was tantamount to fighting Black Wind, worse, to siding with the same Anglos who'd attacked one of their *gowaa* just days ago. Some of Black Wind's warriors were blood relatives of people still in the camp.

And . . . offering the whites of the town the location of the lost silver mine in exchange for their help? The People would lose the mountain that had become sacred to them. Rain Blossom's mother and father feared that they would lose their girl.

Some others feared they would lose their souls, the

spirit that bound them together as a people. They'd promised their *gan* to stay here and serve them. More, they doubted that the Hunters were flesh and blood, as Macklin insisted. Creatures so nightmarish, so outlandishly different from anything known on this world, creatures who killed by throwing *ittendi*, lightning itself, *must* be spirit creatures that could never be killed by mortal weapons.

Some continued to insist that the spirit-devils were the People's mountain *gan*, but angry, unpredictable . . . as nature itself often was. Attacking them, even with an army of white-eye soldiers to help, would be as productive as attacking a sudden lightning storm . . . and far more dangerous.

"Let me ask you this," Macklin said at last, speaking in slow, somewhat halting Apache. He was beginning to trust the flow of words from that hidden part of himself buried behind the amnesiac wall inside. "If the devil-spirits were truly mountain *gan*, if they truly controlled the lightning, why would they resort to kidnapping a child to offer in exchange for me? Wouldn't they be able to find me no matter where I was hiding? Wouldn't they be able to take me or kill me without needing the People's help?"

"It is not right to question the way of *gan*."

"Then the People are slaves, who are not allowed to think for themselves. I pity them!"

"White devil!" someone snapped, and an angry outburst followed. For a moment, Macklin thought he'd gone too far . . . but as the argument raged on, he could sense it turning in his favor. The debate continued, but in the end it was agreed. Everyone in the camp had seen the attacking Hunters, had heard their threats. If these were gods, they were gods of blood and terror . . . not gods any sane people would want to follow.

And those who refused in principle to ask the whites for help were already gone with Black Wind. After several hours of argument, Iron Bear declared that Macklin would go to the town for help.

"They want to arrest me," Macklin pointed out. He'd been thinking that it would be better if he went to Fort Huachuca.

"You will go with Great Bear and Water-on-Rock. Both have some of the Anglo tongue. The fact that you go, knowing the white eyes in the town hate you, will be proof you are sincere. Tell them we will show them where the silver mine they seek lies hidden, if they will send men and guns to help us get Rain Blossom back."

"What about Fort Huachuca?"

Iron Bear looked at Tzit-dijin. "*This* one knows the soldiers' ways—"

"Uh-uh!" Tzit-dijin exclaimed. "Not me! No way! Man, they want me back jes' so's they can *shoot* me!"

"You were a buffalo soldier once."

"I ain't one now! I'se a *'Pache* now, not no soldier!" In Apache, he added, "I am of the People. The white eyes are nothing to me. But they seek my death. I cannot go."

"What about me?" Cissy said. "I can go to the fort."

"You are a woman." Iron Bear looked at her in surprise. "Will they listen to you?"

"Believe me, Chief," she said. "A damsel in distress? They'll listen!"

"They won't believe you if you tell them we need help fighting creatures from the stars," Macklin said.

"Don't I know it! I figure we can tell them there are some renegade Apaches up here plannin' on attacking the town. *That's* true enough, anyway! I have a feelin' they'd like to have a little talk with Black Wind and his people! I'll need some of your men though, Chief, so's I can find the place."

"You will have them. Hawk-Takes-Prey and Yellow Snake will go with you."

That would serve several purposes, Macklin thought.

The escorts Iron Bear was offering would be there as much to make sure that Rain Blossom's ransom—him—returned as anything else. He thought that Iron Bear, Na-a-cha, and Tze-go-juni all trusted him, but for most of the others, he was at best an unknown quantity.

At worst, he was still a *white eye.*

"This is bad," one of the warriors said from the crowd. "Can we trust them? They are white eyes!"

"If we keep the woman," another said, pointing at Cissy, "we know Moon Eagle will return."

"You'll have to trust us," Macklin said. "You don't really have much of a choice."

"The warriors we send with you will in part be our trust," Iron Bear said. He looked at Macklin. "We must know you will return, Moon Eagle, and within three days. Rain Blossom's life depends upon it."

"Yeah. Like I said, I'm going to have to be the bait. But first we have to stop Black Wind from starting a war. Then we need enough people to help us take on the Hunters. After that, well . . . all I can say is that you can trust me. I promise that I *will* be back, no matter what happens with the white men."

"Of what value," one hard-to-convince brave said in snarled Apache, "is a white man's promise?"

And Macklin honestly didn't know how to answer him.

SEVENTEEN

✧ **1** ✧

It was nearly dawn after a night without sleep when Macklin, Great Bear, and Water-on-Rock rode down out of Guindani Canyon and turned north toward the town of Apache Peak. "We should try to talk to them outside of town," Macklin told the others. "Once we're inside Apache Peak, there's no place to run if they try to take us prisoner. And I can't afford to hang around down here as a prisoner if they won't listen to reason. I have to be on the mountain in three days."

"White eyes *never* listen to reason," Water-on-Rock said. Then he glanced at Macklin, sheepish. "I did not mean . . ."

"Not a problem. I suppose I—"

"Moon Eagle! Look there!"

The sky was bright enough now that they could see all the way to the town. Riders were coming out, raising a cloud of dust as they urged their mounts into an all-out gallop.

"Well, it looks like they've seen us," Macklin said. He pulled his Winchester out of the saddle sheath and cocked it to chamber a .44-40 round, but he held it then in one hand, muzzle pointed at the sky. "Remember. Don't point your rifles right at them . . . but make sure they see them. We don't want them thinking they can just take us down."

Macklin and the two Apaches waited, motionless, at the top of a small rise, as the five riders galloped toward them. Minutes later, Macklin could see that the man in the lead was Pete Smethers.

"Good morning, Sheriff," Macklin called as the riders approached on winded horses. "You're up awfully early."

"What the *devil* are you playing at, Macklin?" Smethers demanded.

"We can take 'em!" one of Smethers' men said. He drew his Colt revolver.

Macklin dropped the muzzle of his Winchester so it was pointing at the man's chest. "Easy, there. We want to talk."

"Got nothing to say to you," Smethers said. He gave a cold glance to the Apaches. "Or your friends! You've got a sweet nerve comin' back here, 'specially after stealin' Johnny Osborn's horse like that!"

"We-all's got special ways of dealin' with horse thieves 'round here," another of the sheriff's men said, grinning.

"Well, please tell Mr. Osborn that I'll return his horse as soon as I can. I needed to borrow it. Or . . . I'll buy it, if he wants."

"You also damned near gave poor Jim and Zeke concussions when you hit 'em." Smethers leaned forward in his saddle, lowering his voice. "Look, Macklin. We don't want your kind around here. We don't want *them*. You *know* I let you go yesterday."

"Oh?"

"Well, it was mostly Cissy's idea. But you saw that crowd in El Camino yesterday. They were ready to string you up from the nearest tree. I figured the best way to get you out of my hair and uphold my authority in this town was to let her help you escape. Cissy's got a soft heart. I knew she'd take care of things."

"She did that."

"Is she okay? I didn't expect her to run off herself like that."

"She's fine, last time I saw her," Macklin said truthfully. No sense in giving them too much information. "She wants a chance to start over someplace else. Can't say I blame her much."

"She's a sweet kid. Okay, Macklin. I take it from these two friends of yours that you're not coming in to give yourself up."

"Nope. Came to warn you. *And* to make you an offer."

"A warning, huh? About what?"

"The Chokonen band up there," Macklin said, jerking a thumb over his shoulder at the mountains, "don't want war. Their *nantan*, Shoz-pesh, is tired of war and wants to live in peace."

"He can just go back to the reservation like a good little Indian, then, can't he?" one of Smethers' men said. "What do *we* got to do with it?"

"Easy, Clem," Smethers said. "Let him speak his piece."

"Shoz-pesh and most of his people want peace," Macklin continued, "but there are a few of his people who didn't agree last night. They're going on the warpath, and their likely targets are either your town or your mine . . . the one where Mr. Osborn was kind enough to loan me his horse. I'm told they won't attack at night . . . but you'll notice it's almost full light now. They could be getting ready to attack right this minute."

"Son of a bitch!" Clem exclaimed. He turned in his saddle, studying the rocks and wooded hills to the north. All of the riders looked a lot more nervous now.

"You're just plumb full of good news, Macklin,"

Smethers said. "You mentioned an offer. What's that about?"

"You might be interested in knowing," Macklin said easily, "that Shoz-pesh knows where the lost Bennett Mine is. And he's willing to show you its location and let you mine there, if his people can continue to live in these mountains in peace."

"I dunno," Smethers said, rubbing his jaw. "I don't have authority for stuff like that. All the Apaches hereabouts are supposed to be on the reservation up at San Carlos."

"Shoot, Pete," one of the men said. "If the Injuns are just gonna up and give us the mine . . . !"

"Y'know, that might not be such a bad deal at that, Sheriff," Clem said grudgingly. "We get everything we want . . ."

"*If* we can trust the damned savages," one of the other white men muttered.

Great Bear spat an Apache phrase . . . one that Macklin's AI hadn't heard before, but no translation was needed. Macklin guessed it had something to do with the man's ancestry.

"You can trust them," Macklin said. He wasn't entirely sure he could trust the white men, however. The turnaround in attitude, from a lynch-mob mindset to a willingness to accept Iron Bear's offer, was nothing less than startling.

Greed, it seemed, could do wonderful things in the arena of attitude adjustment.

"Ain't so sure we can trust you," Clem replied. "Y'coulda gone renegade."

"No reason to start name-calling," Smethers said. "None less than the Earp brothers themselves vouched for this guy, and that's enough for me."

"Mebee we should see what th' judge an' th' mayor got t'say," one of the men suggested.

"We'll do that," Smethers said. He started to pull his horse's head around. "You come with us, Macklin?"

"Not sure that's such a good idea, Sheriff," Macklin replied. "Considering the reception I got in Apache Peak yesterday."

"My word, Macklin: You come talk to the judge, and you walk away afterward. But I'm not sure they'll hear it from me."

Macklin chuckled. "Well, I'd think they'd be a lot less likely to listen to *me*. A horse thief and an escaped prisoner?"

Three gunshots in the distance interrupted Smethers' answer . . . one sounding by itself, two more in quick succession. Echoes rolled back from the mountains. The sheriff's party urged their mounts around. By the light of the sun just rising above the Dragoon Mountains in the east, across the San Pedro Valley, Macklin could see several figures dashing across the main street of town, running toward the adobe building. A puff of smoke appeared at the adobe's roof . . . followed, long seconds later, by the sound of the shot.

"Son of a bitch!" Smethers shouted. "We gotta get back there!"

"Hang on, Sheriff," Macklin said. "I might have a plan. . . ."

⋄ **2** ⋄

IN THE THREE HOURS SINCE SHE'D LEFT THE INDIAN CAMP, Cissy had left the mountains and was riding south now along the western side of the San Pedro Valley. For most of the ride, she'd had to walk Macklin's roan carefully down narrow trails in near-total darkness, often stopping to dismount and lead the horse by hand. The Indians with her, Yellow Snake and Hawk-Takes-Prey, said little beyond telling her which path to take when the trail forked, and she had the feeling they were coming along to make sure she didn't run away, as much as to lend any support to her arguments when she got to the fort.

Once out of the mountains, she stopped and took a long and longing look across the San Pedro, toward Tombstone. Maybe there she could get the new start she needed.

But Snake and Hawk, as she thought of them now, weren't about to let her abandon her mission. Besides, she'd promised. Hell, she'd volunteered.

And . . . who knew? Maybe once she'd told the soldiers her tale, she'd be able to stay at the fort. As a distressed citizen—being captured by Apaches certainly qualified as "distressed" in these parts—they might put her up for a few days, maybe even arrange for her to get back to Tucson.

And from there . . .

She sighed as the horse walked south under a dawn-lit sky. From there, she would have to start getting money together if she was ever to make it back home. And that meant another saloon job, supplemented by working on her back in a crib or a back room.

Or she could still meet someone respectable and marry him.

Someone respectable . . .

She thought of Macklin. He wasn't respectable, exactly, not in the sense that you could point to his job or his clothes or his family and say, "Now *there's* a respectable man." But he was kind and gentle and good. She knew men well enough to pick up on that. During the whole time she'd been alone with him yesterday, he hadn't once tried to take advantage of her, hadn't made reference to what she did for a living, hadn't treated her as anything but a lady.

That was unusual. Cowboys—most men in these parts—treated women with an exaggerated sense of courtesy and deference. Ladies were still rare enough birds in southern Arizona Territory to be treated with extreme respect. She smiled, remembering a story she'd heard once about a cowboy who'd had to take a cow from his boss's ranch to a neighboring ranch owned by a young woman in order to get the animal serviced by the woman's bull. "Bull," however, was too harsh and vulgar a word for a lady's ears, and so the embarrassed hand had asked if his cow could "visit for a spell with the gentleman cow."

But Cissy was no lady. She'd left that behind in Philadelphia six years ago when she set out to marry a man she'd never met, whom she'd talked with only in letters. By the time she'd *serviced* her first hundred men or so and taken their money for it, she knew she would never be able to apply the word *lady* to herself again. Still, she was determined that she had nothing to be ashamed of. She'd done what she needed to do to survive, and would do it again if she had to.

But by crossing that invisible but oh-so-high and solid barrier between proper ladies and what she was—a member of a separate class that included prostitutes, military post laundresses, and actresses—she'd surrendered the right to be treated as a respectable person. The miners in town treated her and the seven other girls who'd followed the sweet scent of easy riches from Tucson down to Apache Peak as possessions of a sort. Some treated them kindly, some were rough, abusive, even violent. Most paid their money and received her attentions with scarcely a word spoken or an acknowledgment that she was a person at all.

And for most of the men she'd been with, that arrangement was just fine. Still, she dreamed of something more.

John Macklin was so nice. She wondered if . . . maybe . . .

Ahead and to the right, a small boulder rested beside the path. As she guided the horse toward it, the animal shied suddenly, ears pricking, nostrils flaring. It whinnied, tossed its head, then backed away.

"C'mon, damn you," Cissy told the animal, kicking its sides with her boot heels. "What's the matter with you?" She caught a whiff of something sour, like burnt gunpowder or rotten eggs.

Macklin's horse was a gentle, tractable animal, but it balked now, refusing to advance. The Indians came up on either side of Cissy, and their mounts shied as well, terrified, eyes rolling back in their heads.

Snake growled something at his mount and slapped it on the back of its neck. The horse reared, and since he was riding nothing more substantial than a blanket, Snake had to grab hold of the mane to stay on.

The boulder was changing. . . .

Cissy screamed. She couldn't help it, though she hated the weakness as terror and bewilderment wrenched the sound from her. The rock seemed to blur, its shape changing, and for just a moment, she had a glimpse of the thing she'd see outside of Apache Peak one day . . . a body the size of a small pony, humpbacked, and more like a panther in its lines; an upper body with two long arms, each ending in wickedly curved scythe-like claws; a head similar to a snake's or an alligator's, huge and toothy and golden-eyed, but sprouting things like black branches from the sides of the head.

And in the next instant, the monster was gone, fading away to an uneasy invisibility. In its place was a tall, bearded man in a three-piece suit and a string tie, and he was holding an odd-looking device like a black-metal pipe in one hand. "You vill come mit me," the man said, pointing the pipe at her. What was that accent? German?

Hawk-Takes-Prey brought his gun, a heavy Sharps buffalo rifle, to his shoulder, but before he could pull the trigger, there was a flash of something like lightning, a thunderclap of sound, and the N'de warrior pitched back off his horse, his face a hideously exploded ruin.

"No!" Cissy screamed. Yellow Snake swung his horse around and lunged into a gallop, racing away from the horror, toward the north. The German man—or whatever he or it really was—raised the pipe, taking aim . . . but Cissy's horse, spooked by the loud report and the stink of burned meat, sidestepped into the thing's line of aim and reared, nearly throwing Cissy to the ground.

Moving with a speed and a grace that was decidedly not human, the creature moved past Cissy, aimed at the fleeing Yellow Snake, and fired again. The Apache was riding low, clinging to the horse's neck and melding his body with the animal's, galloping full tilt up the path. A clump of mesquite burst into flame as he passed it. The creature was lining up for another shot when Cissy, deliberately this time, moved her horse into its line of sight. "Please!" she cried. "Don't!"

She was under no illusions that she could ride like that, and she knew she was dead if she tried. But at least she'd given Yellow Snake a chance to get away, with word of what had happened to her.

She wondered what *was* going to happen to her, as the creature reached for her with a not-entirely-convincing illusion of a human arm. Its hand felt . . . odd as it grabbed her arm and pulled her down from the horse, which, driven mad by the smell or the simple proximity of the thing—Cissy wasn't sure which—bolted then and followed Yellow Snake at a wild gallop.

Cissy raised herself on hands and knees, looking up at her captor. "You know Macklin," it said.

"Y-yes." There was no way to deny it. The creature's words had sounded like a statement, not a question, and she had the damndest feeling that it was looking right into her soul, that it would *know* if she was speaking the truth.

"You vill come. This way."

"Who . . . what are you?"

It smiled at her, but the feeling behind that simple bar-
ing of teeth filled her with fear. "I am Karl Freis. I have
business with Macklin. You vill help me, *ja*?"

"Please don't hurt me!"

"Come." The thing was offering no guarantees.

But Cissy had no choice as it took her arm once more,
and guided her back toward the rocks. Beyond was a . . .
thing, a device like nothing she'd ever seen before, like
an enormous egg, richly carved and manufactured from
something that shone like metal, but with a softer luster
to its death-black finish. A carriage of some sort, but enclosed . . . with no wheels, no horse, and no visible means
of propulsion.

I guess, she thought, *that's it for getting the cavalry to
ride to the rescue.*

❖ 3 ❖

BLACK WIND'S APACHES HAD APPROACHED THE TOWN
through the woods from the west, where they had good
cover and could get loose without being seen by the
armed lookouts on top of the adobe building. Macklin's
idea had been to slip into the woods to the south and circle
around to the west so that they would approach the town
from the same direction as Black Wind's warriors.

As Macklin, Smethers, and their men grew nearer, the
sounds of gunfire picked up, a steady, crackling bang-and-
thunder as Apaches poured fire into the camp, and the
miners fought back.

Macklin turned to Great Bear and Water-on-Rock.
"Stay here!" he said, then spurred his horse forward, without waiting to see if he would be obeyed, or to be caught
up in an argument. He didn't know how keen his two
Apache watchdogs might be on fighting their own kin . . .
but one thing that was certain, they couldn't ride into the

mining camp now, not without becoming targets for the miners' fire.

"We will be here, Moon Eagle!" Great Bear called out.

Good. They understood. And they trusted him, at least to an extent.

Ahead, Macklin saw at least ten mounted Apaches riding through the town, apparently circling the adobe where nearly a dozen or so men had holed up and were firing back, from the roof, and through the tall, narrow slit windows in the adobe's walls. More Apaches lay under cover at the edge of the woods, dismounted, firing at whatever targets presented themselves. Not all of the miners in the town had made the safety of the adobe, however. Macklin saw two bodies stretched out on the ground between the adobe and the sheriff's office, and two Apaches were emerging from one of the tents, dragging a screaming man.

As Macklin and Smethers galloped forward, their charge flushed a number of dismounted Apaches out of the woods and into the open. Whooping like Indians themselves, the mounted party emerged from the woods, firing wildly at the Apaches around them, and at the Indian riders at the center of town.

Macklin took aim with his revolver at the Apaches struggling with the white man in front of the tent. He fired twice, then realized that it was going to be almost impossible to hit *anything* from the back of a moving horse. He reined his horse around, however, and gave it a quick double kick, galloping toward the fight. The Apaches saw him coming and dropped the white man. One aimed a rifle and fired, and Macklin felt the snap of the bullet as it cracked past his left ear.

Then he was there, among them, his horse rearing as he fired down at one of the Apaches from almost point-blank range. The man threw up his arms, twisted, and collapsed; the other Apache turned and ran.

Macklin reached down and grabbed the white man's arm; he clutched at Macklin's saddle and got one foot on Macklin's boot, lifting himself clear of the ground as Macklin urged the big chestnut toward the adobe. Crashing through the line of mounted Apaches, Macklin delivered the man practically to the adobe's front door, dropping him off, then reining around to face the swarming Indians. One was charging, holding a rifle in one hand as he leaned against his horse's neck. Macklin took careful aim and fired; the round struck the horse, which went down in a wildly kicking tumble of legs and hooves, throwing the Apache hard. He hit, rolled, then was on his feet again, running for the woods.

All of the Apaches were running, Macklin saw now, a few on horseback, the rest on foot. Smethers and his six riders, plus the two braves with Macklin, were in a swirling, chaotic, mounted fight, and Black Wind's people, unwilling to face more or less even odds in what they'd thought would be an attack on an easy, undefended target, were running.

Macklin looked for Black Wind. He was the leader of this renegade group, and if he could be caught or killed, there was a chance that this rebellion could be crushed before it was properly started.

There he was . . . on horseback, but near the woods, signaling to his men with an upraised rifle. He hadn't risked himself in the actual attack, but had stayed back, possibly to allow himself to oversee the entire battle.

"Sheriff!" Macklin yelled. When Smethers turned to look, he pointed. "That's the leader!"

Smethers nodded, rallied Clem and another of the men with him, and galloped toward the distant figure. Black Wind watched them for a moment, then turned his horse and vanished into the trees. Macklin knew they weren't going to find him, not if the Apache war leader knew this terrain as well as Macklin thought he did.

Gunfire erupted from the tree line, and one of Smethers' riders toppled from his horse. Clem and the sheriff fired back, then broke off their charge, galloping back into town.

"You sure called the Indian attack right," Smethers said, pulling up his horse next to Macklin. "If you're as right about this Apache chief's willingness to let us at the Bennett Mine, maybe we can deal."

"I hope so," Macklin said. He was looking past the sheriff, at the bodies sprawled in the street. He saw four white men there, one of them still moving, and two Apaches, with several more Indians dead in and near the woods. "Enough people have died on this mountain, don't you think?"

"Could be you're right. Come on. Let's find the mayor." He saw Macklin's hesitation and shook his head. "Don't worry. I ain't gonna arrest you, and nobody else'll touch you in this town either. I saw what you did for Larry Briscoll. You're all right, Macklin. Even if you do have some strange ideas about the Apaches."

"Maybe it's time to try some strange ideas, Sheriff. I don't think the sane ones have been working all that well."

"Could be you're right. C'mon."

They dismounted and walked into the adobe.

✧ 4 ✧

Na-a-cha felt his heart sink as he watched Yellow Snake dismount from a trembling, lathered horse and walk toward the rock shelter. Where was Hawk-Takes-Prey? Where was the white-eye woman?

Tzit-dijin stood at his side. "Oh, man," the deserter said. His hand went up to the bugle he wore slung over his chest. "Oh, *man*, dis be bad! Where'd the white girl go?"

"I don't know," Na-a-cha said in Apache. "But we're about to find out."

"I fought the demon monster!" Yellow Snake said, eyes wide, hands slashing as he relived a vivid, hand-to-hand confrontation with one of the devil-spirits. "I fought it for a long, a very long time! Hawk-Takes-Prey fought, too, and bravely, but the spirit-devil was too strong! It fired lightning from its mouth and eyes, and screeched like an owl, but loud as thunder, and Hawk-Takes-Prey died!"

"How did you get away, Yellow Snake?" Iron Bear asked. By this time, every man, woman, and child in the camp had gathered around, listening to Yellow Snake's tale.

"I fought very hard! The monster, it was a rock, a big rock beside the path but then it used its *gan*-magic to change into a horrible beast like the ones that took Rain Blossom last night. Then it changed into a white eyes, but it still was very powerful, still shot lightnings from its eyes. It called me by name and commanded that I obey, but I said 'No! No, devil-spirit, I will *not* do as you command!' And it said, 'Then you will die, Yellow Snake, you and all your people!' And I took my rifle and fired at it, killing it! But then it leaped back to life again and chased me, and my horse panicked and ran, and I had to hang on, but I kept shooting it as it chased me, and each time it died and came back to life again. . . ."

Na-a-cha felt the uneasy stirring of the crowd, sensed the growing panic as they listened to Yellow Snake's words. Na-a-cha knew Yellow Snake well, knew his parents well. He was a good man, a brave warrior, but he did have a tendency to boast. Na-a-cha had the feeling that he was stretching things out a bit, possibly to make himself look brave . . . or like less of a coward, in his own eyes and in the eyes of the band.

Most likely, Yellow Snake had run . . . and who could

blame him? Against such enemies, able to command the lightning Powers themselves . . .

"You did well to face the monster," Na-a-cha told Yellow Snake. He had to stop him from scaring the people in the camp to the point where they would be unable to face these things. "We will talk about the beast's powers later. What happened to the white woman?"

"It ate her!" he said, eyes wide. "It ate her, like Tze-go-juni says it ate Running Bird!"

"How did it eat her when it was chasing you, getting shot, and coming back to life?"

"I . . . I don't know. Maybe there were two of them. Or three!"

"That must have been it," Na-a-cha said, nodding. He placed a hand on Yellow Snake's shoulder. "Truth. If you think about it, I believe you will realize that the beasts were not coming back to life, for they are flesh and blood, like us. There were just several chasing you. An easy mistake to make, given the strange nature of these beasts from the stars!"

"I . . . yes. You may be right."

"And the white woman is dead?"

"I believe so, *diyi*." Then, as Na-a-cha continued to hold Yellow Snake with his eyes, he dropped his gaze. "I did not see her eaten, *diyi*. Not exactly. But one of the beasts had her in its grasp. Why else would it want her?"

"I don't know, and I wish I did. Where did this happen?"

Yellow Snake told him.

"It is almost as though the devil-spirits had left one— or several—of their number there to watch the road to the white man's fort. Watching to see if anyone would ride there for help."

"No help will come from the soldiers," Yellow Snake said.

"And I do not know if Moon Eagle's plan will work

without them," Na-a-cha replied. "Come. You will tell us more of what you saw."

He led Yellow Snake into the rock shelter, leaving Tzit-dijin, Iron Bear, and the rest outside.

EIGHTEEN

✦ 1 ✦

OTHER MINERS WERE ENTERING THE ADOBE, TAKING AD-
vantage of the Apaches' retreat to come out of hiding in
their tents and ramshackle lean-tos and shacks to make
for the sturdier protection of the adobe building. Two men
stooped to carry in the badly wounded man Macklin had
seen in the street. He, Smethers, Clem, and the others filed
in after them.

"Wounded man, here!" someone called. Others crowded
around to help.

The inside of the adobe building was cool and dark,
with a packed-down earth floor and tables made of planks
set across barrels. It had the look of a storehouse, with all
of the crates, barrels, and boxes stacked about, but it was
filled now with a couple of dozen hard-faced men, standing by slit windows with shotguns, buffalo rifles, and
Winchester .44-40s. Buckets of water had been carried
into the building from an outside well, and were situated
at strategic points around the room, for drinking, and just
in case the Apaches tried to use fire against them.

Four women, with hair hanging free and haunted eyes,
loaded rifles and revolvers at a plank table in the back of

the room, while three more attended the wounded—the badly hurt man they'd just brought in from the street, and another with a blood-stained bandage around his left arm, and the arm in a makeshift sling. A ladder led up through a hole in the ceiling to the building's second floor. The men spoke in low and earnest tones as they gripped their weapons, peering out through the slits and into the bright morning light.

As Macklin took in the scene, he felt the other side of the conflict between native and invading cultures. The men and women here had begun to build something, a community founded on hopes, dreams, blood, and—yes—greed, but noble despite the baser drives within the foundation. They'd built it, nurtured it, and now they were fighting for the chance to see it through. A chance at wealth, true . . . but, more, a chance at a new life. Like Cissy, most of the men and women here must have left old lives to pursue a dream on the Western frontier.

A very few had already found wealth, and the power that goes with it. Judge Thornton leaned back in a ladder-back chair, puffing his cigar. Mayor Norden sat beside him, looking worried. "Macklin!" Norden cried as Macklin entered. "What in the tarnation are you doing back here?"

"Macklin here just saved our tails," Smethers told them. "Led us in from the woods and caught the Apaches from behind, dead to rights!"

"Saved my life," Larry Briscoll said. He came over to Macklin and pumped his hand. "I thought I was a goner there, Macklin. Thank you!"

"Glad I could help."

"Listen, you tunnel rats!" Larry called out. "Macklin here is okay in my book! Y'hear me?"

The others cheered, or slapped Macklin on the shoulder as the sheriff led him toward the back of the room. Smethers was right. Their mood had changed completely since yesterday. Well . . . most of them, anyway. He caught a few dark glances, and heard a lone muttered "Injun lover," as he passed.

Some hatreds, he reflected, would never die.

"So we have you t'thank for breaking that attack, eh?" Thornton said, puffing his cigar.

"In a way, he did more than that," Smethers said. He turned to Macklin. "Hell, you got us all up and moving in time for the attack. Our lookouts spotted you coming out of the canyon and gave the alarm. Thought you were an Apache war party at first. If it hadn't been for that, the damned redskins might've been all over us before we knew what was happening, sneaking out of the woods that way."

"It isn't over yet," Macklin warned. "Most of the Apaches want peace, but about twenty have followed a renegade medicine man named Black Wind. He wants to start a war with the whites. He wants you out of these mountains, and he'll drive you out if he can."

"Jes' let him try!" a grizzled miner to Macklin's left growled. Macklin felt a start of recognition. It was Tom Crittenden. Dan Granger was with him.

"Howdy, Tom," he said. "Hi, Dan. I guess the job you offered didn't turn out quite the way I expected it."

"Well, life's like that, sometimes," Granger replied.

"Macklin here has some interesting news, though," Smethers added. "Tell 'em, Macklin. Tell 'em about what the good Indians want to do."

"Hell," the man with the bandaged arm growled. "Th' only good Indian is a dead'un."

"Quiet, Jubal. Let him talk."

Macklin began telling them about Iron Bear's desire to live in peace with the white men, and how he might be persuaded to give them access to the lost mine.

"Yeah, but how do we know we can trust him?" Tom said. "Th' murderin' bastards killed a bunch of our men up on that mountain when they went up lookin' fer the place."

"That wasn't Iron Bear," Macklin told them. "There's . . . someone else up on that mountain."

"What?" Tom said, and then he cackled. "Ghosts?"

"The Indians call them devil-spirits," Macklin said. "They're not human, and they have no love for us, white man *or* Apache."

" 'Devil-spirits,' huh?" one miner said. "That might explain some of the weird stuff people've been seein' up there!"

"What have people been seeing?"

"Huh. Spook lights and moving stars. Funny lights, like the aurora borealis, up Alaska way, but brighter. C'mon, boys, you all seen those things."

"Superstitious nonsense!" Dan Granger spat. "Indian myths and spook stories!"

"Yeah," Tom said.

"What about the Flatrock Monster?" Clem said.

"Flatrock Monster?" Macklin asked.

"Coupla the boys was explorin' the big peak, back there, a few weeks back. Ben Gaither an' George Doyle. There's a place they called Flatrock Canyon. Followed wagon ruts in that made 'em think they might be close to the Bennett Mine. Only then, Ben, he ups and sees somethin' like a horse, only it's got a snake's head, he says, and arms and teeth and claws and, oh, yeah! It was quite a monster, the way he told it!"

"Ben had just gotten into the liquor stores, is all," Norden said.

"Well, *somethin'* sure spooked him," Clem said. "He come runnin' back down that mountain, him and Doyle, and he was white as a ghost and shakin' like all get-out! George, he said he didn't see nothin', but he sure believed Ben had!"

"Where's Ben now? Macklin asked.

"Went back up lookin' fer the Bennett Mine," Tom said, " 'long with George and a coupla others, last week. They didn't come back. We figured the Apaches got 'em."

"It wasn't Apaches," Macklin said. He wondered how to explain. He remembered something Ned Buntline had told him. "Anyone here ever hear about something called the Great Moon Hoax? It goes back a ways . . . almost fifty years, in fact."

"Moon Hoax?" Tom rubbed his jaw. "My daddy told me somethin' a long time ago 'bout that. He read in the newspapers 'bout how some scientist types built a telescope big enough to let 'em see people living on the moon! It was all a crock, of course."

"Men on the moon!" someone guffawed.

"Well, you can laugh all you want," Macklin said, "but there are other worlds circling other suns . . . the stars in the night sky. Some of those worlds have life on them, and people . . . only those people, most of them, don't look much like anything we know here on Earth. Some of them can come here. Some of them *are* here. I think that's what Ben's Flatrock Monster was."

The room had grown quiet as he spoke. "Mister, that's just plain loco," someone said into the flat silence as Macklin finished.

"Don't be so sure, Billy," Clem said. "*I* seen some strange things up there m'self. Most of us have! You've all heard the stories."

"Yeah, and I don't believe a word of 'em!"

"Too many of you boys've been chewin' jimson weed," Dan said. He grinned. "Or hitting the rye whiskey too hard. Those Indian stories've got you all spooked."

Some of them, Macklin thought, were already convinced. Others would never believe, no matter what proof was offered. The majority, as ever, wavered between the two. Possibly it wasn't necessary that any of them believe completely, if he could just get them moving in the right direction.

"Maybe they are just tall tales, then," Macklin said. "Ghost stories. Imaginary monsters. Indian superstitions. The fact is, Iron Bear and his people believe them, whether you do or not. And he's willing to show you where the Bennett Mine is, and let you work it, if you help him against these ghosts . . . and if you agree to let him and his people live up in these mountains peacefully."

"I'll need to talk to the territorial governor," Norden said. "Or maybe the military governor at San Carlos. *I* can't give those Indians permission to live off the reservation."

Thornton wore a shrewd look on his face. "You sure you want to do that, Mayor? I mean, it would mean government people down here, snooping around. Looking into our business."

"Least we could do is help our neighbors," Smethers said, with a wink. "Maybe later, after all the claim legalities are straightened out, nice and neat, we can talk to somebody and straighten out the legal stuff then. . . ."

"Lots of Apaches are workin' with the Army as scouts," someone said. "If they want to work for us, it suits me."

"Ha! *'Specially* if they take us to th' Lost Bennett!" someone shouted.

The enthusiasm for the idea was building.

"Well, I'll tell you what, Macklin," Thornton said. "We'll certainly take the offer under advisement. I presume you wouldn't mind continuing to handle the negotiations with the Indians for us?"

"They seem to trust me, sir. I think that would be a fine idea."

"Well, all things considered—"

"Hey! Ground floor!" a shout came down from the upper story. "Lookouts say there's a fire in the town!"

Macklin followed Smethers, Clem, Norden, and a few others up the ladder to the next floor. There were more men crouched by narrow windows here, a number of beds and some more boxes, but little else in the way of furnishings.

A second ladder led to a square hole in the roof, looking through into bright blue sky. They climbed the last ladder and emerged on the adobe's roof.

This was the highest point inside the town, though the mountains towered above Apache Peak like giants. The buildings of the town were clustered around the adobe like chicks around a hen, with a single broad corridor down the middle, running north and south, which served as Main Street.

Black smoke boiled into a pristine sky on the north edge of the town. It looked like a number of tents and shacks were on fire there. Figures ran between the tents, some carrying torches.

Norden unfolded a small, brass pocket telescope and held it to his eye. "Looks like the bad Indians are trying to burn us out, Macklin," he said.

"Is there anything we can do about it?" Clem asked.

"Not unless you want to go out there and take the fight to them," Smethers said. "And that could be damned expensive."

"We can hold them off from in here," Norden said. "We might lose the rest of the town, but, hell, if we're going to find the Lost Bennett at last, we can rebuild, right?"

The next attack began ten minutes later, as snipers among the rocks and trees at the base of East Peak began taking potshots at the adobe. No one was hit, but the gunfire grew heavy, a galling, steady crack and bang mingled with the shrill whine of ricochets that wore on the nerves. The men on the roof came down the ladder, because gunmen on the mountain, high enough up to be able to look down on the roof, were getting just a bit too accurate with their shooting.

The fire in the camp, meanwhile, grew worse, and heavy smoke began drifting south, spreading across the town and filtering in through the narrow windows of the adobe. Before long it was apparent that the Apaches weren't just trying to burn the town. They were trying to smoke the defenders of the adobe out into the open as well.

"What about the mine?" Macklin asked Thornton after a time. "How many men are up there? Why haven't they come back?"

"They're probably holed up in the rocks, either under attack themselves, or waiting to see if they're gonna be attacked. No one wants to be out and on the move when the Apaches strike."

"The Apaches probably feel the same way," Macklin pointed out. "If someone could get to the mine, get those people together, and bring them back here, we might be able to break the Apache attack for good."

"I dunno," Thornton replied. "These people aren't gunfighters, you understand. They're miners, most of 'em, or farmers and storekeepers who thought they'd make more money digging for silver than doing what they knew."

"That's why we hired you, Macklin," Norden said. "Remember?"

"I remember."

Black Wind's Apaches wouldn't know those men were storekeepers and miners, though, Macklin thought. And if they stayed put out there by the mine, sooner or later the Apaches would begin to see them as an easier target than the adobe.

It was time to do something about the situation, instead of crouching inside the building, reacting to what happened outside.

The smoke was getting thicker outside. Within the

adobe, some of the men and women had tied kerchiefs soaked in water over their faces, and the sound of coughing was almost constant now.

"I'm going to get those other miners," Macklin told Thornton. "At least it will give Black Wind something extra to think about."

"Okay, Macklin," Thornton said after a moment's thought. "I think you're crazy, but if you make it . . ."

Norden had been listening. "What if the mine is also under attack?" he asked. "You'll be stuck out there, with all those Apaches wandering around."

"I don't think the Apaches will have hit both the town and the mine," Macklin said, shaking his head. "Black Wind only has about forty braves, at the most. He knows he can't take on that many of you at the same time. At the most, he'll post a rifleman or two to make the miners keep their heads down. I might be able to sneak up behind them . . . or convince the miners to come out in force."

"The foreman out there, this shift, is Roger Craig," Thornton said. "He's a good man. You tell him that I said he should get his ass back here with as many men as have guns, pronto!"

"I'll tell him."

Norden was still thinking. "Y'know, it's a long ride, but it might make more sense for him to head south. Get to Fort Huachuca and fetch back the cavalry."

"Never work," Thornton said. "Four, five hours there, five hours back. We can't hold out much longer here." He coughed, as if to make the point. "Certainly not eight or nine hours."

Macklin smiled. "All you have to do is hold out until this afternoon," Macklin told him. "Maybe another five hours."

"Yeah? What happens then?"

"Remember Cissy?"

"Yeah."

"She's riding to Fort Huachuca to get help. She left about the same time I did, before dawn this morning. I imagine she's almost there by now. And the fort is what . . . a five-hour ride you said?"

Thornton's face brightened. "Maybe less, if they come running. My God, Macklin, you're a miracle worker!"

"Well, just try to hold out until the soldiers get here." He hadn't wanted to tell them about Cissy, because he didn't want to build up false hope. There was no telling what Cissy would find when she reached Fort Huachuca . . . maybe a troop of cavalry ready to ride, and maybe she'd find the fort manned by a skeleton force because the troop was out on patrol somewhere, with no help at all to send north.

And that was assuming she made it that far. Having Yellow Snake and Hawk-Takes-Prey with her was a good guarantee that she wouldn't get lost, but Black Wind might have people patrolling that road, just to keep someone from riding that way for help. It was a long shot . . . and Macklin wished now that she hadn't been so damned determined to go, when Tzit-dijin had refused the job.

But at the moment, he thought the hope of reinforcements would help the embattled defenders of Apache Peak more than the letdown would hurt them later.

For one thing, if he couldn't get help, there wasn't going to be a *later* to worry about.

"Okay," he said. He drew his revolver, and checked to see that all of the chambers were loaded. He would leave his rifle here. They needed it . . . and he wouldn't be able to shoot much with it the way he was planning on riding. "I'll be back with help as soon as I can."

"Luck, Macklin," Thornton told him.

"You want me to come with you?" Smethers asked.

"No thanks, Sheriff. They need all the good guns here they can get. But keep an eye out for when I come back.

If I have the other miners with me, the Apaches may redeploy to attack us, and that could give you a chance to break out and hit them where it hurts."

"I'll be looking forward to that, Macklin," Smethers said with a grim nod. "Good luck, then."

"Thanks."

The smoke was heavy outside, lying in a thick gray pall. Several horses, including Macklin's chestnut, were still tied to the hitching line out front, though they were all snorting and stamping nervously as they breathed the drifting smoke.

Though he could scarcely see across the street to the sheriff's office, Macklin was sure the Apaches must have moved close enough to keep the adobe building under observation. They would be foolish not to. As if in answer to his thought, a rifle cracked from somewhere out in the smoke, and the bullet shrieked off adobe blocks somewhere above and behind his head.

Ducking low, pistol in his hand, Macklin swung under the hitching line as he untied the reins, put boot to stirrup, and swung into the saddle. Another shot rang out . . . and then a whole volley of gunfire. He dropped over and pressed his body against the chestnut's mane as he urged the animal into a trot, then a gallop, swinging around the south side of the adobe and heading east.

A few hundred yards farther on, the smoke thinned to a pale haze as he skirted the rolling brown ground of the San Pedro Valley. Turning north then, he raced along with the smoke pall of burning Apache Peak on his left. It looked as though the Apaches had managed to set fire to most of the tents and temporary structures. The townspeople were going to have a hell of a big rebuilding job in front of them, once this was all over.

He had to swing west again, toward the looming shadow of East Peak just visible through the smoke haze, if he was going to find the narrow defile leading to the mine. The Apaches might be watching for him, and he was going to have to be careful.

Slipping back into the smoke, he slowed his pace a bit, feeling his way west with the mountain's shadow as a guide. He thought he recognized the shape of those huge blocks of stone that looked as though they'd fallen away from the Whetstones proper, creating a walled-in valley running north.

He wasn't about to ride into that valley, though. If the Apaches wanted to stop anyone from getting from the town to the mine, all they had to do was post a man or two right about . . . *there*. Or over there. Among the boulders, high up on either side of the pass. As if to prove him right, a small figure in white pants and a blue shirt with a bright red bandanna moved then, close beside one of the spots that Macklin had chosen. Smoke puffed among the boulders, and then Macklin heard the shot.

He rolled off the horse, which shied and cantered off toward the east. Either it would find some weeds to graze on, or someone—Apache or townsman—would round it up sooner or later. Macklin stayed low and, pistol in hand, began crawling toward the rocks.

Even this far from the town, the smoke haze was thick enough that visibility was uncertain. The Apache sentinel up there might well think he'd killed the man who'd ridden up on horseback. Macklin couldn't see his opponent now, and though that wasn't a guarantee that the other man couldn't see him, it gave Macklin a starting point from which to develop the tactical situation.

He reached a tumbledown of boulders, part of the eastern ridge of huge granite blocks that had fallen away from the mountain during some geological upheaval eons past. The rock was water-smoothed but there were plenty of cracks and crevices. Macklin holstered his pistol and started climbing.

He stopped frequently to listen.

It wasn't sound he was listening to, however, but a kind of inner voice or sense. He'd felt it before, more than once. When he'd first arrived in Tucson, and was following the Kra'agh, disguised as one of Clanton's gunnics. Or later, as he'd moved down the alley toward Apache Slim's store, and felt with cast-iron certainty that a trap lay ahead.

He was learning to trust that voice. It might be intuition . . . but he suspected that it actually was connected with his AI, that "second self" Na-a-cha had somehow sensed inside him back at the rock shelter, and which seemed to be reaching out in various ways now, to help him survive, helping him learn the Apache language, helping him now, perhaps, with senses that Macklin couldn't even guess at, to feel the presence of someone else up there among the boulders, someone who was trying to kill Macklin.

He thought he could sense the other man, in *that* direction, a little above him, and perhaps thirty yards away.

Macklin climbed, trying to blend speed with silent stealth. Going up the east face of the boulder spill this way, he felt nakedly exposed, but he kept climbing until he was able to slither over the top on his belly, emerging on the top of several house-sized boulders strung along the wall in an uneven line, like badly spaced teeth. He looked back toward the mouth of the valley, in the direction his inner sense had been pointing him. Sure enough, there was the other man, an Apache in white pantaloons and a blue shirt, crouched behind a boulder as he scanned the smoky terrain to the south and east, rifle in hand.

Silently, Macklin crept up on him from the north.

He had no compunctions about firing from ambush. The old adage about a "fair fight," with two men facing one another in an empty street and going for the fast draw was largely myth. It certainly didn't apply in a situation like this, where chivalry toward a deadly enemy could only be equated with sheer stupidity.

However, Macklin was armed only with a handgun, a weapon with an accurate range of perhaps ten or fifteen yards. He was a good shot with the weapon, and he'd been practicing a lot lately in Tombstone back-lots and in the desert outside of town, but it would be a waste of ammo, not to mention stupid, to try to take that Apache rifleman at twice that range. Drawing the pistol again and cocking it, he began moving closer.

He almost made it. Macklin was just fifteen yards or so from the Apache sentry when the man caught a whisper of sound or a scent and spun suddenly. His eyes met Macklin's, and the rifle came up to his shoulder.

Macklin fired as he dropped to the left. His shot went wild and the Apache fired back, the bullet chipping across the surface of the boulder next to Macklin with a loud whine, scattering a stinging cloud of tiny fragments in its wake.

Lying on hard rock, now, Macklin took more careful aim as the Indian cocked his Winchester's lever, chambering another round. The bullet hit the man in the side, but he managed to get off a second shot. Macklin fired a third time, gripping his gun hand wrist with his free hand to steady it, and the Apache toppled over the side of the boulder, dropping to the rocks and earth twenty feet below.

"Macklin!"

He spun at the call, pistol coming up as he caught sight of another Apache standing behind him. It was Water-on-Rock, just a few yards away, unarmed and smiling.

"Jeez, you scared the hell out of me!" Macklin said. His heart was pounding furiously. He started to lower the pistol, then stopped. Something was wrong. . . .

Water-on-Rock had never called him Macklin. To those within the band, he was Moon Eagle. They knew his white man name was Macklin, to be sure . . . but the slip was just warning enough to put him on his guard.

The breeze, from the north, carried just a hint of a familiar scent, like rotten eggs.

Water-on-Rock lunged forward, a weapon of some kind in his . . . in *its* hands. Macklin fired, cocked, and fired again, guessing at where within the illusion cast by the Hunter its vulnerable hump might lie. Kra'agh could take a hell of a lot of punishment before they went down, and Macklin was painfully aware that he had only one bullet left. If he could hit the massive hump over its shoulders, which Dorree had once told him housed the thick block of bone protecting the Kra'agh's brain, he would be able to kill it, or at least stun it badly enough to give him a fighting chance.

At his second shot, Water-on-Rock screamed, the sound an unearthly keening that grated on the nerves and sent shivers down the spine. The image of the Apache brave wavered, fading out, and for a moment Macklin could see the Kra'agh as it really was, a thrashing, many-limbed creature with wicked claws and a flat, serpent's head, widely distended jaws revealing far too many needle-slender teeth. A beamer, one of the unearthly weapons the Kra'agh favored, lay a few feet away on the ground, dropped as the monster convulsed.

Macklin ducked forward, raising the pistol and drawing back the hammer above his last round. The horror in front of him keened and shrilled, lashing at him with one long, blade-tipped arm. Macklin wanted to reach the beamer, but the Hunter lunged, falling across it. Its head darted forward, golden eyes ablaze, and the black and gnarled branches of its feeder arms, the four small arms growing from the sides of its head, reached out to grab him and drag him toward those teeth. Macklin sidestepped the lunge and jumped forward, past the surprised alien's head, ramming the muzzle of his Colt up against its shaggy hump and pulling the trigger.

The detonation convulsed the Hunter as though it had

been hit by a jolt of electricity. Macklin heard the brain case crack, and the Kra'agh twisted away, rolling almost to the edge of the boulder.

But it was still alive. Macklin stepped back, out of the reach of the thrashing limbs. The beamer lay on the rock nearby. He scooped it up, looking at the oddly shaped press points on its slick, faintly oily surface, and wondered how the hell the thing worked.

"Ma . . . klin . . ."

The wounded Kra'agh was gone. Water-on-Rock stood there instead, looking perfectly healthy, though his words were strained.

"Give it up, Kra'agh," Macklin told it. "You've lost. Before long, everyone on this planet will know who and what you are, and they'll be ready for you!"

The image of Water-on-Rock smiled—weakly, Macklin thought. The food beasts of this world cannot avoid their destiny, which is to feed the race. As for you . . ."

Suddenly, Macklin heard another voice . . . Cissy's. "John! John! Where are you? These . . . these things have me! Please . . ." And then she screamed.

Macklin lunged forward, pressing the beamer into the Water-on-Rock image. He felt nothing, no resistance, as the weapon vanished a few inches into the projection's belly. "What have you done with her?"

"It, the female . . . is with us," the Kra'agh said. The image of the Apache faded once more, and again Macklin stared at the eldritch horror, clinging to the edge of the boulder cliff. "There will . . . be no help . . . from the soldiers . . . in their fort to the south." The strange being seemed to be having trouble breathing. Flaps were opening and closing fitfully behind the base of the feeder arms, behind the jaws, and he wondered if it was breathing through those instead of its mouth.

"Is she still alive? Or was that voice some sort of recording?"

"It lives. For now. If you come to us, we will release it and the N'de juvenile."

"I'll be there," Macklin promised. "I was going to come anyway. But you'd better take good care of them. If anything happens to either one—"

"You are not in a position . . . to bargain . . . human. But they are . . . of no importance. We will release them . . . if you come to us. Unless . . ." It began wheezing.

"Unless what?" Macklin demanded.

"Unless one of us gets hungry."

"Damn you! I'm the one you want. Let them go!"

There was no reply. Cautiously, Macklin nudged the thing's head with the tip of the beamer. One arm dropped away limply, three-fingered hand wide open, but the golden eyes remained fixed and unseeing. The slits on its neck had stopped pulsing as well.

He had to take the Kra'agh at its word. The Hunters had Cissy, and no help would be coming from Fort Huachuca.

So far today, things were not going according to plan at all.

NINETEEN

✧ **1** ✧

ROGER CRAIG WAS A MASSIVE, BURLY MAN WITH A CHEST-length beard, a vile-smelling cigar, and hands that looked like they could wrestle raw ore from the rocks without benefit of pick or shovel. He met Macklin with a double-barreled shotgun that looked like a toy in his hands and a dozen more armed miners backing him up.

"Thank God you got through, Macklin," Craig told him when introductions were complete. "We knew something was going on back at the town. We could hear the shooting. But the red devils've been taking potshots at us all day from the mountain, keeping us holed up down here. We couldn't all come, and we didn't see much sense in whittling ourselves down a little at a time, so we decided to hunker down and wait for someone to make it through from the town."

"The town's pretty much waiting on you the same way," Macklin said. He went on to tell them about the attack, the burning of the tents and shacks, and the situation inside the make-do adobe fort. He did not bother to tell them about the attempt to raise the cavalry at Fort Huachuca, though. Apache Peak was on its own.

He'd encountered two more Apaches blocking the only approach to the mine. He'd tried using the Kra'agh beamer, but the thing had shifted oddly, squirming in his hand like a living thing, and he'd been unable to find a firing switch or trigger, so he'd had to do it the old-fashioned way. He was carrying the Winchester dropped by the first Apache warrior at the mouth of the canyon, and so was able to work his way into a good position almost a hundred yards away, and take down one of the sentries before he'd even spotted Macklin. The other sentinel had run, making his way up the rocks on the sheer face of East Peak as nimbly as a mountain goat and vanishing among the boulders at the top.

The way was then open to the mine.

"I figure we can put together about twenty of the boys with guns," Craig told him. "That'll leave ten more armed men to hold the mine, and take care of the rest of my people who aren't armed."

"Twenty may do it," Macklin said. "Black Wind has got to be hurting by now, and from what I've seen, the Apaches don't like prolonged, stand-up fights."

"That's true enough," Craig told him. "They like to use hit-and-run tactics. Sneak in, hit you where you're weakest, grab what they can and skeedaddle."

"In other words," one of the other miners said, "they don't fight *fair*!"

"If it works," Macklin said, "what's the point of fair? When the other guy is trying to kill you, you don't want to give him an even chance!"

"Listen to this guy," Craig told the others, nodding. "He knows what it's all about."

Macklin was looking over the carts, crates, and supplies scattered about the mine entrance. He noticed one wagon half full of ore, another next to it that was empty. "Can you people hitch up that empty wagon and bring it along?" he asked.

"Sure,"

Craig replied. "You have an idea?"

"There's something lying near the mouth of this canyon," he explained, "that I'd like to take with us back to town." The body of the Hunter he'd killed would go a long way toward convincing Thornton and the others of the Kra'agh's reality. Whether it would help rally them all to go help the Apaches get Rain Blossom and Cissy back, or whether it would so terrify them that they all fled, he didn't know. He did know that he was tired of people looking at him like he was crazy every time he began describing the Kra'agh threat to this planet.

He had one other piece of evidence as well, and that was the enigmatic Kra'agh weapon, the device Dorree had once called a beamer. While Craig was organizing his men and hitching up the wagon, Macklin excused himself and went off behind some boulders to try to figure the device out. With this, he thought, they had a real chance, *if* he could work out how to use the thing. It changed shape slightly when he squeezed the grip. It was showing something that might be a firing button now, but it remained stubbornly inert when he aimed it at distant rocks and pressed it.

He studied the design carefully. The grip was oddly shaped with three deep grooves circling it, evidently made to fit the three-fingered Kra'agh feeder hand. He found pressure points within those grooves and decided that they were some sort of grip safety; squeeze them while pressing the top button, and the weapon should fire. He couldn't do it with one hand, but he managed to squeeze all the right spots with two.

And still nothing happened . . . except that the grip squirmed beneath his hands as though trying to change shape.

Now there were other buttons and pressure points in the smooth, oily casing of the device, but Macklin didn't have the time to try all possible combinations. He was beginning to think that the weapon was smarter than it looked. It might draw power from the harness that the Kra'agh always wore . . . or perhaps it could simply tell by touch or body temperature or even the owner's thoughts whether or not a Kra'agh was trying to operate it. Maybe it changed shape in response to his thoughts. It made sense, Macklin reflected. If the Kra'agh were in the habit of moving in on primitive worlds and taking them over as vast ranches for raising food and game, they would want to have weapons that would not do the game animals any good if they fell into the wrong hands. In fact . . .

The grip, Macklin noticed, was growing warm . . . very warm, and he could hear a high-pitched whine building from within the device. Acting almost without thinking, he arced his arm back and around and flung the weapon as hard and as far as he could, hurling it past some large boulders in the opposite direction from the mine and dropping in the same moment to lay face-down on the rock, arms curled protectively over his head.

The explosion was shattering, deafening, a single thunderclap assaulting his ears, his body, his whole being. He was just rising from the ground, ears ringing, when Craig and a half dozen other miners swarmed up the path from the mine.

"What the hell!" Craig exclaimed. "Macklin, was you using *dynamite* up here?"

"I thought . . . some Apaches were trying to sneak down from the side of the mountain over there," he lied. He couldn't exactly answer the question directly, or honestly.

"Donny. Frank. Check it."

"Ain't nothin' over here but a hole in the ground," one of the men called back a moment later. "What'd you use, mister? Ten, twelve sticks?"

"You gotta be real careful with that stuff, Macklin," Craig warned. "We've got a lot of high explosives stored around here, and one blast can set the rest off real easy like. Sympathetic detonation. And you want to be careful about other boys around, and yell 'fire in the hole' if they're in the blast area."

"Sorry," Macklin said. "There wasn't time for more."

"No harm done, and if you was right about the Indians, you sure as hell scared 'em off. Good job. You ready to go?"

"All set."

"Right. Let's roll. Donny? Let's bring a couple crates of boom sticks along. Macklin here had a pretty good idea."

They mounted up and rode back toward town, Macklin riding with Ted Joslyn in the wagon. At the mouth to the canyon, though, when they pulled up to find the body of the Kra'agh, Macklin was in for another disappointment. Though he and two other men climbed the rocks and searched carefully for a you'll-know-it-if-you-see-it, as Macklin described it, there was no sign of the Kra'agh body. They found the Apache Macklin had killed nearby, but either the Hunter had gotten up and walked away—a disturbing thought—or its friends had come and picked it up.

The Kra'agh, obviously, were still being very careful about revealing themselves openly on Earth. A few had seen them—Tze-go-juni and her captors, Cissy during her walk near Apache Peak, the men who'd seen the Flatrock Monster—but most of those sounded like accidents, or Kra'agh who planned on killing or capturing their victims and didn't care if those victims got a look at them or not. The one exception seemed to be the three who'd invaded the Apache camp and taken Rain Blossom hostage.

Macklin guessed that they'd let the Indians see them in their true form because they hoped to overawe them, playing on superstition or religious belief. Perhaps they'd collected the thoughts of Indian victims like Jiminez and knew some Apaches believed they somewhat resembled their mountain *gan*.

In any case, Macklin was certain now that the Hunters' caution about being seen, about leaving bodies or equipment lying around loose, in letting themselves be known openly, probably meant that there were so few of them around that they faced a very real danger of being defeated by the local humans . . . even if they were armed with weapons that by comparison to a beamer were almost laughably primitive. That meant that Macklin had a real chance of upsetting Kra'agh plans for Earth, and it also gave him a possible weapon against them. If the Kra'agh feared humans, despite their obvious technological superiority, Macklin was pretty sure he could find a way to turn that fear against them.

They approached the town of Apache Peak, which was still mantled in a low-lying haze of smoke from dozens of fires. The men grew increasingly angry as they passed the all-too-evident signs of the Apache rampage—a woman's hat, dress, and other apparel scattered on the ground . . . a trunk dragged into the open and smashed apart, the books and clothing inside strewn wildly about . . . a man, dead from half-a-dozen wounds, his body stripped naked and savagely mutilated . . .

"Murdering savages," Ted Joslyn muttered, flicking the reins on the wagon's team. "That was Sonny Clay, a buddy of mine!"

Macklin said nothing. Talk about living in peace with the Indians was one thing; it was different when you saw your friends and neighbors lying butchered on the ground.

He led them back along the tree line on the west side of town, whooping and hollering and firing their weapons. A group of ten Apaches was there, emerging from among the trees and rocks, then fleeing as the miners approached.

The opened fire, and for a desperate few moments, the two parties blazed away at each other, with some of the hostile fire coming from the rocks above. The Apaches began to melt back in among the boulders, though, when one of their number collapsed on the ground.

Craig rode up to the wagon, took a stick of dynamite from an open crate, and tamped a fuse and blasting cap into one end. Lighting the fuse from his cigar, he grinned at Macklin and shouted, "Not a bad idea at all!" before galloping on ahead. A few moments later, a thunderous explosion sounded from among the rocks, the crack echoing down from the mountains in slow-fading repetitions.

But one of the miners was hit, knocked from his horse by rifle fire as he charged after an Indian fleeing on foot. As more Apaches arrived from the burning town, the miners began dismounting and finding cover for themselves among the rocks.

Macklin jumped off the wagon as Ted pulled it up close to the boulders and fallen tree trunks that had become their impromptu fortress. Several miners formed a chain to pass the dynamite crates down and get them under cover, as the rest lay down a devastating, crackling barrage that kept the Apaches at bay.

Bullets whined off the boulders, and a few arrows with sharp, steel tips snicked into the circle and buried their heads in the earth or trunks of trees. Explosions rocked the ground as Craig's men hurled sticks of dynamite at the enemy. They stopped that, though, when one of the sticks was snatched up and tossed back. Craig picked it up, grabbed the short stub of sputtering fuse, and pulled it out of the blasting cap before it could detonate, calmly puffing on his cigar all the while.

Another stick tossed at the Apaches flew back, hitting the ground and bouncing twice to end up sputtering and smoking almost at Macklin's feet. He didn't bother trying to disarm the thing; instead, he snatched it up and hurled it back again, then ducked behind a rock as it exploded, still in midair.

Macklin was worried. He'd managed to lead the mine contingent into a situation even more dangerous than that of the men and women still holed up in the adobe, pinned down . . . and without water or more than a few dozen rounds of ammunition apiece. He'd thought that the Apaches would run when Craig's force arrived, but they appeared to be gathering in greater numbers than ever. Two more men were hit, one badly.

In the distance, to the south, he saw Black Wind, mounted on a dark gray horse, once again watching from the edge of the fight.

"Hold off on the dynamite for a bit," he called to Craig. "I want to try something." Before the miner could reply, Macklin leaped astride one of the horses inside the miners' perimeter and with a loud "Ha!" spurred it forward. Leaping some small boulders and fallen timber, he broke into a full gallop, racing directly toward Black Wind. An Apache fired at him, the bullet snapping past his head.

Black Wind was the key to the renegade Apache threat. Get him, and the attack would be ended. Macklin leaned far over, pressing his body against the horse's neck, trying to get close enough for a clear shot at the Apache war leader. More bullets snicked past or ricocheted from the rock nearby with shrill shrieks, but he ignored the galling fire and kept moving, trying to keep himself and his horse under the cover of the rock ledge they were on, trying to get closer to Black Wind. It looked as though the Apache was waving his men on, using a long lance with colorful feathers tied behind its head as a pointer. From the expression on his face, though, he was having less than total success. His war party was melting away even as he tried to rally them.

Then he saw Macklin. He drew back the spear, then hurled it as hard as he could. Macklin swerved his horse

and ducked, and the spear flew past his head. Macklin had
his Colt out, and as he galloped closer, he took aim and
fired . . .

. . . demonstrating once again that it's next to impossible to hit *anything* from moving horseback.

Black Wind shouted to one of his followers on the
ground, and caught a rifle tossed to him. He took aim as
Macklin came still closer, and fired.

The shot missed.

And then a fresh barrage of gunfire and wild shouts
sounded from the south.

At first, Macklin thought the U.S. Cavalry was arriving
after all, as horsemen thundered closer on furiously driven
mounts. Then they got close enough that he could resolve
the figures astride the lathered animals . . . Apaches.

For perhaps the first time in the history of the American West, a troop of Apache Indians was riding at full
gallop to the rescue of a beleaguered band of white
men. . . .

⋄ **2** ⋄

BLACK WIND STARED AROUND HIM, AT HIS MEN VANISHING
back into woods and rocks, fleeing the sudden charge by
their brothers. He took a last look, too, at Macklin, now
only thirty yards away, then wheeled his horse and galloped off.

Macklin was following. Good! Black Wind would lead
the white man deeper into the mountains, find a place to
dismount, and wait in ambush until the white man rode
past. Simple! He could then strike a deal with the mountain *gan*, trade Macklin for Rain Blossom, and return a
hero of the band.

Simple . . .

✧ 3 ✧

SHERIFF SMETHERS RODE UP TO THE MINERS' PERIMETER, a Colt in his hand.

"I thought *we* were supposed to be rescuin' *you*!" Craig shouted, laughing.

"It's the damned Apaches who rescued both of us!" Smethers said, shaking his head in wonder. "Never thought I'd see the day!"

"Ain't much left of the town, though," Craig said, looking about. The smoke was slowly clearing now, and only the adobe and a few scattered shacks and tents were left standing. The bits and pieces of fragmented civilization—clothing strewn about on the ground, a dropped mantel clock, books, papers, broken furniture, pulled-down tents, the bodies of men and horses—added an eerie sense of forlorn abandonment and melancholy to the scene.

"We can build again, Rog," Smethers said. "We *will* build again. . . ."

A tall, lean Apache rode up, bareback on a white mare. "Where is Macklin?" he demanded.

"Uh, last I saw, he was chasing one of your people," Craig said. He pointed. "Went that-a-way."

The Apache nodded and, without another word, nudged his horse with his heels and galloped off after Macklin.

"Maybe," Smethers said, "we should follow along."

"I think you might be right."

They would not all go, however, Smethers decided. Twenty men, all well armed, were detailed from the town and from the perimeter.

They mounted up and set off, Sheriff Smethers in the lead.

✧ 4 ✧

BLACK WIND FLED THE SITE OF THE BATTLE, RIDING HIS horse through the twisting maze of pathways and arroyos up into the rugged terrain forming the southern shoulder of East Peak. He was pretty sure that Macklin was still following him. All he needed to do was find the right spot to turn the tables on his persistent foe.

That tumble of rocks up ahead, for instance . . .

He rode closer, looking for a place to hide. One of the rocks, a little apart from the others, began *changing*. . . .

✧ 5 ✧

"MOON EAGLE!"

The shout snapped Macklin's attention back from the trail. He reined up, turning in his saddle. Great Bear rode up the path behind him, leading a half dozen other Apache warriors.

"Great Bear! I thought you were dead! Water-on-Rock is—"

"I know. The evil *gan* have taken him. One came at us out of the rock while we waited for you. I . . . ran . . ."

"It's okay, Great Bear. I've fought these things before. It's almost impossible not to run. They're very hard to kill, and more dangerous than any enemy you've ever fought."

"Water-on-Rock tried to fight it. He called to me, 'Get away!' If I stay, I am taken, too. So . . . I run."

"If it's any help, I met the Hunter that killed Water-on-Rock, and killed it."

"How do you know it was the same?"

"The Star Hunters have a way of making themselves look like other things. A rock. A tree. If they catch a man and use a device they carry to copy his thoughts before they kill him, they can make themselves look and sound and act like him, at least if you don't get too close and the light's not too bright. I met what looked like Water-on-Rock . . . but it turned out to be a Hunter. That's how I knew Water-on-Rock was dead."

Great Bear nodded.

"C'mon," Macklin told him. "Black Wind went up this way. . . ."

"We should not follow, Moon Eagle. That was why we came after you, to tell you that the evil *gan* are in these hills. It would serve no purpose if they took you here. For any of us."

Macklin knew what he was obliquely referring to. If Macklin was taken here, the Chokonen band would lose their one small bit of leverage for making the Kra'agh release Rain Blossom.

He wanted to keep riding. If he could just catch Black Wind . . .

But his inner warning system was speaking as well. There was an indefinable but oppressive menace to those brown, boulder-strewn hills ahead, almost as though something were watching him from among the rocks.

"Okay," he told Great Bear. "Let's go back down. But we'll be back. . . ."

Turning their horses, they started back down the path.

⋄ 6 ⋄

DEATHSTALKER COMPLETED DRAINING THE APACHE DIYI that called itself Black Wind. This explained much. The N'de taken and patterned already had been primitively superstitious in many ways, with confused notions as to what they really believed and underlying thoughts thickly encrusted with bizarre mythologies and confused impressions of gods, spirits, and beings that were not wholly spirit nor simply material.

This one, however, was a medicine man of consider-

able power and knowledge. It knew secrets of earth, fire, water, and sky, knew the secret names of the gods, knew how to use the tzi-ditindi, *or sounding wood, to call them, and the use of* hoddentin *to purify and make holy, knew the secrets of Killer-of-Enemies and Changing Woman and the* ga he, *or mountain spirits, knew, in fact, a host of things about the universe within which the N'de lived.*

There was a philosophy among the Kra'agh, the nga m'zegre, *or Created Worlds, which stated that every creature of mind, even semiintelligent food beasts, created its own world through its perceptions, thoughts, and beliefs. Like most Kra'agh, Deathstalker took a materialistic, common-sense view of the universe and had little patience with the nonsensical musings of philosopher-physicists and theoreticians.*

Still, Deathstalker had hunted on many worlds, had patterned food beasts representing a broad and unnervingly diverse spectrum of belief and worldview. Some, the dull ones, saw nothing to the universe more interesting than food to crop and water to drink; some, like these humans, possessed numerous different ways of looking at the world around them, ways often diametrically opposed to one another. It could be confusing, sometimes, to possess so many different ways of thinking within one mind.

How a creature viewed its world depended largely in what it believed about itself and that world. The N'de saw themselves as caretakers, of a sort, of a world created for them by Usen, the Life-Giver. To understand the created world, it was necessary to see it through a system of belief that saw gods and spirits everywhere.

An immature girl took on the essence of Changing Woman to become a mature adult. In like manner, Deathstalker was taking on the essence of Black Wind, acquiring its . . . no, his *power over natural forces and the* chidin-bi-kungua, *the House of Spirits.*

There was no scientific or rational basis for it, but

Deathstalker felt . . . more powerful. More in control.
More deadly.
It knew that Macklin wanted Black Wind. Excellent.
That would be yet another bit of bait for the trap.
Ll'graaz, *it thought.* The trap closes.

⋄ 7 ⋄

IT WAS, MACKLIN THOUGHT, A SCENE HE'D NEVER EX-
pected to witness. By midafternoon, forty men had gathered around a large fire beneath the rock shelter, squatting
on the ground as they talked with one another . . . half of
them white men from Apache Peak, the other half Chokonen Apache. Na-a-cha was there to speak for the Chokonen, while Vic Norden represented the miners. Macklin
stood between the two groups—"between the worlds," as
Na-a-cha had told him once— serving as translator and
mediator . . . and making sure both groups shared *understanding* as well as mere language.

"We're all agreed, then," Macklin said. "Norden and
his people will have access to the Bennett Mine, and can
work it without interference from the Apache. The N'de
will be allowed to stay in these mountains, and to keep
their holy places on the peaks to themselves alone.

"In addition, both groups will work together to help
rescue an Apache girl being held by evil *gan* on the west
slope of the mountain called Apache Peak."

"I still don't know what to make of these imaginary
gan-things you're talking about," Norden said. "But it
sounds like we have to help out if the Apaches are going
to be willing to help us."

"The *gan* are not imaginary," Na-a-cha said. "You will
learn that soon enough!"

"He's right," Macklin added. "The Hunters are all too
real, I'm afraid."

"Don't matter none," Tom Crittenden said. "If'n they can be killed, we'll kill 'em!"

"So where do you want us to go?" Norden asked.

"You swear, then, to help us?" Na-a-cha asked.

Norden raised his right hand. "As duly appointed mayor of Apache Peak, and as an official on the board of the Apache Peak Mining Consortium, yes, I swear!"

"And we swear by these mountains that this new friendship shall remain true."

"Right. So . . . where are we supposed to find these critters?"

"As it happens," Macklin told them, "the place where the Hunters are holding Rain Blossom and Cissy, and your lost mine, are in the same place. From what Na-a-cha has told me, it sounds like the Hunters have moved into the mine shaft itself."

"Son of a bitch!" one of the miners said, snorting. "We've been hornswoggled!"

"Not really, Hank," Norden said. "Hold your damned tongue."

"Yeah, but they got us to help them clear up their little *gan* problem by offering us back our own mine!"

"Which we would have had to fight for anyway, as it turns out," Norden reminded him. "Now shut the hell up and let's hear what they have to say."

"The mine is located on the west slope of Apache Peak, about two thirds of the way to the top," Macklin told them, passing on what Na-a-cha had told him just a few hours earlier. "That's only about a mile from here. The Chokonen will be able to lead us there along a trail that they say will let us sneak up pretty close without being seen.

He was gambling at this point. Everything he knew about the Kra'agh told him that they had other ways of monitoring an approaching force than eyes alone. What he was counting on was that the Hunters would detect the mixed group of Anglos and Apaches but not be able to know their thoughts.

"Now, here's what I want to try. . . ."

Macklin began laying out his plan. As he did so, he became increasingly aware of just how exhausted he was. He hadn't gotten any sleep last night . . . and precious little before that. Mostly, though, he was scared . . . scared down to the deepest, most private marrow of his deepest-buried bones. The terror of what he was about to do was draining him, leaving him weaker by far than did the simple lack of sleep.

He wondered if his AI companion could feel fear, and if it knew what the two of them were about to face. Macklin was under no illusions about what was about to happen. He would have to offer himself to the Kra'agh to get them to release both Cissy and Rain Blossom. This impromptu army he was organizing would be his guarantee, he hoped, that the Kra'agh didn't simply grab him, and go ahead and kill the two women anyway.

And if the Kra'agh did get him, if he couldn't talk or fight his way out of their grasp, the Apache-white army was his one small hope that the people of Earth could be alerted to the alien threat, and learn, somehow, to fight back.

As he looked at the miners—scruffy, dirty, greedy, opportunistic, stubborn, individualistic, suspicious, scared—and as he looked at the N'de—superstitious, grim, stubborn, individualistic, suspicious, scared—he knew how slim Earth's chances were right now. Hurt the Kra'agh badly enough, and they might think twice about an invasion. But how to hurt beings so powerful, so advanced . . . and so nightmarishly terrifying?

Macklin didn't know.

All he could do was lead . . . for as long as he was able to do so.

TWENTY

✧ 1 ✧

MACKLIN STOOD AT THE EDGE OF A BROAD, FLAT, ROCK-floored valley, shaped like a bowl with sides that were gentle at first, but then which swiftly grew steep on the east and north sides. Trees and boulders hemmed the space in, though a trail rutted with wagon-wheel tracks led down the slope toward the southwest.

Directly ahead, a canyon opened in a sheer rock wall along the north side of the bowl, decorated with oddly carved stone shapes. One in particular made an impressive monument—a huge flat rock as large as the adobe building in the mining camp, balanced precariously on a cylindrical column of banded sandstone forty feet high, standing like a guardian pillar just to the right of the canyon entrance. This, Macklin decided, must be the flat rock immortalized in tales of the Flatrock Monster. It also marked the entrance to the lost Bennett Mine; Na-a-cha had assured him that the shaft entrance was perhaps fifty yards down that dark box canyon. If the Apache *diyi* was to be believed, the devil-*gan* had been seen here frequently, and strange lights regularly passed in and out of the canyon mouth. The canyon itself was so tight and slender that it was virtually a cave without a roof. In fact, fallen timber and overgrowth in places turned the canyon into the next best thing to a cave, with sheer walls and a floor perpetually wreathed in sunless gloom.

It was, in short, a perfect hiding place for the Kra'agh, who shunned bright light and who'd hoped to keep their activities on this world secret, both from the natives, and from the offworlder Monitors of the Associative.

Behind Macklin stood Na-a-cha and Norden. The mayor of Apache Peak was interested in the rock wall they were standing next to, which showed an unusual black stain against the paler gray granite. "See this?" he said. "Silver. Sure sign. Probably copper, and maybe some gold, too . . . but the rocks are very rich in silver. This is what must've given old Bennett his first idea that there was pay dirt here."

Na-a-cha wore a shuttered expression masking his feelings. Clearly, he didn't share the white man's fascination for grubbing about in the earth. At the moment, he was more concerned about Rain Blossom . . . and Macklin. "It should not be much longer," he said, but Macklin suspected he was trying to reassure himself.

"I imagine they're watching us now," Macklin said. "They have . . . devices, machines that let them see far distances."

"I know such machines," Na-a-cha said. "Telescopes . . ."

"These machines are more like cameras," Macklin explained. "The boxes white men use to record images and landscapes? But these pictures would move, and have color. This scene here, say, could be transmitted instantly to a screen thousands of miles away, to be viewed by someone there."

Na-a-cha shook his head. "I do not see why such a thing would be wanted."

"For one thing, they could be watching us through a camera the size of your thumb, while they are safely buried away deep underground where we can't get at them."

Na-a-cha had no reply to that. Moments later, however, they all became aware of something moving in front of the canyon mouth. At first, it was nothing more than a wisp of shadow all but invisible against the deeper shadows within the canyon. Then the shadows coalesced and hardened, and Macklin found himself looking across the bare rock at Black Wind.

"Black Wind!" Na-a-cha said, stiffening. "If he has allied himself with the Star Hunter devil-*gan* . . ."

"It might not be Black Wind," Macklin told him. "Just guessing, mind you, but from the way he just appeared, I'd say that that is one of the *gan*. If so, Black Wind is dead. They killed him."

The image of Black Wind was unarmed. It held out its empty hands. "You have brought Macklin?" it asked, speaking Apache.

"We have Macklin," Na-a-cha said in the same language. He took a step forward, guiding Macklin by the left arm. Macklin stepped with him, his wrists tied behind his back. "But you must release Rain Blossom as you promised." He paused, then added in English, "You must release both of your prisoners!"

"That's right," Norden called out. "You've got Cissy Colburn in there. We want her back, too!"

"You shall have them," Black Wind said. "Send Macklin forward."

"Not until you give us Cissy and the squaw!" Norden bellowed. He drew his Colt and pressed the muzzle against Macklin's head. "Macklin here's broken half a dozen of our laws, including breaking jail and stealing horses. I'd just as soon shoot the son of a bitch than give him over to you. If I do, I don't expect he'll be any good to you, will he?"

Black Wind appeared to consider this. "We want Macklin's death, above all. I would be willing to watch you kill it."

"Send out Cissy, and you can kill him yourself."

"And Rain Blossom!" Na-a-cha added. "We want both women in exchange for Macklin, alive."

Again, Black Wind hesitated. "Very well. There are things that Macklin knows that we must know. It will be impossible to extract the information if you scramble its brains with a pistol bullet. The two women are of no importance to us. You may have them. *After* you give us Macklin."

"No!" Na-a-cha said. "You are spirit-*gan*, and have great powers. You have ways of seeing far, of flying through the air, of controlling the lightning. If we give you Macklin first, we have no way to make you keep your promise. If you give us the women first, you can easily enforce your will upon us."

This, Macklin thought, was the most deadly part of the encounter, each side maneuvering to see what it could get away with. The trouble was that the aliens really did hold all the cards. They could simply come grab him and burn down N'de and miners alike, and not even worry about an exchange. The only thing keeping them from doing so right now was the possibility that Macklin would be killed in the ensuing scuffle . . . and the sight of Norden's revolver pressed to his temple.

"Send out the women, and you can have this bastard!" Norden yelled. "But you'd better hurry! My trigger finger's getting mighty tired!"

"Here are the women," Black Wind said.

They emerged from the cave mouth, looking small and ragged, clothing torn, faces pale, their hands, like Macklin, tied behind their backs.

"Bring Macklin here!" Black Wind's image called.

Na-a-cha started forward, pushing Macklin along. Norden paced them, keeping his gun to Macklin's head.

"Rain Blossom!" Na-a-cha called out in Apache. "Come this way! You're free!"

"C'mon, Cissy!" Norden added in English. "Get the hell over here!"

Neither woman moved, or even seemed to see the approaching trio. They stood silently, hands behind their backs, looking down at the ground near their feet. Rain Blossom started once, and looked up . . . but not at Black Wind and not at the three walking slowly toward her.

"It's a projection of some kind," Macklin said quietly. "Same sort of thing they use to make you see Black Wind or a rock instead of one of them. They're trying to trick us."

The three men stopped, five yards from the canyon entrance. "Now send out the *real* women!" Norden bellowed. "Not just those fancy pictures!" He ground the pistol painfully against Macklin's head. "I *mean* it, goddamn it! You freaks are making me lose my temper!"

Everything seemed to happen at once, then.

Something bright and very shiny emerged from the canyon, vaguely egg-shaped, but with swellings, domes, ridges and cupolas on its surface that gave it an organic, almost living feel, making it look at once like a simple shape, but with an ornate and complex surface. It flew, hovering several feet off the ground, and its surface gave off a pulsing white light so brilliant that it was hard to see the thing's surface detail.

The two women winked out, as though they'd never been there . . . which, in fact, they hadn't. The image of Black Wind shimmered as well, replaced momentarily by the alien nightmare form of a Kra'agh Star Hunter.

And something like a straight-line bolt of lightning seared from the side of the flying craft, striking Norden's head with a thunderclap and exploding it in a spray of red mist and chips of white bone. Na-a-cha dropped to the ground as if struck by a club, as Norden's headless body collapsed in a bloody heap; Macklin dove forward, running toward the image of Black Wind.

As he ran, he tugged at the rope binding his wrists, letting it unravel and fall. His Colt was slung in its holster, tucked down into the seat of his pants with the handle hidden beneath the blouse of his shirt. Hands free now, he drew the revolver, aiming as he ran, pulling back the hammer with his thumb and then squeezing the trigger.

Black Wind's image faded away . . . but there was no Kra'agh remaining in its place. Black Wind, like the women, had been pure illusion, a ruse to draw them onward.

Behind him, the flying craft pivoted, and descended. Part of the side seemed to dilate open with a ripple like a stone tossed into a pond, and two Hunters emerged. Macklin raised the pistol and fired, striking one . . . then dropped flat to the ground as someone in the hills behind him shouted, "Moon Eagle! Down!"

During the past few hours, Apache riflemen had infiltrated the heights surrounding the bowl, hiding among the trees and rocks higher up on the slopes of Apache Peak. They opened fire now from cover, dozens of smoke puffs appearing in a ragged half-circle around the rim of the rock-sided bowl.

Macklin looked up and saw other bullets flashing into white-hot brilliance as they struck the side of the flying craft . . . no, they were vaporizing inches away from the vehicle's side. Apparently there was some sort of field or shield made of energy protecting the craft's hull.

The two Kra'agh were closer and more threatening, though. The one that Macklin had shot had been slowed, but not badly hurt. It staggered now, however, as bullet after bullet struck home from the surrounding cliffs. The second Kra'agh dashed forward, grabbing Macklin with one large, clawed hand, and dragging him back toward the hovering vehicle. Concerned only with getting back under cover fast, it didn't appear to realize at first that

Macklin was armed. Possibly it didn't recognize the Colt as a weapon; possibly it had other things on its mind.

As it dragged him into the gaping opening in the side of the craft, which now was hovering just inches off the ground, Macklin swung his revolver up, jamming the muzzle against the Hunter's hump and pulling the trigger.

The shot convulsed the being, knocking it down. Its sinuous neck writhed and twisted, the jaws gaping as it swung to bite Macklin. He fired again, this time straight down the thing's yawning throat, then ducked aside as the creature's death struggles slammed it against the craft's interior bulkhead.

Macklin looked around wildly; the interior of the craft was softly lit, but he couldn't tell where the light was coming from. Ceiling, walls, and floor all glowed in soft orange light; a hatch in one wall dilated open, revealing a third creature in a kind of seat and harness combination behind an array of controls. Though he'd seen no windows on the outside of the craft, the bulkhead from this side appeared transparent . . . or perhaps this was another illusion of some sort. The craft evidently was flying through the narrow canyon now very fast, though Macklin felt neither a sense of speed nor movement as it swerved left or right to follow the twists of the stone-walled corridor.

The pilot twisted its head about and vented a shrill, hissing shriek as it saw Macklin standing on the aft deck astride the body of its companion. Macklin raised the pistol and fired four rounds before the hammer clicked dead on an empty cartridge. The pilot writhed and slumped in its harness; two of his wildly fired bullets had missed, striking the instrument panel, and now the craft was leaning far to the left, if the view outside was anything to go by. Oddly, Macklin could still feel neither the craft's evident speed nor its tilt to the side. In the next instant, it struck the side of the canyon and the view outside spun wildly, still without any of the sensations of movement or crashing penetrating to the interior.

The craft struck the canyon wall again, then plowed nose-first into soft dirt.

The pilot was still alive, though wounded, and was unsnapping its seat straps. Dropping the revolver, Macklin stooped and pulled the beamer from the dead Hunter's harness, desperately willing the thing to behave. Again, the alien weapon shifted and writhed in his hands, but he managed a clumsy, two-handed grip . . . and when he thumbed one of the exposed buttons, lightning crackled from the front of the device, connecting with the pilot and snapping and flickering in a deadly, blue-white spray of radiance. The pilot shrieked, snapped back, and collapsed, a gaping black hole smoking in the upper part of its torso.

Macklin stared at the weapon, bemused. The mere intent to kill seemed to be what controlled it, making it hold its shape and discharge its bolt.

Outside, five more of the monsters ran past the downed ship, racing for the canyon mouth. Na-a-cha's certainty that there were only three of the nightmares to contend with had obviously been a bit optimistic. There were two dead right here inside the ship, plus the third outside the canyon and a fourth Macklin had killed earlier outside of the town. These . . . and were there more?

As his eyes adjusted to the relative gloom at the bottom of the canyon, he realized what he was looking at. There, a dozen yards ahead, the canyon came to an abrupt end in a rock wall that climbed straight up toward the sun. There was a cave in that wall just ahead, and something huge and black with menace crouched just within the cavern opening.

The cavern, he realized with a start, had been the mouth of the Bennett mine, but the Hunters had enlarged it dramatically, cutting through rock and timbering, the remnants of which were still lying about on the ground. The obsidian-black shape, he could see now, was the prow of a ship, a craft of some sort like this one, but *much* larger. He could only see the end, but guessed that it was cigar-shaped, richly decorated with sharp angles and edges everywhere. The small craft must be the equivalent, Macklin thought, of a ship's boat. There, buried in the mine shaft, was the real Kra'agh ship, and it was enormous, big enough for dozens of the creatures.

It was not a pleasant thought.

Closer at hand, just opposite the canyon from the spot where the small flyer had come to ground, part of the canyon wall had been cut away to create a storage area of some sort. Macklin saw boxes, stacks of timbers . . . and with a jolt of recognition, he saw two human shapes hanging from the rock wall, two feet off the ground. It was Rain Blossom and Cissy. They were tied hand and foot and appeared to have been suspended somehow from the sheer rock face. Both were moving, though, and very much alive. The ground below them, though, was covered by what looked like white bones, and he saw several skeletons suspended on the rock wall to either side of the living prisoners.

It took several moments of frustrated and frantic experimenting to figure out how to open the hatch in the downed flyer's side. A panel glowing more brightly than the rest of the interior bulkhead hummed when he touched it, and the door rippled open. As he stepped through, he felt a sudden, stomach-twisting vertigo. The field or effect that had kept him from feeling the flyer's movement inside gave way to a normal gravity, and the twist between the two left him dizzy and ill.

No matter. He could be sick later. Still clutching the stolen beamer, he dashed across the canyon floor to the cut-stone alcove.

"John!" Cissy cried. "Get me down from here!"

"Help me, please!" Rain Blossom cried out in Apache.

Reaching up, Macklin grasped Rain Blossom by her waist, lifted, then eased her down. He was relieved to see that the only fastening was a metal hook driven into stone; the back of her richly fringed and decorated buckskin dress had been snagged over the hook, keeping her up, immobile, and out of the way.

Thunderous explosions echoed down the canyon from the south. The five Hunters must have emerged . . . and run straight into the trap.

The Apaches were superb at moving in unnoticed and setting an ambush, and he'd used Na-a-cha's men in just that capacity. The miners, though, he'd held in reserve until after the fighting had begun. As soon as they'd heard the shooting, they'd moved in from above the bowl-shaped valley, taking up positions on the cliff tops above the canyon mouth. From there, they were in the perfect position to shoot down on any Kra'agh emerging from the canyon . . . and to drop lit sticks of dynamite on them. From the quick-paced rumble of explosions, it sounded like the Kra'agh had emerged into a storm of raining dynamite.

Rain Blossom appeared weak and scared, but unhurt. He pulled Cissy down next, laying her among the skeletons and bones on the ground. Those, he thought, must belong to the original Bennett Mine crew, and possibly to some of the later searchers as well. He had a pocket knife. He used that to snick through the bindings, which appeared to be of some soft, translucent, but very tough material he didn't recognize. It cut, however, and in a few moments, the women's wrists and ankles were free.

"Oh, God, thank you!" Cissy cried, and she hugged him. Rain Blossom looked scared and grateful and shy all at once.

"Come on," he told them. "We have to find a way out of here!"

"John!" Cissy screamed, pointing past his shoulder. "Look!"

He turned. The squat, angular, black shape within the mine was moving, emerging into the canyon. The hull was glowing now. A hatchway with a short ramp extended yawned open beneath the thrusting prow, spilling a dim orange radiance from within. Macklin could sense a dull, distant rumbling throb. Rocks spilled from either side of the mineshaft, dislodged by that deep-set thrumming vibration in the air.

Two more Kra'agh emerged from the mine shaft's mouth. Macklin propelled both women toward the open end of the canyon but stood his ground, raising the beamer. He grasped it uncomfortably with both hands, thought about killing, and squeezing the firing button.

Again, lightning stabbed from the weapon's blunt muzzle, striking the rock wall beside one of the Hunters. They both returned fire, the beams going high, striking the rock above and behind him with snapping, hissing blasts that pelted him with flecks of hot gravel. Both Kra'agh then dashed up the ramp, vanishing into the belly of the slowly advancing ship.

Macklin fired again, dragging lightning across the ship's hull, but without obvious effect. The lightning cut off in mid bolt, however, and as much as he stabbed at the buttons, he could get no response.

He knew what to expect, though. He ran forward, toward the ship, closing the distance in a few long, hard strides. He could feel the tingling vibration in the grip of the alien weapon, feel it growing warm. He ran as long as he dared, then hurled the weapon as hard as he could, sending it spinning end for end in a long, flat arc toward the huge ship.

The front hatch was irising shut now, but the beamer spun through the opening at the last moment, vanishing inside.

A moment later, the tail of the ship emerged from the enlarged mineshaft, and the vessel started to rise. Then, a dazzling, blinding flash lit the ship from within, visible as violent blue-white stabs of light emerging from portholes or other openings along the sides. The ship drifted higher for a moment, then began to settle again, drifting toward the canyon floor. Macklin had already turned and was running as fast as he could down the canyon. He caught up with the women and urged them along faster. At their backs, the ship—as large as a fair-sized building—grounded on the canyon floor, hitting hard enough to split its belly open, releasing the pent-up glare of an exploding sun.

The blast picked the three of them up off their feet and hurled them forward. Macklin shot from the mouth of the canyon like a bullet emerging from the muzzle of a gun, landing on hard rock and skidding, managing to leave a fair amount of cloth and skin behind as he did so.

As he rolled to a stop, dazed and torn, he felt the ground convulse beneath his back, legs, and elbows. The canyon appeared to be collapsing; no, it was the mountain beyond the canyon that was expanding, a dome of rock rising slowly, then subsiding as unthinkable forces were released far underground.

The walls of the canyon were collapsing as well. The precariously balanced flat rock slipped from its perch and tumbled, dropping edge-on into the canyon mouth ten yards from the sprawled bodies of Macklin, Rain Blossom, and Cissy. The sound of the avalanche was as loud and boomingly deep as thunder, and clouds of dust boiled out and engulfed them in a choking cloud.

But then, almost miraculously, it was quiet. . . .

Nearby, torn and flame-blackened alien bodies lay in a twitching, hideous splatter of body parts and gore. Very slowly, Macklin rose to a sitting position, then made it up to his knees. His arms hurt terribly where he'd skinned them on the rock. His head throbbed. His left leg felt like he'd wrenched it badly, and the pain burned in his knee and hip.

But he could only stare at the alien bodies nearby . . . or what was left of them. They were scarcely recognizable as things that had once been living. Thirty yards away, a line of blue-clad men, *black* men like Tzit-dijin, knelt in a ragged line, their rifles held rigidly at their shoulders, all aiming at Macklin.

"Mistuh," a grizzled sergeant called out, his head not rising from the breech of the Sharps carbine he was aiming at Macklin. "You'd better move real slow and keep your hands where we can see 'em. Sheriff? Is that your man?"

"Are you real, Macklin?" Smethers asked, eyes narrowed with hard suspicion. The Colt in his hand never wavered as he aimed it at Macklin's head.

"Hell," Macklin said, struggling to his feet. "I wouldn't hurt this much if I wasn't." His legs gave way and he dropped again, unable to stand. Smethers came closer, prodding him with the toe of a boot.

"It's okay," Smethers called out. "He's real!"

"Check the women," Macklin told him. "They've been through hell."

"They both look okay. A little scraped up and burned, but okay. Macklin, I don't know what to say. You did a hell of a job!"

"You boys did okay yourselves." He pulled himself upright again. "Where'd the cavalry come from? Cissy didn't get through to raise them."

"Sergeant Davies, sir," the graying cavalry noncom said. "Actually, we were following one of our own."

"One of . . . your own?"

"We're C Troop," he said, pride in his voice. "Tenth Cavalry, out of Fort Huachuca. We were on patrol this afternoon north of the fort, when we saw this rider approaching from the mountains. He looked like one of us, a buffalo soldier, but he was pretty ragged. He rode up to just out of pistol shot, pulled up his bugle, and sounded the charge. As we started after him, he galloped off, leading us back toward the mountains.

"We were pretty sure he was a deserter. Not many buffalo soldiers go over the hill, but a few do, and we don't like it. We were going to bring that fellow back. At the same time, we had to be careful. He might have been working with the Apaches and, if so, he could be leading us smack into a trap."

Macklin took in the dark, sweat-beaded faces, the hard look of ebony-chiseled competence. These were tough men, warriors as hard and as deadly as any the Apaches were able to field.

Yes, he could imagine them wanting to take care of a wayward one of their own.

"In fact, though," Davies continued, "he led us all the way to what was left of Apache Peak. We saw the town had been burned to the ground, and the miners there told us about renegade Apaches up in the mountains, and how some of the miners had gone up with a bunch of good Apaches to try to bring them down. There was also . . . I don't know, crazy talk about Indian legends and monsters and strange-looking beasts.

"We started up the trail, following you. We were at the Apache camp by a big rock overhang when we heard gunshots ahead. We came on at the gallop . . . and found ourselves in the middle of the damndest fight I've ever seen. We saw these . . . these things, like living nightmares, and both the whites and the Apaches were shooting at them, throwing dynamite . . . it was a sight, I tell ya! We fell into line and opened up on the things. Turned out they weren't as tough as they looked, between our rifles and all that dynamite! The sheriff, here, he told us they could make themselves look like humans, though, so that's why we were waiting when you three came flying out like that.

"So that's our story, mistuh," the sergeant concluded. "And now, I'd be very pleased if someone would tell me just what in the blue blazing *hell* is going on up here!"

Macklin told him. He told him most of the story, anyway, leaving out some of what he knew or guessed of Kra'agh intentions, of Associative Monitors, of his own role in the unfolding story of Earth's involvement in a far-flung web of galactic politics and food service; he wasn't sure how much would be believed, and he knew that if the sergeant decided that any part of what he said was a lie, well, he'd probably conclude that the rest was a lie as well.

He didn't say anything about Tzit-dijin, either. Obviously, the buffalo soldier deserter had ridden off for Fort Huachuca when he'd learned that Cissy had been captured, even though he knew he risked being captured and hung as a deserter. He'd gone anyway, and brought back some of his former comrades. He was probably hiding up in the mountains now; Macklin figured he'd earned any peace he wanted to find.

But he told Davies of other worlds circling suns so distant they were nothing but stars in the night sky. He said that some of those other worlds had life, people of their own, though few looked even remotely like the people of Earth.

And as on Earth, some were warriors, some were hunters, and many were not at all pleasant to know. The Kra'agh were Star Hunters, and they thought of humans as nothing more than cattle, as edible and sometimes challenging beasts, for entertainment and for food. The creatures Davies and his men had seen and helped dispatch had been advance scouts for a much larger invasion force.

The main force would be arriving someday soon, coming in from the stars to transform the entire Earth into a huge, free-range game preserve.

By the time his story was over, the sun had set in a red blaze in the west, and the clear blue sky above was growing dark. Davies looked up at the first stars just beginning to appear in the east, and shivered.

"I always thought the stars looked damned cold," he said.

"Don't worry, boys," Smethers said happily. "We got the bastards! We got 'em, all! Thanks to Macklin and the U.S. Cavalry!"

"But the Bennett Mine's lost again!" Craig said. "That whole canyon's done caved in and collapsed over the entrance! It's gonna take months to clear it out . . . or to find a way to dig a fresh shaft!

"We'll do it, by God," Smethers said. "We'll find a way, and we'll *do* it! I think right now I'm more interested in finding what's left of the Hunter base down there. Or that flying machine. The hell with silver! There could be *real* money in a genuine flying machine, or those things that spit lightning!"

The others were arguing back and forth about how expensive it might be to clear the mine entrance again . . . and what might be done with what was inside. The consensus was that the explosion must have rendered any Kra'agh artifacts useless.

But still, wasn't it worth a look to be sure?

"Nobody's gonna believe this," Davies said.

"We have to tell people," Macklin said. "Have to warn them."

"How you gonna do that?" Davies asked. "Ain't no way they'll believe the word of an old Nigra like me. Ain't *no* way." He shrugged. "They won't believe my men, won't believe those silver-happy miners, sure as hellfire won't believe no Injuns. All you got is those burned-up bodies, and they won't last long. So how you gonna get anybody to even listen to you, huh?"

How indeed? With Mankind and his world in the balance, Macklin would have to convince them all of a tale wilder than the Great Moon Hoax.

Macklin took a torch and went off by himself, leaving the argument and the nervous jesting behind him. He wanted to see those torn alien bodies again.

There was so little left . . . not enough, even, to make an autopsy possible, not one that would prove to an unbelieving world that monsters walked its surface. The rotten-egg stink was overpowering, eye-watering.

Still Macklin breathed with shallow, gentle breaths, and stared for a long time at the burned and torn mess that had been five alien Kra'agh.

Or . . . were there only four bodies here? Craig's boys with their dynamite had done just a little too thorough a job. There was nothing left in that reeking mess that could definitively prove that there were five bodies there . . . or fewer.

Macklin felt a cold crawling at the base of his neck. The story might not yet be over. . . .

⋄ 2 ⋄

IT WAS NOT OVER, NOT YET. THE SLASHERCLAW SHIP THAT Deathstalker and the others had been using as a base was destroyed. It was alone now, cut off from its own kind, marooned on a hostile world.

No matter. There were other Hunters here, and it knew how to reach them. And reach them it would, to warn them of this new and unfortunate development. The two human factions—primitive N'de and slightly less primitive Anglos—had unexpectedly stopped fighting each other and united, and apparently were now fully aware of the Kra'agh presence and their intentions, and determined to stop them at any cost. This was not good.

But not insurmountable. The main Kra'agh invasion fleet would be here soon, and then, at last, the humans would find their true place... at the bottom of the Kra'agh food chain.

It was really only a matter of time.

Epilogue

✧ **1** ✧

Macklin returned to Tombstone.

It was clear that the Apache Peak Consortium was going nowhere. Thornton had come up with some more money to sink a test shaft above the ruin of the Bennett Mine . . . but two volunteers had gone down into the rubble of the collapsed outer canyon, and when they'd come back, they were vomiting blood and so weak they couldn't stand. Within the next few days their hair started to fall out and hideous blisters appeared on their skin, and by the time their friends had taken them by wagon back up to Benson to see a doctor, they were dead.

A curse, some of the other miners said. *You won't catch me going down into the old Bennett! No sir! I heard there was an Apache curse on the place . . . !*

The word was, Big Nate Thornton was finding it impossible to hire men to work anywhere on what some were calling "that accursed mountain."

Macklin rode to Tombstone a week after the events on Apache Peak. Cissy Colburn rode with him. There would be work there, of one sort or another . . . and Marshal Evans would still want him eventually in Tucson.

Somewhere on this planet, there were other Monitors. Macklin knew he would find one, somehow. In the meantime, he had a world to cxplore, and a new sense of self-awareness. The thing in his chest, he thought, was beginning to wake up. . . .

⋄ **2** ⋄

NA-A-CHA STOOD FOR THE FINAL TIME ON THE MOUNTAIN. The N'de were leaving after all, following their brothers south to Mexico. Go-yath-lay, He-Who-Yawns, whom the Anglos called Geronimo, was there, and he needed help fighting the Mexicans.

And the *gan*, it seemed, were gone from the sacred mountain.

Perhaps the evil *gan* had overcome the good mountain *gan*, the *ga he* of Na-a-cha's people. No matter. They would take the good spirits with them to the south. Somehow, they would find a way.

He thought of Macklin, and his search for himself and the *gan* he carried within. Na-a-cha's search was no different. Macklin's *gan*, his Powers, were inside, made manifest in the black circle in his chest. He needed only to learn how to tap them to find his place in a hostile world.

He stretched out his arms and he sang the prayer that traditionally followed the songs of the *ga he*.

Great Blue Mountain Spirit in the east,
The home made of blue clouds,
The cross made of blue mirage,
There, you have begun to live,
There, is the life of goodness,
I am grateful for that made of goodness there.

Great Yellow Mountain Spirit in the south,
Your spiritually hale body is made of yellow clouds;
Leader of the Mountain Spirits, holy Mountain Spirit,
You live by means of the good of this life.

Great White Mountain Spirit in the west,
Your spiritually hale body is made of the white
    mirage;
Holy Mountain Spirit, leader of the Mountain Spirits,
I am happy over your words,
You are happy over my words.

Great Black Mountain Spirit in the north,
Your spiritually hale body is made of black clouds;
In that way, Big Black Mountain Spirit,
Holy Mountain Spirit, leader of the Mountain Spirits,
I am happy over your words,
You are happy over my words,
Now it is good.
Now it is good.

Na-a-cha turned his back on the mountain and started
on the long trek south. There was goodness there, as
everywhere. Life for the N'de, the People.
    Life for the People of Earth.
    In the darkening sky above, a falling star flared briefly,
brilliantly, and winked out.